THE GIRL
WITH ALL
THE GIFTS

M. R. CAREY

www.orbitbooks.net

ORBIT

First published in Great Britain in 2014 by Orbit

Copyright © 2014 by M. R. Carey

A CIP catalogue record for this book
is available from the British Library.

HB ISBN 978-0-356-50273-1
C format 978-0-356-50284-7

Typeset in Bembo by Palimpsest Book Production Limited,
Falkirk, Stirlingshire
Printed and bound by CPI Group (UK) Ltd,
Croydon CR0 4YY

Papers used by Orbit are from well-managed
forests and other responsible sources.

MIX
Paper from
responsible sources
FSC
www.fsc.org   FSC® C104740

Orbit
An imprint of
Little, Brown Book Group
100 Victoria Embankment
London EC4Y 0DY

An Hachette UK Company
www.hachette.co.uk

www.orbitbooks.net

For Lin, who opened the box

1

Her name is Melanie. It means "the black girl", from an ancient Greek word, but her skin is actually very fair so she thinks maybe it's not such a good name for her. She likes the name Pandora a whole lot, but you don't get to choose. Miss Justineau assigns names from a big list; new children get the top name on the boys' list or the top name on the girls' list, and that, Miss Justineau says, is that.

There haven't been any new children for a long time now. Melanie doesn't know why that is. There used to be lots; every week, or every couple of weeks, voices in the night. Muttered orders, complaints, the occasional curse. A cell door slamming. Then, after a while, usually a month or two, a new face in the classroom – a new boy or girl who hadn't even learned to talk yet. But they got it fast.

Melanie was new herself, once, but that's hard to remember because it was a long time ago. It was before there were any words; there were just things without names, and things without names don't stay in your mind. They fall out, and then they're gone.

Now she's ten years old, and she has skin like a princess in

1

a fairy tale; skin as white as snow. So she knows that when she grows up she'll be beautiful, with princes falling over themselves to climb her tower and rescue her.

Assuming, of course, that she has a tower.

In the meantime, she has the cell, the corridor, the classroom and the shower room.

The cell is small and square. It has a bed, a chair and a table. On the walls, which are painted grey, there are pictures; a big one of the Amazon rainforest and a smaller one of a pussycat drinking from a saucer of milk. Sometimes Sergeant and his people move the children around, so Melanie knows that some of the cells have different pictures in them. She used to have a horse in a meadow and a mountain with snow on the top, which she liked better.

It's Miss Justineau who puts the pictures up. She cuts them out from the stack of old magazines in the classroom, and she sticks them up with bits of blue sticky stuff at the corners. She hoards the blue sticky stuff like a miser in a story. Whenever she takes a picture down, or puts a new one up, she scrapes up every last bit that's stuck to the wall and puts it back on the little round ball of the stuff that she keeps in her desk.

When it's gone, it's gone, Miss Justineau says.

The corridor has twenty doors on the left-hand side and eighteen doors on the right-hand side. Also it has a door at either end. One door is painted red, and it leads to the class-room – so Melanie thinks of that as the classroom end of the corridor. The door at the other end is bare grey steel and it's really, really thick. Where it leads to is a bit harder to say. Once when Melanie was being taken back to her cell, the door was off its hinges, with some men working on it, and she could see how it had all these bolts and sticking-out bits around the edges of it, so when it's closed it would be really hard to open. Past the door, there was a long flight of concrete steps going up and up. She wasn't supposed to see any of that stuff, and Sergeant said, "Little bitch has got way too many eyes on her" as he shoved her chair into her cell and slammed the door shut. But she saw, and she remembers.

She listens, too, and from overheard conversations she has a sense of this place in relation to other places she hasn't ever seen. This place is the block. Outside the block is the base, which is Hotel Echo. Outside the base is region 6, with London thirty miles to the south and then Beacon another forty-four miles further – and nothing else beyond Beacon except the sea. Most of region 6 is clear, but the only thing that keeps it that way is the burn patrols, with their frags and fireballs. This is what the base is for, Melanie is pretty sure. It sends out burn patrols, to clear away the hungries.

The burn patrols have to be really careful, because there are lots of hungries still out there. If they get your scent, they'll follow you for a hundred miles, and when they catch you they'll eat you. Melanie is glad that she lives in the block, behind that big steel door, where she's safe.

Beacon is very different from the base. It's a whole great big city full of people, with buildings that go up into the sky. It's got the sea on one side of it and moats and minefields on the other three, so the hungries can't get close. In Beacon you can live your whole life without ever seeing a hungry. And it's so big there are probably a hundred billion people there, all living together.

Melanie hopes she'll go to Beacon some day. When the mission is complete, and when (Dr Caldwell said this once) everything gets folded up and put away. Melanie tries to imagine that day; the steel walls closing up like the pages of a book, and then . . . something else. Something else outside, into which they'll all go.

It will be scary. But so amazing!

Through the grey steel door each morning Sergeant comes and Sergeant's people come and finally the teacher comes. They walk down the corridor, past Melanie's door, bringing with them the strong, bitter chemical smell that they always have on them; it's not a nice smell, but it's exciting because it means the start of another day's lessons.

At the sound of the bolts sliding and the footsteps, Melanie runs to the door of her cell and stands on tiptoe to peep through the little mesh-screen window in the door and see the people when they go by. She calls out good morning to them, but they're not supposed to answer and usually they don't. Sergeant and his people never do, and neither do Dr Caldwell or Mr Whitaker. And Dr Selkirk goes by really fast and never looks the right way, so Melanie can't see her face. But sometimes Melanie will get a wave from Miss Justineau or a quick, furtive smile from Miss Mailer.

Whoever is going to be the teacher for the day goes straight through into the classroom, while Sergeant's people start to unlock the cell doors. Their job is to take the children to the classroom, and after that they go away again. There's a procedure that they follow, which takes a long time. Melanie thinks it must be the same for all the children, but of course she doesn't know that for sure because it always happens inside the cells and the only cell that Melanie sees the inside of is her own.

To start with, Sergeant bangs on all the doors and shouts at the children to get ready. What he usually shouts is "Transit!" but sometimes he adds more words to that. "Transit, you little bastards!" or "Transit! Let's see you!" His big, scarred face looms up at the mesh window and he glares in at you, making sure you're out of bed and moving.

And one time, Melanie remembers, he made a speech – not to the children but to his people. "Some of you are new. You don't know what the hell you've signed up for, and you don't know where the hell you are. You're scared of these frigging little abortions, right? Well, good. Hug that fear to your mortal soul. The more scared you are, the less chance you'll screw up." Then he shouted, "Transit!" which was lucky because Melanie wasn't sure by then if this was the transit shout or not.

4

After Sergeant says "Transit", Melanie gets dressed, quickly, in the white shift that hangs on the hook next to her door, a pair of white trousers from the receptacle in the wall, and the white pumps lined up under her bed. Then she sits down in the wheelchair at the foot of her bed, like she's been taught to do. She puts her hands on the arms of the chair and her feet on the footrests. She closes her eyes and waits. She counts while she waits. The highest she's ever had to count is two thousand five hundred and twenty-six; the lowest is one thousand nine hundred and one.

When the key turns in the door, she stops counting and opens her eyes. Sergeant comes in with his gun and points it at her. Then two of Sergeant's people come in and tighten and buckle the straps of the chair around Melanie's wrists and ankles. There's also a strap for her neck; they tighten that one last of all, when her hands and feet are fastened up all the way, and they always do it from behind. The strap is designed so they never have to put their hands in front of Melanie's face. Melanie sometimes says, "I won't bite." She says it as a joke, but Sergeant's people never laugh. Sergeant did once, the first time she said it, but it was a nasty laugh. And then he said, "Like we'd ever give you the chance, sugar plum."

When Melanie is all strapped into the chair, and she can't move her hands or her feet or her head, they wheel her into the classroom and put her at her desk. The teacher might be talking to some of the other children, or writing something on the blackboard, but she (or he, if it's Mr Whitaker, the only teacher who's a he) will usually stop and say, "Good morning, Melanie." That way the children who sit way up at the front of the class will know that Melanie has come into the room and they can say good morning too. Most of them can't see her when she comes in, of course, because they're all in their own chairs with their neck straps fastened up, so they can't turn their heads around that far.

This procedure – the wheeling in, and the teacher saying

good morning and then the chorus of greetings from the other kids – happens nine more times, because there are nine children who come into the classroom after Melanie. One of them is Anne, who used to be Melanie's best friend in the class and maybe still is except that the last time they moved the kids around (Sergeant calls it "shuffling the deck") they ended up sitting a long way apart and it's hard to be best friends with someone you can't talk to. Another is Kenny, who Melanie doesn't like because he calls her Melon Brain or M-M-M-Melanie to remind her that she used to stammer sometimes in class.

When all the children are in the classroom, the lessons start. Every day has sums and spelling, and every day has retention tests, but there doesn't seem to be a plan for the rest of the lessons. Some teachers like to read aloud from books and then ask questions about what they just read. Others make the children learn facts and dates and tables and equations, which is something that Melanie is very good at. She knows all the kings and queens of England and when they reigned, and all the cities in the United Kingdom with their areas and populations and the rivers that run through them (if they have rivers) and their mottoes (if they have mottoes). She also knows the capitals of Europe and their populations and the years when they were at war with Britain, which most of them were at one time or another.

She doesn't find it hard to remember this stuff; she does it to keep from being bored, because being bored is worse than almost anything. If she knows surface area and total population, she can work out mean population density in her head and then do regression analyses to guess how many people there might be in ten, twenty, thirty years' time.

But there's sort of a problem with that. Melanie learned the stuff about the cities of the United Kingdom from Mr Whitaker's lessons, and she's not sure if she's got all the details right. Because one day, when Mr Whitaker was acting kind of

funny and his voice was all slippery and fuzzy, he said something that worried Melanie. She was asking him whether
1,036,900 was the population of the whole of Birmingham
with all its suburbs or just the central metropolitan area, and
he said, "Who cares? None of this stuff matters any more. I
just gave it to you because all the textbooks we've got are
thirty years old."

Melanie persisted, because she knew that Birmingham is the
biggest city in England after London, and she wanted to be
sure she had the numbers exactly right. "But the census figures
from—" she said.

Mr Whitaker cut her off. "Jesus, Melanie, it's irrelevant. It's
ancient history! There's nothing out there any more. Not a
damn thing. The population of Birmingham is zero."

So it's possible, even quite likely, that some of Melanie's lists
need to be updated in some respects.

The children have lessons on Monday, Tuesday, Wednesday,
Thursday and Friday. On Saturday, they stay locked in their
rooms all day and music plays over the PA system. Nobody
comes, not even Sergeant, and the music is too loud to talk
over. Melanie had the idea long ago of making up a language
that used signs instead of words, so the children could talk to
each other through their little mesh windows, and she went
ahead and made the language up, which was fun to do, but
when she asked Miss Justineau if she could teach it to the
class, Miss Justineau told her no, really loud and sharp. She
made Melanie promise not to mention her sign language to
any of the other teachers, and especially not to Sergeant. "He's
paranoid enough already," she said. "If he thinks you're talking
behind his back, he'll lose what's left of his mind."

So Melanie never got to teach the other children how to
talk in sign language.

Saturdays are long and dull, and hard to get through. Melanie
tells herself aloud some of the stories that the children have
been told in class, or sings mathematical proofs like the proof

for the infinity of prime numbers, in time to the music. It's okay to do this out loud because the music hides her voice. Otherwise Sergeant would come in and tell her to stop.

Melanie knows that Sergeant is still there on Saturdays, because one Saturday when Ronnie hit her hand against the mesh window of her cell until it bled and got all mashed up, Sergeant came in. He brought two of his people, and all three of them were dressed in the big suits that hide their faces, and they went into Ronnie's cell and Melanie guessed from the sounds that they were trying to tie Ronnie into her chair. She also guessed from the sounds that Ronnie was struggling and making it hard for them, because she kept shouting and saying, "Leave me alone! Leave me alone!" Then there was a banging sound that went on and on while one of Sergeant's people shouted, "Christ Jesus, don't—" and then other people were shouting too, and someone said, "Grab her other arm! Hold her!" and then it all went quiet again.

Melanie couldn't tell what happened after that. The people who work for Sergeant went around and locked all the little screens over the mesh windows, so the children couldn't see out. They stayed locked all day. The next Monday, Ronnie wasn't in the class any more, and nobody seemed to know what had happened to her. Melanie likes to think there's another classroom somewhere else on the base, and Ronnie went there, so she might come back one day when Sergeant shuffles the deck again. But what she really believes, when she can't stop herself from thinking about it, is that Sergeant took Ronnie away to punish her for being bad, and he won't let her see any of the other children ever again.

Sundays are like Saturdays except for chow time and the shower. At the start of the day the children are put in their chairs as though it's a regular school day, but with just their right hands and forearms unstrapped. They're wheeled into the shower room, which is the last door on the right, just before the bare steel door.

In the shower room, which is white-tiled and empty, the children sit and wait until everybody has been wheeled in. Then Sergeant's people bring chow bowls and spoons. They put a bowl on each child's lap, the spoon already sticking into it.

In the bowl there are about a million grubs, all squirming and wriggling over each other.

The children eat.

In the stories that they read, children sometimes eat other things – cakes and chocolate and bangers and mash and crisps and sweets and spaghetti and meatballs. The children only eat grubs, and only once a week, because – as Dr Selkirk explains one time when Melanie asks – their bodies are spectacularly efficient at metabolising proteins. They don't have to have any of those other things, not even water to drink. The grubs give them everything they need.

When they've finished eating, and the bowls have been taken away again, Sergeant's people go out, close the doors and cycle the door seals. The shower room is completely dark now, because there aren't any lights in there. Pipes behind the walls start to make a sound like someone trying not to laugh, and a chemical spray falls from the ceiling.

It's the same chemical that's on the teachers and Sergeant and Sergeant's people, or at least it smells the same, but it's a lot stronger. It stings a little, at first. Then it stings a lot. It leaves Melanie's eyes puffy, reddened and half blind. But it evaporates quickly from clothes and skin, so after half an hour more of sitting in the still, dark room, there's nothing left of it but the smell, and then finally the smell fades too, or at least they get used to it so it's not so bad any more, and they just wait in silence for the door to be unlocked and Sergeant's people to come and get them. This is how the children are washed, and for that reason, if for no other, Sunday is probably the worst day of the week.

The best day of the week is whichever day Miss Justineau

teaches. It isn't always the same day, and some weeks she doesn't come at all, but whenever Melanie is wheeled into the classroom and sees Miss Justineau there, she feels a surge of pure happiness, like her heart flying up out of her into the sky.

Nobody gets bored on Miss Justineau days. It's a thrill for Melanie even to look at her. She likes to guess what Miss Justineau will be wearing, and whether her hair will be up or down. It's usually down, and it's long and black and really crinkly so it looks like a waterfall. But sometimes she ties it up in a knot on the back of her head, really tight, and that's good too, because it makes her face sort of stand out more, almost like she's a statue on the side of a temple, holding up the ceiling. A caryatid. Although Miss Justineau's face stands out anyway because it's such a wonderful, wonderful colour. It's dark brown, like the wood of the trees in Melanie's rainforest picture whose seeds only grow out of the ashes of a bushfire, or like the coffee that Miss Justineau pours out of her flask into her cup at break time. Except it's darker and richer than either of those things, with lots of other colours mixed in, so there isn't anything you can really compare it to. All you can say is that it's as dark as Melanie's skin is light.

And sometimes Miss Justineau wears a scarf or something over her shirt, tied around her neck and shoulders. On those days Melanie thinks she looks either like a pirate or like one of the women of Hamelin when the Pied Piper came. But the women of Hamelin in the picture in Miss Justineau's book were mostly old and bent over, and Miss Justineau is young and not bent over at all and very tall and very beautiful. So she's more like a pirate really, except not with long boots and not with a sword.

When Miss Justineau teaches, the day is full of amazing things. Sometimes she'll read poems aloud, or bring her flute and play it, or show the children pictures out of a book and tell them stories about the people in the pictures. That was how Melanie got to find out about Pandora and Epimetheus and the box full of all the evils of the world, because one day Miss J showed them a picture in the book. It was a picture of a woman opening a box and lots of really scary things coming out of it. "Who is that?" Anne asked Miss Justineau.

"That's Pandora," Miss Justineau said. "She was a really amazing woman. All the gods had blessed her and given her gifts. That's what her name means – 'the girl with all the gifts'. So she was clever, and brave, and beautiful, and funny, and everything else you'd want to be. But she just had the one tiny fault, which was that she was very – and I mean *very* – curious."

She had the kids hooked by this point, and they were loving it and so was she, and in the end they got the whole story, which started with the war between the gods and the Titans and ended with Pandora opening up the box and letting all the terrible things out.

Melanie said she didn't think it was right to blame Pandora for what happened, because it was a trap that Zeus had set for mortals and he made her be the way she was on purpose, just so the trap would get sprung.

"Say it loud, sister," Miss Justineau said. "Men get the pleasure, women get the rap." And she laughed. Melanie made Miss Justineau laugh! That was a really good day, even if she doesn't know what she said that was funny.

The only problem with the days when Miss Justineau teaches is that the time goes by too quickly. Every second is so precious to Melanie that she doesn't even blink; she just sits there wide-eyed, drinking in everything that Miss Justineau says, and memorising it so that she can play it back to herself later, in her cell. And whenever she can manage it, she asks Miss Justineau questions, because what she most likes to hear, and to remember, is Miss Justineau's voice saying her name, Melanie, in that way that makes her feel like the most important person in the world.

2

One time, Sergeant comes into the classroom on a Miss Justineau day. Melanie doesn't know he's there until he speaks, because he's standing right at the back of the class. When Miss Justineau says, ". . . and this time, Pooh and Piglet counted three sets of footprints in the snow," Sergeant's voice breaks in with, "What the hell is this?"

Miss Justineau stops and looks round. "I'm reading the children a story, Sergeant Parks," she says.

"I can see that," Sergeant's voice says. "I thought the idea was to put them through their paces, not give them a cabaret."

Miss Justineau tenses. If you didn't know her as well as Melanie knows her, and if you didn't watch her as closely as Melanie watches her, you'd most likely miss it. It's gone again really quickly, and her voice when she speaks sounds just the same as it always does, not angry at all. "That's exactly what we're doing," she says. "It's important to see how they process information. But there has to be input, so there can be output."

"Input?" Sergeant repeats. "You mean facts?"

"No. Not just facts. Ideas."

"Oh yeah, plenty of world-class ideas in *Winnie-the-Pooh*."

Sergeant is using sarcasm. Melanie knows how sarcasm works; you say the opposite of what you really mean. "Seriously, you're wasting your time. You want to tell them stories, tell them about Jack the Ripper and John Wayne Gacy."

"They're children," Miss Justineau points out.

"No."

"Psychologically speaking, yes. They're children."

"Well, then fuck psychology," Sergeant says, sounding kind of angry now. "That, what you said right there, that's why you don't want to read them *Winnie-the-Pooh*. You carry on that way, you'll start thinking of them as real kids. And then you'll slip up. And maybe you'll untie one of them because he needs a cuddle or something. I don't need to tell you what happens after that."

Sergeant comes out to the front of the class then, and he does something really horrible. He rolls up his sleeve, all the way to the elbow, and he holds his bare forearm in front of Kenny's face; right in front of Kenny, just an inch or so away from him. Nothing happens at first, but then Sergeant spits on his hand and rubs at his forearm, like he's wiping something away.

"Don't," says Miss Justineau. "Don't do that to him." But Sergeant doesn't answer her or look at her.

Melanie sits two rows behind Kenny, and two rows over, so she can see the whole thing. Kenny goes really stiff, and then his mouth gapes wide and he starts to snap at Sergeant's arm, which of course he can't reach. And drool starts to drip down from the corner of his mouth, but not much of it because nobody ever gives the children anything to drink, so it's thick, half solid, and it hangs there on the end of Kenny's chin, wobbling, while Kenny grunts and snaps at Sergeant's arm, and makes kind of moaning, whimpering sounds.

And bad as that is, it gets worse — because the kids on either side of Kenny start doing it too, as though it's something they've caught from Kenny, and the kids right behind twitch and shake as though someone is poking them really hard in the stomach.

"You see?" Sergeant says, and he turns to look at Miss Justineau's face to make sure she gets his point. And then he blinks, all surprised, and maybe he wishes he hadn't looked at her, because Miss Justineau is glaring at him like she wants to smack him in the face, and Sergeant lets his arm fall to his side and shrugs like none of this was ever important to him anyway.

"Not everyone who looks human is human," he says.

"No," Miss Justineau agrees. "I'm with you on that one."

Kenny's head sags a little sideways, which is as far as it can move because of the strap, and he makes a clicking sound in his throat.

"It's all right, Kenny," Miss Justineau says. "It will pass soon. Let's go on with the story. Would you like that? Would you like to hear what happened to Pooh and Piglet? Sergeant Parks, if you'll excuse us? Please?"

Sergeant looks at her, and shakes his head really hard. "You don't want to get attached to them," he says. "You know what they're here for. Hell, you know better than—"

But Miss Justineau starts to read again, like she can't hear him, like he's not even there, and in the end he leaves. Or maybe he's still standing at the back of the classroom, not speaking, but Melanie doesn't think so because after a while Miss Justineau gets up and shuts the door, and Melanie thinks that she'd only do that right then if Sergeant was on the other side of it.

Melanie barely sleeps at all that night. She keeps thinking about what Sergeant said, that the children aren't real children, and about how Miss Justineau looked at him when he was being so nasty to Kenny.

And she thinks about Kenny snarling and snapping at Sergeant's arm like a dog. She wonders why he did it, and she thinks maybe she knows the answer because when Sergeant

14

wiped his arm with spit and waved it under Kenny's nose, it was as though under the bitter chemical smell Sergeant had a different smell altogether. And even though the smell was very faint where Melanie was, it made her head swim and her jaw muscles start to work by themselves. She can't even figure out what it was she was feeling, because it's not like anything that ever happened to her before or anything she heard about in a story, but it was like there was something she was supposed to do and it was so urgent, so important that her body was trying to take over her mind and do it without her.

But along with these scary thoughts, she also thinks: *Sergeant has a name.* The same way the teachers do. The same way the children do. Up until now, Sergeant has been more like a god or a Titan to Melanie; now she knows that he's just like everyone else, even if he is scary. He's not just Sergeant, he's Sergeant Parks. The enormity of that change, more than anything else, is what keeps her awake until the doors unlock in the morning and the teachers come.

In a way, Melanie's feelings about Miss Justineau have changed too, after that day. Or rather, they haven't changed at all, but they've become about a hundred times stronger. There can't be anyone better or kinder or lovelier than Miss Justineau anywhere in the world; Melanie wishes she was a god or a Titan or a Trojan warrior, so she could fight for Miss Justineau and save her from Heffalumps and Woozles. She knows that Heffalumps and Woozles are in *Winnie-the-Pooh*, not in a Greek myth, but she likes the words, and she likes the idea of saving Miss Justineau so much that it becomes her favourite thought. She thinks about it whenever she's not thinking about anything else. It makes even Sundays bearable.

So one day when Miss Mailer unstraps everybody's right arms from the elbow down, slots the tray tables on to their chairs and tells them to write a story, that's the story that Melanie writes. Miss Mailer is only interested in their vocabulary, of course, and doesn't care much at all what their stories are about. This is really obvious because she gives out a word list alongside the assignment and tells the class that every word from the word list they use correctly gets them an extra point in the assessment.

Melanie ignores the word list and cuts loose.

When Miss Mailer asks who would like to read their story aloud, she's the first to wave – as far as you can wave with just your forearm free – and say "Me, Miss Mailer! Pick me!"

So she gets to read her story. Which goes like this.

Once upon a time there was a very beautiful woman. The most beautiful and kind and clever and amazing woman in all the world. She was tall and not bent over, with skin so dark she was like her own shadow, and long black hair that curled around so much it made you dizzy to look at her. And she lived in ancient Greece, after the war between the gods and the Titans, when the gods had already won.

And one day, as she was walking in a forest, she was attacked by a monster. It was a frigging abortion, and it wanted to kill her and eat her. The woman was really brave, and she fought and fought, but the monster was very big and very fierce and it didn't matter how many times she wounded it, it just kept on coming.

The woman was afraid. She hugged her fear to her mortal soul.

The monster broke her sword, and her spear, and it was about to eat her.

But then a little girl came along. She was a special little girl, made by all the gods, like Pandora. And she was like Achilles too, because her mother (the beautiful, amazing woman) had dipped her in the water of the River Styx, so she was all invulnerable except for one little part of her (but it wasn't her heel because that's obvious; it was a place that she kept secret so the monster couldn't find it).

And the little girl fought the monster and killed it and cut

off its head and its arms and legs and all the other bits of it.
And the beautiful woman hugged her to her mortal soul, and
said, "You are my special girl. You will always be with me, and
I will never let you go."

And they lived together, for ever after, in great peace and
prosperity.

The last sentence is stolen word for word from a story by
the Brothers Grimm that Miss Justineau read to the class once,
and some of the other bits are sort of borrowed from Miss
Justineau's Greek myths book, which is called *Tales the Muses
Told*, or just from cool things she's heard people say. But it's
still Melanie's story, and she's very happy when the other kids
all say how good it is. Even Kenny, in the end, says he liked
the part where the monster got chopped up.

Miss Mailer seems happy too. The whole time Melanie was
reading the story out, she was scribbling in her notebook. And
she recorded the reading on her little hand recorder machine.
Melanie hopes she'll play it back to Miss Justineau, so Miss
Justineau will get to hear it too.

"That was really interesting, Melanie," Miss Mailer says. She
puts the recorder down on Melanie's tray table, right in front
of her, and asks her a lot of questions about the story. What
did the monster look like? How did the girl feel about the
monster when it was alive? How did she feel about it after it
was dead? How did she feel about the woman? And lots of
stuff like that, which is kind of fun because it feels almost like
the people in the story are real somewhere.

Like she saved Miss Justineau from a monster, and Miss
Justineau hugged her.

Which is better than a million Greek myths.

17

3

One day Miss Justineau talks to them about death. It's because most of the men in the Light Brigade have just died, in a poem that Miss Justineau read to the class. The children want to know what it means to die, and what it's like. Miss Justineau says it's like all the lights going out, and everything going really quiet, the way it does at night – but for ever. No morning. The lights never come back on again.

"That sounds terrible," says Lizzie in a voice like she's about to cry. It sounds terrible to Melanie too; like sitting in the shower room on Sunday with the chemical smell in the air, and then even the smell goes away and there's nothing at all for ever and ever.

Miss Justineau can see that she's upset them, and she tries to make it okay again by talking about it more. "But maybe it's not like that at all," she says quickly. "Nobody really knows, because when you're dead, you can't come back to talk about it. And anyway, it would be different for you than it would be for most people because you're—"

And then she stops herself, with the next word sort of frozen halfway out of her lips.

"We're what?" Melanie asks.

It's a moment or two before Miss Justineau says anything. It looks to Melanie like she's thinking of something to say that won't make them feel any worse than they do already. "You're children. You can't really imagine what death might be like, because for children it seems like everything has to go on for ever."

That isn't what she was going to say, Melanie is pretty sure. But it's really interesting, just the same. There's a silence while they think about it. It's true, Melanie decides. She can't remember a time when her life was any different than this, and she can't imagine any other way that people could live. But there's something that doesn't make sense to her in the whole equation, and so she has to ask the question.

"*Whose* children are we, Miss Justineau?"

In most stories she knows, children have a mother and a father, like Iphigenia had Clytemnestra and Agamemnon, and Helen had Leda and Zeus. Sometimes they have teachers too, but not always, and they never seem to have sergeants. So this is a question that gets to the very roots of the world, and Melanie asks it with some trepidation.

Again Miss Justineau thinks about it for a long time, until Melanie is sure she won't answer. Then she says, "Your mother is dead, Melanie. She died when you were very little. Probably your daddy's dead too, although there isn't really any way of knowing. So the army is looking after you now."

"Is that just Melanie?" John asks. "Or is it all of us?"

Miss Justineau nods slowly. "All of you."

"We're in an orphanage," Anne guesses. (The class heard the story of Oliver Twist once, on another Miss Justineau day.)

"No. You're on an army base."

"Is that what happens to kids whose mum and dad die?" This is Steven now.

"Sometimes."

Melanie is thinking hard and putting all these facts together inside her head, like they're pieces of a puzzle. "How old was I," she asks, "when my mother died?" Because she must have been very young if she can't remember her mother at all.

"It's not easy to explain," Miss Justineau says, and they can see from her face that she's really not comfortable talking about this stuff.

"Was I still a baby?" Melanie asks.

"Not really. But almost. You were very young."

"And did my mother give me to the army?"

Another long silence.

"No," Miss Justineau says at last. "The army pretty much helped itself."

It comes out quick and low and almost hard. Miss Justineau changes the subject then, and the children are happy to let her do it because nobody is very enthusiastic about death by this point.

So they do the periodic table of the elements, which is easy and fun. Starting with Miles in the front row at the very end, everyone takes turns to name an element. First time around they do it in straight number order. Then they reverse it. Then Miss Justineau shouts out challenges like "Has to start with the letter N!" or "Actinides only!"

Nobody drops out until the challenges get really hard, like "Can't follow in group or period, and has to start with a letter that's in your name!" Zoe complains that that means people with long names have more chances, and she's right, obviously, but still she's got zinc, zirconium, oxygen, osmium, einsteinium, erbium and europium to choose from, so she's not doing too badly.

By the time Xanthi wins (with xenon), everyone is laughing and it looks as though all the death stuff is forgotten. It isn't, of course. Melanie knows her classmates well enough to be sure that they're turning Miss Justineau's words over and over in their minds, the same way she is – shaking them and worrying at them, to see what insights might fall out. Because the one thing they never learn about, really, is themselves.

And by this time, Melanie has thought of the big exception to that rule about kids having mothers and fathers – Pandora, who didn't have a mother or a father because Zeus just made her out of gloopy clay. Melanie thinks that would be better, in some ways, than having a mother and a father who you never even got to meet. The ghost of her parents' absence hovers around her, makes her uneasy.

But she wants to know one more thing, and she wants it badly enough that she even takes the chance of upsetting Miss Justineau some more. At the end of the lesson, she waits until Miss Justineau is close to her and she asks her question really quietly.

"Miss Justineau, what will happen when we're grown up? Will the army still want to keep us, or will we go home to Beacon? And if we go there, will all the teachers come with us?"

All the teachers! Yeah, right. Like she cares if she ever sees Mr Slippery-Voice-Whitaker again. Or boring Dr Selkirk, who looks at the ground the whole time like she's scared of even seeing the class. She means *you, Miss Justineau, you, you, you,* and she wants to say it, but at the same time she's scared to, like saying the wish out loud will make it not happen.

And she knows, again extrapolating from the stories she's read or heard, that children don't stay in school for ever. They don't set up home with their teachers and live there and be there with them when school is finished. And although she doesn't really know what those words mean, what school being finished could possibly be like, she accepts that it will someday happen and therefore that something else will start.

So she's ready for Miss Justineau to say no. She's hardened herself to let nothing show in her face, if that's the answer. She really just wants the facts, so she can prepare herself for the grief of separation.

21

But Miss Justineau doesn't answer at all. Unless the quick movement of her hand is an answer. She puts it up in front of her own face as though Melanie has thrown something at her (which Melanie never, ever would do in a million years!).

Then the siren whoops three times to signal the end of the day. And Miss Justineau ducks her head, pulling herself together after that imaginary blow. And it's sort of a strange thing, but for the first time Melanie realises that Miss Justineau always wears red, somewhere on her. Her T-shirt, or her hairband, or her trousers, or her scarf. All the other teachers and Dr Caldwell and Dr Selkirk wear white, and Sergeant and Sergeant's people wear green and brown and greeny-brown. Miss Justineau is red.

Like blood.

Like something about her is wounded, and not healing, and hurting her all the time.

That's a stupid idea, Melanie thinks, because Miss Justineau always smiles and laughs and her voice is like a song. If something was hurting her, she wouldn't be able to smile so much. But right then, Miss Justineau isn't smiling at all. She's staring down at the ground, and her face is all twisted up like she's angry, sad, sick – like something bad is going to come out of her anyway, and it might be tears or words or vomit or all three.

"I'll stay," Melanie blurts. She's desperate to make Miss Justineau feel okay again. "If you have to stay here, I'll stay with you. I wouldn't want to be in Beacon without you there."

Miss Justineau lifts her head and looks at Melanie again. Her eyes are very shiny, and her mouth is like the line on Dr Caldwell's EEG machine, changing all the time.

"I'm sorry," Melanie says quickly. "Please don't be sad, Miss Justineau. You can do whatever you want to do, of course you can. You can go or stay or . . ."

She doesn't get another word out. She crashes into total, tongue-tied silence, because something completely unexpected and absolutely wonderful happens.

22

Miss Justineau puts out her hand and strokes Melanie's hair.

She strokes Melanie's hair with her hand, like it was just the most natural and normal thing in the world.

And lights are dancing behind Melanie's eyes, and she can't get her breath, and she can't speak or hear or think about anything because apart from Sergeant's people, maybe two or three times and always by accident, nobody has ever touched her before and this is Miss Justineau touching her and it's almost too nice to be in the world at all.

Everybody in the class who can see is watching. Everybody's eyes and mouths are big and wide. It's so quiet, you can hear Miss Justineau draw a breath, with a little tremor at the end of it, as though she's shivering from cold.

"Oh God!" she whispers.

"Here endeth the lesson," says Sergeant.

Melanie can't turn her head to look at him, because of the neck strap on her chair. Nobody else seems to have seen Sergeant come into the room either. They're all just as surprised and scared as she is. Even Miss Justineau looks scared, which is another one of those things (like Sergeant having a name) that changes the architecture of the whole world.

Sergeant walks into Melanie's line of sight, right behind Miss Justineau. Miss Justineau has already snatched her hand away from Melanie's hair, as soon as Sergeant spoke. She ducks her head again, so Melanie can't see her face.

"They go back now," Sergeant says.

"Right." Miss Justineau's voice is very small.

"And you go on a charge."

"Right."

"And maybe you lose your job. Because every rule we got, you just broke."

Miss Justineau brings her head up again. Both her eyes are wet with tears now. "Fuck you, Eddie," she says, as quietly and calmly as if she was saying good morning.

She walks out of Melanie's line of sight, very quickly. Melanie

23

wants to call her back, wants to say something to make her stay: *I love you, Miss Justineau. I'll be a god or a Titan for you, and save you.* But she can't say anything, and then Sergeant's people come and start to wheel the kids away one by one.

4

Why? Why did she do that?

Helen Justineau has no good answer, so she just keeps on asking herself the question. Stands forlorn in her room in the luxuriously appointed civilian block, a foot on every side bigger than a regular soldier's room, and with an en suite chemical toilet. Leaning against the mirror on the wall, avoiding her own sick, accusing gaze.

She scrubbed her hands until they were raw, but she can still feel that cold flesh. So cold, as though blood never ran in it. As though she was touching something that had just been dredged up from the bottom of the sea.

Why did she do it? What happened in that laying on of hands?

Nice cop is just a role she plays – observing and measuring the children's emotional responses to her so she can write mealy-mouthed reports for Caroline Caldwell about their capacity for normal affect.

Normal affect. That's what Justineau is feeling now, presumably.

It's like she dug a pit trap, nice and deep, squared off the edges, wiped her hands. Then walked right into it.

Except that it was test subject number one, really, who dug the pit. Melanie. It was her desperate, obvious, hero-worshipping crush that tripped Justineau up, or at least threw her far enough off balance that tripping became inevitable. Those big, trusting eyes, in that bone-white face. Death and the maiden, all wrapped up in one tiny package.

She didn't turn the compassion off in time. She didn't remind herself, the way she does at the start of every day, that when the programme wraps up, Beacon will airlift her out of here the same way they airlifted her in. Quick and easy, taking all her things with her, leaving no footprint. This isn't life. It's something that's playing out in its own self-contained subroutine. She can walk out as clean as when she came in, if she just doesn't let anything touch her.

That horse, however, may already have bolted.

5

Every once in a while in the block, there's a day that doesn't start right. A day when all the repeating patterns that Melanie uses as measuring sticks for her life fail to occur, one after another, and she feels like she's bobbing around helplessly in the air – a Melanie-shaped balloon. The week after Miss Justineau told the class that their mothers were dead, there's a day like that.

It's a Friday, but when Sergeant and his people arrive they don't bring a teacher with them and they don't open the cell doors. Melanie already knows what's going to happen next, but she still feels a prickle of unease when she hears the clacking of Dr Caldwell's high-heeled shoes on the concrete floor. And then a moment or two later she hears the sound of Dr Caldwell's pen, which Dr Caldwell will sometimes keep clicking on and off and on and off even when she doesn't want to write anything.

Melanie doesn't get up off the bed. She just sits there and waits. She doesn't like Dr Caldwell very much. That's partly because the rhythms of the day get disrupted whenever Dr Caldwell shows up, but it's mostly because she doesn't know what Dr Caldwell is for. The teachers teach, and Sergeant's people take the kids back and forth between the classroom and the cells, and feed them and shower them on Sundays. Dr Caldwell just appears, at unforeseeable times (Melanie tried to work out once if there was a pattern, but she couldn't find one), and everyone stops doing what they were doing, or what they're meant to do, until she's gone again.

The clacking of the shoes and the clicking of the pen get louder and louder and then stop.

"Good morning, Doctor," Sergeant says, out in the corridor. "To what do we owe the pleasure?"

"Sergeant," Dr Caldwell answers. Her voice is almost as soft and warm as Miss Justineau's, which makes Melanie feel a little bit guilty about not liking her. She's probably really nice if you get to know her. "I'm starting a new test series, and I need one of each."

"One of each?" Sergeant repeats. "You mean, a boy and a girl?"

"A what and a what?" Dr Caldwell laughs musically. "No, I don't mean that at all. The gender is completely irrelevant. We've established that much. I meant high and low end of the bell curve."

"Well, you just tell me which ones you want. I'll pack them up and bring them over."

There's a rustling of papers. "Sixteen should do fine for the lower end," Dr Caldwell says. Her heel taps on the floor of the corridor a few times, but she's not walking because the sound doesn't get louder or softer. Her pen clicks.

"You want this one?" Sergeant asks. His voice sounds really close.

Melanie looks up. Dr Caldwell is looking in through the grille in her cell door. Her eyes meet Melanie's, for a long time, and neither of them blinks.

"Our little genius?" Dr Caldwell says. "Wash your mouth out, Sergeant. I'm not going to waste number one on a simple stratum comp. When I come for Melanie, there'll be angels and trumpets."

Sergeant mutters something Melanie can't hear, and Dr Caldwell laughs. "Well, I'm sure you can supply some trumpets at least." She turns away, and the *click-clack-click* of her heels recedes along the corridor.

"Two little ducks," she calls. "Twenty-two."

Melanie doesn't know the cell numbers for all the kids, but she remembers most of them from when a teacher has called someone in the class by their number instead of their name. Marcia is number sixteen and Liam is number twenty-two. She wonders what Dr Caldwell wants them for, and what she'll say to them.

She goes to the grille and watches Sergeant's people go into cell 16 and cell 22. They wheel Liam and Marcia out, and down the corridor – not towards the classroom, but the other way, towards the big steel door.

Melanie watches them as far as she can, but they go further than that. She thinks they have to have gone through the door, because what else is down at that end of the corridor? They're seeing with their own eyes what's outside the door!

Melanie hopes it's a Miss Justineau day, because Miss Justineau lets the kids talk to each other about stuff that's not in the lesson, so when Liam and Marcia come back she'll be able to ask them what Dr Caldwell talked to them about, and what they did, and what's on the far side of the door.

Of course, she hopes it will be a Miss Justineau day for a lot of other reasons too.

And it turns out it is. The children make up songs for Miss Justineau to play on her flute, with complicated rules for how long the words are and how they rhyme. They have great fun, but the day goes on and Liam and Marcia don't come back. So Melanie can't ask, and she goes back to her cell that night with her curiosity, if anything, burning even brighter.

Then it's the weekend, with no lessons and no talking. All

29

through Saturday Melanie listens, but the steel door doesn't open and nobody comes or goes.

Liam and Marcia aren't in the shower on Sunday.

And Monday is Miss Mailer, and Tuesday is Mr Whitaker, and somehow after that Melanie feels afraid to ask because the possibility has opened up in her mind, like a crack in a wall, that Liam and Marcia might not come back at all, the same way Ronnie didn't come back after she shouted and screamed that time. And maybe asking the question will change what happens. Maybe if they all pretend not to notice, Liam and Marcia will be wheeled in one day and it will be like they never went away. But if anyone asks, "Where did they go to?" then they'll really be gone and she'll never see them again.

6

"Okay," Miss Justineau says. "Does anyone know what today is?"

It's Tuesday, obviously, and more important than that, it's a Miss Justineau day, but everyone tries to guess what else it might be. "Your birthday?" "The *king's* birthday?" "The day when something important happened, years ago?" "A day with a palindromic date?" "A day when someone new is coming?"

They're all excited, because they know it's got something to do with the big canvas bag that Miss Justineau brought in with her, and they can see that she's just as excited to show them what's inside. It's going to be a good day – one of the best days, probably.

But it's Siobhan, in the end, who gets it. "It's the first day of spring!" she shouts from behind Melanie.

"Good for you, Siobhan," Miss Justineau says. "Absolutely right. It's the twenty-first of March and, for the part of the world where we live, that's . . . what? What's the big deal about the twenty-first?"

"The first day of spring," Tom repeats, but Melanie, who's kicking herself for not seeing this sooner, knows that Miss

31

Justineau is looking for more than that. "It's the vernal equinox!" she says quickly before anyone else can.

"Exactly," Miss Justineau agrees. "Give the lady a big hand. It's the vernal equinox. Now, what does that mean?"

The kids all clamour to answer. Usually nobody bothers to tell them what date it is, and of course they never get to see the sky, but they're familiar with the theory. Ever since the solstice, way back in December, the nights have been getting shorter and the days have been getting longer (not that the kids ever see night and day, because the rooms in the block don't have any windows). Today is the day when the two finally balance. The night and the day are both exactly twelve hours long.

"And that makes it kind of a magical day," Miss Justineau says. "In olden times, it meant the long dark of winter was finally over, and things would start growing again and the world would be renewed. The solstice was the promise – that the days wouldn't just keep on getting shorter until they disappeared altogether. The equinox was the day when the promise was fulfilled."

Miss Justineau picks up the big bag and puts it on the table. "And I was thinking about this," she says slowly, knowing they're all watching, knowing that they're aching to see what's in the bag. "And it occurred to me that nobody ever showed you, really, what spring is all about. So I climbed over the perimeter fence . . ."

Gasps from the children. Region 6 may be mostly cleared, but outside the fence still belongs to the hungries. As soon as you're out there, they can see you and smell you – and once they get your scent, they're never going to stop following you until they've eaten you.

Miss Justineau laughs at the horrified expressions on their faces. "Only kidding," she says. "There's actually a part of the camp where the soldiers didn't bother to finish clearing when they set up this base. There's lots of wild flowers there, and

32

even a few trees. So . . ." – and she pulls the mouth of the bag wide open – "I went over there, and I just grabbed what I could find. Would have felt like vandalism, before the Breakdown, but the wild flowers are doing okay for themselves these days, so I just thought what the hell."

She reaches into the bag and takes something out. It's a sort of stick, long and twisted, with smaller sticks coming off it in all directions. And the smaller sticks have smaller sticks, and so on, so it's a really crazy, complicated shape. And all over it there are these little green dots – but as Miss Justineau turns the stick in her hand, Melanie can see that they're not dots. They bulge right out from the stick, as though they're being forced up from inside it. And some of them are broken; they've split in the middle and they're sort of peeling into ever-so-slender green lips and brackets.

"Anyone know what this is?" Miss Justineau asks.

Nobody speaks. Melanie is thinking about it hard, trying to match it up with something she's already seen, or maybe been told about in class. She's just about to get it, because the word means what it says – the way the big stick breaks into smaller sticks, and again and again, so there's more and more of them, like breaking down a great big number into the long list of its prime factors.

"It's a branch," Joanne says.

Dummy, dummy, dummy, Melanie scolds herself. Her rainforest picture is just full of branches. But the real branch looks different somehow. Its shape is more complicated and broken up, its textures rougher.

"You're damn right it's a branch," Miss Justineau agrees. "I think it's an alder. A couple of thousand years ago, the people who lived around here would have called this time of year the alder month. They used the bark of the tree for medicine, because it's really rich in something called salicin. It's kind of a natural pain relief drug."

She goes around the class, unstrapping the children's right

33

arms from their chairs so that they can hold the branch and look at it right up close. It's kind of ugly, Melanie thinks, but absolutely fascinating. Especially when Miss Justineau explains that the little green balls are buds – and they'll turn into leaves and cover the whole tree in green, as though it's put a summer dress on.

But there's a lot more stuff in the bag, and when Miss Justineau starts to unpack it, the whole class stares in awe. Because the bag is full of colours – starbursts and wheels and whorls of dazzling brightness that are as fine and complex in their structures as the branch is, only much more symmetrical. Flowers.

"Red campion," Miss Justineau says, holding up a spray that's not red at all but sort of purple, each petal forked into two like the footprint of an animal in a tracking chart Melanie saw once.

"Rosemary." White fingers and green fingers, all laced together like your hands clasped together in your lap when you're nervous and you don't want to fidget.

"Daffodils." Yellow tubes like the trumpets angels blow in the old pictures in Miss Justineau's books, but with fringed lips so delicate they move when Miss Justineau breathes on them.

"Medlar." White spheres in dense clusters, each one made out of overlapping petals that are curved and nested on themselves, and open at one end to show something inside that looks like a tiny model of more flowers.

The children are hypnotised. It's spring in the classroom. It's equinox, with the world balanced between winter and summer, life and death, like a spinning ball balanced on the tip of someone's finger.

When everyone has looked at the flowers, and held them, Miss Justineau puts them in bottles and jars all around the classroom, wherever there's a shelf or a table or a clear surface, so the whole room becomes a meadow.

She reads the class some poems about flowers, starting with

34

one by Walt Whitman about lilacs and how spring always comes back again, but Walt Whitman hasn't got very far at all before he's talking about death and offering to give his lilacs to a coffin that he's seen, so Miss Justineau says let's quit while we're ahead and reads Thomas Campion instead. He even has the same name as a flower, Melanie thinks, and she likes his poem a whole lot better.

But maybe the most important thing that comes out of this day is that Melanie now knows what date it is. She doesn't want to stop knowing again, so she decides to keep count.

She clears a place in her mind, just for the date, and every day she goes to that place and adds one. She makes sure to ask Miss Justineau if this is a leap year, which it is. Once she knows that, she's good.

Knowing the date is reassuring in some way she can't quite figure out. It's like it gives her a secret power – like she's in control of a little piece of the world.

It's not until then that she realises she's never had that feeling before.

7

Caroline Caldwell is very skilled at separating brains from skulls. She does it quickly and methodically, and she gets the brain out in one piece, with minimal tissue damage. She's reached the point now where she could almost do it in her sleep.

In fact, it's been three nights since she slept, and there's an itchiness behind her eyes that isn't eased by rubbing them. But her mind is clear, with only the very slightest sense of a hallucinatory edge to that clarity. She knows what she's doing. She watches herself do it, approving the virtuosity of her own technique.

The first cut is to the rear of the occipital bone – easing her slimmest bone-saw into the gap that Selkirk has opened up for her, through the peeled-back layers of flesh and between the nubs and buds of exposed muscle.

She extends that first cut out to either side, taking care to maintain a straight horizontal line corresponding to the widest part of the skull. It's important to have enough room to work in, so she doesn't squash the brain or leave part of it behind when she takes it out. She journeys on, the bone-saw flicking lightly back and forth like the bow of a violin, through the parietal and temporal bones, keeping the same straight line, until she comes at last to the superciliary ridges.

At that point, the straight line ceases to matter. Instead, X marks the spot; Dr Caldwell draws the saw down from top left to bottom right, then up again from bottom left to top right, making two slightly deeper incisions that cross at the midpoint between the subject's eyes.

Which flicker in rapid saccades, focus and defocus in restless busy-work.

The subject is dead, but the pathogen that controls his nervous system isn't even slightly deterred by the loss of a steering consciousness. It still knows what it wants, and it's still the captain of this sinking ship.

Dr Caldwell deepens the intersecting cuts at the front of the skull, because the subject's sinuses in effect create a double thickness of bone there.

Then she puts down the bone-saw and picks up a screw-driver – part of a set that her father received as a free gift from the *Reader's Digest* publishing company when he subscribed to some of their products more than thirty years previously.

The next part is delicate, and difficult. She probes the cuts with the tip of the screwdriver, levering them further open where she can, but making sure that she never inserts the screwdriver's business end deep enough to damage the brain beneath.

The subject sighs, although he has no need for oxygen any more. "Soon be done," Dr Caldwell says, and feels foolish a half-second later. This is not a conversation, or a shared experience of any kind.

She sees Selkirk watching her, with a slightly guarded expression. Piqued, she snaps her fingers and points, making Selkirk pick up the bone-saw and hand it back to her.

Now she's engaged in a ballet of infinitesimal increments – testing the skull with the tip of the screwdriver to see where it moves, going in with the saw again where there's resistance, and gradually levering the whole top of the skull loose in one piece.

Which is the hardest part, now done.

Lifting the front of the calvarium, Caldwell snips loose cranial nerves and blood vessels with a number ten pencil-grip scalpel, lifting the brain gently from the front as it comes free. Once the spinal cord is exposed, she cuts that too.

But she doesn't try to lift the brain all the way out. Now that it's free, she hands the scalpel back to Selkirk and accepts a pair of snub-nosed pliers, with which she removes, very carefully, the few jagged edges of bone that stand proud from the rim of the hole she's made in the skull. It's all too easy to gouge troughs in the brain as you lift it through that makeshift trapdoor, and then it's of such limited use you might as well throw it away.

Now she lifts it; with both hands, from underneath, teasing it up with the tips of her fingers through the opening in the skull without ever letting it touch the edge.

And sets it down, with great care, on the cutting board.

Subject number twenty-two, whose name was Liam if you accept the idea of giving these things a name, continues to stare at her, his eyes tracking her movements. It doesn't mean he's alive. Dr Caldwell takes the view that the moment of death is the moment when the pathogen crosses the blood–brain barrier. What's left, though its heart may beat (some ten or twelve times per minute), and though it speaks and can even be christened with a boy's name or a girl's name, is not the host. It's the parasite.

And the parasite, whose needs and tropisms are very different from human needs and human instincts, is a diligent steward. It continues to run a wide range of bodily systems and networks without reference to the brain, which is just as well seeing as the brain is about to be cut into thin slices and set between glass plates.

"Shall I take the rest of the spinal cord out?" Selkirk asks.

She has that tentative, pleading tone in her voice that Caldwell despises. She's like a beggar on a street corner, asking not for money or food but for mercy. *Don't make me do anything nasty or difficult.*

Dr Caldwell, who is prepping the razor, doesn't even look around. "Sure," she says. "Go ahead."

She's brusque in her manner, even surly, because this part of the procedure, more than any other, hurts her professional pride. If anything were ever to make her shake her fist at the untenanted heavens, it would be this. She's read about how brains were sliced and mounted in the good old days, before the Breakdown. There was a device called an ATLUM – an automated lathe ultramicrotome – which with its diamond blade could be calibrated to slice brains into perfect cross-sections of single-neuron thickness. Thirty thousand slices per millimetre, give or take.

The best that Dr Caldwell's guillotine can manage, without smearing and crushing the fragile structures she wants to look at, is about ten slices per millimetre.

Mention Robert Edwards to Dr Caldwell. Mention Elizabeth Blackburn, Günter Blobel or Carol Greider, or any cellular biologist who ever got the Nobel prize, and see what she says.

More often than not she'll say: I bet he (or she) had an automated lathe ultramicrotome. And a TEAM 0.5 transmission electron microscope, and a live-cell imaging system, and an army of grad students, interns and lab assistants to handle the dull routine of processing so the Nobel laureate would be free to waltz in the moonlight with his frigging muse.

Dr Caldwell is trying to save the world, and she feels like she's wearing oven mitts instead of surgical gloves. She had her chance once to do it in style. But nothing came of it, and here she is. Alone, but complete unto herself. Still fighting.

Selkirk gives a bleat of dismay, jolting Caldwell out of her profitless reverie. "Spinal cord is severed, Doctor. Level with the twelfth vertebra."

"Toss it," Dr Caldwell mutters. She doesn't even try to hide her contempt.

8

One hundred and seventeen days have passed since the day when Liam and Marcia were taken away and didn't come back.

Melanie continues to think about it and worry at it, but she still hasn't asked Miss Justineau – or anyone else – what happened to them. The closest she's come is to ask Mr Whitaker what two little ducks means. She remembers Dr Caldwell saying those words on the day when it all happened.

Mr Whitaker is having one of those up-and-down days when he brings his bottle into class – the bottle full to the brim with the medicine that makes him first better and then worse. Melanie has watched this strange and mildly disturbing progress enough times that she can predict its course. Mr Whitaker comes into class nervous and irritable, determined to find fault with everything the children say or do.

Then he drinks the medicine, and it spreads through him like ink through water (it was Miss Justineau who showed them what that looks like). His body relaxes, losing its tics and twitches. His mind relaxes too, and for a little while he's gentle and patient with everyone. If he could only stop at that point, it would be wonderful, but he keeps drinking and the miracle is reversed. It's not that Mr Whitaker gets grumpy again. What he gets is something worse, something quite awful, that Melanie doesn't have a name for. He seems to sink in on himself in total misery, and at the same time try to shrink away from himself as though there's something inside him that's too nasty to touch. Sometimes he cries, and says he's sorry – not to the children, but to someone else who isn't really there, and whose name keeps changing.

Knowing this cycle well, Melanie times her question to coincide with the expansive phase. What might those two little ducks be, she asks Mr Whitaker, that Dr Caldwell mentioned? Why did she mention them right then, on the day when she took Marcia and Liam away?

"It's from a game called bingo," Mr Whitaker tells her, his voice only a little blurred around the edges. "In the game, each player gets a card full of numbers from one to a hundred. The caller calls out numbers at random, and the first player to have all their numbers called wins a prize."

"Are the two little ducks one of the prizes?" Melanie asks him.

"No, Melanie, they're one of the numbers. It's sort of a code. Every number has a special phrase or group of words attached to it. Two little ducks is twenty-two, because of the shapes the numbers make on the page. Look." He draws them on the whiteboard. "They look just like ducks swimming along, you see?"

Melanie thinks they look more like swans actually, but the game of bingo doesn't interest her very much. So all Dr Caldwell was doing was saying twenty-two twice, once in ordinary numbers and once in this code. Saying two times over that she was choosing Liam instead of someone else.

Choosing him for what?

Melanie thinks about numbers. Her secret language uses numbers – different numbers of fingers held up with your right hand and your left hand, or your right hand twice, if

42

your left hand is still tied to the chair. That makes six times six different combinations (because holding up no fingers is a signal too) – enough for all the letters of the alphabet and special signs for all the teachers and Dr Caldwell and Sergeant, plus a question mark and a sign that means "I'm joking".

A hundred and seventeen days means that it's summer now. Maybe Miss Justineau will bring the world into the classroom again – will show them what summer looks like, the way she did with spring. But Miss Justineau is different these days, when she's with the class. She sometimes forgets what she's saying, breaks off mid-sentence and goes quiet for a long time before she starts up again, usually with something completely different.

She reads from books a lot more, and organises games and sing-songs a lot less.

Maybe Miss Justineau is sad for some reason. That thought makes Melanie both desperate and angry. She wants to protect Miss Justineau, and she wants to know who'd be so horrible as to make her sad. If she could find out who it was, she doesn't know what she'd do to them, but it would make them very sorry.

And when she starts to think about who it might be, there's really only one name that comes into her mind.

And here he is walking into the classroom now, at the head of half a dozen of his people, his scowling face half crossed out by the wobbly diagonal of his scar. He puts his hands on the handles of Melanie's chair, swivels it around and pushes it out of the classroom. He does it really fast and jerky, the way he does most things. He wheels the chair right past the door of Melanie's cell, then he backs in, pushing the door open with his bottom, and spins the chair around so sharply and suddenly it makes Melanie dizzy.

Two of Sergeant's people come in behind him, but they don't go anywhere near the chair. They stand to attention and wait until Sergeant nods permission. One of them covers

Melanie with his handgun while the other starts to undo the straps, the neck strap first and from behind.

Melanie meets Sergeant's gaze, feeling something inside her clench like a fist. It's Sergeant's fault that Miss Justineau is sad. It has to be, because she only started to be sad after Sergeant got mad with her and told her she'd broken the rules.

"Look at you," he says to Melanie now. "Face all screwed up like a tragedy mask. Like you've got feelings. Jesus Christ!"

Melanie scowls at him, as fierce as she can get. "If I had a box full of all the evils of the world," she tells him, "I'd open it just a little way and push you inside. Then I'd close it again for always."

Sergeant laughs, and there's surprise in the laugh – like he can't believe what he just heard. "Well, shit," he says, "I'd better make sure you never get hold of a box."

Melanie is outraged that he took the biggest insult she could think of and laughed it off. She casts around desperately for a way to raise the stakes. "She loves me!" she blurts. "That's why she stroked my hair! Because she loves me and wants to be with me! And all you do is make her sad, so she hates you! She hates you as bad as if you were a hungry!"

Sergeant stares at her, and something happens in his face. It's like he's surprised, and then he's scared, and then he's angry. The fingers of his big hands pull back slowly into fists.

He puts his hands on the arms of the chair and slams it back against the wall. His face is very close to Melanie's, and it's all red and twisty.

"I will fucking dismantle you, you little roach!" he says in a choking voice.

Sergeant's people are watching all this with anxious looks on their faces. They look like they think there's something they should be doing but they're not sure what it is. One of them says, "Sergeant Parks . . ." but then doesn't say anything else.

Sergeant straightens up and steps back, makes a gesture that's halfway to being a shrug. "We're done here," he says.

"She's still strapped in," says the other one of Sergeant's people.

"Too bad," says Sergeant. He throws the door open and waits for them to move, looking at one of them and then the other until they give up and leave Melanie where she is and go out through the door.

"Sweet dreams, kid," Sergeant says. He slams the door shut behind him, and she hears the bolts shoot home.

One.

Two.

Three.

9

"I'm concerned about your objectivity," Dr Caldwell tells Helen Justineau.

Justineau doesn't answer, but her face probably says *excuse me?* all by itself.

"We're examining these subjects for a reason," Caldwell goes on. "You wouldn't necessarily know it from the level of support we get, but our research programme is incalculably important."

Justineau still says nothing, and Caldwell seems to feel a need to fill the vacuum. Maybe to overfill it. "It's no exaggeration to say that our survival as a race might depend on our figuring out why the infection has taken a different course in these children – as opposed to its normal progression in the other ninety-nine point nine nine nine per cent of subjects. Our survival, Helen. That's what we're playing for. Some hope of a future. Some way out of this mess."

They're in the lab, Caldwell's workshop of filthy creation, which Justineau doesn't often visit. She's only here now because Caldwell summoned her. This base and this mission may both be under military jurisdiction, but Caldwell is still her boss, and when that call comes, she has to answer. Has to leave the classroom and visit the torture chamber.

Brains in jars. Tissue cultures in which recognisably human limbs and organs spawn lumpy cloudscapes of grey fungal matter. A hand and forearm – child-sized, of course – flayed and opened, the flesh pinned back and slivers of yellow plastic inserted to prise apart muscle and leave interior structures open to examination. The room is cluttered and claustrophobic, the blinds always drawn down to keep the outside world at a clinically optimum distance. The light – pure white, unforgivingly intense – comes from fluorescent tubes that lie flush with the ceiling.

Caldwell is preparing microscope slides, using a razor blade to take slivers of tissue from what looks like a tongue.

Justineau doesn't flinch. She takes care to look at everything that's there, because she's a part of this process. Pretending not to see would, she believes, take her past some point of no return, past the event horizon of hypocrisy into a black hole of solipsism.

Christ, she might turn into Caroline Caldwell.

Who almost got to be part of the great big save-the-human-race think tank, back in the early days of what came to be called the Breakdown. A couple of dozen scientists, secret mission, secret government training – the biggest deal in a rapidly shrinking world. Many were called, and few were chosen. Caldwell was one of the ones at the front of the line when the doors closed in her face. Does that still sting, all these years later? Is that what drove her crazy?

It was so long ago now that Justineau has forgotten most of the details. Three years after the first wave of infections, when the freefalling societies of the developed world hit what they mistakenly thought was bottom. In the UK the numbers of infected appeared briefly to have stabilised, and a hundred initiatives were discussed. Beacon was going to find the cure, reclaim the cities, and restore a much-longed-for status quo.

47

In that strange false dawn, two mobile labs were commissioned. They weren't built from scratch – there wasn't time enough for that. Instead they were jury-rigged quickly and elegantly by refitting two vehicles already owned by the London Natural History Museum.

Intended to house travelling exhibitions, Charles Darwin and Rosalind Franklin – Charlie and Rosie – now became huge roving research stations. Each was the length of an articulated truck, and almost twice as wide. Each was fitted with state-of-the-art biology and organic chemistry labs, together with berths for a crew of six researchers, four guards and two drivers. They also benefited from a range of refurbishments approved by the Department of Defence, including the fitting of caterpillar treads, inch-thick external armour and both forward- and rear-mounted field guns and flame-throwers.

The great green hopes, as they were called, were unveiled with as much fanfare as could be mustered. Politicians hoping to be the heroes of the coming human renaissance made speeches over them and broke champagne bottles off their bows. They were launched with tears and prayers and poems and exordiums.

Into oblivion.

Things fell apart really quickly after that – the respite was just a chaos artefact, created by powerful forces momentarily cancelling each other out. The infection was still spreading, and global capitalism was still tearing itself apart – like the two giants eating each other in the Dalí painting called *Autumn Cannibalism*. No amount of expertly choreographed PR could prevail, in the end, against Armageddon. It strolled over the barricades and took its pleasure.

Nobody ever saw those hand-picked geniuses again. They're left with the second division, the substitutes' bench, the runners-up. *Only Caroline Caldwell can save us now!* God fucking help us.

"You didn't bring me here to be objective," Justineau reminds her superior, and she's surprised that her voice sounds almost level. "You brought me in because you wanted psychological evaluations to supplement the raw physical data you get from your own research. If I'm objective, I'm worthless to you. I thought my engaging with the children's thought processes was the whole point."

Caldwell makes a non-committal gesture, purses her lips. She wears lipstick every day, despite its scarcity, and she wears it to good effect; puts up an optimal front to the world. In an age of rust, she comes up stainless steel.

"Engaging?" she says. "Engaging is fine, Helen. I'm talking about something beyond that." She nods towards a stack of papers on one of the work surfaces, in among the Petri dishes and stacked slide boxes. "That top sheet, there. That's a routine file copy of a request you made to Beacon. You wanted them to impose a moratorium on physical testing of the subjects."

Justineau has no answer, apart from the obvious one. "I asked you to send me home," she says. "On seven separate occasions. You refused."

"You were brought here to do a job. The job still remains to be done. I choose to hold you to your contract."

"Well, then you get the whole deal," Justineau says. "If I was back in Beacon, maybe I could look the other way. If you keep me here, you have to put up with minor inconveniences like me having a conscience."

Caldwell's lips narrow down to a single ruled line. She reaches out and touches the handle of her razor, moves it so that it's parallel with the edge of the table. "No," she says. "I really don't. I define the programme, and your part in it. And that part is still a necessary one, which is why I'm taking the time to talk to you now. I'm concerned, Helen. You seem to have made a fundamental error of judgement, and unless you can step away from it, it will taint all your observations of the subjects. You'll be worse than useless."

An error of judgement. Justineau considers a remark about the

49

reliability of Caldwell's own judgement, but trading insults isn't going to win this. "Isn't it apparent to you by now," she says instead, "that the children's responses are all within the normal human range? And mostly displaced towards the top end of that range?"

"You're talking cognitively?"

"No, Caroline. I'm talking across the board. Cognitively. Emotionally. Associatively. The works."

Caldwell shrugs. "Well, 'the works' would have to include their hard-wired reflexes. Anyone who experiences a feeding frenzy when they smell human flesh isn't testing entirely within normal parameters, wouldn't you agree?"

"You know what I mean."

"Yes. And you know that you're wrong." Caldwell hasn't raised her voice, shows no sign of being angry or impatient or frustrated. She might be a teacher, exposing a pupil's sophomoric lapse of logic so that they can correct and improve. "The subjects aren't human; they're hungries. High-functioning hungries. The fact that they can talk may make them easier to empathise with, but it also makes them very much more dangerous than the animalistic variety we usually encounter. It's a risk just having them here, inside the perimeter – which is why we were told to set up so very far from Beacon. But the information that we're hoping to gain justifies that risk. It justifies anything."

Justineau laughs – a harsh and ugly spasming of breath that hurts her coming out. It's got to be said. There's no way around it. "You carved up two children, Caroline. And you did it without anaesthetic."

"They don't respond to anaesthetic. Their brain cells have a lipid fraction so small that alveolar concentrations never cross the action threshold. Which in itself ought to tell you that the subjects' ontological status is to some extent in doubt."

"You're dissecting *kids*!" Justineau repeats. "My God, you're like the wicked witch in a fairy tale! I know you've got form.

50

You cut up seven of them, didn't you? Back before I got here. Before you requisitioned me. You stopped because there were no surprises. You weren't finding anything you didn't already know. But now, for some reason, you're ignoring that fact and starting up again. So yeah, I went over your head because I was hoping there might be somebody sane up there."

Justineau registers her own voice, realises that she's too loud and too shrill. She falters into silence, waits to be told that she's cashiered. It will be a relief. It will all be over. She'll have taken it as far as she can, and she'll have lost, and they'll send her away. It will become somebody else's problem. Of course she'd save the kids if she could, if there was any way, but you can't save people from the world. There's nowhere else to take them.

"I'd like you to see something," Caldwell says.

Justineau doesn't have any answer. She watches with an eerie sense of dislocation as Caldwell crosses to another part of the lab, comes back with a glass fish tank in which she's set up one of her tissue cultures. It's an older one, with several years of growth. The tank is about eighteen inches by twelve by ten inches high, and its interior is completely filled with a dense mass of fine, dark grey strands. Like plague-flavoured candy floss, Justineau thinks. It's impossible even to tell what the original substrate was; it's just lost in the toxic froth that has sprouted from it.

"This is all one organism," Caldwell says, with pride and perhaps even a perverse kind of affection in her voice. She points. "And we know now what kind of organism it is. We finally figured it out."

"I thought it was pretty obvious," Justineau says.

If Caldwell hears the sarcasm, she doesn't appear to be troubled by it. "Oh, we knew it was a fungus," she agrees. "There was an assumption at first that the hungry pathogen had to be a virus or a bacterium. The swift onset, and the multiple vectors of infection, seemed to point in that direction. But

51

there was plenty of evidence to support the fungal hypothesis. If the Breakdown hadn't come so quickly, the organism would have been isolated within a matter of days.

"As it was . . . we had to wait a little while. In the chaos of those first few weeks, a great many things were lost. Any testing that was being done on the first victims was curtailed when those victims attacked, overpowered and fed on the physicians and scientists who were examining them. The exponential spread of the plague ensured that the same scenario was played out again and again. And of course the men and women who could have told us the most were always, by the nature of their work, the most exposed to infection."

Caldwell speaks in the dry, inflectionless tone of a lecturer, but her expression hardens as she stares down at the thing that is both her nemesis and the focal point of her waking life.

"If you grow the pathogen in a dry, sterile medium," she says, "it will eventually reveal its true nature. But its growth cycle is slow. Quite astonishingly slow. In the hungries themselves, it takes several years for the mycelial threads to appear on the surface of the skin – where they look like dark grey veins, or fine mottling. In agar, the process is slower still. This specimen is twelve years old, and it's still immature. The sexual or germinating structures – sporangia or hymenia – have yet to form. That's why it's only possible to catch the infection from the bite of a hungry or direct exposure to its bodily fluids. After two decades, the pathogen still hasn't spored. It can only bud asexually, in a nutrient solution. Ideally, human blood."

"Why are you showing me this?" Justineau demands. "I've read the literature."

"Yes, Helen," Caldwell agrees. "But I wrote it. And I'm still writing it. Through the cultures I took from badly decayed hungries – cultures like this one – I was able to establish that the hungry pathogen is an old friend in a new suit. *Ophiocordyceps unilateralis*.

"We encountered it first as a parasite on ants. And its

52

behaviour in that context made it notorious. Nature docu-mentaries dwelled on every lurid detail."

Caldwell proceeds to dwell on every lurid detail, but she really doesn't need to. Back when she first identified the hungry pathogen as a mutant *Cordyceps*, she was so happy that she just had to share. She persuaded Beacon to approve an educational programme for all base personnel. They filed into the canteen in groups of twenty, and Caldwell started the show by playing a short extract from a David Attenborough documentary, date-line twenty years or so before Breakdown.

Attenborough's perfectly pitched voice, honey from an English country garden, described with incongruous gentleness how *Ophiocordyceps* spores lie dormant on the forest floor in humid environments such as the South American rainforest. Foraging ants pick them up, without noticing, because the spores are sticky. They adhere to the underside of the ant's thorax or abdomen. Once attached, they sprout mycelial threads which penetrate the ant's body and attack its nervous system.

The fungus hot-wires the ant.

Images on the screen of ants convulsing, trying in vain to scrape the sticky spores off their body armour with quick, spasmodic sweeps of their legs. Doesn't help. The spores have commenced digging in, and the ant's nervous system is starting to flood with foreign chemicals – expert forgeries of its own neurotransmitters.

The fungus gets into the driving seat, puts its foot on the accelerator and drives the ant away. Makes it climb to the highest place it can reach – to a leaf fifty feet or more above the forest floor, where it digs in with its mandibles, locks itself immovably to the leaf's spinal ridge.

The fungus spreads through the ant's body and explodes out of its head – a phallic sporangium skull-fucking the dying insect from the inside. The sporangium sheds thousands of spores, and falling from that great height they spread for miles. Which of course is the point of the exercise.

Thousands of species of *Cordyceps*, each one a specialist, bonded uniquely with a particular species of ant.

But at some point a *Cordyceps* came along that was a lot less finicky. It jumped the species barrier, then the genus, family, order and class. It clawed its way to the top of the evolutionary tree, assuming for a moment that evolution is a tree and has a top. Of course, the fungus might have had a helping hand. It might have been grown in a lab, for any number of reasons; coaxed along with gene-splicing and injected RNA. Those were very big jumps.

"This," Caldwell is saying, tapping the sealed lid of the fish tank, "is what's inside the subjects' heads. Inside their brains. When you walk into that classroom, you think you're talking to children. But you're not, Helen. You're talking to the thing that killed the children."

Justineau shakes her head. "I don't believe that," she says.

"I'm afraid it doesn't matter what you believe."

"They exhibit behavioural responses that have no bearing on the fungus's survival."

Caldwell shrugs off-handedly. "Yes, of course they do. For the moment. Waste not, want not. *Ophiocordyceps* doesn't devour the entire nervous system all in one go. But if one of those things you think of as your pupils smells human flesh, human pheromones, it's the fungus that you'll be dealing with. The first thing it does is to consolidate its control of the motor cortex and the feeding reflex. That's how it propagates itself – in saliva, mainly. The bite gives nourishment to the host and spreads the infection at the same time. Hence the extreme caution we take in the handling of the test subjects. And hence" – she sighed – "the need for this lecture."

Justineau feels an intense desire to assert herself against a judgement that's already been made. She takes hold of the lid of the fish tank and wrenches it open.

Caldwell gives a wordless yell as she recoils, hand clasped to her mouth.

54

Then she thinks about what she's doing, and lowers her hand. She glares at Justineau, her cool detachment holed below the waterline.

"That was very stupid," she says.

"But not dangerous," Justineau points out. "You said it yourself, Caroline. No sex organs yet. No spores. No way for the fungus to spread in air. It needs blood and sweat and spit and tears. You see? You're just as likely as anyone to make a false assessment – to see a risk where there really isn't any."

"It's a poor analogy," Caldwell says. There's an edge in her voice you could part a hair on. "And overestimating risk isn't even an issue here. The danger – all the danger – lies in ignoring it."

"Caroline." Justineau tries one last time. "I'm not arguing that we should stop the programme. Just that we should switch to other methods."

Caldwell smiles, brittle, precise. "I'm open to other methods," she tells Justineau. "That's why I asked for a developmental psychologist to join the team in the first place." The smile fades out, an inevitable ebb tide. "*My* team. Your methods are adjuncts to mine, called on when I need them. You don't dictate our approach, and you don't talk to Beacon over my head. Has it occurred to you, Helen, that we're here under military rather than civilian jurisdiction? Do you ever think about that?"

"Not much," Justineau admits.

"Well, you should. It makes a difference. If I do decide that you're compromising my programme, and if I inform Sergeant Parks of that fact, you won't be sent home."

She fixes Justineau with a stare that's incongruously gentle and concerned.

"You'll be shot."

Silence falls between them.

"I am interested in what's going on inside their heads," Caldwell says at last. "Mostly I find I can determine that by examining physical structures under a microscope. When I

55

can't, I look at your reports. And what I expect to find there is clear, rational assessment building to an occasional well-justified conjecture. Do you understand that?"

A long pause. "Yes," Justineau says.

"Good. In that case, and as a starting point, I'd like you to list the subjects in order of their importance to your assessments – as of now. Tell me which ones you still need to observe, and how much you need them. I'll try to take your priorities into account when I'm choosing the next subjects to be brought over here and dissected. We need masses of comparative measurements. We're stonewalled, and the only thing I can think of that might bring us any new insights is bulk data. I want to process half the cohort in the next three weeks."

Justineau can't take that blow without flinching. "Half the class?" she repeats faintly. "But that's . . . Caroline! Jesus . . .!"

"Half the cohort," Caldwell insists. "Half of our remaining supply of test subjects. *The class* is a maze you've built for them to run through. Don't reify it into something that merits consideration on its own account. I need the list by Sunday, but earlier is better. We'll begin processing on Monday morning. Thanks for your time, Helen. If there's anything that I or Dr Selkirk can do to help, just let us know. But the final decision is yours, of course. We won't encroach on that."

Justineau finds herself in the open air, walking in some random direction. Sunlight hits her face, and she swerves away from it. Her face is hot enough already.

Half of our remaining . . .

Her mind collides with the words, sends them careening out of reach.

Another time she might admire Caldwell's brutal honesty about her own failings. *We're stonewalled.* She identifies with the project so completely that vanity on her own account is impossible.

On the other hand: *the final decision is yours.* That's pure sadism. Serve at my altar, Helen. You even get to choose the sacrifices, so how cool is that?

Half of . . .

Things will fall apart, and the centre won't hold. Perforated with fears and insecurities, the class will tear along every fold. They'll finally ask the questions Justineau can't answer. She'll have to choose between confession and evasion, and either one will probably kick her right over the edge of the catastrophe curve.

Which is maybe where she deserves to be. Child-killer. Facilitator of mass murder, smiling a Judas smile as she ticks the boxes. The thought of Parks putting a gun to her head has its own peculiar appeal at that moment.

Then she walks right into him, hard enough that they both stagger. He recovers first, grips her shoulders lightly to steady her.

"Hey," he says. "You all right, Miss Justineau?"

His broad, flat face, made asymmetrical and inconceivably ugly by the scar, radiates friendly solicitude.

Justineau pulls out of his grasp, her own face twisting as her anger finds its level. Parks blinks, seeing the visceral emotion, uncertain where it came from or where it might be going.

"I'm fine," Justineau says. "Get out of my way, please."

The sergeant gestures over his shoulder, towards the fence at his back. "Sentry clocked some movement in the woods over there," he says. "We don't know if it's hungries or what it is. Either way, perimeter's off-limits for now. Sorry. That was why I tried to head you off."

Movement in the middle distance, in the direction where he's pointing, distracts her for a second so that she has to wrench her attention back.

She faces him, trying to take a breath that's long and level, trying to pull all the slopping emotions back inside so he won't see them in her face. She doesn't want to be understood by this man, even on such a superficial level.

57

And thinking about what he's already seen, what he might know or think he knows of her, makes her suddenly see the timing of her humiliation in a new perspective. When Parks saw her breaking the no-contact rule, he threatened to put her on a charge. But then nothing happened. Until now.

Parks went and told tales about her to Caroline Caldwell. She's sure of it. The four-month gap between the Melanie incident and this dressing-down doesn't dent that conviction. Things percolate slowly through bureaucracies, take their own sweet time.

She has to fight the urge to punch Parks full in his ruin of a face. Maybe find the flaw, the pressure point that will make him crumble into pieces and be gone out of her life.

"I'm still here, Sergeant," she tells him, stung into defiance. "You took your best shot, and all she did was smack my hand and set me extra homework."

Parks' forehead creases, in the areas where it still can – where the scar tissue doesn't render it permanently creased. "Sorry?" he says.

"Don't be." She starts to walk around him, remembers that she can't keep going in this direction and turns, so she's broadside on to him for a moment.

"I didn't take any shot at all," the sergeant says quickly. "I don't report to Dr Caldwell, if that's what you think."

He sounds like he means it. He sounds like he really wants her to believe him.

"Well you should," Justineau says. "It's an excellent way of pissing me off. Don't mess up your perfect score, Sergeant."

Something like distress shows in Parks' face now. "Look," he says, "I'm trying to help you. Seriously."

"To help me?"

"Exactly. I've clocked up a lot of years in the field. And I've survived more grab-bagger sweeps than almost anyone. I mean hard-core shit. Inner city."

"So?"

58

Parks shrugs massively, is silent for a second as though he's hit the limits of his vocabulary – which doesn't strike her as too unlikely. "So I know what I'm talking about," he says at last. "I know the hungries. You don't live that long outside the fence unless you work out the moves. What you can get away with, and what's going to get you killed."

Justineau lets her utter indifference show in her face. She knows somehow that it will get deeper into him than any show of anger could. His agitation shows her the way to a high ground of cold disdain. "I'm not outside the fence."

"But you're handling them. You're dealing with them every day. And you're not keeping your guard up. Shit, you had your hands on that thing. You touched it." He falters on the words.

"Yes," Justineau agrees. "I did. Shocking, isn't it?"

"It's stupid." Parks shakes his head as if to dislodge a fly that's landed on him. "Miss Justineau . . . Helen . . . the regs are there for a reason. If you take them seriously, they'll save you. From your own instincts, as much as anything."

She doesn't bother to answer. She just stares him down.

"Okay," Parks says. "Then I'll have to take this into my own hands."

"You'll have to what?"

"It's my responsibility."

"Into your own hands?"

"This base's security is my—"

"You want to lay hands on me, Sergeant?"

"I won't touch a hair on your head," he says, exasperated. "I can keep order in my own damn house." And she reads it, suddenly, in his face. She can see that he's talking around something. Something that's fresh in his mind.

"What have you done?" she demands.

"Nothing."

"What have you done?"

"Nothing that concerns you."

59

He's still talking when she walks away, but it's not hard to shut the words out. They're just words.

By the time she gets to the classroom block, she's running.

10

When there's nothing to do, and you can't even move, time goes a lot more slowly.

Melanie's legs and her left arm, still strapped into the chair, have cramped agonisingly, but that happened a long time ago and now the pain of the cramp has faded and it's like her body has stopped bothering to tell her how it feels, so she doesn't even have the pain to distract her.

She sits and thinks about Sergeant's anger and what it means. It could mean a lot of things, but the starting point is the same in every case. It was only when she talked about Miss Justineau that Sergeant got angry – when she said that Miss Justineau loved her.

Melanie understands jealousy. She's jealous, a little bit, every time Miss Justineau talks to another boy or girl in class. She wants Miss Justineau's time to belong to her, and the reminders that it doesn't sting a little, make her heart do a gentle drop and thud in her chest.

But the idea of Sergeant being jealous is dizzying. If Sergeant can be jealous, there are limits to his power – and she herself stands at one of those limits, looking back at him.

That thought sustains her, for a while. But nobody comes, and the hours drag on – and though she's good at waiting, at doing nothing, the time is hanging heavy on her. She tries to tell herself stories, but they fall apart in her mind. She sets herself simultaneous equation puzzles and solves them, but it's too easy when you've made the problems up yourself. You're halfway to the answer before you've started to think about it properly. She's tired now, but her enforced position in the chair doesn't allow her to rest.

Then, after a long, long time, she hears the key turning in the lock, the bolts drawn back. Heavy steel door clanging. Footsteps running on concrete, raising a whisper farm of echoes. Is it Sergeant? Has he come back to dismantle her?

Someone unlocks Melanie's door and pushes it open.

Miss Justineau stands in the doorway. "It's okay," she says. "I'm here, Melanie. I'm here for you."

Miss Justineau steps forward. She wrestles with the chair, like Hercules wrestling with a lion or a snake. The arm strap is partway undone, and it opens up really easily. Then Miss J goes down on her knees and she's working on the leg straps. Right. Then left. She mutters and curses as she works. "He's frigging insane! Why? Why would anyone do this?" Melanie feels the constriction lessen, and sensation returns to her legs in a tingling rush.

She surges to her feet, her heart almost bursting with happiness and relief. Miss Justineau has saved her! She raises her arms in an instinct too strong to resist. She wants Miss Justineau to lift her up. She wants to hold her and be held by her and be touching her not just with her hair but with her hands and her face and her whole body.

Then she freezes like a statue. Her jaw muscles stiffen, and a moan comes out of her mouth.

Miss Justineau is alarmed. "Melanie?" She stands, and her hand reaches out.

"Don't!" Melanie screams. "Don't touch me!"

Miss Justineau stops moving, but she's so close! So close! Melanie whimpers. Her whole mind is exploding. She staggers back, but her stiff legs don't work properly and she falls full length on the floor. The smell, the wonderful, terrible smell, fills the room and her mind and her thoughts, and all she wants to do is . . .

"Go away!" she moans. "Go away go away go away!"

Miss Justineau doesn't move.

"Go away, or I'll fucking dismantle you!" Melanie wails. She's desperate. Her mouth is filled with thick saliva like mud from a mudslide. Her jaws start to churn of their own accord. Her head feels light, and the room sort of goes away and then comes back again without moving.

Melanie is dangling on the end of the thinnest, thinnest piece of string. She's going to fall and there's only one direction to fall in.

"Oh God!" Miss Justineau sobs. She gets it at last. She takes a step back. "I'm sorry, Melanie. I didn't even think!"

About the showers. Among the sounds that Melanie heard, one big absence: no hiss of chemical spray falling from the ceiling to settle on Miss Justineau and layer on its own smell to hide the Miss Justineau smell underneath.

What Melanie feels right then is what Kenny felt when Sergeant wiped the chemicals off his arm and put it right up close to Kenny's face. But she only just caught the edge of it that time, and she didn't really understand it.

Something opens inside her, like a mouth opening wider and wider and wider and screaming all the time – not from fear, but from need. Melanie thinks she has a word for it now, although it still isn't anything she's felt before. It's hunger. When the children eat, hunger doesn't factor into it. The grubs are poured into your bowl, and you shovel them into your mouth. But in stories that she's heard, it's different. The people in the stories want and need to eat, and then when they do eat they feel themselves fill up with something. It gives them a satisfaction nothing else can give them. Melanie thinks of a song the children learned and sang one time: *You're my bread when I'm hungry.* Hunger is bending Melanie's spine like Achilles bending his bow. And Miss Justineau will be her bread.

"You have to go," she says. She thinks she says. She can't be sure, because of the heart sounds and breath sounds and blood sounds that are crashing in her ears. She makes a gesture. *Go!* But Miss Justineau is just standing there, trapped between wanting to run and wanting to help.

Melanie scrambles up and lunges, arms stretched out. And it's almost like that other gesture, a moment ago, when she asked to be picked up, but now she presses her hands against Miss Justineau's stomach

touching touching touching her

and pushes her violently away. She's stronger than she ever guessed. Miss Justineau staggers back, almost trips. If she trips, she'll be dead. Be bread.

Melanie's muscles are tensing, knotting, coiling inside her. Gathering themselves for some massive effort.

She diverts them into a bellowing roar.

Miss Justineau scrambles, stumbles, is out through the door and wrenching it closed.

Melanie is moving forward and pulling backward at the same time. A man with a big dog on a leash and she's both of them, straining against the tether of her own will.

The first bolt slides home exactly as she hits the door. The smell, the need, fill her from toe to crown, but Miss Justineau is safe on the other side of the door. Melanie claws at it, wondering at her own stupid, hopeful fingers. The door won't open now, but some animal inside her still thinks it might.

It's a long time before the animal gives up. And then, exhausted, the little girl sinks to her knees next to the door, rests her forehead against cold, unyielding concrete.

From above her, Miss Justineau's voice. "I'm sorry, Melanie. I'm so sorry."

64

She looks up groggily, sees Miss J's face at the mesh window. "It's all right," she says, weakly. "I won't bite."

It's meant to be a joke. On the other side of the door, Miss Justineau starts to cry.

11

For a great many reasons, the events of that day will eventually become a soggy, undifferentiated mass in Helen Justineau's mind. But three things will stand out clear for her until the day she dies.

The first is that Sergeant Parks was right all along. Right about her, and about the risks that her behaviour has exposed her to. Seeing the child turn into the monster, right before her eyes, has made her understand at last that both are real. There is no future in which she can set Melanie free, or save her, or remove that cell door from between them.

The second is that some things become true simply by being spoken. When she said to the little girl "I'm here for you", the architecture of her mind, her definition of herself, shifted and reconfigured around that statement. She became committed, or maybe just acknowledged a commitment. It has nothing to do with guilt for earlier crimes (although she has a pretty fair understanding of what she deserves), or any hope of redemption. It's just the outermost point on an arc. She's risen as far as she can, and now she's falling again, no longer in control (if she ever was to start with) of her own movements.

The deadline that was set for her is coming on at a rush. She's expected to choose which of the class will be disassembled on Caroline Caldwell's table. She has no idea what she'll do now. All her options seem to be barred in one way or another.

The third thing is almost banal, in comparison. It's just that the movement she saw over Parks' shoulder, when he was warning her away from the perimeter, was on the wrong side of the fence. That was what had distracted her, thrown her off her stride for a moment, after the two of them ricocheted off one another and recoiled.

A human figure had been watching the fence from the edge of the woods, almost out of sight among the trees and the waist-high undergrowth.

Not a hungry. A hungry wouldn't hold a branch aside with his hand to maintain a clear line of sight.

A junker, then. A wild man, who never came inside.

And therefore, she reasons, not a threat.

Because all the threats she's concerned about right now relate to friendly fire.

12

If Eddie Parks knows one thing, it's that he's sick of this detail.

He was okay with the retrieval runs, as far as that went. The grab-bagging, the soldiers called it. Dirty work, and about as dangerous as you can get, but so what? You knew what the risks were going to be, and the rewards. You weighed them in your hands, and they made sense. You could see why you were doing it.

And that was what *kept* you doing it, week in and week out. Going into areas where you knew damn well there'd be hungries around every corner. The inner cities, where the population density was highest and the infection spread quicker than the fear of it.

And your life was on the line with every choice you made, every step you took, because there were all kinds of situations you could walk into and not walk out of. The hungries in the city, Christ fucking Jesus . . . they're like statues, most of the time, because they don't move unless something else moves. You're sprayed from head to foot with e-blocker, so they can't smell you, and you can walk right by them as long as you do it slow enough and smooth enough that you don't flip their trigger.

You can get yourself in really deep.

Then some clumsy bastard trips over a loose paving stone, or sneezes, or just scratches his ass, and one of the hungries whips its head round, on the sound or the movement or whatever the hell, and once one of them clocks you, it's monkey-see-monkey-do for all the rest. They go from zero to sixty in half a heartbeat, and they're all running in the same direction. So then you've got three choices, two of which will reliably get you killed.

If you freeze, the hungries will roll over you like some kind of gangrenous tsunami. They've got your number now, and they won't be fooled no matter what you smell like.

If you turn and run, they'll take you down. You can build up a bit of a lead at first, and even think you're winning, but a hungry can keep up that same loping run pretty much for ever. He's never going to stop, he's never going to slow down, and over the distance he will take you.

So you fight.

Broad sweeps, below the waist, full automatic. Bust their legs, and they've got to drag themselves on their hands to get to you. Changes the odds a little. And if you can get yourself into a narrow place, where they can only come at you one or two at a time, that helps too. But you would not believe how much damage those fuckers will take and still keep moving.

And some days you'll stir up a different kind of opposition. Junkers. Survivalist arseholes who refused to come into Beacon when the call went out, preferring to live off the land and take their chances. Most of the junkers stay well away from the cities, like any sane person would, but their raiding parties still tend to see any built-up area for fifty miles around their camp as their very own preserve and property.

So when a Beacon grab-bagger patrol meets a troop of junker scavengers, the fur is going to fly every time. It was a junker who gave Sergeant Parks his scar, which isn't romantic and understated like a duelling scar but a horrific, pucker-edged trench that crosses his face like a bend sinister on an old coat of arms. Parks tends to gauge the mettle of a new recruit by how long they can look him in the eye first time around, before that monstrous thing makes them take a desperate, abiding interest in their own boots.

But what makes all the aggravation of grab-bagging worthwhile is the stuff that's still sitting around in all those houses and all those offices, waiting to be taken. Old tech, computers and machine tools and comms hardware that hasn't been touched since the Breakdown – stuff that you can't even make any more. They've got people back at Beacon, tech people, who know exactly how this stuff works, but the knowledge isn't any good without the infrastructure. It's like there used to be a whole factory for every frigging circuit board and every frigging piece of plastic. And the people who used to work in those factories are the ones who right now are so eager to chew their way through your Kevlar to the tender parts underneath.

So that old stuff is literally priceless. Parks gets that. They're trying to find a way to remake the world twenty years after it fell apart, and the goodies that the grab-bag patrols bring home are . . . well, they're a rope bridge over a bottomless canyon. They're the only way of getting from this besieged *here* to a *there* where everything is back in good order.

But he feels like they lost their way somewhere. When they found the first of the weird kids, and some grunt who'd obviously never heard about curiosity and the cat called in a fucking observation report.

Nice going, soldier. Because you couldn't keep from *observing*, the grab-baggers suddenly get a whole slew of new orders. Bring us one of those kids. Let's take a good long look at him/her/it.

And the techies looked, and then the scientists looked, and they got the itch to kill a few cats too. Hungries with human reactions? Human behaviours? Human-level brain functions?

70

Hungries who can do something besides run and feed? And they're running naked and feral through the streets of the inner cities, right alongside the regular variety? What's the deal?

More orders. Requisition a base, a long way from anywhere. Mount a perimeter, and stand by. They'd been raiding the ragged hinterlands of Stevenage and Luton, so RAF Henlow seemed to fit the bill. It was more or less intact, it offered plenty of space both above the ground and in reinforced bunkers underneath it, and it had a functional airstrip.

They dropped in, and then they dug in. Disinfected. Decorated. Waited.

And in due course Dr Caldwell came along with her white coat and her bright red lipstick and her microscope, and a letter from Beacon with a whole lot of signatures and authorisations on it. "This is my show now, Sergeant," she said. "I'll take that building over there and the sheds on either side of it. Go get me some more of those kids. As many as you can find."

Just like that. Like she was ordering fast food, back in the days when there was fast food and you could order it.

Looking back on it, that was the point where Parks' life stopped making sense. When he stopped being a grab-bagger and became a hunter and trapper.

It's not like he wasn't good at it. Hey, he was shit-hot. He realised right out of the gate that you could spot the oddballs, the kids who were different, by the way they moved. Hungries toggle between two states. They're frozen in place most of the time, just standing there like they're never going to move again. Then they smell prey, or hear it, or catch sight of it, and they break into that terrifying dead sprint. No warm-up, no warning. Warp factor nine.

But the weird kids move even when they're not hunting, so you can tell them apart. And they react to stuff that isn't food, so you can get their attention – with a mirror, say, or the beam of light from a torch, or a piece of coloured plastic.

71

Cut them out of the pack. Not that there's a pack exactly, because the hungries always treat other hungries like they're part of the scenery. But get them to come out where they're alone, and exposed. Then drop the nets.

He and his team took thirty in the space of about seven months. It wasn't even hard once they got into the rhythm of it. Then Caldwell told them to stand down and wait for further orders. Said she had enough material to work with.

And how messed up is this? Suddenly Parks is in charge of a kindergarten. He finds himself defending a base that isn't doing a damn thing apart from nursemaiding these little hungries. They've got their own rooms, the same pallet beds as the soldiers, weekly feeding (which if you ever want to eat again yourself, you don't want to see), even a schoolroom.

Why a schoolroom?

Because Caldwell wants to know if these spooky little monsters can learn. She want to see inside their heads. Not just the hardware – she's got her operating table for that side of things – but the squishy stuff too. Like, what are they thinking?

Here's what Parks is thinking. The regular hungries are *clean* compared to these kid-shaped monstrosities. At least you can tell that the regular hungries are animals. They don't say "Good morning, Sergeant" when you kneecap them.

There isn't a whole lot more of that he can choke down, to be honest. The blonde one . . . Melanie. She's test subject number one, for some reason, even though she was about the eleventh or the twelfth one he bagged. She scares the shit out of him, and he can't explain why. Or maybe he can, and he doesn't like to think about it. Certainly a part of it is that unfailing good-little-girl smarminess she's got. An animal like that, even if it looks like a human being, should make meaningless sounds or no sounds at all. Hearing it talk just muddies the waters.

But Parks is a soldier. He knows how to shut up and do

72

what he's told. In fact, that's his speciality subject. And he gets what Caldwell is doing. These kids — presumably the kids of junker families that got trapped and bitten and infected — seem to have some kind of partial immunity to the hungry pathogen. Oh, they're still flesh-eaters. Still react in the same way to the smell of live meat, which is the sign by which ye shall frigging well know them. But the light inside their heads didn't go out, for some reason — or not all the way out. They were living like animals when the grab-baggers found them, but they rehabilitate really nice and they can walk and talk and whistle and sing and count up to big numbers and all the rest of it.

Whereas their mummies and daddies are in the wind. If they all got taken and fed on as a family unit, the adults just went the same way as everyone else who gets bitten. They turned into full-on brain-dead monsters.

The kids got stuck halfway. So maybe they're the best hope of finding an actual cure.

See? Parks is no fool. He knows what's being done here, and he's served that purpose silently and uncomplainingly. He's served it for the best part of four years now.

Rotation was meant to happen after eighteen months.

There are other people in the same boat, and it's fair to say that Parks is more worried about them than he is about himself. That's not bleeding-heart bullshit; it's just that he knows his own limits better than he knows theirs. There are twenty-eight men and women under his command (he doesn't count Caldwell's people, who mostly don't know what an order is), and with that small a number, base security needs all of them to be combat-fit and ready to respond if a situation develops.

Parks has doubts about half his muster, at this point.

Doubts about himself too, insofar as he's a non-commissioned officer effectively acting as a field commander for a unit main-taining a fixed post with civilian liaison. The minimum rank for that billet, if you go by regs, is lieutenant.

Parks has his own scripture, which doesn't meet regs at many points. But he knows when his centre of gravity is compromised. And just recently that's how he feels more days than not.

That's how he feels today, when he takes Gallagher's report.

Gallagher, K., Private, 1097, 24 July, 17.36

In the course of a routine clearance sweep of the woodland north-west of base, I was involved in an incident which transpired as follows immediately below.

I was bait, Devani was pacing me with the heavy auto, and Barlow and Tap were clean-up.

We verified a large group of hungries stationary in the Hitchin Road, close to the Airman roundabout. They were skin and bone, mostly, but none of them looked too far gone to be a threat.

We set up in the wood, as per operational parameters, and Devani dropped me off at the roundabout. On Lance Bombardier Tap's orders, I was not wearing e-blocker.

I proceeded to go upwind of the hungries and waited until they clocked me.

Whereupon, having clocked me, they pursued me for several hundred yards, off the road and into the woodland, where I proceeded to—

"Jesus wept," Parks says, putting the report down on his desk. "You proceeded to proceed? Just tell me what happened, Gallagher. Save this bollocks for your autobiography."

Gallagher blushes to the roots of his red hair. His freckles disappear in the general incandescence. On anyone else, that blazing face would mean a consciousness of having screwed up, but there's a long list of things that would make Gallagher blush like a schoolgirl, including for example a dirty joke, any exertion more taxing than a parade march, or a single sip of bootleg gin. Not that you tend to see this soldier drinking all that often – he's as skittish around alcohol as if the army he signed up with was the one that offers you salvation. Parks extends the benefit of the doubt a little bit further and a little bit thinner.

"Sir," Gallagher says, "the hungries were right up my arse. I mean, they were close enough so I could *smell* them. You know that sour stink they get, when the grey threads start showing through their skin? It was strong enough so my eyes were watering."

"Thready ones don't normally get this far out from the cities," Parks muses, not liking the news.

"No, sir. But I'm telling you, this bunch was ripe. Couple of them had their faces all fallen in. Clothes had mostly rotted off them. One of them had lost an arm. Don't know whether it had been eaten off of him, back when he first got infected, or if it had fallen off since, but yeah, these weren't newbies.

"Anyway, I was running back towards where Tap and Barlow were set up, behind that big stand of beech trees. There's a hedgerow there, and it's pretty solid. You've got to pick your spot – go through it where it's thin enough not to slow you down too much. And you can't see what you're running into, obviously."

Gallagher hesitates, seeming to wince slightly. His memories have hit a barrier a lot more solid than that hedge.

"What did you run into?" Parks prompts.

"Three blokes. Junkers. They were just walking along on the far side of the hedge, where they couldn't be seen from the road. There are blackberry bushes all along that stretch, so maybe they were picking fruit or something. Except that one of the three – boss man, I reckoned, on account of his kit – he had a pair of binoculars. And all three of them were armed. Boss man's got a handgun; the other two have got machetes.

"I broke out of the hedge about fifty yards away, heading right at them." Gallagher shakes his head in unhappy wonder. "I shouted at them to run, but they didn't take any notice. The bloke with the gun drew down on me, and he was this close to blowing my brains out.

"Then the hungries burst through the hedge right behind me, and he sort of lost his concentration. But the three of them were still blocking my way, and this nutcase still had his gun pointed right at me. So I barged him. It's not like there was anywhere else to go. He got one shot off, but he managed to miss me. Don't know how, at that range. Then I hit him full on with my shoulder and kept right on going."

The soldier stops again. Parks waits, letting him get it out in his own words. It's clear that this whole thing has freaked him out badly, and it's part of Parks' job, sometimes, to take confession. Gallagher is one of the greenest of the buck privates. If he was born at all when the Breakdown came, he was still sucking on his mother's tit. You've got to make allowances for that.

"Ten seconds later, I'm back in the trees again," Gallagher says. "I looked over my shoulder and didn't see anything. But I heard a scream. One of the junkers, obviously. And he went on screaming for a hell of a long time. I stopped. I was thinking about going back, but then the hungries popped up right behind me and I had to get going again."

Gallagher shrugs.

"We completed the mission. Tap and Barlow had set the traps up right on the finish line. Hungries ran into them, got themselves stuck in the barbed wire, and after that it was just clean-up."

"Petrol or lime?" Parks asks. He can't keep from asking, because he's told Nielson no more petrol for routine bake-offs, but he knows for a fact the quartermaster is still signing off on ten-gallon drums.

"Lime, sir." Gallagher is reproachful. "There's a pit by the road there that we dug out back in April. We didn't even half fill it yet. We rolled them in and shovelled three bags in on top of them, so they should render down nicely so long as it doesn't rain."

This purely operational stuff perks Gallagher up a little, but he becomes sombre again as he gets back to his own story. "After we were done, we went back to the hedge. The boss

76

man and one of the other two were lying there on the ground, right where I'd seen them before. They were really badly chewed up, but they were still twitching. Then the boss man opened his eyes, and I verified—" Gallagher catches himself slipping back into report-speak, stops and starts again. "He was crying blood, the way they do sometimes when the rot's just getting into them. It was obvious they were both infected."

Parks is impassive. He saw that punchline coming. "Did you finish them off?" he asks – the bluntness deliberate. Call a spade a spade. Make Gallagher see that it's all just business as usual. It won't help him now, but it might take the edge off later.

"Barley – Private Barlow – decapitated them both with the second bloke's machete."

"Mask and gloves on?"

"Yes, sir."

"And you retrieved their kit?"

"Yes, sir. Handgun is well maintained, and there were forty rounds of ammo in one of the packs. Binoculars are a bit cack, to be honest, but the boss man had a walkie-talkie too. Nielson thinks it might work with our long-range sets."

Parks nods approval. "You handled a tricky situation really well," he tells Gallagher, and he means it. "If you'd frozen when you came through that hedge, the civilians would still have died – and most likely they'd have held you up long enough to kill you too. This is a better outcome all round."

Gallagher says nothing.

"Think about it," Parks persists. "These junkers were less than a mile away from our perimeter, armed and tooled up for surveillance. Whatever they were doing, they weren't just out taking the air. I know you feel like shit right now, Private, but what happened to them isn't down to you. Even if they were lily-white. Junkers choose to live outside the fences, so they take what comes with that.

"Go and get drunk. Maybe pick a fight with somebody or get yourself laid. Burn it off. But do not waste a bastard second

77

of my time or yours with feeling guilty about this bullshit. Drop a penny in the poor box, move along."

Gallagher comes to attention, seeing the dismiss looming.

"Now dismiss."

"Yes, sir."

The private rips off a smart salute. Mostly they don't bother these days, but it's his way of saying thanks.

Truth is, Gallagher may be green, but he's far from the worst of an indifferent-to-sod-awful bunch of soldiers, and Parks can't afford to have him join the walking wounded. If the lad had killed the junkers himself, gutted them and made balloon animals out of their colons, Parks would still have done his best to put a positive spin on it. His own people are his priority here, first and last.

But somewhere in the stack, he's also thinking this: junkers? On his doorstep?

Like he didn't have enough to bloody worry about.

13

The week goes by, slow and inexorable. Three Mr Whitaker days in a row reduce the class to unaccustomed lethargy.

Whether by accident or design, Sergeant stays away from Melanie. She hears his voice yelling transit in the mornings, but he's never visible when she's taken out from her cell, or when she's brought back to it. Each time, she feels a surge of anticipation. She's ready to fight him again, and declare her hate for him, and defy him to hurt her some more.

But he doesn't come into her line of sight, and she has to swallow all those feelings back into herself the way a rat or a rabbit will sometimes reabsorb into its womb a litter of young that it can't safely give birth to.

Friday is a Miss Justineau day. Normally this would be a cause of intense and uncomplicated joy. This time, Melanie is afraid as well as excited. She almost ate Miss Justineau. What if Miss Justineau is angry about that, and doesn't like her any more?

The start of the lesson does little to reassure her. Miss J has come back unhappy and preoccupied, folded in on herself so that her emotions are impossible to read. She says good morning to the class as a whole, not to each individual boy and girl. She makes no eye contact.

She tests the children with short-answer and multiple-choice questions for most of the day. Then she sits at her desk and marks their answers, writing the test scores down in a big notebook while the class works on sums.

Melanie isn't thinking much about the sums, which she finishes in a few minutes. They're just easy calculus, most of them with single variables. Her attention is focused on Miss Justineau, and to her horror she sees that Miss Justineau is crying silently as she works.

Melanie searches her mind frantically for something to say. Something that might comfort Miss J, or at least distract her from her sorrows. If it's the marking that's making her sad, they can switch to a different activity that's easier and more fun.

"Can we have stories, Miss Justineau?" she asks. Miss Justineau doesn't seem to have heard. She goes on tallying up the test scores.

Some of the other kids sigh or tut or fidget. They can see that Miss Justineau is sad, and they clearly think that Melanie shouldn't be bothering her with selfish demands. Melanie sticks to her guns. She knows the class can make Miss J happy again if she'll only talk to them. Her own happiest times have always been here, like this, so how can they not be Miss Justineau's happiest times too?

She tries again. "Can we have myths of Ancient Greece, Miss Justineau?" she asks louder.

This time Miss J hears. She looks up, and shakes her head. "Not today, Melanie," she says, and her voice is as sad as her face. For a few moments she just stares out at the class, almost like she's surprised to see them there. "I have to finish these assessments," she says.

But she doesn't go back to the notebook. She keeps looking at the class. There's kind of a frown on her face. It's like she's the one who's doing hard sums, not them, and she's reached one that she just can't work out.

"Who the hell am I kidding?" she asks really quietly.

She tears up the tests, which is surprising but the kids don't really mind, because who cares about test results? Only Kenny and Andrew, when they're trying to outscore each other, which is really lame and stupid because Melanie is the best in the class and Zoe is the second best, so the boys are only fighting for third place.

Then Miss J tears up the notebook. She rips the pages out a few at a time, and shreds them with her hands until they're too small to tear any more. She drops the pieces into the waste-paper basket, only they're too small and light to fall straight. They turn in the air, spread out, make a mess on the floor all around it. Miss Justineau doesn't mind. She starts to throw the pieces up in the air, instead of just dropping them, so they spread out even further.

She's not happy exactly, but she's stopped crying. It's a good sign.

"You want stories?" she asks the class.

They all do.

Miss Justineau gets the Greek myths book out of the book corner and brings it to the front. She reads them the story of Actaeon, which is scary, and Theseus and the Minotaur, which is even scarier. At Melanie's request, she winds up with Pandora again, even though they all know it. It's a good way to finish off the day.

When Sergeant's people come, Miss Justineau doesn't look at them. She sits on the corner of the teacher's desk, turning the Greek myths book over and over in her hands.

"Goodbye, Miss Justineau," Melanie says. "See you soon, I hope."

Miss Justineau looks up. It seems as though she's about to say something, but there's a bump right then as someone – one of Sergeant's people – gets hold of Melanie's chair from behind and takes the brakes off. The chair starts to turn.

"I need this one for a moment," Miss Justineau says. Melanie can't see her any more, because she's been turned mostly away, but Miss Justineau's voice is loud, like she's very close by.

"Okay." The soldier sounds bored, like it's all the same to him. He moves on to Gary's chair.

"Good night, Melanie," Miss Justineau says. But she doesn't go away. She leans down over Melanie, her shadow falling on the arms of the chair and on Melanie's hands.

Melanie feels something hard and angular being shoved down between her back and the back of the chair. "Enjoy," Miss Justineau murmurs. "But keep it to yourself."

Melanie leans back, as hard as she can, squaring her shoulders against the chair's bare metal plates. The something is wedged against the small of her back – completely out of sight. She has no idea what it could be, but it's something that came from Miss Justineau's hand. Something Miss Justineau has given to her, and only her.

She stays in that position all the way back to her cell, and all through her straps being untied. She doesn't move a muscle. She keeps her gaze fixed on the floor, not trusting herself to meet the eyes of Sergeant's people without giving the secret away.

Only when they've gone, and the bolts have shot closed on the cell door, does she reach behind her back and slide out the foreign object that's been lodged there, registering first the solid weight of it, then the rectangular shape, and finally the words on the cover.

Tales the Muses Told: Greek Myths, by Roger Lancelyn Green.

Melanie makes a strangled sound. She can't help it, even though it might bring Sergeant's people back into the cell to find out what she's doing. A book! A book of her own! And *this* book! She runs her hands over the cover, riffles the pages, turns the book in her hands to look at it from every angle. She smells the book.

That turns out to be a mistake, because the book smells of Miss Justineau. On top, strongest, the chemical smell from her fingers, as bitter and horrible as always; but underneath, a little, and on the inside pages a lot, the warm and human smell of Miss Justineau herself.

The feeling – the bullying, screaming hunger – goes on for a long time. But it's not nearly as strong as it was when Melanie was smelling Miss J herself, right up close, with no chemical spray at all. It's still scary – a rebellion of her body against her mind, as though she's Pandora wanting to open the box and it doesn't matter how many times she's been told not to, she's just been built so she *has* to, and she can't make herself stop. But finally Melanie gets used to the smell the way the children in the shower on Sunday get used to the smell of the chemicals. It doesn't go away exactly, but it doesn't torment her in quite the same way; it becomes kind of invisible, just because it doesn't change. The hunger gets less and less, and when it's all gone, Melanie is still there.

The book is still there too; Melanie reads it until daybreak, and even when she stumbles over the words or has to guess what they mean, she's in another world.

She will think of that later – only a day later – after the world she knows has gone away.

14

Monday has come and gone, and the list that Dr Caldwell requested has not been forthcoming. Justineau has not spoken to her, or sent a memo. She has not explained the delay, or requested additional time.

Clearly, Caldwell thinks, her initial assessment was correct. Justineau's emotional identification with the subjects is interfering with the proper performance of her duties. And since her duties are owed to Caldwell, are factored into Caldwell's clinical plans, Caldwell has to take that dereliction seriously.

She calls up her own database on the test subjects. Where to start? She's looking for reasons why *Ophiocordyceps* has shown such unlikely mercy in this tiny handful of cases. Most people infected with the pathogen experience its full effect almost instantaneously. Within minutes, or hours at most, sentience and self-awareness shut down permanently and irrevocably. This happens even before the threads of the fungus penetrate the tissue of the brain; its secretions, mimicking the brain's own neurotransmitters, do most of the dirty work. Tiny chemical wrecking balls pounding away at the edifice of self until it cracks and crumbles, falls apart. What's left is a clockwork toy, that only moves when *Cordyceps* turns the key.

These children were infected years ago, and they can still think and talk. Even learn. And their brains are mostly in a reasonably sound condition; mycelial threads are widely dispersed through the nerve tissue, but they don't seem able to feed on it. There's something in the children's body chemistry which is retarding both the spread of the fungus and the virulence of its effects.

Partial immunity.

If she could find the reason why, Caldwell would be halfway – *at least* halfway – to a full cure.

When she thinks of it like that, the decision is made for her. She needs to start with the child who shows least impairment of all. The child who, despite having as high a concentration of fungal matter in her blood and tissue as any of the others, and more than most, somehow retains a genius-level IQ.

She needs to start with Melanie.

15

Sergeant Parks gets his orders, and he's about to pass them down the line. But really, there's no reason for him not to do this himself. He's doubled perimeter sweeps since he heard Gallagher's tale of woe, afraid that the junkers might have some incursion in mind, so his people are weary and wired. A bad combination.

There's half an hour to go before the daily circus gets under way. As duty officer, he signs out the keys from the secure cupboard. Then he countersigns as base commander. He takes the thick ring off its hook and walks on over to the block.

Where his ears are assaulted by the hyperactive bombast of the 1812 Overture. He turns the rubbish off. It was Caldwell's idea to play music to the abortions when they're in their cells, out of a vaguely benign impulse – music soothing the savage breast, or some such bullshit. But they were limited to the music they could find, and a lot of it didn't fall into the soothing category.

In the silence, made louder by contrast, Parks walks along the corridor to Melanie's cell. She's looking out through the grille. He waves her away from it.

"Transit," he tells her. "Go sit in your chair. Now."

She does as she's told, and he unlocks the door. Standing orders call for at least two people to be present when the kids are strapped into their chairs or let out of them, but Parks is confident that he can do it by himself. His hand is on the stock of his pistol, but he doesn't draw it. He's assuming that the habit of countless mornings will kick in automatically.

The kid is staring at him with those big, almost lidless eyes – flecks of grey in the baby blue reminding him of what she is, in case he was ever disposed to let that slip his mind.

"Good morning, Sergeant," she says.

"Keep your hands on those armrests," he tells her. He doesn't need to say it. She's not moving. Except for her eyes, tracking him as he straps up her right hand, then her left.

"It's early," Melanie says. "And you're on your own."

"You're going to the lab. Dr Caldwell wants to see you."

The kid goes very quiet for a moment or two. He's working on her legs now.

"Like Liam and Marcia," she says at last.

"Yeah. Like them."

"They didn't come back." There's a tremor in the kid's voice now. Parks finishes with the legs, doesn't answer. It's not the sort of thing that seems to need an answer. He straightens up again, and those big blue eyes fix him to the spot.

"Will I come back?" Melanie asks.

Parks shrugs. "Not my decision. Ask Dr Caldwell."

He goes around behind the chair and finds the neck strap. This is the part where you've got to watch your step. Easy to get your hand in reach of those teeth, if you let your guard down. Parks doesn't.

"I want to see Miss Justineau," Melanie says.

"Tell Dr Caldwell that."

"Please, Sergeant." She twists her head, at the worst possible moment, and he's forced to pull his hand away sharply, out of reach, dropping the strap, which is only half threaded through.

87

"Face front!" he raps. "Don't move your head. You know not to do that!"

The kid faces front. "I'm sorry," she says meekly.

"Well, don't do it again."

"Please, Sergeant," she mumbles. "I want to see her before I go. So she knows where I am. Can we wait? Until she comes?"

"No," Parks says, tightening the neck strap. "We can't." The kid's secured now, and he's able to relax. He turns the chair, aims it at the door.

"Please, Eddie," Melanie says quickly.

Sheer surprise makes him stop. It's like a door just slammed inside his chest. "What? What did you say?"

"Please, Eddie. Sergeant Parks. Let me talk to her."

The little monster found out his name somehow. She's sneaking up inside his guard, waving his name like a white flag. *Mean you no harm.* It's like if one of those paintings that looks like a real door in a real wall opened right in front of you, and a bogeyman leered out of it. Or like you turn over a stone and see the things crawling there, and one of them waves at you and says "Hi, Eddie!"

He can't help himself. He reaches down and grips her throat – which is just as big an offence against regulations as Justineau stroking her like a fucking pet. "Don't ever do that," he says, between his bared teeth. "Don't ever use my name again."

The kid doesn't answer. He realises how hard he's pressing on her windpipe. She probably can't answer. He takes his hand away – it's shaking badly – and puts it back where it belongs, on the handle of the wheelchair.

"We're going to Dr Caldwell now," Parks says. "You got any questions, you save them up for her. I don't want to hear another peep out of you."

And he doesn't.

88

16

But that's partly because the next thing he does is to wheel the chair out through the steel door and – backwards all the way, bump, bump, bump – up the stairs beyond.

For Melanie, this is like sailing over the edge of the world.

The steel door has marked the furthest horizon of her experience for as long as she can remember. She knows she must have come in through there, sometime in the distant past, but that feels like a story from a really old book, written in a language that nobody can speak any more.

This feels more like that passage in the Bible that Dr Selkirk read to them once, where God makes the world. Not Zeus, but the other god.

The steps. The vertical space they're climbing through (like the corridor, but laid on its end so it points upwards). The smell of the space, as they get higher and higher and the chemical disinfectant smell of the cells starts to fade. The sounds from outside, coming from above them through a door that isn't quite closed.

The air. And the light. As Sergeant pushes the door open with his backside and drags her out into the day.

Total overload.

Because the air is warm, and it's breathing; moving against Melanie's skin like something that's alive. And the light is so intense it's like someone dipped the world into a barrel of oil and set it alight.

She's lived in Plato's cave, staring at the shadows on the wall. Now she's been turned around to face the fire.

A sound is forced out of Melanie. A painful exhalation from the centre of her chest – from a dark, damp place that tastes of bitter chemicals and the acetone tang of whiteboard markers.

She goes limp. The world pours in through her eyes and ears, her nose, her tongue, her skin. There's too much of it, and it never stops coming. She's like the drain in the corner of the shower room. She closes her eyes but the light still hits her eyelids, makes patterns of spangled colour dance inside her brain. She opens them again.

She endures, and collates, and begins to understand.

They pass buildings made of wood or shiny metal, set on concrete foundations. The buildings are all the same shape, rectangular and blocky, and mostly the same colour – dark green. Nobody's tried to make them look nice. Their function is what matters.

The same is true of the chain-link fence that rises in the distance to a height of four metres, completely enclosing all the structures that Melanie can see. It's topped with razor wire, held outwards from the main fence at an angle of about thirty degrees by elbowed concrete pylons.

They pass some of Sergeant's people, who watch them go by and sometimes raise their hands to salute Sergeant. But they don't speak to him, and they don't move from where they're standing. They carry rifles at the ready. They watch the fence, and the gates in the fence.

Melanie lets these facts run together in her mind. Their possible meanings form spontaneously at the points of confluence.

They come to another building, where two of Sergeant's people are on guard. One of the two opens the door for them. The other – a man with red hair – salutes crisply. "You need a guard detail for that one, sir?" he asks.

"If I need anything, Gallagher, I'll ask for it," Sergeant growls.

"Yes, sir!"

They go inside, and immediately the sound of Sergeant's footsteps changes, gets louder, with a hollow reverberation. They're on tiles. Sergeant waits, and Melanie knows what he's waiting for. This is a shower, like the one in the block. The chemical spray starts up, pouring down over the both of them.

It takes longer than the shower in the block. The shower heads actually move, sliding down the walls on metal tracks, angling as they descend to spray every inch of their bodies from every direction.

Sergeant endures this with his head down, eyes tight shut. Melanie, who's used to the pain and knows her eyes will sting just as much whether they're shut or open, keeps watching. She sees that there are steel shutters at the end of the shower area through which they've just entered. A simple ratchet-based mechanism allows them to be raised or lowered by the turning of a handle. This building can be sealed off from the base outside, can become a fortress. What goes on here must be very, very important.

All this time Melanie is trying hard not to think about Marcia and Liam. She's scared about what might happen to her here. She's scared of never being able to go back to her friends, and the classroom, and Miss Justineau. Perhaps it's that fear, as much as the novelty, that makes her so acutely aware of her surroundings. She's registering everything she sees. She's also doing her best to memorise it all, especially the route they've taken. She wants to be able to find her way back, if she's free at any point to do that.

The chemical spray dribbles and sputters to a stop. Sergeant wheels her forwards, through a double swing door, along a corridor, to another door over which a bare red light bulb shines. A sign on the door reads: NO ADMITTANCE TO UN-AUTHORISED PERSONNEL. Sergeant stops there, presses a buzzer and waits.

After a few seconds, the door is opened from the inside by Dr Selkirk. She's in her usual white gown, but she's also wearing green plastic gloves, and around her throat there's a thing like a white cotton necklace. She raises this now with a tug of her index finger and thumb. It's a mask, made of white gauze, that fits over the lower part of her face.

"Good morning, Dr Selkirk," Melanie says.

Dr Selkirk looks at her for a moment as though she's deciding whether or not to answer. In the end, she just nods. Then she laughs. It's a hollow, unhappy sound, Melanie thinks. The laugh you'd make if you rubbed out a mistake in a sum you were doing and accidentally tore the paper.

"Postman," Sergeant Parks says laconically. "Where do you want this?"

"Right," Dr Selkirk says, her voice muffled by the mask. "Yes. You can bring her in. We're ready for her." She stands aside and pulls the door wide so Sergeant can wheel Melanie inside.

This room is the strangest thing Melanie has ever seen. Of course, she's starting to realise that she hasn't seen all that much, but there are more things here of more baffling variety than she would have thought the whole world could hold. Bottles and tanks and jars and boxes; surfaces of white ceramic and stainless steel that gleam in the harsh radiance of strip lights overhead.

Some of the things in the bottles look like parts of people. Some of them are animals. Closest to her is a rat (she recognises it from a picture in a book) suspended head down in clear liquid. Thin grey strings like shoelaces – hundreds of them – have exploded from the rat's body cavity and filled most of the interior space of the bottle, wrapped loosely around

92

and around the little corpse as though the rat had decided to try to be an octopus and then hadn't known how to stop.

One bottle along from the rat is an eyeball with gaudy streamers of nerve tissue attached behind.

These things fill Melanie's mind with wild surmise. She says nothing, drinks it all in.

"Transfer her to the table, please." It's not Dr Selkirk who says this, it's Dr Caldwell. She's standing at a work surface on the far side of the room, arranging shiny steel objects in a precise order. She touches some of them several times over, as though the distance and angles between them matter a great deal to her.

"Good morning, Dr Caldwell," Melanie says.

"Good morning, Melanie," Dr Caldwell says. "Welcome to my laboratory. The most important room on the base."

With Dr Selkirk's help, Sergeant transfers Melanie from her chair on to a high table in the centre of the room. It's a complex manoeuvre. They untie her hands from the armrests and handcuff them in front of her. They lock her feet to a restraint bar. Then they undo the neck strap and lift her on to the table. She weighs almost nothing, so they don't have any trouble carrying her.

Once she's sitting on the table, they strap her feet into harnesses low down on its sides, which Dr Selkirk adjusts carefully so that they're tight. Then they remove the restraint bar, which is no longer needed.

"Lie down, Melanie," Dr Caldwell says. "And hold out your hands." The women take one hand each, and as Sergeant unlocks the cuffs, they carefully set her wrists in two more harnesses. Dr Caldwell ties them up.

Melanie is completely immobile now, apart from her head. She's grateful that there's no neck strap like the one on the chair.

"You need me?" Sergeant asks Dr Caldwell.

"Emphatically not."

Sergeant wheels the chair back to the door. Melanie takes this in, and reads it right. She won't be needing the chair again. She won't be going back to her cell. *Tales the Muses Told* is lying under her mattress back there, and she crashes head first into the realisation that she may never see it again. Those pages that smell of Miss Justineau are now, and perhaps for ever, inaccessibly distant.

She wants to cry out to Sergeant to wait – or ask him to carry a message to Miss J. She can't say a word. Misgivings are crowding in on her. She's in uncharted territory, and she fears the blank, inscrutable future into which she's being rushed before she's ready. She wants her future to be like her past, but knows it won't be. The knowledge sits like a stone in her stomach.

The door closes behind Sergeant. The two women begin to undress her.

They use scissors, cutting her out of her cotton shift.

17

For Helen Justineau, the first hint that something is wrong is when she's walking down the corridor from the shower to the classroom. She looks for Melanie's face in the mesh window of her door, but Melanie doesn't appear.

She unlocks the classroom and stands at her desk while the children are wheeled in one by one. She says hello to each in turn. The twentieth child (the twenty-first, until Marcia was taken) ought to be Melanie, but it's Anne. One of the deadpan soldier boys deposits her and immediately heads for the door.

"Hold on," Justineau says.

The private stops, turns back to face her with minimal civility. "Yes, miss?"

"Where's Melanie?"

He shrugs. "One of the cells was empty," he offers. "I went on to the next one. Is there a problem?"

Justineau doesn't answer. She leaves the classroom, walks out into the corridor. She goes to Melanie's cell. Nothing to be seen there. The door of the cell stands open. The bed and the chair are both empty.

Nothing about this feels right. The soldier is at her back,

asking her again if there's a problem. She ignores him and heads for the stairs.

Sergeant Parks is standing at the top, talking in a low voice to a group of three soldiers who all look very scared – very far from business as usual. At another time that might give Justineau pause. At another time she'd at least wait for him to finish, but she barges right in.

"Sergeant," she says. "Has Melanie been moved?"

Parks has seen her walk up, but he stares at her now as though he's only just registered who she is. "I'm sorry, Miss Justineau," he says. "We've got something of an emergency. Potentially. We're clocking large number of hungries close to the perimeter."

"Has Melanie been moved?" Justineau repeats.

Sergeant Parks tries again. "If you go back to the classroom, we can talk about this as soon as—"

"Just answer me. Where is she?"

Parks glances away, just for a second, then looks her square in the eyes. "Dr Caldwell asked for her to be sent over to the lab."

Justineau's stomach free-falls. "And you . . . you took her?" she asks stupidly.

He nods. "About half an hour ago. I would have told you, obviously, but class hadn't started and I didn't know where you were."

But she should have known as soon as she saw the empty cell. Once it's said, it becomes so blindingly obvious that she curses herself for wasting these few precious minutes. She's off at a run toward the lab complex. Parks is shouting at her – something about needing to get inside – but there'll be time for him later.

If she's too late, all the time in the worthless fucking world.

18

Dr Caldwell and Dr Selkirk wash Melanie all over her body, very thoroughly, with disinfectant soap that smells just like the spray from the showers. She submits to this in silence, her thoughts racing.

"Do you like learning about science, Melanie?" Dr Caldwell asks her. Dr Selkirk shoots Dr Caldwell a slightly startled look.

"Yes," Melanie says guardedly.

When she's clean, Dr Caldwell picks up some sort of tool about the size of a blackboard rubber. She presses on it, and it starts to hum in her hand. She puts it against the side of Melanie's head, draws it across her scalp in short, straight lines. It sends vibrations through her skin into her skull.

Melanie is about to ask what this thing is, but then she sees Dr Selkirk lift up a handful of blonde hair and drop it into a plastic bin.

Dr Caldwell is thorough, going over the whole of Melanie's head twice. The second time she presses harder and it actually hurts, just a little. Dr Selkirk scoops away more drifts of Melanie's hair. Then she wipes her hands carefully with a wet paper towel taken from a dispenser on the wall.

Dr Caldwell applies bright blue paint to Melanie's scalp, from a plastic jar labelled BACTERICIDE GEL E2J. Melanie tries to imagine what she must look like now, bareheaded and blue. She must be a little bit like a Pictish warrior. Mr Whitaker showed them some pictures of Picts, one time when his voice was blurry, and he couldn't stop laughing at the phrase *pictures of Picts*. If someone went into battle naked, the Picts said he was sky-clad. Melanie has almost never been naked. It's not a nice feeling at all, she decides; it makes her feel vulnerable and ashamed.

"I don't," she says.

"What?" Dr Caldwell sets down the brush and wipes her fingers against her white coat, leaving sky-blue streaks.

"I don't like learning about science. I want to go back to the classroom, please."

Dr Caldwell meets her gaze, for the first time. "I'm afraid that's not possible," she says. "Close your eyes, Melanie."

"No," Melanie says. She's certain that if she does, Dr Caldwell will do something mean to her. Something that will hurt.

And suddenly, like seeing the other side of an optical illusion, she knows what that something will be. They're going to cut her up and put pieces of her in jars like these pieces of other people all around her.

She throws her weight against the straps, struggles desperately, but they don't move at all.

"Should we try some isoflurane?" Dr Selkirk asks. Her voice is unsteady. She sounds like she might be going to cry.

"They don't respond," Dr Caldwell says. "You know that. I refuse to waste one of our last few cylinders of general anaesthetic making the experimental subject feel vaguely drowsy. Please remember, Doctor, that the subject presents as a child but is actually a fungal colony animating a child's body. There's no place for sentiment here."

"No," Dr Selkirk agrees. "I know."

She picks up a knife, of a kind that Melanie has never seen before. It has a very long handle and a very short blade – the blade so thin that when it's edge-on to her, it's almost invisible. She holds it out to Dr Caldwell.

"I want to go back to the classroom," Melanie says again.

The knife slips through Dr Selkirk's fingers and falls to the floor just before Dr Caldwell can take it. It makes a ringing sound as it hits, and again as it bounces. "I'm sorry, I'm sorry," Dr Selkirk yelps. She bends to pick it up, hesitates, straightens again and takes another from the instrument tray instead. She flinches from Dr Caldwell's glare as she hands it over.

"If the noise is troubling you," Dr Caldwell says, "I'll remove the pharynx first." And she puts the cold edge of the blade against Melanie's throat.

"It'll be the last fucking thing you ever do," says Miss Justineau's voice.

The two women pause in their work and look towards the door. Melanie can't at first, because if she raises her head she'll cut her own throat on the blade of the knife. But then Dr Caldwell moves her hand away, and she's free to bend her neck and take a peek.

Miss Justineau is standing in the doorway. She's holding something in her hands – a red cylinder with a black tube attached to one side of it. It seems to be pretty heavy.

"Good morning, Miss Justineau," Melanie says. She's dizzy with relief, but the ridiculous, inadequate words are hard-wired into her. She couldn't keep them in if she tried.

"Helen," Dr Caldwell says. "Please come in, won't you? And close the door. This isn't exactly an antiseptic environment, but we're doing our best."

"Put the scalpel down," Miss Justineau says. "Now."

Dr Caldwell frowns. "Don't be absurd. I'm in the middle of a dissection."

Miss Justineau advances into the room, stopping only when she comes to the bottom end of the table where Melanie's bare feet are strapped down. "No," she says, "you're at the start of a dissection. If you were in the middle of it, we wouldn't be talking right now. Put the scalpel down, Caroline, and nobody gets hurt."

"Oh dear," Dr Caldwell says. "This isn't going to end well, is it?"

"That's kind of up to you."

Dr Caldwell glances at Dr Selkirk, who hasn't made a move or said a word since Miss Justineau came into the room. She's just standing there with her mouth half open, her hands clasped to her chest. She looks like someone who's staring at a hypnotist's watch and is about to go under.

"Jean," Dr Caldwell says. "Call security, please, and tell them to come and remove Helen from the theatre."

Dr Selkirk glances at the phone on the work surface and takes a half-step in that direction. Miss Justineau swings round a lot faster and brings the fire extinguisher down on the phone. The handset breaks in two with a dry, complicated crunching sound. Dr Selkirk jumps back.

"Yeah, look at it, Jean," Miss Justineau tells her. "The next time you move, you're getting this right in your face."

"And you'll make the same threat if I try to go to the door, or the window, I suppose," Dr Caldwell says. "Helen, I don't think you've thought this through. It really doesn't matter whether I call off this procedure or not. You can take Melanie out of the lab, but you can't take her out of the base. Every gate is guarded, and outside the gate there are perimeter patrols. There is no way you can stop this."

Miss Justineau doesn't answer, but Melanie knows that Dr Caldwell is wrong. Miss Justineau can do anything she wants to do. She's like Prometheus, and Dr Caldwell is like Zeus. Zeus thought he was big and clever because he was a god, but the Titans weren't scared of him at all. Of course, in the story, the Titans lost in the end – but Melanie is in no doubt about who's going to win this battle.

"I'll take it one step at a time," Miss Justineau growls. "Jean, undo those straps."

100

"Don't," Dr Caldwell says quickly, "do anything of the kind." She gives Dr Selkirk a brief, fierce stare as she says this, then turns her full attention back to Miss Justineau.

And softens on the instant. "Helen, you're not well. The situation here has put all of us under terrible strain. And this fantasy of rescuing the test subject . . . well, it's part of your response to that stress. We're all friends, and colleagues. Nobody is going to be reported. Nobody is going to be punished. We're going to work this out, because really there isn't any alternative."

Miss Justineau hesitates, lulled by this gentleness.

"I'm going to put the scalpel down," Dr Caldwell says. "I'm asking you to do the same with your . . . weapon."

And Dr Caldwell does what she promised. She shows the scalpel, holds it high for a second, then sets it down on the edge of the table, close to Melanie's left side. She does this slowly, with exaggerated care. So Miss Justineau is watching the hand with the scalpel. Of course she is.

With her other hand, Dr Caldwell takes something small and shiny from the pocket of her lab coat.

"Miss Justineau!" Melanie shrieks. Too late. Much too late.

Dr Caldwell thrusts the shiny something into Miss Justineau's face. There's a sound like the hiss of the shower spray, and a smell on the air that's sour and scalding and takes your breath away. Miss Justineau gurgles, the sound cut off very suddenly. She drops the fire extinguisher, and she's clawing at her face. She sinks slowly to her knees, then topples sideways on to the floor of the lab, where she twitches and writhes, making noises like she's choking.

Dr Caldwell stares at her dispassionately. "Now go and get a security detail," she says to Dr Selkirk. "I want this woman under military arrest. The charge will be attempted sabotage."

Melanie slumps back on to the table with a moan of anguish – both for herself and for Miss Justineau. Despair fills her, makes her heavy as lead.

Dr Selkirk heads for the door, but that means she has to skirt around Miss Justineau, who is still on her knees, wheezing and moaning as she tries to draw a breath through the burning miasma of whatever it was that Dr Caldwell hit her with. It's heavy in the air, and Dr Selkirk starts coughing too.

Entirely out of patience, Dr Caldwell reaches out her hand to pick up the scalpel again.

But right then, something happens that makes her stop. Two things, really. The first is an explosion, loud enough to make the windows rattle in their frames. The second is an ear-splitting scream, like a hundred people shrieking all at the same time.

Dr Selkirk's face looks first blank, then terrified. "That's general evacuation," she says. "Isn't it? Isn't that the evacuation siren?"

Dr Caldwell doesn't waste time answering her. She crosses to the window and hauls up the blinds.

Melanie sits up again, as far as she can, but she's too low down. Mostly what she can see is the sky outside.

Both the doctors are staring out of the window. Miss Justineau is still on the floor, her hands clasped to her face, her back and shoulders shaking. She's oblivious to everything except her pain.

"What's happening?" Dr Selkirk bleats. "There are people moving out there. Are they—"

"I don't know," Dr Caldwell snaps. "I'm going to lower the emergency shutters. We can hold out here until the all-clear sounds."

She reaches out to do it. She puts her hand on the switch.

That's when the window shatters.

And the hungries swarm over the sill.

102

19

Long before Sergeant Parks has come up with any kind of a counter-attack, the fences are down.

It's not that it happens fast; it's just remorseless. The hungries that Gallagher clocked in the trees on the eastern perimeter suddenly come out of there at a flat run. They're not hunting anything, they're just running – and the strangeness of that maybe makes Parks hesitate for a second or two, while he tries to figure it out.

Then the wind changes and the smell hits him. A rank wave of decomposition, so intense it's almost like a punch in the face. Soldiers on either side of him gasp. Someone swears.

And the smell tells him, even before he sees it. There are more of them. A lot more. That's the smell of a whole herd of hungries, a frigging tidal wave of hungries. Too many to stop.

So the only option is to slow them down. Blunt that head-long charge before they reach the fence.

"Aim for the legs," he shouts. "Full auto." And then "Fire!"

The soldiers do as they're told. The air fills with the angry punctuation of their guns. Hungries fall, and are trampled under by more hungries coming behind them. But there are too many, and they're too close. It's not going to stop them.

Then Parks sees something else, at the back of the moving wall of undead. Junkers. Junkers so thickly padded with body armour that each of them looks like the Michelin man. Some are carrying spears. Others are wielding what look like cattle prods, which they jam into the neck or back of any hungry who slows down. At least two are holding flame-throwers. Jets of flame fired to right and left hem in the hungries and keep them from straying too far off the target.

Which is the fence, and the base beyond.

Two bulldozers are also rolling along on the flanks of the herd, their blades set obliquely. When the hungries straggling at the edges get too close, they either turn back towards the central mass or else they're ploughed under.

This isn't a stampede. It's a cattle drive.

"Oh God!" says Private Alsop in a strangled voice. "Oh Jesus!"

Parks wastes another moment in marvelling at the sheer genius of the assault. Using the hungries as battering rams, as weapons of war. He wonders how the junkers rounded up so many, and where they corralled them before this forced march, but that's just logistics. The idea of doing something like this – it's nothing short of majestic.

"Target the live ones!" he bellows. "The junkers! Fire on the junkers!" But they only get in a couple of ragged volleys before he yells at them to fall back, to get away from the fence.

Because the fence is going to give, and they're going to be neck deep in rotting cannibals.

They retreat in good order, firing as they go.

The wave hits. It doesn't even slow. Hungries slam full-tilt into the mesh and into the concrete stanchions that support it. It leans inwards, groans and creaks, but seems to be holding. The front ranks of walking corpses are treading water.

But more and more hungries fetch up behind them, push

against them, transmit their own weight and momentum to the point of impact, the flimsy barricade of woven wire links.

The concrete posts themselves are starting to list drunkenly. A stretch of fence goes down, suddenly unviable, as a fence post tilts clean out of the ground along with a hemispheric divot of earth.

Dozens of the don't-know-they're-dead come down with it, trampled and ground down and compressed to mincemeat. But there are plenty more where they came from. They rush forward, their pistoning feet threshing the remains of the fallen.

As quick as that, the hungries are through.

20

Justineau tries to stand. It's not easy, because her guts are churning, her lungs are full of acid and the floor under her feet heaves like the deck of a ship. Her face feels like a mask of white-hot iron, fitted way too tight over her skull.

Things are moving around her, quickly, with no accompanying narrative apart from panting breath and a single muffled shriek. She's been blind since Caldwell sprayed her, and although the initial rush of tears washed most of the pepper spray out of her eyes, they're still swollen half shut. She sees blurred shapes, crashing against each other like flotsam in the wake of a flood.

She blinks furiously, trying to dredge up some more moisture from her now dry-baked tear ducts.

Two of the shapes resolve. One is Selkirk, on her side on the floor of the lab, her legs jackknifing in furious staccato. The other is a hungry which is kneeling astride her, stuffing her spilled intestines into its mouth in pink, sagging coils.

More hungries surge in from all sides, hiding Selkirk from view. She's a honey-pot for putrescent bees. The last Justineau sees of her is her inconsolable face.

Melanie! Justineau thinks. *Where's Melanie?*

The room is a sea of scrambling, clutching bodies. Justineau backs away from the feeding frenzy, almost backs into another. By the window of the room, Caroline Caldwell is fighting for her life with silent ferocity. Two hungries who came over the sill crawling on hands and knees, leaving pieces of themselves on the jagged edges of the broken glass, have gripped her legs and are swarming up her body. Their jaws are working like the interlocking scoops of mechanical diggers. Caldwell has got her hands on the tops of their heads, as though in benediction, but what she's actually doing is pushing against them as hard as she can, trying desperately to stop them from bending forward and sinking their teeth into her. She's losing that battle, inch by inch.

Justineau finds the fire extinguisher where she dropped it, its bright red paint calling out to her across the lab's anodyne whites and greys. She picks it up, turns like a hammer-thrower and swings it underarm. It makes contact with a hollow clang, and the head of one of the hungries sags sideways, the neck snapped cleanly. It still doesn't let go, but Caldwell's right hand is freed because the thing's jaws can't be brought to bear now that its neck is no longer pulling its weight.

With the strength and resolution of sheer terror, Caldwell uses her free hand to grip a slender triangle of glass that's still adhering to the window frame, and pulls it loose. Her own blood wells up between her fingers as she slashes at the other hungry again and again, flaying its face off its skull in broad strips.

Justineau leaves her to it. With the window right in front of her, she can orientate herself. She turns to face the operating table. Amazingly, her line of sight is clear. Most of the hungries are fighting over scraps of Jean Selkirk, which means they're down on hands and knees, snouts in the trough.

The operating table is empty. The plasticated straps that had held Melanie immobile now hang useless, sheared clean

107

through. The scalpel that Caldwell put down before she used the pepper spray is lying discarded at the head end of the table.

Justineau looks around wildly. She makes a sound like a moan, which is lost in the liquid snuffling sounds of the monsters' banquet. The chaos of the room has resolved itself into simplicity. Selkirk hosting the feast. Caldwell carving at the face and upper body of the hungry that's still blindly trying to ascend her, until it finally falls away, effectively peeled.

Melanie is nowhere.

Caldwell is free now, and she's frantically gathering up notes and samples with her blood-slicked hands, trying to pile up too many things in her arms until they fall to the floor in a clattering cascade. The sound is loud enough to rouse the hungries who are eating Selkirk. Their heads jerk up and turn, left and then right, in eerie synchrony.

Caldwell is down on one knee, picking up the fallen treasures. Justineau grips her by her collar and hauls her upright.

"Come on!" she shouts. Or she tries to shout. But she's swallowed some of the pepper spray, so her tongue is three times its normal size. She sounds like Charles Laughton in *The Hunchback of Notre Dame*. Doesn't matter. She's hauling Caldwell to the door like a mother dragging a wilful child as the hungries surge up from the floor and trample over what's left of Dr Selkirk in their eagerness to reach this new food source.

Justineau slams the lab door in their faces. It's not locked, but that's a detail. Hungries are no better with locks than wild dogs would be. The door shudders from their repeated assaults, but it doesn't open.

The women are in a short corridor, with the shower unit at the other end of it. Justineau is heading for the shower and the doors beyond, which she left wide open when she came in, but she slows and stops before she gets there. In the space between this block and the vehicle sheds, a running firefight is going on. The men she can see ducking and shooting and taking cover behind the angle of the next building are not

108

Sergeant Parks' men, in the khaki she's always hated; they're savages in motley, their hair blacked and sculpted with tar, machetes tucked into their belts.

Junkers.

While Justineau is still staring, two of the men leap into the air, back-flipping at impossible speed. The flash and roar of the grenade comes half a second later, and the peristaltic shudder of the shockwave a heartbeat after that.

Caldwell points to another door – maybe she says something too, but the wild carillon in Justineau's ears blots out all other sounds. The door is locked. Caldwell rummages in her pockets, leaving dark red Bézier curves of blood on her white lab coat. Her hands, Justineau sees, are in a really bad state, flaps of skin hanging loose from deep incisions where she gripped the jagged glass sliver to hit out with it.

Pocket after pocket. Caldwell can't find the key. She tears open the coat at last, tries her trouser pockets, and it's there. She gets the door open and they're in what turns out to be a storeroom, filled with a dozen or more identical grey steel shelf units. It's a refuge.

It's a trap. As soon as Caldwell locks the door from the inside, Justineau realises she can't stay here. Melanie is wandering around somewhere outside, like Red Riding Hood in the deep, dark woods, surrounded by men who are firing automatic weapons.

Justineau has to find her. Which means she has to get outside.

Caldwell leans against the end of a shelf unit, either pulling herself together or retreating into some inner space that's nicer than this one. Justineau ignores her, checks out the narrow room. There are no other doors, but there's a window, high up on the wall. It will open on to the side of the building that's closest to the perimeter fence and furthest from the fighting. From there, she could maybe make a run for it – back to the classroom block, where Melanie will have gone to ground if she was able to find her way back there.

109

Justineau starts to empty the nearest shelf unit, sweeping boxes and bottles, bags of surgical gauze, rolls of paper towel off the shelves on to the floor. Caldwell watches her in silence as she pulls the unit over to the window, where it can serve as a ladder.

"They'll kill you," Caldwell says.

"*Theb fhtay hhhere*," Justineau snarls over her shoulder. But when she starts to climb, Caldwell steadies the unit with her shredded hands – then clambers up after her, emitting a little gasp of pain every time she has to grip the cold metal of the unit.

The window secures with a catch. Justineau releases it and tilts it open an inch. Outside, just a stretch of untrodden grass. The shouts and gunshots are deadened by distance.

She pushes the window fully open and climbs through, dropping down on to the grass. It's still wet with morning dew, cold against her ankles. The ordinariness of that feeling is like a telegram from the other side of the world.

Caldwell has more trouble getting out, because she's trying not to use her injured hands to support her weight. She falls heavily, unable to keep her balance, and sprawls full length in the grass. Justineau helps her up, none too gently.

From the corner, they can see right across the parade ground to the classroom block and the barracks proper. There are hungries everywhere, in tight groups and running hard. Justineau thinks they're running at random, but then she sees the junker herders in their weird armour, driving them on with spear points, Tasers and good old-fashioned fire.

Clinically she notes that the junkers are all plastered with tar – not just their hair, but the flesh of their arms and hands, the weave of their Kevlar vests. It must do something similar to what the e-blocker spray does, masking the smell of their endocrine sweat so that the hungries don't turn and swim up that chemical gradient all the way to their tormentors' throats.

But mostly she thinks: *hungries as bioweapons!* Win or lose, the base is done for.

"I'm going to try to get across to the classroom block," she tells Caldwell. "You should probably give it a few seconds, then head for the fence. At least some of them will be looking the other way."

"The classroom block is underground," Caldwell snaps. "There's only one way in or out. You'll be trapped."

What a wonderful pair of scientists the two of them are. Assembling known facts into valid inferences. Forensic minds refusing to quit in the face of this utter fucking nightmare.

Justineau doesn't bother to answer. She just runs. She's plotted a course and she sticks to it, giving the nearest pack of hungries a wide berth as they sweep on past her, heading for the barracks. The junkers who are herding them are too busy with what they're doing to turn aside for her.

And their comrades, coming up behind them, are taking fire from both sides: Parks' people are using the terrain, turning the open spaces between the wooden huts into killing grounds.

Justineau has to swerve away from three soldiers who are running right towards her, rifles in their hands, and then she's sideways on to another stampeding wedge of hungries. She tacks and weaves, and only realises she's lost her way when she rounds another corner and what's in front of her is about a dozen spike-haired men, their limbs black and shiny with tar that must still be liquid, firing from behind a makeshift barricade of overturned dumpsters.

The junkers turn and see her. Most of them turn right back again and keep on firing, but two immediately stand and walk towards her. One pulls a knife from a sheath at his belt and hefts it in his hand. The other just levels the gun he's already carrying.

Justineau freezes. No point in running, turning her back to the gun, and when she tries to come up with another response, her brain floods with a cold flush of nothing at all.

111

The knife man kicks her legs out from under her, sends her sprawling. He grips the sleeve of her shirt, hauls her half upright, and holds her out to the other as though he's offering her up as a gift.

"Do it," he says.

Justineau raises her head. Usually a bad idea to make eye contact with a wild animal, but if she's going to die anyway, she wants to die telling him to go screw himself and – if she has time – exactly how and where.

It's the gunner whose gaze she meets. And she realises with an almost surreal jolt of surprise how young he is. Still in his teens, probably. He moves the gun from her head to point it at her chest, maybe because he doesn't want to go home from this with the image of her exploded face hanging in the gallery of his dreams.

There's something ritualistic about all this, the way the older man holds her still and waits for the other to dispatch her. It's a rite of passage – a bonding moment, maybe, between a father and a son.

The youngster steels himself, visibly.

Then he's gone. Knocked off his feet. Something dark and subliminally fast has whipped by and taken him with it. He writhes on the asphalt, struggling with an enemy that despite its tiny size spits and mewls and claws at him like an entire sackful of pissed off cats.

It's Melanie. And she's not taking any prisoners.

The man – boy, rather – gives a scream that tails off into a liquid gurgle as her jaws close on his throat.

21

The shock of that first taste of blood and warm flesh is so intense that it almost makes Melanie faint. Nothing in her life has ever been this good. Not even having her hair stroked by Miss Justineau! The rush of pleasure is bigger than she is. The part of her that can think bends in that cataract, broadsided, and clings to whatever it can to keep from being swept away.

She tries to remind herself what's at stake. She attacked the man because he was going to hurt Miss Justineau, not because of the irresistible fresh meat smell; she didn't catch a whiff of that until she was astride him, and she bit down before she'd even thought about doing it. Her body didn't need her permission for this, and it wasn't prepared to wait. Now she bites and tears and chews and swallows, the sensations filling her and battering her like the torrent of a waterfall pouring into a cup held right under it.

Something hits her hard, dislodging her from her prey, from her meal. Another man stands over her, leans down towards her, a knife raised in his hand. Miss Justineau tackles him from behind, her hands beating at his head. He has to turn to defend himself, and Melanie is able to get a solid grip on his leg. She wraps herself around him, lifts herself effortlessly off the ground with her strong arms, locks to him like a limpet.

The man bellows incoherent curses and hammers at her frantically. The blows hurt, but they don't matter. Melanie finds the point where leg joins body, driven by some instinct so deep she can't even tell where it comes from. She fastens her teeth on to the man and bites through the leg of his pants until the blood wells thick and spurting into her mouth. She knew it would. She sensed the artery singing to her through folds of flesh and fabric.

The man's scream is a scary sound, shrill and wobbly. Melanie doesn't like it at all. But oh, she likes the taste! Likes the way his opened thigh becomes a fountain, as though raw meat was a magic garden, a hidden landscape that she never glimpsed until now.

It's too much, finally. Her stomach and her mind aren't big enough. The whole world isn't big enough. Numbed with delight, with repletion that melts her muscles and her thoughts, she doesn't resist this time when hands pluck her loose and lift her up.

From under the reek of chemicals comes the Miss Justineau smell, familiar and welcome and wonderful. Pressed to Miss Justineau's chest, she emits a satiated purr. She wants to curl to sleep there, like an animal in its burrow.

But she can't sleep, because Miss Justineau is moving, running fast. Each footfall jars Melanie. And the full feeling doesn't last. Her torpid hunger rallies quickly, prods at the edges of her mind with eager intimations. Already the smell means something different, is urging her to feed again. She turns and wriggles in a grip too weak to contain her, butts with her head against the underside of Miss J's arm, mouth open to bite again.

But she can't she mustn't she can't! This is Miss Justineau, who loves her. Who saved her from the table and the thin, scary knife. Melanie can't stop her jaws from closing but she jerks

114

her head back, at the last moment, so they close on air instead of flesh.

A growl wells up from inside her, from the same place that mewled like a kitten only a few moments ago.

has to

mustn't

has to

She wrestles with a wild animal, and the animal is her.

So she knows she's going to lose.

22

Justineau is running again. But now she has no idea where she's running to. The familiar geography of the base has been rendered arcane by the smoke of explosions, the din of gunfire and running feet.

Melanie makes it even harder to focus, squirming and thrashing in her grip. Justineau remembers lifting her from the body of the young junker boy, like plucking a blood-gorged tick from a dog's belly, and has to fight the urge to drop her.

Why fight it? Not because Melanie saved her. But then, in a sense, yes. Because she's turned her back on something inside herself, and Melanie is the sign of that – the anti-Isaac she snatched from the fire to prove to God that he doesn't always get to call the shots.

Fuck you, Caroline.

Melanie is making noises a human throat isn't properly configured for, and her head is levering backwards and forwards, butting at Justineau's arm. There's astonishing strength in the little girl. She's going to break free. She's going to bring the both of them down.

Justineau glimpses the steel door of the classroom block, unexpectedly close by, and swerves towards it.

Realises immediately that it's no use to her. The door is closed, and the locks engage automatically when it's in that position. There's no possible way she can get inside.

Hungries loom on her right, a dozen or so, coming from the direction of the lab. Maybe they're the same ones she originally fled from, still following her scent. Either way, they can smell her now and they want her. They're coming towards her, legs rising and falling in tireless, mechanical syncopation.

Nothing for it but to turn tail. To run away from them as fast as she can, and pray that she gets somewhere before they catch her.

She does. She gets to the fence. It's suddenly right there in front of her, blocking her way like a wire-mesh Everest. She's finished.

She turns, at bay. The hungries are coming on at that same merciless, metronomic sprint. To right and left, there's nothing. Nowhere to hide, or to run to. She lets go of Melanie, sees her fall like a cat falls, righting herself in the air to land on starfish-spread hands and feet.

Justineau balls her fists, braces herself, but an enormous exhaustion hits her and darkness rushes in from the corners of her vision as the adrenalin wave deserts her. She doesn't even throw a punch as the first hungry gapes his jaws and reaches out to pull her down.

With a wet crunch, he's slammed to the ground and ploughed under.

A wall slides smoothly across Justineau's field of vision. It's metallic, painted in dull green and there's a window in it. From the window, a monster's face stares out at her. Sergeant Parks' face.

"Get inside!" he bellows.

The thing in front of her resolves itself, like a puzzle picture. It's one of the base's Humvees. Justineau grabs the door handle and tries all the wrong ways to make it open, twisting and pulling before she finally pops it with a single squeeze of the catch release on the handle's inner face.

She throws the door open as the hungries round the back of the vehicle and start towards her. One of Parks' boy soldiers, a kid half her age with a mass of red hair like an autumn bonfire, is up on the roof manning the Humvee's pedestal gun. He swings it wildly, stitching the air with stinging metal. It's not clear what he's aiming at, but on one of the down-swings he intersects the nearest hungries and knocks them right off their feet.

Justineau holds the door, but doesn't move – because Melanie doesn't move. Crouched on the ground, the little girl stares into the vehicle's dark interior with animal mistrust.

"It's fine!" Justineau yells. "Melanie, come on. Get inside. Now!"

Melanie makes up her mind – makes a standing jump past Justineau and in through the door. Justineau clambers in after her, slams the door tight shut.

Turns to see Caroline Caldwell's pale, sweating face staring right at her. Her hands are folded under her armpits and she's lying on the floor of the Humvee like a bolt of firewood. Melanie cowers away from her, presses against Justineau again, and mechanically Justineau embraces her.

The Humvee wheels around. Through the window, they can briefly see a kaleidoscope of smoke and ruin and running figures.

They drive through the fence without slowing, but almost don't make it across the ditch beyond. The Humvee belly-flops on the far side, shudders for a few seconds like a washing machine on spin before it gets enough traction to drag its rear end up over the rim.

For the next few miles, it's chased by five yards of chain-link and a concrete post, bounding along behind it the way a wedding car trails tin cans.

118

23

Parks would prefer to drive straight across country – the Humvee doesn't need roads all that much – but the scrape and grind from behind him tells him that all isn't well with the rear axle. So he shifts down to get a bit more push out of the engine, floors the gas and drives with reckless speed down the empty B roads around the base, swerving left and right at random. He figures that the best way for them not to be found is – for the time being – to be lost themselves.

At least there's no pursuit that he can see. That's something to be profoundly grateful for.

He finally brings the Humvee to a halt about ten miles from the base, pulling off the road on to a rutted, overgrown field. He turns off the ignition and gets his breath back, leaning over the wheel as the engine cools. The sounds it's making are not happy sounds. He grabbed the vehicle from the workshop, the only place he could get to without crossing a parade ground full of hungries, and he wonders – now that it's too late – what it was in there for.

Gallagher climbs down from the pedestal, folds the gun down after him and locks the hatch. He's shaking like he's got a fever, so these simple actions take him quite a while. When he's finally sitting in the shotgun seat he gives the sergeant a terrified stare, looking for orders or explanations or anything that will help him to keep it together.

"Good work," Parks tells him. "Check on the civilians. I'm going to do a quick recce."

He opens the door, but he doesn't get any further than that. Glancing over into the back seat, Gallagher gives a short, pained yell. "Sarge! Sergeant Parks!"

"What is it, son?" Parks asks wearily. He turns to look into the back with a sinking feeling, expecting to see that one of the two women has sustained a gut wound or something similar – that they're going to have to watch her die.

But it's not that. Dr Caldwell's coat is saturated with blood, but most of it seems to be from her hands. And Helen Justineau looks pretty much fine, apart from her red, puffed-up face.

No, what made the boy shout out is their third passenger. It's one of the little hungry kids – the monsters from the containment block. Parks recognises her, with a palpable shock, as the one he just took over to the meat market, to Dr Caldwell's lab. She's changed since then. She's crouching on the floor of the Humvee, buck naked, shaved bald, and painted like a savage, her vivid blue eyes flicking backwards and forwards between the women. The curve of her back speaks both tension and the imminence of movement.

Awkwardly, because of the angle, Parks grabs his sidearm and takes aim, thrusting it between the seat backs so that it points directly at the little girl's head. A head shot is his best chance of putting her down, at this sort of range.

Their eyes meet. She doesn't move. Like she's asking him to do it.

It's Helen Justineau who stops him, interposing her body between them. In the narrow confines of the Humvee, she makes a pretty unanswerable barricade.

120

"Move aside," Parks tells her.

"Then put the gun down," Justineau says. "You're not killing her."

"She's already dead," Dr Caldwell points out from the floor, her voice uneven. "Technically speaking."

Justineau shoots a sidelong glance at the doctor, but doesn't bother to answer her. Her gaze comes back immediately to Parks. "She's not a danger," she says. "Not right now. You can see that. Let her out of the car, let her get some distance from you – from all of us – and take it from there. Okay?"

What Parks can see is that the nightmare-that-walks-like-a-girl is wide-eyed and trembling, barely in control of itself. Everyone in the car is chemmed up, e-blocker from hairline to socks, but there's enough blood kicking around – on Caldwell's hands and arms and clothes, on the kid herself – to be pushing her triggers anyway. He's never seen a hungry in a meat frenzy and not acting on it. It's a novelty, but he's not going to bet his life on it being a long-term trend.

He either shoots her now, or he does what Justineau says. And if he shoots her, he takes the risk of killing one or both of the civilians.

"Do it," he says. "Quickly."

Justineau throws the door open. "Melanie . . ." she says, but the kid doesn't need to be told. She's out of there like a bullet, running away from the Humvee and across the field, her spindly legs a blur.

She goes upwind, Parks can't help but notice. She gets away from the smell of them. From the smell of the blood. Then she crouches down in the long grass, almost lost to view, and hugs her knees. She turns her face away.

"Good enough?" Justineau demands.

"No!" Caldwell says quickly. "She's got to be restrained and brought with us. We have no idea what happened to the rest of the subjects. If the base is lost, and my records along with it, she's all we've got to show for a four-year programme."

121

"Which says a lot for your programme," Justineau says. Caldwell glares. The air between them is thick with bad vibes.

Parks gestures to Gallagher — a jerk of the head — and gets out of the vehicle, leaving the womenfolk to it. He's worried about the Humvee's rear axle and he wants to look at it right away. No telling when they might have to move again.

24

Melanie is coming down.

At first she can't think at all. Then, when thoughts come back, she shrinks away from them, like Mr Whitaker when his bottle is almost empty. Her mouth is haunted by memories that want to be real again. Her mind is reeling from what she's done.

And her body is wracked with a million tics and shakes – each cell reporting in unfit for duty, demanding what it can't have.

She's always been a good girl. But she ate pieces of two men, and very probably killed them both. Killed them with her teeth.

She was hungry, and they were her bread.

So what is she now?

These conundrums come and go as the residual hunger allows her to focus on them. Sometimes they're very big and very clear, sometimes far away and seen through skeins of fuzz and smoke.

Something else that comes and goes: a memory. When she was lying on the table, tied down, and sawing at the plastic band that held her left wrist – left hand twisted round, the scalpel held awkwardly between the very tips of her fingers – one of the hungries loomed over her.

She froze at once. Stared up, breathless, into that savage, vacant face. There was nothing she could do, not even scream. Not even close her eyes. Free will fled away along the vectors of her fear.

For a strained second which then broke, abruptly, into pieces. The hungry gaped, slack-jawed, head hanging down and shoulders hunched up like a vulture. Its gaze slid away from Melanie's, to the left and then to the right. It put out its tongue to taste the air, and then it stumbled on around the table, heading for a writhing mass of motion on the lab's floor, almost out of Melanie's field of vision.

It had only met her stare for that one second by blind chance.

After that it didn't even seem to know she was there.

What with the withdrawal effects and with worrying at this puzzle, it's a long while before Melanie notices the world she's sitting in.

Wild flowers surround her. A couple of them – daffodils and campion – are familiar from Miss Justineau's lesson on the day of the vernal equinox. The rest are completely new, and there are dozens of them. She turns her head, very slowly, staring at one after another.

She registers the tiny buzzing things that fly between them and guesses that they're bees, because of what they're doing – visiting one flower after another, bullying their way into the core of each one with a shrugging, rocking gait, and then backing out again and taking off for the next.

Something much bigger flies across the field in front of her. A black bird that might be a crow or a jackdaw, its song a hoarse, thrilling war cry. Sweeter and softer songs weave around it, but she can't see the birds – if they are birds – that make those sounds.

124

The air is heavy with scents. Melanie knows that some of them are the scents of the flowers, but even the air seems to have a smell – earthy and rich and complicated, made out of things living and things dying and things long dead. The smell of a world where nothing stops moving, nothing stays the same.

Suddenly she's an ant all scrunched up on the floor of that world. A static atom in a sea of change. The immensity of earth envelops her, and enters into her. She sips it, with each gulp of heady, supercharged atmosphere.

And even in this dazed, strung-out state, even with those memories of meat and monstrous violence lying thwart across her mind, she really, really likes it.

The smells, especially. They affect her very differently from the smell of people, but they still excite her – wake something in her mind that must have been asleep until then.

They help her to push the meat hunger and the memories away into a middle distance where they don't hurt and shame her so very much.

By degrees, she comes back to herself. Which is when she realises that Miss Justineau is standing a little way away from her, watching her in silence. Miss Justineau's face is wary, full of questions.

Melanie chooses to answer the most important one. "I won't bite, Miss Justineau.

"But you'd better not get any closer than that," she adds quickly, scrambling back as Miss J takes a step towards her. "You smell all . . . and there's blood on you. I don't know what I'll do."

"Okay." Miss Justineau stops where she is, and nods. "We'll find a place to wash, and then we'll freshen up the e-blocker. Are you okay, Melanie? It must have been really frightening for you." Her face is full of concern, along with something else. Fear, maybe.

And she should be afraid. They're outside the fence, in region 6, and they must be miles and miles away from the base. They're out among the monsters, the hungries, with no refuge close to hand.

"Are you okay?" Miss Justineau asks again.

Melanie nods, but it's a lie. She's not okay, not yet. She doesn't know if she'll ever be okay again. Being strapped down on the table with Dr Caldwell's knife in front of her eyes was the scariest thing that ever happened to her. Until she saw Miss J about to be killed, and then that became the scariest thing. And now, it's the thought of biting and eating pieces of those two men.

However you look at it, it hasn't been a good day at all. She wants to ask the question that's burning a hole through her heart. Because Miss Justineau will know. Of course she will. Miss Justineau knows everything. But she can't ask, because she can't make the words come out. She doesn't want to admit that there's a doubt, a question there.

What am I?

So she says nothing. She waits for Miss Justineau to speak. And after a long time, Miss Justineau does. "You were very brave. If you hadn't come along when you did, and if you hadn't fought those men, they would have killed me."

"And Dr Caldwell was going to kill me and chop me up into pieces and put me in jars," Melanie reminds her. "You saved me first, Miss Justineau."

"Helen," Miss J says. "My name is Helen."

Melanie considers this statement.

"Not to me," she says.

25

When he gets down under the Humvee and takes a good look at the rear axle, Parks swears.

Bitterly.

He's only a middling mechanic, but he can tell that it's pretty much screwed. It's taken a good whack just off centre, presumably when they leapt the security ditch, and it's all bent into a shallow V, with a small but visible crack in the metal at the impact point. They're lucky to have got this far without it breaking in two. They sure as hell won't make it much further. Not on their own, anyway. And Parks has done enough shout-outs by this time, on normal and emergency frequencies, to know that there's no help coming from the base.

He debates with himself whether it's worth looking at the engine. There's something wrong there, too, that he might have a better chance of fixing, but the axle's probably going to give long before that becomes an issue.

Probably. But not certainly.

With a sigh, he crawls out from under the Humvee and goes around to the front. Private Gallagher trails after him like a lost puppy, still begging for orders.

"Is it okay, Sarge?" he asks, anxiously.

"Just pop the bonnet for me, son," Parks says. "We need to take a look at the insides, too."

The insides look okay, remarkably. The straining sounds from the engine have an obvious cause, which is that one of the motor mounts has been unscrewed. The engine block is hanging at an angle, vibrating against the top of the wheel arch where it's touching. It would have torn itself to pieces eventually, but it doesn't seem to have done much real damage yet. Parks gets the socket set out of the tool locker on the side of the vehicle and puts a new bolt through the mount, locking the engine back into place.

He takes his time, because once he's finished, he's got to start making decisions about all this other shit.

He holds the briefing inside the Hummer to lengthen the odds against nasty surprises, and he makes the little hungry kid sit outside on the bonnet.

That's the way he thinks of it, as a briefing. He's the only soldier here except for Gallagher, who's too young to have an opinion, let alone a plan. So it's going to have to be Parks who calls the shots.

That's not how it goes down, though. The civilians have ideas of their own − always an omen of disaster and heartache in Parks' book − and they're not shy about expressing them.

Starting from when Parks says they're going to head south. It makes perfect sense − most likely it's their only chance − but as soon as he says it, they're up in his face.

"All my notes and samples are at the base!" Dr Caldwell says. "They have to be retrieved."

"There are thirty kids there, too," Justineau adds. "And most of your men. What are we going to do? Just walk away from them?"

"That's exactly what we're going to do," Parks tells them. "If you shut up, I'll tell you why. I've been up on that radio

128

every ten or fifteen minutes since we stopped. Not only is there no answer from the base, there's no answer full stop. Nobody else got out of there. Or if they did, they got out without wheels or comms, which means they might just as well be on another planet as far as we're concerned. There's no way to get their attention right now without getting the junkers bouncing at us too. If we meet them on the road, that's great. Otherwise, we're alone, and the only sensible thing to do is to head for home fires. For Beacon."

Caldwell doesn't answer. She's unfolded her arms for the first time and she's taking a furtive, fearful look at her injuries, like a poker player lifting the corners of his cards to see what Lady Luck has sent along.

But Justineau just keeps going at it, which is pretty much what Parks expects from her by this point. "What if we wait for a few days, and then start back towards the base? We can take it slowly, and scout out the ground as we go. If the junkers are still in possession, we back off. But if it's clear, we can go on in. Maybe just me and Dr Caldwell, while you stay back and cover us. If the kids are still alive in there, I can't just leave them."

Parks sighs. There's so much craziness in this one short speech, it's hard to know which way to come at it. "Okay," he says. "First off, they were never alive to start with. Second—"

"They're children, Sergeant." There's a vicious edge to her voice. "Whether they're hungries or not isn't the issue."

"Begging your pardon, Miss Justineau, it's very much the issue. Being hungries, they can live for a really long time without food. Maybe indefinitely. If they're still locked up in that bunker, they're safe. And they'll stay safe until someone opens it up. If they're not, the junkers probably just added them into that stampede they've got going, in which case they're not our problem any more. But I'll tell you what is. You're talking about sneaking up close to that base. Scoping it out. How exactly do you propose to do that?"

"Well, we come up through . . ." Justineau starts, but she stops right there because she's seen it.

"No way to be quiet if we bring the Hummer," Parks says, voicing what she's just now getting around to thinking. "They'll hear us coming from a couple of miles off. And if we do it without the Hummer, then we're bollock naked in an area that's just had a couple of thousand hungries set loose in it. I wouldn't give much for our chances."

Justineau says nothing. She knows he's right, and she's not going to argue for suicide.

But now here comes Dr Caldwell again. "I think it's a question of strict priorities, Sergeant Parks. My research was the entire reason for the base's existence. However much risk is involved in retrieving the notes and samples from the lab, I believe we need to do it."

"And I don't," Parks says. "Same thing applies. If your stuff is okay, it's okay because they left it. I think they most likely did, because they wouldn't have been looking for paper – except maybe to wipe their arses on. They were looking for food, weapons, petrol, stuff like that." Unless they were looking for payback for the guys that Gallagher got killed, but he's not going to say that right now.

"The longer we leave it—" Caldwell starts to object.

"So I'm making a judgement call." Parks cuts her off. "We go south, and we keep on the radio. Soon as we're close enough to get a ping from Beacon, we tell them what went down. They can airlift some people in – with some real firepower to back them up. They'll get the stuff from your lab, and then probably swing by and pick us up on their way home. Or worst case, we don't manage to make contact from the road, so we have to report once we get there. Same thing happens, but it happens a day or so later. Either way, everyone's happy."

"I'm not happy," Caldwell says, coldly. "I'm not happy at all. A delay of even a day in recovering those materials is unacceptable."

"What if I went to the base by myself?" Justineau demands. "You could wait for me here, and then if I didn't come back—"

"That's not going to happen," Parks snaps. He doesn't mean to rain on her parade, but he's had enough of this bullshit. "Right now, those motherfuckers don't know how far we got, which way we went, or even whether we're alive or dead. And that's how I want it to stay. If you go back and they catch you, right away they've got a line on us."

"I won't tell them anything," Justineau says, but he doesn't even have to say anything to shoot that one down. They're all grown-ups here.

Parks waits for further objections, because he's pretty sure they're coming. But Justineau is looking through the glass now at the little hungry girl, who seems to be drawing something in the dust on the Hummer's bonnet. There's a look on the kid's face like she's trying to figure out a hard word on a smudged page. And the same look, now he comes to think of it, on Justineau's face. That gives him a slightly queasy feeling. Meanwhile, Caldwell is flexing her fingers as if she's checking out whether they still work, so he gets a free pass on that one.

"Okay," he says, "here's what we'll do. There's a stream a couple of clicks west of here that was still running clean last I heard. We'll drive there first, pick up some water. Then we go to one of the supply caches and get ourselves provisioned. We need food and e-blockers, mainly, but there's a lot of other stuff that would come in pretty useful. After that, we light straight out. East until we hit the A1, then south all the way to Beacon. Either we skirt around London or we push straight through, depending. We'll scope out the situation there once we get closer. Any questions?"

There are a million questions, he knows damn well. He's also got a pretty shrewd hunch as to which one is going to come first, and he's not disappointed.

"What about Melanie?" Justineau demands.

"What about her?" Parks counters. "She's running no risk

131

here. She can live off the land, like any hungry does. They prefer people, but they'll eat any kind of meat once they get the scent of it. And you know first-hand now how quick they run. Quick enough to bring down most things, over the distance."

Justineau stares at him like he's talking in a foreign language. "Do you remember back just now when I used the word *children*?" she says. "Did it sink in at all? I'm not concerned about her intake of proteins, Sergeant. I'm concerned about the rat-bastard ethics of leaving a little girl alone in the middle of nowhere. And when you say she's safe, I presume you mean from other hungries."

"They ignore their own," Gallagher pipes up – the first time he's spoken. "Don't even seem to realise they're there. I think they must smell different."

"But she's not safe from the junkers," Justineau goes on, ignoring him. "And she's not safe from any other refusenik human enclaves there might be around here. They'll just trap her and douse her with quicklime without even realising what she is."

"They'll know bloody well what she is," Parks says.

"I'm not leaving her."

"She can't ride with us."

"I'm not leaving her." The set of Justineau's shoulders tells Parks that she means it – that they're at match point here.

"What if she rides on the roof?" Caldwell says, cutting through the impasse. "With the damage to the axle, I imagine we'll be travelling quite slowly, and there are rails up there for her to hold on to. You could even put up the pedestal for her, perhaps." They all look at her, and she shrugs. "I thought I'd made my position clear. Melanie is part of my research – possibly the only part that's left. If we have to go to some trouble to bring her along with us, it's worth it."

"You're not touching her," Justineau says tersely.

"Well, that's an argument we can leave until we reach Beacon."

132

"Agreed," Parks says quickly. "No to the pedestal – it opens up to the inside of the vehicle. But she can ride on the roof. I don't have any problem with that, as long as she keeps a reasonable distance from all of us whenever we have to open the doors."

And that's what they finally agree, just when he's starting to think they'll sit here and argue until their brains bleed out of their frigging ears.

Justineau goes out to tell the monster what's what.

Parks details Gallagher to keep that little moppet in his line of sight at all times, and not ever to find himself away from his rifle or sidearm. He'll be watching her himself, of course, but a little overkill never hurts.

26

"What do you want to do?" Miss Justineau asks her.

For a moment Melanie doesn't even understand the question. She waits for Miss J to clarify, and eventually – a little haltingly – she does.

"We're driving south, towards Beacon. But you could go anywhere. The soldiers trapped you, in Luton or Bedford or somewhere like that, where you were living. You could go back there if you wanted, and be with . . . well, with your own . . ."

She hesitates. "What?" Melanie prompts. "With who?"

Miss Justineau shakes her head. "Be on your own, I mean. Be free to do what you want. In Beacon, you wouldn't be free. They'd only put you in another cell."

"I liked my cell. I liked the classroom."

"But there probably wouldn't be any more lessons, Melanie. And Dr Caldwell would be in charge of you again."

Melanie nods. She knows all this. And it's not that she isn't afraid. It's just that the fear makes no difference.

"It doesn't matter," she explains to Miss J. "I want to be where you are. And I don't know the way back to wherever

I was before, anyway. I don't even remember it. All I remember is the block, and you. You're . . ." Now it's Melanie's turn to hesitate. She doesn't know the words for this. "You're my bread," she says at last. "When I'm hungry. I don't mean that I want to eat you, Miss Justineau! I really don't! I'd rather die than do that. I just mean . . . you fill me up the way the bread does to the man in the song. You make me feel like I don't need anything else."

Miss J doesn't seem to have an answer for that. She doesn't have any answer at all for a few moments. She looks away, looks back, looks away again. Her eyes fill up with tears and she can't speak at all for a while. When she can finally meet Melanie's gaze, she seems to have accepted that the two of them are going to stay together – if not for ever, at least for now. "You're going to have to ride up on the roof," she tells Melanie. "Are you okay with that?"

"Yes," Melanie says at once. "Sure. That's fine, Miss Justineau."

It's better than fine. It's a relief. The thought of getting back inside the Humvee has been terrifying Melanie ever since she realised it was a possibility, so it's purely wonderful that they've thought of an alternative. Now she doesn't have to ride with Dr Caldwell, who scares her so badly it's like scissors cutting into her chest. But more importantly, there's no danger that she'll get hungry again with Miss Justineau sitting right next to her.

Now Miss Justineau is looking at the picture Melanie drew in the dust on the Humvee's bonnet. Blobs and blocks, with a single wavy line threading through them. She gives Melanie a curious glance. "What's this?"

Melanie shrugs. She doesn't want to say. It's the route she memorised, from Dr Caldwell's lab all the way back to the stairs that lead down to the block. To her cell. It's the way home, and she drew it even though she knows that she's never going to retrace those steps, to sit in the classroom with the other children. Knows that home is just an idea now to be

135

visited in memories but not ever again found in the way that you find your ground and stand on it and know that it's yours.

All she has – to describe to herself how she feels now – is stories she's been told, about Moses not getting to see that land where there was all the milk, and Aeneas running away after Troy fell down, and a poem about a nightingale and a sad heart standing in alien corn.

It all comes together inside her, and she can't begin to explain. "It's just a pattern," she says, feeling bad because it's a lie. She's lying to Miss Justineau, who she loves more than anyone in the world. And of course the other part of the feeling, that's even harder to say, is that they're each other's home now. They have to be.

If only she didn't have the memory of that terrible hunger, coming up from inside her. The horrifying pleasure of blood and meat in her mouth. Why hasn't Miss Justineau asked her about that? Why wasn't she surprised that Melanie could do those things?

"Those men . . ." she says tentatively.

"The men at the base?"

"Yes. Them. What I did to them . . ."

"They were junkers, Melanie," Miss Justineau says. "Killers. They would have done worse to you, if you'd let them. And to me. You shouldn't feel bad about anything that happened. You couldn't help it. You're not to blame for any of it."

In spite of her fears, Melanie has to ask. "Why? Why am I not to blame?"

Miss J hesitates. "Because of your nature," she says. And when Melanie opens her mouth on another question, she shakes her head. "Not now. There's no time now, and this is really deep stuff. I know you're scared. I know you don't understand. I promise I'll explain, when we've got the time. When we're safe. For now . . . just try not to worry, and try not to be sad. We won't leave you. I promise. We'll all stick together. Okay?"

Melanie considers. Is it okay? This is a scary subject, so it's

136

a relief in some ways to let it drop. But the question is hanging over her like a weight, and she can't be content until it's answered. Finally, uncertainly, she nods. Because she's found a way of looking at it that makes it not so bad at all – a thought that's lying at the bottom of the sadness and the worry like hope lying underneath all the terrible things in Pandora's box.

From now on, every day will be a Miss Justineau day.

27

They skirt the edge of Shefford and drive across open fields to Sergeant Parks' stream, which is actually a shallow stretch of the river Flit. They fill a dozen ten-gallon plastic drums with water and load them into the lockers on the Humvee that are designed to hold them.

While they're there, Justineau takes off her sweater and washes it in the quick-flowing water, squeezes it out against a rock, washes it some more. The blood gradually detaches itself from the fibres, rust-brown clouds swirling and dissipating in the turbulence. She ties it to the Humvee's radio antenna to dry. It's heavy enough to bend the antenna almost horizontal.

Melanie uses water from the river to wash the blue gel off her body. Its smell reminds her of the lab, she tells Justineau, and it makes her look really silly besides.

From the river, they go to a set of coordinates that Parks reads off from a file on his mobile phone. They're looking for one of the supply caches that were set up when they first took over the base, intended to provision a retreat to Beacon in the event of an emergency like the one that just happened. The cache would have contained food, guns and ammunition, medical supplies, tubes of e-blocker gel, water purification tablets, maps, comms gear, ultra-light blankets – everything they could possibly need. But it's academic now, because there's just a hole in the ground where the cache should be. Junkers have found it, or someone else has. Best-case scenario: they weren't the only ones who escaped from the base, and some other group has beaten them to it. But Sergeant Parks doesn't think so, because there wouldn't have been time to dig all the way down to the cache and then get clear before they arrived. This was probably done long before.

So they're limited to what they've got in the vehicle. They go and take inventory now, throwing open all the lockers inside and out to see which are full and which are empty. According to regs, Parks explains, they should all be full. He leaves the other half of that thought unspoken; after this many years in the field, regs don't count for much.

There's good news and there's bad. The Humvee boasts a well-stocked first aid kit and an intact weapons locker. The rations locker, though, is three-quarters empty. Between the five of them, they've got enough food sachets for a couple of days at best. There are also two backpacks, five water canteens and a flare gun that carries seven pre-loaded slugs.

Maybe the most worrying thing is that they've got only three tubes of e-blocker gel between them, one of which is already started.

Justineau wrestles against a humanitarian impulse, and loses. She takes out the first aid kit and indicates Caldwell's hands with a nod of her head. "We might as well get some bandages on those," she says. "Unless you've got something else you should be doing."

The injuries to Caldwell's hands are very severe. The cuts go all the way to the bone. The flesh of her palms hangs in ragged flaps, partially sliced away, as though she was a Sunday roast that someone took a clumsy pass at. The skin around these areas is swollen and red. The blood that's dried on them is black.

Justineau washes the wounds as best she can with water from a canteen. Caldwell doesn't cry out, but she's trembling and pale as Justineau carefully wipes away the dried blood with cotton wool swabs. This makes the wounds bleed again, but Justineau suspects that's a good thing. Infection is a real possibility out here, and blood plays its part in flushing germs out from the surface of a wound.

Then she disinfects. Caldwell moans for the first time as the astringent liquid bites into her newly opened flesh. Sweat stands out on her forehead, and she bites her lower lip to keep from crying out.

Justineau puts field dressings on both of the doctor's hands, leaving the fingers free to move as far as she can, but making sure that all the injured areas are well covered. She took a first aid course once, a couple of years back, so she knows what she's doing. It's a good, workmanlike job.

"Thank you," Caldwell says when she's finished.

Justineau shrugs. The last thing she wants is civilities from this woman. And Caldwell seems to recognise this, because she doesn't take the civilities any further.

"All aboard," Parks says, as Gallagher slams the boot shut. "We should get moving."

"Give me a minute," Justineau says. She takes the sweater down from the radio antenna and inspects it. There are still a few stains on it, but it's mostly dry. She helps Melanie to wriggle into it.

"Is it too scratchy?" she asks.

Melanie shakes her head, and gives a smile – weak, but sincere. "It's really soft," she says. "And warm. Thank you, Miss Justineau."

"You're welcome, Melanie. Does it . . . smell okay?"

"It doesn't smell of blood. Or of you. It doesn't smell of anything very much."

"Then I guess it will do for now," Justineau says. "Until we can find something better."

Parks has been waiting all this time, not even trying to look patient. Justineau climbs into the Humvee, giving Melanie a final wave. As soon as the door is closed, Melanie swarms up the outside of the vehicle and finds herself a comfortable place, wedged in behind the cover of the pedestal gun. She holds on tight as the Humvee starts to roll.

Now they're doubling back on their own tracks, eastwards, to the ancient north–south slash of the A1. They take it slow, to avoid giving the rear axle any further shocks. And they're careful to skirt around the towns. That's where you always get the heaviest concentrations of hungries, Parks says, and the noise of the Humvee would bring them running. But all the same, they're making good time.

For about five miles.

Then the Humvee rocks and yaws like a dinghy on a wild sea, pitching them out of their seats on to the floor. Caldwell gives an anguished howl as she steadies herself, unthinking, with her injured hands. She goes into a tight crouch around them, hugging them against her chest.

There's a single, jolting crash, after which the Humvee starts up a different kind of shuddering, intense and agonising. A shriek like an air-raid siren splits the air. The axle's gone, and they're dragging their backside across the tarmac.

Parks slams on the brakes and brings them to a dead stop. They slew over, settle onto the road with a hydraulic sigh, more like an animal lying down than anything mechanical.

Parks sighs too. Braces himself.

Justineau has never felt anything for the sergeant up to now apart from resentment and suspicion – spiking into real hatred when he delivered Melanie into Caldwell's hands – but in this moment she admires him. The loss of the Humvee is a crushing blow, and he doesn't even take the time to curse about it.

He gets them moving. Gets them out of their dead transport. First thing Justineau does is to check on Melanie, who's managed to hold on through all the bucking and shaking. She

141

takes the girl's hand briefly and squeezes it. "Change of plan," she says. Melanie nods. She gets it. Without being asked, she climbs down again and grabs some distance, just as she did at the cache site.

Sergeant Parks throws open the boot, takes a backpack for himself and gives the other one to Gallagher. They'll need as much water as they can take with them, but there's no way they can carry those big drums. Everyone gets a canteen, fills it from one of the drums. Parks takes the fifth canteen himself (the possibility of him giving it to Melanie is never raised). Everyone except Melanie has a good, long swig from the half-empty drum, until their stomachs are uncomfortably full. When it's mostly empty, Parks offers it to Melanie to finish, but she's never drunk water in her life. The little moisture her body needs, she's used to taking from live meat. The thought of pouring water into her mouth makes her wrinkle up her face and back away.

Everyone gets a knife and a handgun, the sheath and holster clipping right on to their belts. The soldiers take rifles too, and Parks scoops up a double handful of grenades like strange black fruit. The grenades are smooth-sided, not sculpted into lozenges like the ones Justineau has seen in old war movies. Parks also helps himself – after a moment's thought – to the flare gun, which he slips into the backpack, and to a pair of walkie-talkies from under the Humvee's dash. He gives one of these to Gallagher and hooks the other into his belt.

Into the backpacks too go the meagre food supplies, divided evenly between them. Justineau adds the first aid kit, despite its awkward bulk. Chances are pretty good that they'll need it.

They work with feverish haste, even though the country road they're on is silent except for birdsong. They take their cue from Parks, who is grim-faced and urgent, speaking in monosyllables, chivvying them along.

"Okay," he says at last. "We're good to go. Everybody ready to move out?"

One by one they nod. It's starting to sink in that a journey you could do in half a day on good roads has just become a four- or five-day trek through terra completely incognita, and Justineau presumes that that's as hard for the rest of them to come to terms with as it is for her. She was brought to the base by helicopter, directly from Beacon – and she lived in Beacon for long enough that it became her status quo. Thoughts from before that time, from the Breakdown, when the world filled with monsters who looked like people you knew and loved, and every living soul went scrambling and skittering for cover like mice when the cat wakes up, have been so deeply suppressed, for so long, that they're not memories at all – they're memories of memories.

And that's the world they're going to walk through now. Home is seventy-odd miles away. Seventy miles of England's green and pleasant land, all gone to the hungries and as safe to wander in as it would be to dance a mazurka in a minefield. A bewildering prospect, even if that were all.

And Sergeant Parks' face tells her, even before he speaks, that that's not all.

"You still dead set against cutting the kid loose?" he asks her.

"Yes."

"Then I'm laying down some conditions."

He goes around to the side of the Humvee. There's another locker there, that nobody has opened yet. It turns out to be full of the highly specialised kit that Parks and his people used to use, way back in the day, when they raided the towns of Herts, Beds and Bucks for the high-functioning hungries that Caroline Caldwell was so eager to meet. Restraint harnesses, handcuffs, stun batons, telescoping poles with lasso collars at their business end; a whole chandler's shop full of ways to bring dangerous animals in alive, with minimal risk to their handlers.

"No," Justineau says, her throat dry.

143

But Melanie, when she sees this filthy arsenal, says yes just as quickly, just as firmly. She looks Parks in the eye, appraising, maybe approving. "It's a good idea," she says. "To make sure I can't hurt anyone."

"No," Parks says. "The good idea would be something else entirely. This is just making the best of a bad job." Justineau is in no doubt about his meaning. He'd like to put a bullet in Melanie's head and leave her by the roadside. But given that the civilians have joined forces against him, given that both Caldwell and Justineau, for their different reasons, want Melanie to stay on as a member of their party, this is his grudging compromise.

The two soldiers cuff Melanie's hands behind her back. They attach an adjustable leash to the chain of the cuffs, and play it out to about two metres. Then they put a mask over the lower half of the girl's face, which looks something like a dog's muzzle or a medieval scold's bridle. It's made for an adult but fully adjustable, and they lock it really tight.

When they start to attach a hobble to Melanie's ankles, which will allow her to walk but not to run, Justineau steps in. "Forget it," she snaps. "Do I have to keep reminding you that we're running from junkers as well as hungries? Making sure Melanie can't bite is one thing. Making sure she can't run either – that's just killing her without wasting a bullet."

Which the sergeant clearly wouldn't mind at all. But he thinks about it for a while and finally gives a curt nod.

"You keep talking about *killing* in relation to the test subjects, Helen," Caldwell says, didactic by default. "I've told you this before. In most cases, brain function stops a few hours after infection, which meets the clinical definition of death as far as—"

Justineau turns around and punches Caldwell in the face.

It's a hard punch, and it hurts her hand a lot more than she expects, the shock travelling up her arm all the way to the elbow.

144

Caldwell staggers and almost falls, her arms flailing for balance as she takes one and then two steps back. She stares at Justineau in utter astonishment. Justineau stares right back, nursing the hand she hit with. But she's got one hand left if it turns out to be needed, and of course that's one more than Caldwell has just then.

"Keep talking," she suggests. "I'll knock the teeth out of your mouth one by one."

The two soldiers stand by, interested but impartial. Clearly, they don't have a dog in this catfight.

Melanie also watches, big-eyed, mouth wide open. The anger drains out of Justineau, replaced by a surge of shame at her loss of self-control. She feels the blood rush into her face.

Caldwell's blood is showing too. She licks a trickle of it from her lip. "You're both my witnesses," she says to Parks and Gallagher, her voice thick. "That was an unprovoked assault."

"We saw it," Parks confirms. His tone is dry. "I look forward to being someplace where our witnessing will make a difference. Okay, are we done? Anyone got any speeches they want to make? No? Then let's move out."

They walk on down the lane, due east, leaving the Humvee spavined and silent behind them. Caldwell stands alone for a few moments before joining the exodus. Clearly she's amazed that the attack on her person has elicited so little interest. But she's a realist. She rolls with the bad news.

Justineau wonders if they should have pushed the Humvee into one of the neighbouring fields to hide their trail a little, but she presumes that with the axle broken and the back end of the vehicle hard against the ground, it would be way too heavy to move. And burning it would be a whole lot worse, of course – like sending up a signal flare to tell the enemy exactly where they are.

Plenty of other enemies waiting out there for them without that.

145

28

Melanie builds the world around her as she goes.

This is mostly countryside, with fields on all sides. Rectangular fields, mostly, or at least with roughly squared-off edges. But they're overgrown with weeds to the grown-ups' shoulder height, whatever crops they were once planted with swallowed up long ago. Where the fields meet the road, there are ragged hedges or crumbling walls, and the surface they're walking on is a faded black carpet pitted with holes, some of them big enough for her to fall into.

A landscape of decay – but still gloriously and heart-stoppingly beautiful. The sky overhead is a bright blue bowl of almost infinite size, given depth by a massive bank of pure white cloud at the limit of vision that goes up and up and up like a tower. Birds and insects are everywhere, some of them familiar to her now from the field where they stopped that morning. The sun warms her skin, pouring energy down on to the world out of that upturned bowl – it makes flowers grow on the land, Melanie knows, and algae in the sea; starts food chains all over the place.

A million smells freight the complicated air.

The few houses they see are far off, but even at this distance Melanie observes the signs of ruin. Windows broken, or boarded up. Doors hanging off their hinges. One big farmhouse has its roof all fallen in, the spine of the roof making a perfect downward-pointing parabola.

She remembers Mr Whitaker's lesson, which feels like a very long time ago now. *The population of Birmingham is zero . . .* This world she's seeing was built by people, to meet their needs, but it's not meeting their needs any more. It's all changed. And it's changed because they've retreated from it. They've left it to the hungries.

Melanie realises now that she's been told all this already. She just ignored it, ignored the self-evident logic of her world, and believed − out of the many conflicting stories she was given − only the parts she wanted to believe.

Sergeant Parks is wrestling with a logistical problem, and he still hasn't seen a way out of it.

His initial instinct was to stay clear of the towns on their route − of any built-up area at all − and make this whole stroll strictly cross-country. The argument for doing that is obvious. The hungries mostly stay close to where they were first turned, or infected, or whatever you want to call it. It's not a homing instinct, it's just a side effect of the fact that when they're not hunting, they're mostly standing stock still, like little kids playing Grandmother's Footsteps. So the cities and towns are full of them, the countryside more sparsely populated, exactly the way it used to be before the Breakdown.

But Parks has got three good points to set against that one. The first is the temperature thing − something he noticed when he was out in the field, and teaches to all the soldiers under his command, even though Caldwell says the evidence is still "far from conclusive". The hungries' known triggers are endocrine sweat from an unmasked human body, rapid movement and loud noises. But there's a fourth, which mostly comes into play when the temperature drops at night. They can zero in on you by your body heat, somehow. They can pick you out in the dark like you were a neon sign saying FINE DINING HERE.

And that being the case, point two kicks in. They'll need shelter. If they sleep out in the open, they'll get hungries swarming on them from all directions. Okay, there are other places besides towns that will give you shelter, but most of them presuppose that you've got the time and the manpower to do proper reconnaissance.

Which brings in point three. Time. Ducking and weaving away from any built-up areas will add about twenty extra miles to their route, which doesn't matter all that much as far as the raw numbers go. But the raw numbers aren't worth a shit. What matters is that it will take them across the hardest, slowest terrain, and probably double their journey time. Not to mention the fact that it's hard to run away across a field full of mature brambles with inch-long thorns, or a pasture choked with knee-high knotweed. Hungries don't care if they rip themselves open, and they'll happily keep running if they've got your scent, even as they flay themselves to the bone. Humans will slow down a lot more in that terrain, and get taken that much more easily.

So they're walking right now along a country lane, between two weed-choked fields, and they're about to pass through a village. Or else tack on three extra miles to the journey by slogging all the way around it.

One way or the other, Parks is going to have to make his mind up soon.

Caroline Caldwell goes through the stages of grief, in the prescribed order.

Denial is a stage she goes through very quickly indeed, because her reason strikes down the demeaning, treacherous thought as quickly as it rises. There's no point in denying the truth when the truth is self-evident. There's no point in denying the truth even if you have to wade through thorn thickets and minefields to get to it. The truth is the truth, the only prize worth having. If you deny it, you're only showing that you're unworthy of it.

So Caldwell accepts that her work – the pith and substance of the last decade of her life – is lost.

And lets herself feel the toxic anger and indignation that boils in her like heartburn at that thought. If Justineau hadn't intervened, if she'd been allowed to make that final dissection, would it have made any difference? Of course not. But Justineau ensured that the last minutes of Caldwell's time at the base were wasted. It would be absurd to build anything further on top of that transgression, but it's enough as it stands. Justineau ruined her work, and her work is now gone. Justineau will pay, when they get back to Beacon, with the trashing of her career and with a court-martial that will probably see her shot.

Bargaining is another stage that Caldwell doesn't linger over. She doesn't believe in God, or the gods, or fate, or any higher or lower power that has dominion over her. There's no one to bargain with. But she agrees – even in a deterministic world governed by impartial physical forces – that if the lab is found to be intact and a rescue team from Beacon returns her notes and samples to her in good order, she will light a candle to nobody at all in recognition for the universe having (en passant, by something indistinguishable from chance) been kind to her.

When she holds that thought up to the light and sees how pathetic it is, how cravenly equivocating, she sinks into black depression.

From which she is saved by this thought: there wasn't anything in the lab worth keeping anyway. The samples, possibly, but she has a living sample with her. The notes were mostly descriptive – a very detailed and circumstantial account of the hungry pathogen's life cycle (incomplete, since she's yet to culture a sample to the mature, sexual stage) and the course

149

of the infection both in the regular way of things and in the anomalous state represented by the children. She has this stuff by heart, so the loss of the notes is not crucial.

She has a chance. She's in the field, and opportunities will come.

This could still work out well.

Private Kieran Gallagher knows all about monsters, because he comes from a family in which monsters predominate. Or maybe it's just that his family was more given than most to letting its monsters come out and sniff the air.

The key that let them out was always the same: bootleg vodka, made in a still that his father and older brother had set up in a shed behind an abandoned house about a hundred yards from where they lived. The provisional government in Beacon was officially against unlicensed alcohol, but unofficially they didn't really care so long as you stayed inside your house when you were shit-faced and only beat up your own people.

So Gallagher grew up in a weird microcosm of the wider world outside Beacon. His father, and his brother Steve, and his cousin Jackie looked like normal human beings and even sometimes acted like them, but most of the time they veered between two extremes: reckless violence when they were drinking, and comatose somnolence when the drink wore off.

Ricocheting off that, Gallagher has tried to live the life of the safe and solid middle ground, looking out for the things that make other people go off the rails so he can avoid them assiduously. He was the only soldier on the base who refused the solace of twenty-two per cent proof home-brew beer cooked up in a bucket or a bathtub. The only one who didn't look out for magic mushrooms when he was on wide patrol. The only one who didn't think it was hilarious to watch the antics of that teacher, Whitaker, as he drank himself to death.

And he's always assumed that by steering into the middle of the channel, he was going to manage not to get wrecked.

150

Now he knows you can get wrecked in clear waters too, and he's thinking *oh please, don't let me die. I haven't even lived yet, so it's not fair to let me die.*

He's so scared, he's worried that he might actually piss himself. He's never understood before how being scared could make you do that; but now, thrown into the hungries' world with only Sergeant Parks to back him up and with all those miles to walk before they get back to Beacon, he can feel his nuts tightening and his bladder loosening with every step he takes.

The question is, which is he more afraid of? Dying out here, or going home? They've both got their terrors, about equally vivid in his mind.

He's always had shit-awful luck, from the day he was born. Got the beatings at home and at school, never managed to swap smokes for gropes behind the gym like his brother (the one time he tried, his dad caught him stealing the cigarettes and took it out of him with the end of a belt), got into the army by default to escape from that madhouse, carries a stupid misspelled tattoo (*qui audet piscitur* – "who dares, fishes") because the tattooist was drunk and missed out three letters, caught gonorrhoea from the first girl who ever let him roll her, got the second pregnant and skipped out on her (nothing in excess, not even love), then realised too late that his feelings for her went way beyond sex. If he ever gets back to Beacon and sees her again, he'll try to explain that to her. *I'm a coward and a worthless piece of shit, but if you give me a second chance I'll never run out on you again.*

Not going to happen, is it?

This is what's going to happen. Somewhere between here and Beacon, a hungry will take a bite out of him. Because that's the way his life is set up to work.

He's comforted by something in the thigh pocket of his fatigues. It's a grenade – one that rolled into a corner when Parks was clipping the others into his belt. Gallagher picked

151

it up, intending to hand it to the Sarge, but then on an impulse he swiped it and stowed it instead. He's keeping it for a Hail Mary manoeuvre.

There are so many things in the world that he's scared shit-less about. The hungries might eat him. The junkers might torture or murder him. They might run out of food and water somewhere between here and Beacon and die by inches.

If it comes to it, Gallagher is going to pull the pin on his own life. And to hell with the middle of the road.

Helen Justineau is thinking about dead children.

She can't narrow it down, or doesn't want to. She thinks about all the children in the world who ever died without growing up. There must have been billions of them. Hecatombs of children, apocalypses, genocides of them. In every war, every famine, thrown to the wall. Too small to protect themselves, too innocent to get out of the way. Killed by madmen, perverts, judges, soldiers, random passers-by, friends and neighbours, their own parents. By stupid chance or ruthless edict.

Every adult grew from a kid who beat the odds. But at different times, in different places, the odds have been appall-ingly steep.

And the dead kids drag at every living soul. A weight of guilt you haul around with you like the moon hauls the ocean, too massive to lift and too much a part of you to ever let it go.

If she hadn't talked to the kids about death that day. If she hadn't read them "The Charge of the Light Brigade", and if they hadn't asked what being dead was like, then she wouldn't have stroked Melanie's hair and none of this would have happened. She wouldn't have made a promise she couldn't keep and couldn't walk away from.

She could be as selfish as she's always been, and forgive herself the way everybody else does, and wake up every day as clean as if she'd just been born.

29

Sergeant Parks has made his call. He's heading into Stotfold.

It's a nothing little place on the way to the A1, and he doesn't have any high hopes for it. They won't be able to replenish their supplies there, or find another transport. Anything that was worth having will have been found and taken long before. It's got this one thing going for it, though: that it lies on their route, and with the afternoon wearing down into evening, they're beggars rather than choosers. He wants to be under cover before nightfall.

But they're still two miles out from the town – not even close enough yet to see the chimney of the watermill rising over the trees – when they pass a church.

It's a stupid place to put a church, in Parks' opinion, because it's close to nothing very much. Even before the Breakdown, they couldn't have got any passing trade. And it's useless as a bivouac. Too many big windows, most of them smashed, and the massive arched doorway at the front gaping like a toothless mouth (no telling what happened to the doors).

But there's a breezeblock garage right next to the bigger structure, and Parks likes the look of that. When he goes to check it out up close, telling the others to wait, he likes it even more. The wide, up-and-over door is made of sturdy metal. It won't yield to pushing or clawing, which is mostly what the hungries do when they come up against a door, and is probably rusted into its jamb for added immobility. The other way in, at the side, is a wooden door with a Yale lock. A lot less secure, but the upside is that Parks can knock out the cylinder to open the door from the outside without damaging the wood, and then – if their luck is in – patch it up again or find some other kind of barricade once they're inside.

He waves to Gallagher to come and join him. The two of them go over the church while the women wait out in the road. A first pass shows up no hungries, which is a good sign. Some bones on the floor, near the rood screen, but they look like animal bones. Left there by a fox or a weasel probably, or else by some passing Satanist.

Above the altar, in green spray paint, the words HE'S NOT LISTENING, MORONS. Parks takes that as a given. He's never prayed in his life.

Someone else prayed here, though. In a pew, forgotten, Parks finds a woman's handbag. It contains some loose change, a lipstick, a tiny hymnal, a set of car keys with a built-in locator and a single Xtra-Thin condom. Such blameless everyday objects that they dazzle him a little, raising the spectre of a time when the worst things anyone had to worry about were unsafe sex and forgetting where they parked their car.

Gallagher peers into a side room, a vestry or something, shines his torch around a bit, then slams the door to again. "All clear, Sarge," he calls out.

It might be the door slamming, but more likely it's the words. Something rushes out of the darkness at the back of the church. It hits Gallagher at a flat run, slams him right off his feet, and he goes down with a crash on to the wooden floor.

Parks turns around, sees the two bodies writhing together. He doesn't even have to think about it. He draws his gun,

154

tracks the dark blob of the hungry's head as it lowers into the angle of Gallagher's throat, and squeezes off a shot. The sound is less of a bang, more like the solid *chunk* you get when you bring an axe down on a block of wood.

His aim is spot on. The bullet smacks into the back of the hungry's skull. An ordinary bullet would go right on through. Would hit Gallagher too, or at the very least spray his face and upper body with hungry cerebral tissue – with predictable and depressing consequences an hour or a day or a week down the line. But this is a soft-nosed, steel-aluminium round, designed for minimal penetration. It slows down, spreads out and pulps the hungry's brain to pink milkshake.

Gallagher pushes the limp body to the side and gets out from under it. "Shit!" he pants. "I . . . I didn't see it until it was on top of me. Thanks, Sarge."

Parks verifies the kill. The hungry is completely inert, grey matter oozing from its eyes, nose, ears, pretty much everywhere. In life, it was male, dark-haired, a fair bit younger than Parks himself. It's wearing the mouldering remains of a priest's surplice, so it was probably infected right here. Maybe it's been here ever since, waiting in the dark for a meal to wander by. Or maybe it comes back here after a kill. That does happen, weird as it sounds. Instead of just freezing in place like most of them do, some hungries have a homing instinct for a particular place. Parks wonders if Dr Caldwell knows about this, and if she does, how she squares it with that idea about the host mind dying as soon as the parasite shows up.

Gallagher inspects himself for cuts, bites, and stray hungry bodily fluids. Parks examines him too – minutely. Despite the close encounter, Gallagher checks out clean. He's still thanking Parks, with a post-traumatic shake in his voice. Parks has had so many close calls like this back in his grab-bagging days, he doesn't see it as anything much. He just tells Gallagher not to talk in a threat situation. Hand signals are every bit as good, and a damn sight safer.

They go back outside where the civilians – waiting fifty yards away, at the bottom of the gravel drive – seem to be completely unaware that anything has happened. They must have put the sounds from the church down to a vigorous search.

"Everything okay?" Justineau asks.

"Everything is fine," Parks says. "We're almost done. Just keep an eye on the road and shout if anything comes."

He turns his attention to the garage, which on closer inspection is even better than he thought. He was ready to break the lock with his rifle butt, but he doesn't have to. When he tries the handle of the door, it opens. Whoever was here last left it on the latch.

They go in slowly and carefully, covering each other. Parks drops down on one knee, rifle set to full auto, ready to do a kneecapping sweep. Gallagher gets out his torch and shines it into the corners of the room.

Which is empty. Clean. Nothing for anyone to hide behind, and no scope at all for nasty surprises.

"All good," Parks mutters. "Okay, this will do just fine. Go get them."

Gallagher shepherds the civilians inside and Parks shuts the door, the lock now fully engaged so it closes with a solid click. The civilians are less enthusiastic than Parks was when they see the confined space and inhale its stale, spent air, but they're not inclined to mount much of an argument. Truth is, the two women aren't used to keeping up a quick march, and none of them – including Parks himself, unless you go back a while – are used to being outside of a fence as night comes on. They're freaked and exhausted and starting at shadows. So is he, except that he does his freaking and starting mostly inside, so it doesn't notice as much.

The only sticking point is the girl, which comes as no surprise. Parks suggests that she sleep in the church, and Justineau countersuggests that Parks go fuck himself. "Same point as before," she tells him, getting all pissed off again, which he's thinking now is pretty much Justineau's default setting. And truth to tell, he likes it a lot. If you're going to let yourself feel anything at all, anger's better than most of the alternatives. "Even if hungries were the only threat here," she's saying now, "all of this — all of it — is as strange to Melanie as it is to us. And as scary. We can't leave her tied up in an empty building by herself all night."

"Then stay out there with her," Parks says.

Which has the desired effect of shutting Justineau up for a few seconds. Into that silence he states his manifesto. "We've got a long way to go, so we may as well lay down some ground rules now. You do what I say, when I say it, and you might reach Beacon with your arse still attached. If you keep behaving like you've got a right to an opinion, we'll be dead before this time tomorrow."

Justineau stares at him, speechless. He waits for the apology and the submission.

She holds out her hand. "Keys."

Parks is perplexed. "Which keys? We don't have any keys. The door was—"

"The keys to Melanie's handcuffs," Justineau says. "We're leaving."

"No," Parks says, "you're not."

"What — you think we're all your soldiers now, Sergeant Parks? Seriously?" All of a sudden she doesn't even sound angry any more. She just sounds sourly amused. "We're not. None of us are under your command, except for Private Parts over there. So that 'come with me if you want to live' bullshit doesn't wash. I'd rather take my chances outside than fall in and trust my life to two hard-wired little soldier boys and a certifiable psychopath. Keys. Please. Let's do this. You just said we're a liability, so cut us loose."

"Absolutely not!" Caldwell raps out. "I've already told you, Sergeant. The girl is part of my research. She belongs to me."

157

Justineau shakes her head, staring at the floor. "Do I have to punch you in the head again, Caroline? I don't want to hear from you on this."

Parks is amazed. Appalled. Even a little bit disgusted. He's used to dealing with people who have at least some sort of survival instinct, and he knows that Justineau isn't stupid. Back at the base, he thought of her as the best of Caldwell's exasperating little coterie, and while that isn't saying much, he actually liked and respected her. He still does.

But this is getting them nowhere.

"I'm sorry if I didn't make myself clear," he tells her now. "You're not free to leave; she's not free to stay. My standing orders don't cover any of this, but I'm taking a position. I'm going to get all the human beings here back to Beacon, alive, and after that, someone else can call it."

"You think you can keep me with you against my will?" Justineau asks, putting her hands on her hips.

"Yes." He's sure of it.

"You think you can do it and still keep moving at a decent pace?"

That's a different question, with an uglier answer. He doesn't want to threaten her. He has a sense that if he pushes it, coerces her instead of getting her to cooperate, a line will be crossed and he'll never be able to pull back from it.

He tries a different tack. "I'm open to other suggestions," he says, "so long as they're not stupid. Keeping a hungry in here with us, even if she's cuffed and muzzled, isn't an option. They don't react to physical damage the same way we do, and there's things you can do with cuffs and muzzles if you don't care about disfiguring yourself. She has to stay outside."

Justineau arches an eyebrow. "And if I try to go outside with her, you'll stop me."

He nods. It feels like a softer option than saying yes, even if it means the same thing.

"Okay, then stop me."

She makes for the door. Gallagher steps into her path and quick as a flash she's got her gun – the one Parks gave her – up in his face. A nice slick move. She took advantage of the darkness inside the garage, waited to draw the gun until she was walking right past Parks, so that the angle of her body would cover the movement of her arm. Gallagher freezes, his head tilting back away from the weapon.

"Out of my way, Private," Justineau says quietly. "Or your brains go public."

Parks sighs. He takes out his own sidearm and rests it lightly on her shoulder. He knows from their brief acquaintance that she won't shoot Gallagher. At least, not after just the one warning. But there's no doubting the sincerity of her feelings. "You made your point," he says glumly. "We'll do this some other way."

Because he doesn't want to kill her unless she really forces the issue. He'll do it if he has to, but they're already short-handed, and out of the three of them – Justineau, Gallagher and the doctor – he suspects she might turn out to be the most useful.

So what they do is this. They tie the little girl to the wall with a running rope, attached to the handcuffs. Parks attaches all the canteens to the running rope, along with a whole bunch of stones in a tin bucket that he found outside. There's no way she can move without making a racket that will wake them all.

Justineau is at pains to explain all this to the hungry kid, who's calm and still throughout the whole procedure. She gets it, even if Justineau doesn't – knows why, e-blocker or not, she has to be treated like an unexploded munition. She doesn't complain once.

The food they liberated from the Humvee is the tough and tasteless type 3 carb-and-protein mix, labelled – you have to assume satirically – *Roast Beef and Potatoes*, washed down with water that has an aftertaste of mud, so supper is nobody's idea of a gourmet treat.

Justineau takes an extra spoon and feeds the kid, who therefore has to be released from the muzzle for a few minutes. Parks watches her closely the whole time she's free, his gun in his holster but with the safety off and a round already chambered – but there's no way he could get in there in time if Melanie took it into her head to bite Justineau. He'd just have to shoot the both of them.

But the kid is good as gold, as far as that goes. She swallows the meat chunks from the food mix without even chewing them, spits out the potatoes with a great show of distaste. She's finished inside a minute.

Then Justineau wipes her mouth clean with a corner of cloth torn from God knows what and God knows where, and Parks snaps the muzzle closed again.

"It's looser than before," the hungry kid says. "You should tighten it."

Parks tests it by sliding his thumb inside the strap, up against the back of her neck. She's right, sure enough, and he adjusts it without a word.

The floor is cold and hard, the blankets thin. Their backpacks make pretty lousy pillows. And there's the little monster right there among them, so Parks is tensing all the time for that bang and clatter from the canteens as she reverts to type and goes for them.

He stares up into the featureless dark, thinks of the flash of Justineau's crotch he glimpsed when she was pissing on the gravel outside.

But the future is uncertain, and he can't get up enough enthusiasm even to masturbate.

30

Melanie doesn't dream. At least, she never has before tonight. There were fantasies she indulged, like the fantasy of saving Miss Justineau from monsters, but sleep for her has always been an un-time spent in un-space. She closes her eyes, opens them again and the day recycles.

Tonight, in the garage, it's different. Maybe it's because she's outside the fence, not in her cell. Or maybe it's because the things that have happened to her today are just too vivid and too strange for her mind to let go of them.

Whatever it is, her sleep is lurid and terrifying. Hungries, soldiers and men with knives lurch at her. She bites, and is bitten – kills, and is killed. Until Miss Justineau gathers her in her arms and holds her close.

As her teeth meet in Miss Justineau's throat, she snaps instantly awake, her mind wrenching itself away from that unthinkable prospect. But she can't stop thinking about it. The nightmare lays its stifling folds across her thoughts, and she knows there was something inside the dream images, some hidden payload that she'll sooner or later have to face.

There's a sour metal taste in her mouth. It's like the taste of blood and flesh left behind a vengeful ghost. The mulchy, textureless food that Miss Justineau gave her shifts queasily in her stomach when she moves.

The garage is dark, except for a little filtered light (moonlight, it must be) from around the edges of the door. Silent, except for the level breathing of the four grown-ups.

The red-haired soldier who's one of Sergeant's people murmurs in his sleep – shapeless words that sound like protest or pleading.

After a time of staring into the dark, Melanie's eyes adjust. She can see the outline of Miss Justineau's body, not close but closer to her than the others. She wants to crawl over to her and curl up against her, her shoulders pressed into the precisely right-shaped arc of Miss Justineau's lower back.

But with the atmosphere of that dream on her, she can't. She doesn't dare. And the movement would make the bucket and the canteens clang together anyway, which would wake everyone up.

She thinks about Beacon, and about what she said to Miss Justineau that time in the classroom, after the "Charge of the Light Brigade" lesson. It stands out very clear in her mind, and it's easy to remember the exact words, because this was the conversation that ended with Miss Justineau stroking her hair.

Will we go home to Beacon? Melanie had asked. *When we're grown up?* And Miss Justineau looked so sad, so stricken, that Melanie had immediately started to blurt out apologies and assurances, trying to stave off the effects of whatever terrible thing she'd inadvertently said.

Which she understands now. From this angle, it's obvious. What she'd said, about going home to Beacon, was impossible, like hot snow or dark sunshine. Beacon was never home to her, and never could be.

That was what made Miss Justineau sad. That there never could be a going-home for her that meant being with other boys and girls and grown-ups and doing the things she used

162

to hear about in stories. Still less a going-home that had Miss Justineau in it. She was meant to end up in jars in Dr Caldwell's lab.

This time she's living in now was never foreseen or intended. Not by anyone. That's why they keep arguing about what they're going to do.

Nobody knows. Nobody knows any better than she does where they're really going.

31

Sergeant Parks had planned to let them sleep until the sun's well up, because he knows how hard the next day is going to be, but as things turn out, they wake up early. What rouses them is the sound of engines. A long way off at first, and rising and falling a lot, but it's obvious that whatever the hell it is, it's coming closer.

Under Parks' terse directions they grab their stuff and get the hell out of there. He lets the hungry kid off the running rope and puts her back on the leash, trying hard not to make the buckets clank together. No telling how far the sound will carry in the pre-dawn stillness.

They run out into the luminous half-dark, past the church and into a field behind it, go a good hundred yards or more before Parks signals to them to kneel down among the towering weeds. They could – maybe should – go further but he wants to see what's coming. From here he can get a good view of the road without being seen, and their trampled passage will heal over inside of a minute as the resilient grasses stand up straight again.

They sit and kneel like that for a long time, as the sun

slowly separates from the horizon and low light soaks into the field like water into a rag. They don't speak. They don't move. Justineau opens her mouth at one point, maybe ten minutes in, but Parks gestures her to stay quiet and she does. She can see the urgency in his face.

When the wind shifts, they can hear the shouted voices of people as well as the drone of machines.

It's a strange cavalcade when it finally comes. In the lead, one of the bulldozers Parks saw the day before. As it rolls down the road and turns a bend towards them, he gets a good view of its broad blade, which has been decorated with a flamboyant death's head in metallic spray paint. He hears someone – he thinks it's Gallagher – make a mewling sound of pure fear beside him. But it's low enough that it won't carry, so there's no harm in him voicing what everyone is feeling.

Behind the bulldozer is a Humvee identical to the one they commandeered, and behind that a jeep. All three vehicles are packed with junker men in holiday mood, shouting out to each other and waving a wide variety of offensive weapons. They're chanting something with a strong, repetitive rhythm, but Parks can't make out the words.

The convoy stops at the church, where a couple of the junkers jump down and go inside. There's a shout, and they come out again, looking a little more animated. They've found the dead hungry, Parks guesses. But they don't have any way of telling how long it's been there. Hungry blood doesn't flow much and it's the colour of mud to start with, so drying out doesn't change it. You'd have to look close even to guess how the hungry was taken down, because the entry wound from Parks' pistol was small and discreet and there wasn't any exit wound.

The junkers check the garage too, and Parks tenses because this is where it could all go south. If they've left any trace of their presence there . . . But there are no alarums, and there's no search. After a few minutes the junkers get back on the

165

bulldozer and set off again. The convoy turns another corner and disappears from sight, although they can still hear it for a long time after that.

When everything's gone quiet again, Justineau speaks. "They're looking for us."

"We can't know that," Dr Caldwell objects. "They could be foraging for food."

"Base had plenty of supplies," Parks says, pointing out the obvious. "And they only took it yesterday. I'd have expected them to get the fence back up again and make themselves at home. If they're out here instead, it makes sense to me that they'd be looking for survivors." Which means they've made it personal. He doesn't say it, but he thinks now that the ones Gallagher accidentally got killed might have been important, or popular. The attack on the base could have been totally opportunistic, but this wild hunt was whipped up to settle scores.

But he doesn't say any of this, because he doesn't want Gallagher to feel like he's got all those deaths on his conscience. The boy's sensitive enough that he might go down under the weight of that. Hell, Parks would buckle more than a little himself.

They're all looking scared and shaken, Gallagher most of all, but there's no time for hand-holding. The good news is that the junkers headed north, which means they've got a window for their run to the south and they'd better use it. "Ten minutes," Parks says. "We eat and run."

They go deeper into the long grass, one by one, to relieve themselves and wash and whatever else they need to do, and then they eat a quick, joyless breakfast of carb-and-protein mix 3. The hungry kid is a silent, passive observer to all of this. She doesn't piss and this time she doesn't eat, either. Parks ties her leash to a tree when he goes off to perform his own ablutions.

When he comes back, he finds that Justineau has untied the

leash from the tree and is holding it herself. That's fine by Parks. He'd rather keep his hands free. With a minimum of discussion – a minimum of interaction of any kind – they hit the road. Every face Parks looks at is drawn and scared. They fled from a nightmare, and fuck if it isn't right here again, bumping along behind them. What he knows and doesn't say is that they're heading into worse.

They go east at first, towards Stotfold, but there's no need to stop there now so they detour south, hit the road that used to be the A507 and keep right on going.

This is wild country, for a lot of reasons. In the first days and weeks of the Breakdown, the UK government, like a whole lot of others, thought they could contain the infection by locking down the civilian population. Not surprisingly, this didn't stop people running like rats when they saw what was happening. Thousands, maybe millions, tried to get out of London along the north–south arteries, the A1 and M1. The authorities responded ruthlessly, first with military roadblocks and then with targeted airstrikes.

There are clean stretches still, and some of them are extensive. For miles at a time, though, the two great roads are cratered like First World War battlefields and strewn with rusted hulks like a mechanical version of the elephants' graveyard. You could still walk the road, in between the ruined cars, if you chose to – but only a madman would do it. With visibility down to almost nothing, a hungry could jump out at you from any direction and you wouldn't have more than a heartbeat's warning.

Parks' plan is to join the A1 at junction 10, just north of Baldock. He knows from his grab-bagging days that there's a nice, open corridor there, going south a good ten or fifteen miles. They can do it easily in a day if the weather holds: leave the junkers way behind them. They'll make Stevenage before dark, and hopefully find a good place to sleep without venturing too deep into the urban hinterlands.

For the first few years after the Breakdown, and even after the retreat from London, Beacon used to maintain an armed presence on the main north–south roads. The idea was to allow the grab-baggers a safe passage, both on their outward journey and – more importantly – when they went home again laden down with good things from the land of how-it-used-to-be. But they found out the hard way that there was a down side to those sweet, clear lines of sight. Hungries could spot you from a long way off, and home in on your movements. After a few costly clusterfucks, the permanent posts were dismantled and the grab-baggers took their chances. In recent years they've gone in and out by chopper, when they've gone at all. The roads have been given up for lost.

All of which means that Parks is very watchful as they approach the wide stretch of blacktop, marching in single file up the gentle curve of the old approach road. A sign where they join it points to Baldock services, making a number of unsubstantiated promises: food, petrol, a picnic area, even a bed for the night. From the top of the rise they can see the roofless ruin that used to be the service station, burned out long before. Parks remembers stopping there once, when he was a child, on the way back from a family holiday in the Peak District. Remembers a few highlights anyway: lukewarm hot chocolate with thick sludge at the bottom where it wasn't stirred properly, and a weird man in the gents' toilet, with bulging Marty Feldman eyes, who was singing Bruce Springsteen's "The River" in a scary monotone.

From where Parks is standing, Baldock services was no great loss.

The A1, though, is the same as it ever was. A little weed-choked and pitted, maybe, but as straight as a ruler at this point and pointed due south towards home sweet home. There's a whole lifeless metropolis between here and there, of course, but the sergeant can count his blessings and get as high as two. Right now they've got a good elevation. They can see for miles.

168

And the sun comes out, like a kiss on the cheek from God.

"Okay, listen to me," he says, looking at each of them in turn. Even Gallagher needs to hear this, although most of it's general issue for when you're outside the fence. "Road protocols. Let's get them straight before we go out there. First is, you don't talk. Not out loud. Sound carries, and the hungries home in on it. It's not as strong a trigger for them as smell, but you'd be amazed how good their hearing is.

"Second, you clock any movement, any at all, and you signal. Raise your hand, like this, with the fingers spread. Then point. Make sure everyone sees. Don't just whip your gun out and start shooting, because nobody will know what you're shooting at and they won't be able to back you up. If it's close enough so you can see it's a hungry, and if it's moving towards us, then you can break rule one. Shout *hungry*, or *hungries*, and if you feel like it, give me a range and an address. Three o'clock and a hundred yards, or whatever.

"Third and last, if you do get a hungry after you, then you don't run. There's no way you're going to beat it, and you've got a better chance if you're facing it head-on. Hit it with anything. Bullets, bricks, your bare hands, harsh language. If you're lucky, you'll bring it down. Leg and lower body shots improve your chances of getting lucky, unless it's right in close. In which case, you go for the head so it's got something to chew on besides you."

He catches the eye of the hungry kid. She's watching him as intently as the others, a frown of concentration on her dead pale face. Another time, Parks might have laughed. It's a little bit like a cow listening to a recipe for beef stew.

"I'm assuming there's a different rule for junkers," Helen Justineau says.

Parks nods. "We run into those bastards again, we'll hear them a long time before we see them. In which case we get the fuck off the road and we wait them out, same as last time. As long as they stay in convoy like that, we should be fine."

169

Nobody's got anything else to say about these instructions. They go on up to the road and head south, and for a good couple of hours they walk in complete silence.

It's a glorious summer day, quickly becoming uncomfortably hot as the sun climbs up the sky. A wind rises and falls fitfully, but it doesn't do much to cool them. Worried by their profuse sweating and what it might bring down on them, Parks makes them stop and apply another layer of e-blocker to all the places that need it. Most of those places are underneath their clothes. They turn away from each other by unspoken agreement, forming the vertices of a square at whose centre the hungry kid stands silent, staring not at the grown-ups – the humans – but at the burning spotlight of the sun.

The e-blocker routine is basic but essential. Lay it on thick at crotch and armpits, elbows and the backs of knees. A little bit all over, and a quick-dissolving slimy lozenge of the stuff on your tongue. It's not the sweat that matters; it's mainly the pheromones. The hungries may not have enough brains left to see people as people, but they're shit-hot when it comes to following a chemical gradient.

They move on again. Justineau and the hungry kid walk side by side, the leash slack between them. Caldwell walks behind the two of them, most of the time, with her hands either loose at her sides or crossed against her chest. Gallagher takes the rear position, while Parks himself is on point.

Around about noon, they see something on the road ahead of them. It's just a dark blob at first – not moving, so Parks doesn't flag it up immediately as a danger. But he gestures to them to spread out as they approach it. He's mindful of how easy they are to see on the empty road, the only moving things in a landscape like a still photo.

It's a car. It sits dead centre in the road, but skewed slightly, its nose tilting into what used to be the slow lane. The bonnet is up, the boot likewise, and the four doors are all open. It's not rusted, or burned out. Chances are it hasn't been there very long.

Parks has the others hang back, circles it by himself. It looks empty at first glance, but as he comes around the driver's side he glimpses something in the back seat that looks vaguely human. The rest of the way he's got his gun in his hand and he's hair-trigger, ready to unload on anything that moves.

Nothing moves. The dark, hunched shape used to belong to the species *Homo sapiens*, but it's nothing very much now. You can tell that it was a man, because of his jacket and because of his face, which is mostly intact. The rest of the flesh of his upper body has been eaten away, the head all but detached by a massive apple-coring bite that's been taken out of his throat. In the depths of that old, dry wound, nubs of bone or cartilage show.

Nobody else in the car. Nothing in the boot, apart from a battered pair of shoes and a coil of rope. Lots of stuff scattered on the road all around, though – bags and boxes, a rucksack, and something that looks like a games console or else part of a sound system.

The car tells its own story, as though it were a diorama in a museum. Group of like-minded people share a ride, going . . . somewhere. Somewhere up north. The car starts coughing or banging, or else it just stops. One of the gang gets out to take a look, throws up the bonnet, pronounces the car DOA. So they all start getting their stuff out of the boot. These lackwits can't tell trash from treasure, but there's nothing wrong with the instinct.

They were interrupted. Most of them dropped their shit and ran for the hills. One of them jumped back in the car, and maybe he saved the others by that action, because it looks like a lot more than one hungry partook of him.

"You try turning the key?" Justineau asks. Parks is really pissed off to see her walking right up to the car, even though he hasn't signalled *clear* yet. But the woman's not stupid; on reflection, Parks is aware that his body language changed as he walked around the car – from total threat-readiness to his still

171

cautious but looser business-as-usual. She was just responding to that change a little faster than the others.

"You try it," he suggests.

Justineau leans into the car, goes suddenly still as she sees its other occupant. But if she flinches from that sight, it's only for a heartbeat. She reaches forward, and Parks hears a muted click as the key turns. The engine doesn't make a sound. He didn't really expect it to.

He's looking off to both sides of the road now. There's scrub and bushes to their right, a length of wooden hoarding on the left. Most likely the occupants of the car ran the obvious way, towards the bushes. No telling how far they got, but they didn't come back for their stuff, or to bury their dead. Parks revises his earlier thought, that the sacrifice of the back-seat passenger saved the rest. It's not likely that anyone walked away from this.

The others come up and join them, Gallagher last of all because he waits on Parks' signal. Parks tells them to check the bags and boxes, but it's mostly the kind of precious keepsakes that only mattered to their former owners. Not even clothes, but books and DVDs, letters and ornaments. The few items of food were perishable, and they've perished: withered apples, a rotten loaf, a bottle of whisky that shattered when the bag it was in hit the asphalt.

Justineau opens the rucksack. "Jesus Christ!" she mutters. She dips her hand in and brings out some of the contents. Money. Bundles of fifty-pound notes, bank-fresh in paper sleeves. Completely useless. Twenty-some years after the world went down the toilet, someone still thought it was coming back – that there would come a day when money would mean something again.

"Triumph of hope over experience," Parks observes.

"Nostalgia," Dr Caldwell says categorically. "The psychological comfort outweighs the logical objections. Everybody needs a security blanket."

Only idiots, Parks thinks. Personally, he tends to see security in much less abstract terms.

Gallagher looks from one of them to the other, not sure what's going on. He's too young to remember money. Justineau starts in on an explanation, then shakes her head and gives it up. "Why would I ruin your innocence?" she says.

"There were one hundred pence in a pound," the hungry kid says. "But only after the fifteenth of February 1971. Before that, there were two hundred and forty pence in the pound, but they didn't say pence. They said pennies."

Justineau laughs. "Very good, Melanie." She tears the sleeve from one of the bundles of money, fans out the notes and throws them into the air. "Pennies from heaven," she says as they blow away on the hot wind. The hungry kid smiles, as though the cascade of waste paper is a firework display. She squints into the sun to follow them as they fly.

32

They make, Caroline Caldwell supposes, good progress.

It's hard for her to tell, though, because her time sense is slightly skewed by two extraneous factors. The first factor is a fever that has been rising in her since the evening of the previous day. The second factor is that she allowed herself to become dehydrated as they walked, exacerbating the effects of the first factor.

She watches her own sickness at one remove, not because her scientific vocation conditions everything she does, but because being at one remove actually seems to help. She can observe the sick tiredness of her limbs, identify the ache in her head occasioned by the tiny but repeated jolts of her feet on the asphalt – and still keep moving without a break, because these are purely physiological things, without any bearing in the end on what her mind does.

Which is to turn old questions over and over in the light of new evidence.

She's read many detailed accounts of the hungries' feeding, but never observed it at first hand (the feeding of the test subjects, under artificial and controlled conditions, was an

174

entirely different thing). She finds it striking that the hungries who fed on the man in the car continued to eat until his body was non-viable – until there was almost no flesh left on his upper torso and he had been virtually decapitated.

This is counterintuitive. Caldwell would have expected the hungry pathogen to be better adapted. She would have expected *Ophiocordyceps* to manipulate the cells of the host's hypothalamus more skilfully, suppressing the hunger drive after the first few bites so that the newly infected have a robust chance of survival. That would obviously be far more efficient, since a viable new host will become a new vector in its turn, providing increased opportunities for the pathogen to multiply quickly within a given ecological range.

Perhaps it's a side effect of that very slow maturing: the fact that this strain of *Ophiocordyceps* never reaches its final, sexually seeding stage, but instead reproduces neotenously by asexual budding in the favourable environment of blood or saliva. Logically, you'd expect this to impede the spread of favourable mutations.

Something to consider in the next round of dissections. Examine the cells of the hypothalamus more closely. Look for differential levels of penetration by fungal mycelia.

A mile out of Stevenage – close enough to see the roofs of the houses and the blue-slated spire of a church – Sergeant Parks gives the order to stop. He turns to them and tells them what's going to happen next, pointing at the sky as an unimpeachable witness. "Sun's going down inside the next two hours. Could be those junkers are still looking for us, but either way we need a place to hole up for the night, and this is it. Gallagher and I will go in and disinfect, as far as that's needed. Then we'll come back and get you. Okay?"

Not okay, very obviously. Caldwell can see from Justineau's face that it's not okay for her either, but she chooses to make the point herself because she knows she'll make it more clearly and succinctly.

175

"This isn't going to work," she tells Parks.

"It is if you do as you're told."

Caldwell gestures, cupping the fingers of her hand as though she's holding the man's words up for inspection. The tips of her fingers tingle unpleasantly. "That's exactly *why* it isn't going to work," she says. "Because you're seeing us purely as civilians, with yourself and Private Gallagher as our military escort. In trying to take all the risk on to yourself, you're actually increasing the risk to all of us."

Parks gives her a cold look. "Assessing risk is part of what I do," he tells her.

She's about to explain to him why his assessment is flawed, but Helen Justineau breaks in now, pre-empting her reply. "She's right, Sergeant. We're about to move into a built-up area, where we can expect to find a lot more hungries, at every stage of infection. It's dangerous ground – we won't know how dangerous until we're in it. So what kind of sense does it make for you to cross it three times? You have to go out and do your reconnaissance, then come back here to collect us, then go in again. And what happens to us if those junkers turn up again while you're gone? We wouldn't last a second out here in the open. It's got to be better if we go in with you."

Parks chews on this for a good few seconds. But Caldwell knows him well enough to be confident of his answer. It's not in his repertoire to say no to something just because somebody else thought of it. She and Justineau are right, and that's all there is to it.

"Okay," he says at last. "But the two of you have never done this before, so you'd damn well better follow my lead. Come to think of it," he glances across at the private, "did you ever do a Hitchin run, Gallagher?"

The private shakes his head.

Parks puffs out his breath like a man about to bend down and lift a heavy load. "Okay. Road rules still apply – especially the one about keeping your mouths shut – but this is going to be different. We're almost bound to see hungries, and to be in their line of sight. What you want to do is not trigger them. Move slowly and smoothly. Don't look them directly in the eye. Don't make any loud or sudden noises. As far as you can, you blend into the landscape. If in doubt, look at me and take your cue from me."

Once he's said his piece, he walks on. He doesn't waste any more words or any more time. Caldwell approves of that.

Twenty minutes later, they're coming level with the first buildings. Nobody has sighted any hungries yet, but it's early days. Parks issues whispered commands, and they all stop. The four uninfected humans anoint themselves with e-blocker again.

They head on into town, staying in a tight cluster so that none of them presents a clear and unambiguous human silhouette. These are residential streets, upmarket once, now gone to semi-ruin through a hectic month or so of looting and urban warfare followed by two decades of neglect. The gardens are small pockets of jungle that have broken their borders to colonise parts of the street. Waist-high weeds have smashed and grabbed their way up between tilted flagstones, mature brambles throwing up fist-thick stalks like the tentacles of subterranean monsters. But the shallowness of the soil underneath the pavement has stopped them from uniting their forces and throwing down the houses once and for all. There's a precarious balance of power.

Parks has already told them what he's looking for. Not a house on a street like this, with neighbours on all sides. That would be too difficult to secure. He wants a detached structure standing in its own grounds, with reasonable lines of sight at least out of the upstairs windows, and ideally with the doors intact. He has realistic expectations, though, and he'll take anything that's broadly okay if it means not going too deeply into the town.

But there's nothing he likes here, so they move on.

Five minutes later, keeping up their intent and silent stroll,

177

they come into a wider road into which several streets feed. There's an arcade of shops here. The road surface is crunchy with shattered glass, all the shopfronts broken into and ransacked by looters of a bygone era. Empty tin cans on the ground, rusted to the thinness and delicacy of shells, roll and rattle when the wind comes up a little.

And there are hungries.

Perhaps a dozen of them, widely scattered.

The party of living humans comes to a halt when they see them, only Parks remembering to slow his steps gradually rather than going straight from motion into stillness.

Caldwell is fascinated. She turns her head slowly to examine each of the hungries in turn.

They're a mix of old and new. The older ones can be identified very easily both by their mouldering clothing and by their extreme gauntness. When a hungry feeds, it also feeds the pathogen within it. But if prey can't be found, *Ophiocordyceps* will draw its nutrients directly from the flesh of the host.

Closer to, she can also see the mottled colouring on the older ones. Grey threads have broken the leathery surface of their skin in a network of fine lines, crossing and re-crossing like veins. The whites of the eyes are grey too, and if the hungry's mouth is open you can see a fuzz of grey on the tongue.

The newer hungries are dressed more nattily – or at least their clothes have had less time to rot – and they still have a broadly human appearance. Paradoxically, that makes them a lot more unpleasant to look at, because the wounds and torn flesh through which they contracted the infection in the first place are clearly visible. On an older hungry, the general bleaching and weathering of the skin surface and clothing, along with the overlay of grey mycelia, softens and disguises the wounds; makes something more architectural out of them.

The hungries are in their stationary mode, which is why Caldwell can get away with this unhurried inspection. They

178

stand or sit or kneel at random points along the length of the road, completely motionless, their eyes on nothing and their arms mostly dangling at their sides or − if they're sitting − folded in their laps.

They look like they're posing for paintings, or sunk into such deep introspection that they've forgotten what it was they were meant to be doing. Not like they're waiting; not like a single sound or movement out of place would wake them and launch them into instant motion.

Parks raises his hand, waves the party on with a slow sweep of his arm. The movement serves both as a command and as a reminder of the unhurried pace they need to keep up. The sergeant leads the way, his rifle ready in his hands but pointed at the ground. His gaze is on the ground too for a lot of the time. He scans the visual field with quick, darting glances, his eyes the only part of him at odds with his slow, shambling stride. Caldwell recalls belatedly the hypothesis that hungries retain the rudimentary pattern recognition that all babies are born with − that they're capable of identifying a human face, and respond to it by slipping into a slightly heightened mode of arousal and awareness. Her own researches have failed either to confirm or to refute this, but she is prepared to accept that it might be true for all but the most severely decayed.

So they avoid the eyes of the hungries as they shuffle on down the high street. They look at each other, at the gaping shop windows, at the road ahead or at the sky, letting the macabre still-life figures hover in their peripheral vision.

Except for the test subject. Melanie doesn't seem to be able to look away from her larger counterparts even for a moment; she stares at them as though they exert a hypnotic fascination, almost tripping at one point because she's not looking where she's going.

That stumble causes Sergeant Parks to turn his head − slowly, measuredly − and give her a baleful glare. She understands the reprimand, and the warning. Her own nod, in return, is so gradual that it takes ten seconds to be completed. She wants him to know that she won't make that mistake again.

They pass the first group of hungries and keep on going. More houses, terraced this time, and then another row of shops. A side street that they pass is much more densely populated. Hungries stand silently in a tight cluster, as though awaiting the start of a parade. Caldwell guesses that they converged on a kill, and then when they were done simply remained there, in the absence of a trigger that would induce them to move.

She wonders, walking on, whether the sergeant's strategy is a sound one. They're embedding themselves very deeply. There are now enemies behind them as well as in front and – potentially – on all sides. Parks wears a troubled expression. Probably he's thinking the same thing.

Caldwell is about to suggest that they retrace their steps and – as the least bad of a number of unpleasant options – spend the night in one of the semi-detached houses on the outskirts of the town. They might have hungries for neighbours, but at least they'll have a clear escape route.

But ahead of them, there's an old-fashioned village green – or the remains of one at least. The green itself has run to jungle, but at least it's jungle that seems to have a very sparse hungry population. There are a few of them on the strip of road that surrounds the open space, but not nearly so many as on the street they're on.

Something else too. Private Gallagher sees it first, points – slowly, but emphatically. On the other side of the green is exactly what the sergeant told them to look for: a big detached house, two storeys, standing in its own grounds. It's a mini-mansion of modern design, masquerading as a country house of an earlier age – but given away by its anachronistic excess. It's a Frankenstein's monster of a house, with a half-timbered front, Gothic arches on the ground-floor windows, pilasters framing the front door, gables adhering like barnacles to the roof ridge. The sign on the gate says WAINWRIGHT HOUSE.

"Good enough," Parks says. "Let's go."

Justineau is about to take the direct route, across the over-grown green, but Parks blocks her with a hand on her shoulder. "No telling what's in there," he mutters. "Might startle a cat, or a bird, and get all the deadheads for miles around looking in our direction. Let's stick to the open road."

So they skirt the edge of the weeds and couch grass, instead of going through, and that's why Caldwell sees it.

She slows down, and then she stops. She can't help herself; she stares. It's such a crazy, impossible thing.

One of the hungries is walking down the centre of the road. A female – biological age when she encountered the *Ophiocordyceps* pathogen probably late twenties or early thirties. She seems quite well preserved, unblemished apart from bite damage to the left side of her face. Only the grey threads around her eyes and mouth indicate how long it must have been since she left the human race. She's wearing tan trousers, a white blouse with quarter-length sleeves; stylish summer wear, but the effect is somewhat tarnished by the fact that she's got one shoe missing. In her long, straight, blonde hair there's a single cornrow braid.

She's pushing a baby carriage.

Out of the two things that make this impossible, Caldwell is arrested first by the less remarkable. Why is she walking? Hungries either run, when they pursue prey, or stand still when they don't. There's no intermediate state of leisurely perambu-lation.

And then: why is she clinging to an object? Among the myriad things a human being loses when *Ophiocordyceps* infil-trates the brain and redecorates is the ability to use tools. The baby carriage ought to be as meaningless to this creature as the equations of general relativity would be.

Caldwell can't help herself. She advances, crab-wise, to inter-sect the female hungry's trajectory, careful at these close quar-ters to watch her only out of the corner of her eye. Out of the corner of her other eye, she's aware of Parks raising his hand in a halt gesture. She ignores him. This is too important, and she can't in conscience let it pass.

She stands full in the path of the oncoming carriage, the shambling ex-woman. It bumps against her, with minimal force, and the woman stops dead. Her shoulders slump, her head bows. Now she looks the part: the lights going out, system powering down until something happens to kick-start it again.

Parks and the others have frozen. They're all looking Caldwell's way, watching this play out because there's nothing they can do now to influence it. By the same token, it's too late for Caldwell to worry about whether her e-blockers will work at point-blank range, so she doesn't.

Moving with glacial slowness, she comes around to the side of the carriage. From this angle, she can see that the hungry has more injuries than was immediately apparent. Her shoulder has been torn, flesh hanging there in desiccated strips. The white blouse isn't white at all at the back – it's black from neckline to hem with ancient, crusted blood.

Inside the pushchair there's a row of ducks on an elasticated string, which bob and rock in a desultory dance, and a big yellow blanket, dusty and rucked up, which hides whatever else might be there.

The hungry doesn't seem aware of Caldwell at all. That's good. The doctor makes her movements even more gradual, even more unhurried. Reaches out her hand to the topmost edge of the blanket.

She takes a fold of the thick, stiff fabric between finger and thumb. Slow as a glacier now, she peels it back.

The baby has been dead for a long time. Two large rats, nesting in what's left of its ribcage, start up at once and leap with shrill squeals of protest over Caldwell's left and right shoulders.

Caldwell staggers back with a wordless shriek.

The hungry's head snaps up and round. It stares at Caldwell, eyes widening. Its mouth gapes open on grey rot and black stumps of teeth.

Sergeant Parks fires a single shot into the back of its skull. Its mouth opens wider still, its head tilting sideways. It falls forward on to the carriage, which rolls and pitches it off on to the road's gravelled surface.

On all sides, hungries stir to life, swivelling their heads like range-finders.

"Move," Parks growls. "On me."

Then he bellows:

"*Run!*"

33

They almost die in the first few seconds. Because in spite of Parks' yell, the others freeze.

It just seems like there's nowhere to run to. Hungries are swarming on them from every direction, the gaps between them closing as they converge.

But there's only one direction that matters. And Parks sets to work to open it up again.

Three shots drop three of the sprinting dead in their tracks. Two shots miss. Parks gives Justineau a violent shove, gets her running. Gallagher does the same for Dr Caldwell, and the little hungry kid, Melanie, is already going flat out.

They jump over the fallen hungries, which are scrabbling like cockroaches, trying to right themselves. If Parks had the time, if the seconds that are ticking by weren't shaping up to be the last seconds of their lives, he'd have tried for head shots. As it is, he goes for central body mass and the best odds for sending them down.

Works fine, up until Justineau goes sprawling. One of the holed hungries has grabbed her leg and is swarming up it, hand over hand.

Parks stops long enough to unload a second bullet into the hollow under the ear of the ex-human predator. It lets go. Justineau is up again in an instant, not looking back. Good. Lot's wife should have had that kind of focus.

He's shooting to left and right. Only taking out the closest, the ones that are about to jump or grab. Gallagher is doing the same thing, and – though his hit rate is shit – at least he's not slowing to shoot. That's better than having him aim like Deadeye Dick and stand still long enough to get tackled.

They're at the gates now, and there's no lock on them that Parks can see, but they don't open. Used to be electric, obviously, but bygones are bygones and in the brave new post-mortem world that just means they don't bloody work.

"Over!" he yells. "Up and over!"

Which is easily said. A head-high rampart of ornamental ironwork with functional spear points on top says different. They try, all the same. Parks leaves them to it, turns his back to them and goes on firing.

The up side is that now he can be indiscriminate. Set to full auto and aim low. Cut the hungries' legs out from under them, turning the front-runners into trip hazards to slow the ones behind.

The down side is that more and more of them keep coming. The noise is like a dinner bell. Hungries are crowding into the green space from the streets on every side, at what you'd have to call a dead run. There's no limit to their numbers, and there is a limit to his ammo.

Which he hits, suddenly. The gun stops vibrating in his hands and the noise of his shots dies away through layers of echoes. He ejects the empty magazine, gropes for another in his pocket. He's done this so often he could go through the moves in his sleep. Slap the new mag in and give it a quick, sharp tug, pivoting it on the forward lip so it locks into place. Pull the bolt all the way back.

The bolt sticks halfway. The weapon's just dead weight until he can clear whatever's jamming it – the first round, most likely, elbowed in the chamber. And two hungries are on top of him now, triangulating from left and right. One of them used to be a man, the other a woman. They're about a second away from the world's nastiest three-way.

It's just instinct. Faulty learning. He takes a step back, groping for his sidearm instead of swinging the rifle like a club. Wastes a second that he doesn't have, and it's all over.

Except that it isn't.

In combat, Parks narrows down. It's not even a conscious thing, so much, or a trick he's learned. It just happens. He does the job that's in front of him, and pretty much shunts everything else into a holding pattern.

So he's forgotten about the hungry kid until she's suddenly there, right in front of him. She's inserted herself into the narrowing space between him and his attackers. She's flailing at them with her skinny arms, an atom of defiance with a shrill, shrieking war cry.

And the hungries stop, breakneck sudden. Their eyes defocus. Their heads start to turn to left and right in short arcs, like they're sad or disapproving. They're not looking at Parks any more. They're looking *for* him.

Parks knows the hungries don't hunt or eat each other. Apart from the kids in the classroom, he's never seen a hungry behave like it knows any other hungries are even there. They're alone in a crowd, each one of them answering its own need. They're not pack animals. They're solitaries that cluster accidentally because they're responding to the same triggers.

So he's always assumed that they can't smell each other at all. The smell of a normal man or woman drives them crazy, but other hungries don't register. They're just not on the radar. He realises, in that numbed second, that he was wrong. For each other, the hungries must have a *nothing-to-see-here-move-along* kind of smell, the very opposite of how live people smell. It turns them off, where the live smell turns them on.

186

The kid masked him. Her chemicals blocked his, just for a second or two, so the hungries lost the pheromone trail that ended with their teeth in his throat.

Plenty of others running in, though, that aren't slowing at all. And the two that the kid just windjammed are getting the signal again, eyes locking on target.

But Gallagher's hand clamps on Parks' arm and drags him backwards through the gates, which they've managed to push half open.

They're running again, the house looming ahead of them. Justineau is hauling on the door, throwing it wide. They're through, the hungry kid snaking between his legs to get in ahead of him. Gallagher slams the door shut again, which is just so much wasted time because of the two floor-to-ceiling window panels to either side of it.

"Stairs!" Parks yells, pointing. "Get up the stairs."

They do. To the sound of crazed church bells as the windows shatter.

Parks is bringing up the rear, throwing grenades over his back like strings of beads at a fucking Mardi Gras parade.

And the grenades are going off behind them one after another, barking concussions overlapping in hideous counterpoint. Shrapnel smacks Parks' flak jacket and his unprotected legs.

The last half-dozen treads on the stairs sag and yaw under him like he's stepping on to a rocking boat, but he gets to the top somehow.

And falls, first to his knees, then full-length, sobbing for breath. They all do. Except for the kid, who's staring back down into the gulf of air, as still and quiet as if she's just gone for an afternoon stroll. The stairs are gone, all blown to hell, and they're safe.

No, they're really not. No time for sitting around and swapping stories about the one you got away from. He's got to get them on their feet again at once.

Sure, they found the main gates of this place closed, and the doors not broken in, but there could easily be a back door off its hinges. A window smashed in. A stretch of fence that went down last week or last year. A nest of hungries sitting in one of the rooms up here, perking up at the sound of their approaching footsteps.

So they've got to make themselves a safe base of operations.

And then they've got to search. Make sure there are no hostiles inside their perimeter.

The place looks completely undisturbed, Parks has to admit. But just counting the doors that he can see, he knows there must a shit-load of rooms. He's not prepared to let his guard down until he's made sure that each and every one of them is secure.

They advance up the corridor, trying each door in turn. Most don't open, which is fine with Parks. Whatever's on the other side of a locked door can stay there.

The few that do open lead to tiny bedrooms. The beds are hospital beds with adjustable steel frames and emergency cords at the head end. Tray tables with melamine tops. Tubular steel chairs with faded burgundy seats. En suite bathrooms so small that the shower cubicle is bigger than the floor space outside it. Wainwright House was some kind of private hospital, not a place where people actually lived.

These one-berth wards are way too claustrophobic even for two of them to share, and Parks doesn't think it's a great idea to split up. So they keep looking.

And he's wondering, all this while: did the kid know what she was doing? Was she aware that she could deflect the hungries just by stepping into their path?

It's a troubling thought, because he's not sure what the significance of either a yes or a no would be. He was screwed, and the kid unscrewed him. He turns that around in his mind, but it doesn't look any better no matter which angle he comes at it from. Thinking about it just makes him angry.

They hang a right off the main corridor, then a left, and

eventually they find a day room that's big enough for their needs. Straight-backed chairs line the walls, which are decorated with cheap framed prints of anonymous English pastoral scenes. Haywains predominate. Parks is indifferent to the haywains, and the room's got a few too many doors for his liking, but he's pretty sure by this time that it's the best they're going to find.

"We'll sleep here," he tells the civilians. "But first we've got to check the rest of this floor. Make sure there are no surprises."

The last *we* means himself and Gallagher, mostly, but the quicker the better for this, so he decides to rope Justineau in too. "You said you wanted to help," he reminds her. "Help with this."

Justineau hesitates – looking straight at Dr Caldwell, so it isn't hard to see what's going through her mind. She's worried about leaving Caldwell alone with the kid. But Caldwell was hit worse than anyone by the fight and flight. She's pale and sweating, breath still coming in quick pants long after the rest of them have got their second wind.

"We'll be five minutes," Parks says. "What do you think is going to happen to her in five minutes?" His own voice surprises him; the anger and the tension in it. Justineau stares at him. Maybe Gallagher flashes him a quick look too.

So he explains himself. "Easier to stay in line of sight if there are three of us. Kid's no use because she won't know what to look for. We go out, we come back, and they stay here so we know where to find them. Okay?"

"Okay," Justineau says, but she's still looking at him hard. Like, where's that other shoe, and who's it likely to hit when it drops?

She kneels and puts a hand on Melanie's shoulder. "We're going to take a quick look around," she says. "We'll be right back."

"Be careful," Melanie says.

Justineau nods.

Yeah.

189

34

Alone with Dr Caldwell, the first thing Melanie does is to walk away to the further end of the room and put her back to the wall. She watches every move that Dr Caldwell makes, scared and wary, ready to bolt through the open door after Miss Justineau.

But Dr Caldwell sinks into one of the chairs, either too exhausted or too lost in her own thoughts to pay any attention to Melanie. She doesn't even look at her.

Any other time, Melanie would explore. All day she's been seeing new and amazing things, but Sergeant has set a brisk, steady pace and she's never had time to stop and investigate any of the wonders that went by on both sides of the road: trees and lakes, latticework fences, road signs pointing to places whose names she knows from her lessons, hoardings whose mostly obliterated posters have become mosaics of abstract colour. Living things too – birds in the air, rats and mice and hedgehogs in the weeds alongside the road. A world too big to take in all at once, too new to have names.

And now here she is, in this house that's so different from the base. There must be so many things to discover. This room alone is filled with mysteries both large and small. Why are the chairs only at the edges of the room, when the room is so enormous? Why is there a little wire cradle on the wall next to the door, with a plastic bottle in it and a sign that says CROSS-INFECTION COSTS LIVES? Why is there a faded picture on one of the tables (wild horses galloping across a field) that's been cut up into hundreds and hundreds of wiggly-shaped pieces and then stuck back together again?

But right now, all Melanie wants to do is to go somewhere quiet and be by herself, so she can think about the terrible thing that just happened. The terrible secret she just found out.

Apart from the door that they came in by, there are two more doors out of the room. Melanie goes to the nearest one, keeping Dr Caldwell (who still hasn't moved) always in the corner of her eye. She finds another room, very small and mostly white. There are white cupboards and white shelves, with black and white tiles on the walls. One of the cupboards has a window in it and lots of dials and switches at the top. It smells of old grease. Melanie knows just about enough to guess that the cupboard with a window in it is a cooker. She's seen pictures in books. This must be a kitchen of some kind – a place where you make nice things to eat. But it's too small for her to hide in. If Dr Caldwell came after her, she'd be trapped.

She goes out again. Dr Caldwell hasn't moved, so she walks right past her, giving her a wide berth, and goes to the other door. The next room is very different from the kitchen. Its walls are painted in bright colours, and there are posters, too. One shows ANIMALS OF THE BRITISH HEDGEROWS, and another has words starting with each letter of the alphabet. *Apple. Boat. Cat. Digger. Elephant.* The pictures are cheerful and simple. The boat and the digger have smiling faces at their front ends, which Melanie is almost certain is unrealistic.

There are chairs in here too, but they're smaller and they're all over the place in little clusters, not arranged neatly around

191

the edges of the room. On the floor are toys, strewn as casually as if they were put down a moment before. Girl dolls in dresses and soldier dolls in uniform. Cars and trucks. Plastic building blocks stuck together in the shape of cars or houses or people. Animals made of plush in colours washed out almost to grey.

And books. Lots of them thrown down on chairs, tables, the floor. Hundreds more on a big bookcase to one side of the door. Melanie is in no mood right then to pick them up and read them; the secret weighs heavily on her mind. In any case, even if she wanted to, her hands are stuck behind her back by the handcuffs, and her feet, though they're bare, aren't nearly flexible enough to turn the pages. She scans their titles instead.

The Very Hungry Caterpillar
Fox in Socks
Peepo!
The Cops and the Robbers
What Do You Do With a Kangaroo?
Where the Wild Things Are
The Man Whose Mother Was a Pirate
Pass the Jam, Jim

The titles are like stories in themselves. Some of the books have fallen apart or else been torn, their pages scattered across the floor. It would make her sad, if her heart wasn't full already with a dizzying cargo of emotions.

She's not a little girl. She's a hungry.

It's too crazy, too terrible to be true. But too obvious now to be ignored. The hungry that turned from her at the base, when it could have eaten her . . . that could have been anything. Or nothing. It could have smelled Dr Selkirk's blood and been distracted by that, or it could have been looking for someone bigger to eat, or the blue disinfectant gel could have disguised Melanie's smell the way the shower chemicals always disguised the smell of the grown-ups.

192

But outside, just now, when she stepped in front of Sergeant Parks – impulsive, without thinking, wanting to fight the monsters the same way he did, instead of hiding from them like a big scaredy-cat – they didn't even seem to see her. They certainly didn't hunger for her, the way they did for everyone else. It was like she was invisible. Like there was a bubble of pure nothing where Melanie was.

That's not the big proof, though. That's the little proof that pushes her up against the big proof, which is so very big that she wonders how she could have failed to see it right away. It's the word itself. The name. Hungries.

The monsters are named for the feeling that filled her when she smelled Miss Justineau in the cell, or the junker men outside the block. The hungries smell you, and then they chase you until they eat you. They can't stop themselves.

Melanie knows exactly how that feels. Which means she's a monster.

It makes sense now why Dr Caldwell thinks it was okay to cut her up on a table and put pieces of her in jars.

The door behind her opens, making almost no sound.

She turns to see Dr Caldwell standing in the doorway, staring down at her. The expression on Dr Caldwell's face is complicated and confusing. Melanie flinches back from it.

"Whatever the pertinent factor is," Dr Caldwell says, her voice a quick, low murmur, "you're its apogee. Do you know that? Genius-level mind and all that grey muck growing through your brain doesn't affect it one bit. *Ophiocordyceps* should have eaten out your cortex until all that's left is motor nerves and random backfires. But here you are." She takes a step forward, and Melanie locksteps back away from her.

"I'm not going to harm you," Dr Caldwell says. "There's nothing I can do out here anyway. No lab. No scopes. I just want to look at gross structures. The root of your tongue. Your tear ducts. Your oesophagus. See how far the infection has progressed. It's something. Something to be going on with.

The rest will wait. But you're a crucially important specimen, and I can't just—"

When Dr Caldwell reaches for her, Melanie ducks under her grip and sprints for the door. Dr Caldwell spins and lunges, almost fast enough. The tips of her fingers slide across Melanie's shoulder, but the bandages make her clumsy and she doesn't manage to catch a hold.

Melanie runs as if there's a tiger behind her.

Hearing Dr Caldwell's furious gasp. "Damn! Melanie!"

Out into the big room with the chairs around the edges. Melanie doesn't even know if she's being followed, because she doesn't dare look back. Bile rises in her throat as she thinks of the lab and the table and the long-handled knife.

In her panic, she just runs through the first door she sees, not even sure if it's the right one. It's not. It's the kitchen and she's trapped. She makes a sound inside the muzzle, an animal squeal.

She runs back out into the chair room. Dr Caldwell is on the other side of it. The door to the corridor is halfway between them.

"Don't be stupid," Dr Caldwell says. "I won't hurt you. I just want to examine you."

Melanie starts to walk towards her, head down, docile.

"That's right," Dr Caldwell soothes. "Come on."

When Melanie comes level with the door that leads out to the corridor, she bolts through it.

Since she doesn't know where she's going, it doesn't matter what turns she takes, but she remembers them anyway. Left. Left. Right. She can't help herself. It's the same instinct that made her memorise the return route to the cell block, when Sergeant Parks took her to Dr Caldwell's lab. Home keeps meaning different things, but she has to know her way back to it. It's a need buried too deep in her to be pulled out.

The corridors all look alike, and they offer no hiding places – at least, not to someone who doesn't have the use of their hands. She runs past door after door, all closed.

She goes to ground at last in an alcove, a slight widening of the corridor that creates an angle, a bulwark just wide enough for her body. It would only fool someone who wasn't actually looking for her, since anyone walking by would be able to see her just by turning their head. If Dr Caldwell finds her, she'll run again, and if Dr Caldwell catches her, she'll shout for Miss Justineau. That's her plan – the best she can come up with.

Her ears are straining for the sounds of distant footsteps. When she hears the singing, from much closer, she jumps like a rabbit.

"*Now fetch me . . . my children . . .*"

The voice is so hoarse, it's almost not a voice at all. Breath forced through a crack in a wall, driven by a broken bellows. It's like a song that was left behind here by someone who died, and now it's gone back to the wild.

And it's just those five words. Silence before, and silence after.

For about a minute. Melanie counts under her breath, trembling.

"*And fetch them . . . at speed . . .*"

She doesn't jump this time, but she bites her lip. She can't imagine the mouth that would make that sound. She's heard of ghosts – Miss Justineau told the class some ghost stories once, but she stopped when she got too close to that whole taboo subject of death – and she wonders whether it might be a ghost of someone who died here, singing a song from when he was alive.

"*Bid them hasten . . . or I shall . . . be dead . . .*"

She has to know. Even if it is a ghost, that won't be as scary as not knowing. She follows the sound, out of the alcove and around a bend in the corridor.

Light as red as blood comes through an open door, and it makes her scared for a moment. But as soon as she steps inside, she can see that it's just the light of the sunset coming in through an open window.

195

Just! She's only ever seen it once before, and this one's better. The sky catches fire from the ground on up, and the flames go through every colour, cooling from red-orange to violet and blue at the zenith.

It blinds her, for at least ten or twenty seconds, to the fact that she's not alone.

35

Caroline Caldwell also follows the sound of the strange voice. She's aware, of course, that it's not test subject number one who's singing. But equally she's sure that whoever it is doesn't represent a threat. Until she sees him.

The man sitting on the bed looks like the punchline to a bad joke. He's dressed in a hospital gown that's fallen open, exposing the nakedness beneath. Old wounds criss-cross his body. Deep troughs in the flesh of his shoulders, his arms, his face mark where he's been bitten. Except that bitten doesn't seem to cover it; he's been fed on, lumps of his physical substance torn away and consumed. Scratches and tears ruck his chest and stomach, where the hungries who partially devoured him grabbed him and held on. The two middle fingers of his right hand have been bitten off at the second joint – a defence wound, Caldwell assumes, sustained when he tried to push a hungry away from him and it bit down on his hand.

The blackly comic touch is the bandage on his elbow. This man came to Wainwright House with something trivial like bursitis and – as many people do – experienced complications

197

while he was being treated. In this case, the complications were that hungries feasted on his flesh and made him one of them.

He's still singing, seemingly unaware of Melanie standing directly in front of him, of Caldwell in the doorway of the room.

"The raven . . . croaked . . . as she sat . . . at her meal . . ."

It's so apposite to her thoughts, Caldwell is thrown for a moment. But he's not answering her, he's only singing the last line of the quatrain. She knows the song, vaguely. It's "The Woman Who Rode Double", an old folk ballad as depressing and interminable as most of its type – exactly the sort of song she'd expect a hungry to sing.

Except that they don't. Ever.

Another thing they don't do is look at pictures, but this one is. As he sings, he holds in his lap a wallet, of the kind that has a loose-leaf insert for credit cards. This one holds not cards but photographs. The hungry is trying to flick through them, with one of the remaining fingers of his right hand.

His movements are intermittent, and the gaps, in which he sits still, are very long. Each failure to turn to the next image elicits another line of the song.

"And the old woman . . . knew what . . . he said . . ."

Involuntarily, Caldwell's eyes find Melanie's. The glance they exchange asserts no kinship, unless it's a mark of consanguinity to be a rational and defined thing in the face of the impossible and the uncanny.

Caldwell steps into the room and circles the infected man slowly and warily. The marks of violence he bears are, she sees now, very old. The blood from the wounds has mostly dried and flaked away. Each is rimmed with an embroidery of fine grey threads, the visible sign that *Ophiocordyceps* has made its home within him. There's grey fuzz on his lips, too, and in the corners of his eyes.

It's possible, she thinks clinically, that he's remained in this room, on this bed, ever since he was infected. In that case, some of the bites on his arms might well have been self-inflicted. The fungus needs protein, primarily, and although it can make do with very little, it can't live on air. Auto-cannibalism is an eminently practical strategy for a parasite to which the host's body is only a temporary vector.

Caldwell is utterly fascinated. But she's also, after what happened outside, aware of the need for caution. She retreats back to the door, and beckons for the girl, the test subject, to join her there. Melanie stays exactly where she is. She's identified Caldwell as the greater threat, which is actually far from an unreasonable assumption.

But Caldwell doesn't have time for this bullshit.

She takes out the gun that Sergeant Parks gave her, which up until now has rested undisturbed in the pocket of her lab coat. She thumbs the safety and holds it, in both hands, out towards Melanie. Aiming at her head.

Melanie stiffens. She's seen what guns can do at very close quarters. She stares at the barrel, sickly hypnotised by its nearness, its deadly potentiality.

Caldwell beckons again, this time with a toss of her head.

"*And she . . . grew pale . . . at . . . the raven's tale . . .*"

Melanie takes a long time to decide, but at last she crosses to Caldwell. Caldwell takes one hand off the gun, steers Melanie out through the door with a hand on her shoulder.

She turns back to the male hungry.

"*All kinds of sin I have rioted in,*" she sings. "*And now the judgment must be.*"

The hungry shudders, a quick convulsion running through it. Caldwell steps hurriedly back, swivelling the gun to point it at the centre of the thing's chest. At this range, she can't miss.

But the hungry doesn't charge. It just moves its head from side to side as though it's trying to locate the source of the sound.

"So . . ." it rasps in that almost-not-there voice. "So. So. So."

"Leave him alone," Melanie whispers fiercely. "He's not hurting you."

"*But I secured my children's souls,*" Caldwell croons. "*So pray, my children, for me.*"

"So," the hungry croaks. "So . . ."

"Get out of the way," Sergeant Parks says. His hand is on Caldwell's shoulder, brusquely pushing her aside.

". . . phie . . ." the hungry says.

Parks fires once. A neat black circle, like a caste mark, appears in the centre of the hungry's forehead. It slips down sideways, rolling off the bed. Ancient stains, black and red and grey, mark the place where it has sat for so long.

"Why?" Caldwell wails, in spite of herself. She turns to the sergeant, her arms thrown wide. "Why do you always, always shoot them in the fucking *head*?"

Parks stares back at her, stony-faced. After a moment, he takes her right hand in his left and pushes it down until it's pointing at the ground.

"You want to get demonstrative with a gun in your hand," he says, "you make sure the safety is on."

36

Considering how badly it started, their second night on the road is a lot better than their first, at least in Helen Justineau's opinion.

For starters, they've got food to eat. Even more miraculously, they've got something to cook it with, because the range in the tiny kitchen is powered by gas cylinders. The one that's already hooked up is empty, but there are two full ones standing in the corner of the room and they're both still sound.

The three of them – Justineau, Parks and Gallagher – go through the treasure trove of canned goods in the kitchen cupboards, by the light of electric torches and of a nearly full moon shining in from outside, exclaiming in wonder or disgust at what's on offer. Justineau makes the mistake of checking the best-before dates, which of course are all at least a decade in the past, but Parks insists that they're okay. Or at least some of them will be, by the law of averages. And a can whose contents have oxidised will smell really bad when it's opened, so they can just keep on rolling the dice until their luck is in.

Justineau weighs up the risk against the absolute certainty of protein and carbohydrate mix number 3. She picks up a can opener that she found in a drawer and starts to open the cans.

There are some horrific encounters, but Parks' theory holds. Maybe thirty or forty cans later, they end up with a menu of beef in gravy with baby new potatoes, baked beans and mushy peas. Parks lights the range with a spark struck from a tinderbox – an honest-to-God tinderbox; that has to be centuries old – produced from his pocket with something suspiciously like a flourish, and Gallagher cooks while Justineau wipes dust off plates and cutlery and washes them clean with a dribble of water from one of the canteens.

Melanie and Dr Caldwell play no part in any of this. Caldwell sits on one of the chairs in the day room, laboriously removing and adjusting and rewinding the dressings on her hands. She wears an expression of furious intensity, and doesn't answer when spoken to. You could almost believe she's sulking, but in Justineau's opinion, what they're seeing is raw thought. The doctor is in.

Melanie is in the next room along, which evidently used to be some kind of a play space for kids to hang out in while their parents were here as visitors or inmates. She's been quiet and subdued ever since they arrived. It's hard to get a word out of her. Parks refused absolutely to free her hands, but at least there are posters on the walls for her to look at, and the remains of a bright red beanbag for her to sit on. Her ankle is tethered to a radiator by a short restraint chain, giving her freedom of movement within a circle about seven feet in diameter.

When the food is ready, Justineau takes some through to her. She's sitting on the beanbag, her legs crossed, her bright blue eyes staring with fixed intensity at a poster on the wall depicting voles, shrews, badgers and other British wildlife. There's a light yellow fuzz on the top of her head, Justineau notices. The first hint of hair starting to grow back. It puts her in mind of a newly hatched chick.

She sits with Melanie while she eats. According to Caldwell, hungries can only metabolise protein, so Justineau has washed some cubes of beef clean of the gravy they came in and put them in a bowl.

Melanie is a little freaked out that the meat is hot. Justineau has to blow on each cube before she feeds it to the girl – through the steel grille of her muzzle – on the end of a fork. Melanie doesn't seem impressed, but she thanks Justineau very politely.

"Long day," Justineau observes.

Melanie nods, but says nothing.

Now that the meal is out of the way, Justineau shows Melanie what else she's found. In a few of the rooms there were clothes in the wardrobe or the drawers. One of them must have been occupied by a girl once – probably a bit younger than Melanie, but of a roughly similar size.

Melanie stares at the clothes that Justineau holds out, without comment. Sombre and withdrawn as she is, it's obvious that they still fascinate her. Pink jeans with a unicorn embroidered on the back pocket. A pastel blue T-shirt emblazoned with the motto BORN TO DANCE. An aviator jacket, also pink, with button-up flaps at the shoulders and lots and lots of pockets. White knickers and rainbow-striped socks. Trainers with jewel-spangled laces.

"Do you like them?" Justineau asks. Melanie hasn't spoken, but her gaze flicks backwards and forwards between the strange offerings, studying them or perhaps comparing them.

"Yes," she says. "I think so. But . . ." She hesitates.

"What?"

"I don't know how to put them on."

Of course. Melanie has never worn clothes with buttons or zip fasteners. And then she's got the chain and the handcuffs to contend with. "I'll help you," Justineau promises. "We can't do anything until morning, but before we get moving again, I'll ask Sergeant Parks to untie you for a few minutes. We'll get you out of that mouldy old sweater and into your glad rags."

"Thank you, Miss Justineau." The little girl's face is solemn. "We'll need the other soldier to be there too."

Justineau is a little thrown by this. "They don't need to watch while you change," she says. "I think we'll make them wait in the next room, don't you?"

Melanie shakes her head. "No."

"No?"

"One to untie me, the other to point the gun at me. That's how many it takes."

37

They talk for a little while longer about the things that have happened, wrapping the violence up in careful, delicate words so it feels less horrible. Melanie finds this interesting in spite of herself – that you can use words to hide things, or not to touch them, or to pretend that they're something different than they are. She wishes she could do that with her big secret.

It seems like Miss Justineau thinks that Melanie must be sad because all those hungries got killed, and is trying to make her feel better about it. Melanie *is* sad for them, a little. But she knows enough, now, to be sure that the hungries weren't really people any more, even before they got killed. They were more like empty houses where people used to live.

Melanie tries to reassure Miss Justineau – tries to show her that she's not so very sad about the hungries. Not even about the man who was singing the song, although it seemed to her that there was no reason at all for Sergeant Parks to shoot him. He was just sitting there on the bed, and it didn't look like he could even get up. All he could do was sing and look at his pictures.

But the lady outside had looked harmless too, until Dr

Caldwell screamed. It seemed like hungries could change very quickly, and you had to be careful all the time when you were close to them.

"I'll keep you safe," Miss Justineau says to Melanie now. "You know that, right? I won't let any of them hurt you."

Melanie nods. She knows that Miss Justineau loves her, and that Miss Justineau will try her best.

But how can anyone save her from herself?

38

"I found this," Gallagher says, when Helen Justineau comes
back to the table. Her own food has gone cold by this time,
and the rest of them have almost finished eating, but he felt
like this was something they all had to be there for. He thinks
Helen Justineau has a sexy smile for an older woman, and he
hopes one day she'll use it on him.

He sets down on the table a bottle that he found in a storage
cupboard while they were searching. It was on the floor, covered
with a pile of mouldering J Cloths, and he wouldn't have seen
it at all except that he kicked it by accident and heard the
clink and slosh as its contents were disturbed.

Glancing down, he saw a little of the label, a teasing hint
of brown and gold where the sheltering mound of sky-blue
cloths had slid away. Metaxa three-star brandy. Full and
unopened. On his own account he recoiled from it and from
the poisoned release it represented. He piled the cloths on top
of it again to hide it from sight.

But he kept going back to it. He'd been fretting all day
about this journey. About going back to Beacon and the narrow,
walled-in world he'd been so happy to leave behind. He'd been

207

feeling like he was walking between the rock and the hard place. Maybe, he thought, desperate situations require desperate remedies.

The others stare at the bottle now, their dangling conversation comprehensively hijacked.

"Shit!" Sergeant Parks mutters, with something of reverence in his tone.

"This is the good stuff, right?" Gallagher asks, feeling himself blush.

"No." Sergeant Parks shakes his head slowly. "No, this isn't so great, all things considered, but it's real. Not tin-bucket rotgut." He turns the bottle over in his hands, examines the seal both by eye and by sniffing at it. "Promises well," he comments. "Normally I wouldn't get out of bed for anything less than French cognac, but fuck it. Get some glasses, Private."

Gallagher does.

He doesn't get that smile from Justineau. She's almost as switched off as Dr Caldwell, like all the piled-up crises of the day have strung out her nerves too far and thin for normal stuff.

But what's even cooler than a smile would have been is that the Sarge pours for him first. "Founder of the feast, Private," he says, when he's filled all their glasses. "You get to give the toast."

Gallagher's already hot face gets a bit hotter. He raises the glass. "One bottle for the four of us, thank fuck there are no more of us!" he recites. One of his father's, heard in a roar that carried through thin floorboards to where a pre-teen Kieran Gallagher lay under a single blanket and listened to the grown-ups carouse.

Then call each other cunts.

Then fight.

The toast is accepted, the glasses chinked together. They drink. The raw, sweet booze sears its way down Gallagher's throat. He tries his best to keep his mouth closed on it, but he explodes into coughing. Not as bad as Dr Caldwell, though. She claps her hand to her mouth and — as the cough rises despite her best efforts — sprays brandy and spit out between her fingers.

They all laugh out loud, including the doctor. In fact, she laughs the longest. The laughing takes up each time the coughing stops, and then gives way to it again. It's like alcohol is magic, and they've all suddenly relaxed with each other even though they've only taken a single mouthful of it. Gallagher remembers enough of those family drinking sessions to be sceptical of that particular miracle.

"Your turn," the Sarge says to Justineau, pouring again.

"For a toast? Shit." Justineau shakes her head, but she lifts the brimming glass. "May we live as long as we want. How about that?" She tips it back, drinks the glass empty in one go. The Sarge matches her. Gallagher and Dr Caldwell sip more cautiously.

"It's may we live as long as we want, and never want as long as we live," Gallagher corrects Justineau. He knows this stuff like holy writ.

Justineau sets the glass back down. "Yeah, well," she says. "No point in asking for the moon and the stars, is there?"

The Sarge refills their glasses, tops up Gallagher's and Caldwell's. "Doc?" he asks. Caldwell shrugs. She's not interested in offering any heart-warming exhortations.

Parks taps each of their glasses with his own, three times round.

"To the wind that blows, the ship that goes and the lass that loves a sailor."

"You know any sailors?" Justineau asks sardonically, after they've both emptied their glasses again and Gallagher has sipped politely. They're already making serious inroads into the bottle.

"Every man's a sailor," Parks says. "Every woman's an ocean."

"Horseshit," Justineau exclaims.

209

The Sarge shrugs. "Maybe, but you'd be amazed how often it works."

More laughter, with a slightly wild edge to it. Gallagher stands. This is no good for him, and he was stupid to try it. He's starting to remember things that he steers clear of most of the time, for good and sufficient reasons. Ghosts are rising in his sight, and he doesn't want to have to look them in the eye. He knows them too well already. "Sarge," he says. "I'll swing round one more time, make sure everything's secure."

"Good for you, son," Parks says.

They don't even look at him as he leaves.

He wanders round the corridors of the first-floor level, finding nothing that they didn't find the time before. He covers his mouth and nose as he walks past the room with the dead hungry in it; the stink is really bad.

But it's worse when he gets to the top of the staircase that the Sarge blew out. It's like the breath of hell, right there. There's no sound, no movement. Gallagher stands at the brink and peers down into impenetrable shadow. Eventually he gets up the courage to take the torch from his belt, aim it straight down and click it on.

In the perfect circle of the torchlight, he sees six or seven hungries crammed shoulder to shoulder. The light makes them squirm and surge, but they're too tightly packed to move very far.

Gallagher plays the torch's beam forward and back. The whole length of the hall, they're packed in like sardines. The hungries they were running from a few hours ago, and their friends, and their friends' friends. They move peristaltically as the light passes over them. Their jaws open and close.

The sound of gunshots brought them, from wherever they happened to be. Something loud means something living. Now they're here, and they'll stay here until they score a meal or until the next big thing winds up their fungus-fucked clockwork and sets them moving.

210

Gallagher retreats, sickened and scared. He's lost his enthusiasm for being nightwatchman.

He goes back to the day room. Parks and Justineau are still working their way through the bottle, while Dr Caldwell is stretched out asleep across three chairs.

He thinks maybe he should check in on the hungry kid. Should at least make sure the tether tying her to the radiator is still secure.

He goes through to the room with the toys in it. The kid is sitting on the beanbag, really still and quiet, head down and staring at the floor. Gallagher stifles a shiver; she looks, for a moment, exactly like the monsters filling the downstairs hall.

He props the door open with a chair. He's buggered if he's going to be alone with this thing in the near dark. He walks across to her, making a fair amount of noise so she knows he's coming. She looks up, and it's a relief to him when she does. It's not that rangefinder thing that the hungries do, when they look past you on both sides before zeroing in on you. It's more like what a human being would do.

"What've you got there?" Gallagher asks her. The floor is littered with books, so presumably that's what she was looking at. With her hands cuffed behind her back, looking is all she can do. He picks up the nearest book. *The Water-Babies*, by Charles Kingsley. It looks really old, with a faded dust jacket on the cover, torn at one corner. The picture shows a bunch of cute little fairies rising into the air over the rooftops of a city. London, maybe, but Gallagher has never seen London and doesn't have any way of knowing.

The hungry kid is watching him and not saying a word. It's not an unfriendly look, but it's really intent. Like she doesn't know what he's there for and she's ready for the surprise not to be a nice one.

All she knows of him is that he's one of the people who used to tie her up in that chair all the time, and wheel her in and out of the classroom. Gallagher can't remember now if

211

he's ever spoken to her before this. Consequently, the words come out a little skewed, a little self-conscious. He's not even all that sure why he says it.

"You want me to read this to you?"

A moment's silence. A moment more of that big-eyed stare.

"No," the kid says.

"Oh." That's his entire conversational strategy, shot to shit. He doesn't have a Plan B. He heads for the door again, and the lighted room beyond. He's swung the chair out of the way and he's about to close the door behind him when she blurts it out.

"Can you look on the shelves?"

He turns and steps back inside, replacing the chair. "What?"

There's a long silence. Like she's sorry she spoke, and she's not sure she wants to say it again. He waits her out.

"Can you look on the shelves? Miss Justineau gave me a book, but I had to leave it behind. If the same book is here . . ."

"Yeah?"

"Then . . . you could read me that."

Gallagher hadn't noticed the bookcase before. He follows the girl's gaze now, sees it against the wall next to the door. "Okay," he says. "What was the book called?"

"*Tales the Muses Told.*" There's a quickening of excitement in the girl's voice. "By Roger Lancelyn Green. It's Greek myths."

Gallagher goes over to the bookcase, clicks on his torch and plays it over the shelves. Most of these are picture books for little kids, with stapled spines rather than square ones, so he has to pull them out to see what they're called. There are a few real books, though, and he works his way through them painstakingly.

No Greek myths.

"Sorry," he says. "It's not here. You don't want to try something new?"

"No."

"There's Postman Pat here. And his black and white cat." He holds up a book to show her. The hungry kid gives it a cold stare, then looks away.

Gallagher rejoins her, pulls up a chair at what he considers a safe distance. "My name's Kieran," he tells her. This elicits no response at all. "Is there one story in particular that's your favourite?"

But she doesn't want to talk to him, and he can understand that. Why the hell would she?

"I'm gonna read this one," he says. He holds up a book called *I Wish I Could Show You*. It's got the same kind of pictures in it as *The Cat in the Hat*, which is why he chose it. He used to love that story about the cat and the fish and the kids and the two Things called 1 and 2. He liked to imagine his own house getting trashed like that, and then getting put right again just a second before his dad walked in. For Gallagher, aged about seven, that was a huge, illicit thrill.

"I'm gonna sit here and read this one," he tells the girl again.

She shrugs like that's his business, not hers.

Gallagher opens the book. The pages are damp, so they stick to each other a little, but he's able to pull them apart without tearing them.

"When I was out walking one day in the street," he recites, "I met a young man with red boots on his feet. His belt had a buckle, his hat had a feather. His shirt was of silk and his pants were of leather, and he could not stand still for two seconds together."

The kid pretends not to listen, but Gallagher isn't taken in. It's pretty obvious that she's tilting her head so she can see the pictures.

39

Parks shares out some more of the brandy. It's going fast. Justineau drinks, although she's just reached the stage where she knows it's a bad idea. She'll wake up feeling like shit.

She fans her face, which is uncomfortably hot. Booze always does this to her, even in medicinal amounts. "Jesus," she says. "I've got to get some air."

But there isn't much air to be had. The window is safety-locked and opens all of five inches. "We could go up to the roof," Parks suggests. "There's a fire door at the end of the corridor that leads up there."

"Anything to say the roof is safe?" Justineau asks, and the sergeant nods. Yeah, of course, he would have checked it. Love him or hate him, he's the kind of man who's built his identity around the blessed sacrament of getting the job done. She saw that out on the green, when he saved all their lives by reacting pretty nearly as fast as the hungries did.

"Okay," she says. "Let's see what the roof is like."

And the roof is just fine. About ten degrees cooler than the day room, with a good, stiff wind blowing in their faces. Well, good is maybe overstating it, because the wind smells of rot

214

– like there's a big mountain of spoiled meat right next to them, invisible in the dark, and they're inhaling its taint. Justineau clamps her glass over the lower half of her face like an oxygen mask and breathes brandy breath instead.

"Any idea what that is?" she asks Parks, her voice muffled and distorted by the glass.

"Nope, but it's stronger over here," Parks says, "so I suggest we go over there."

He leads the way to the south-east corner of the building. They're facing London and distant Beacon – the home that flung them out and is now reeling them back in. Justineau lets absence work its usual magic, even though she knows damn well that Beacon is a shit-hole. A big refugee camp governed by real terror and artificially pumped-up optimism – like the bastard child of Butlins and Colditz. It was already well on the way to totalitarianism when she lucked her way out of there, and she's not looking forward to finding out what it's become in the three years that have passed since.

But where else is there?

"The Doc's a real character, isn't she?" Parks muses, leaning over the parapet wall and staring out into the darkness. Moonlight paints the town in woodcut black and white like a picture from a book. Black predominates, turning the streets into unfathomable riverbeds of rushing air.

"That's one word for what she is," Justineau says.

Parks laughs, jokingly raises the glass – like they're toasting their shared opinion of Caroline Caldwell. "Truth is," he says, "in a way I'm glad the whole thing is over. The base, I mean, and the mission. Not glad we're on the run, obviously, and I'm praying we're not the only ones who got away. But I'm glad I don't have to do that any more."

"Do what?"

Parks makes a gesture. In the near dark, Justineau can't see what gesture it is. "Keep a lid on the madhouse. Keep the whole place ticking over, month after month, on string and good intentions. Christ, it's amazing we lasted as long as we did. Not enough men, not enough supplies, no fucking communications, no proper chain of command . . ."

He seems to stop very suddenly, which makes Justineau go back over his words to figure out which ones he wishes he hadn't said. "When did communications stop?" she asks him.

He doesn't answer. So she asks again.

"Last message from Beacon was about five months back," Parks admits. "Normal signalling wavelengths have been empty ever since."

"Shit!" Justineau is deeply shaken. "So we don't even know if . . . Shit!"

"Most likely it just means they relocated the tower," Parks says. "Wouldn't even have to be far. The goosed-together crap we're using for radios, they don't work unless they're pointed right at the signal source. It's like trying to shoot a basketball into a hoop across sixty bloody miles."

They fall silent, contemplating this. The night seems wider now, and colder.

"My God," Justineau says at last. "We might be the last. The four of us."

"We're not the last."

"You don't know that."

"Yeah, I do. The junkers are doing fine."

"The junkers . . ." Justineau's tone is sour. She's heard stories, and now she's seen them for herself. Survivalists who've forgotten how to do anything else besides survive. Parasites and scavengers almost as inhuman in their own way as *Ophiocordyceps*. They don't build, or preserve. They just stay alive. And their ruthlessly patriarchal structures reduce women to pack animals or breeding stock.

If that's humanity's last, best hope, then despair might actually be preferable.

"There've been dark ages before," Parks says, reading her a lot better than she likes. "Things fall down, and people build

216

them up again. There's probably never been a time when life was just . . . steady state. There's always some crisis.

"And then there's the rest of the world, you know? Beacon was in touch with survivor communities in France, Spain, America, all kinds of places. The cities were hit worst – any place where there was a whole bunch of people crammed in together – and a lot of infrastructure fell with the cities. In less developed areas, the contagion didn't spread so fast. There could be some places it never even reached at all."

Parks fills her glass.

"I wanted to ask you something," he says.

"Go on."

"Yesterday, you said you were ready to take the kid and split up from the rest of us."

"So?"

"Did you mean it, by the way? That's not the question, but would you really have cut loose and tried to make it back to Beacon on your own?"

"I meant it when I said it."

"Yeah." He takes a sip of his brandy. "Thought so. Anyway, you called me something, just before you shoved your gun in Gallagher's face. It didn't make sense to me at the time. You said we were hard-wired soldier boys. What does hard-wired mean?"

Justineau is embarrassed. "It's sort of an insult," she says.

"Yeah, well I'd have been surprised if it was a kiss on the cheek. I was just curious. Does it mean like we're really ruthless or something?"

"No. It's a term from psychology. It describes a behaviour that you're born with and can't change. Or that's programmed into you so you don't even think about it. It's just automatic."

Parks laughs. "Like the hungries," he suggests.

Justineau is a little abashed, but she takes it on the chin. "Yes," she admits. "Like the hungries."

"You give good trash talk," Parks compliments her. "Seriously. That's outstanding." He tops up her glass again.

217

And puts his arm around her shoulder.

Justineau pulls away quickly. "What the hell is this?" she demands.

"I thought you were cold," Parks says, sounding surprised. "You were shivering. Sorry. I didn't mean anything by it."

For a long time she just stands there staring at him, in dead silence.

Then she speaks. And there's only one thing she can think of to say.

Spits it out at him, like she wants to spit out, retrospectively, the booze, the memory, the last three years of her life.

"You ever kill a kid?"

40

The question hits Parks squarely between the eyes.

He was feeling pretty mellow up to this point. The brandy has soaked into him, dulling the pain from the many tiny shrapnel wounds he took in his legs and lower back when the stairs went to pieces. And here he thought the two of them were getting along, but no. The teacher's got him clearly defined in her personal encyclopaedia. For *Parks, Sergeant* see *bastard, bloodthirsty*. He's got a range of answers for this one, most of which would involve reminding her how she's been able to stay off the hungries' lunch menu for the last three years. Where her computer came from, and most of the other handy little gadgets that let her do her job. Why Beacon is still standing − if it is − for them to come home to.

But skip it. This isn't going where he was hoping it would, and there's nothing to be gained by telling this very attractive woman that she's both a hypocrite and a whole lot stupider than he thought. It will only make the journey that bit harder.

So he writes it off and heads for the fire door. "I'll leave you to enjoy the view," he says over his shoulder.

"I mean, before the Breakdown," Justineau says to his back.

"It's a straight question, Parks."

Which makes him stop, and turn around again. "What the hell do you think I am?" he asks her.

"I don't know what you are. Answer the question. Did you?"

He doesn't need to think about the answer. He knows where his lines are. They're not built to move, the way some people's are.

"No. I've shot hungries as young as five or six. You don't have much choice when they're trying to eat you alive. But I never killed a kid who you could really say was still alive."

"Well, I did."

Now it's her turn to turn away. She tells him the story without ever making eye contact with him, even though the rampart of a nearby chimney stack throws their faces into shadow and makes eye contact conditional in any case. In the confessional, you never see the priest's face. But Parks is willing to bet that no priest ever had a face like his.

"I was driving home. After a party. I'd been drinking, but not that much. And I was tired. I was working on a paper, and I'd had a couple of weeks of early mornings and late nights, trying to bring it in. None of this matters. It's just . . . you know, you try to make sense of it, afterwards. You look for reasons why it happened."

The words come out of Helen Justineau in a flat monotone. Parks thinks of Gallagher's written report, with its *proceeding to*s and its *thereupon*s. But Justineau's bowed head and the tightness of her grip on the parapet wall add their own commentary.

"I was driving along this road. In Hertfordshire, between South Mimms and Potters Bar. A few houses, every now and then, but mostly miles of hedges, then a pub, then some more hedges. I wasn't expecting . . . I mean, it was late. Way after midnight. I didn't think anyone at all would be out, still less . . .

"Someone ran into the road in front of me. He came through a gap in one of the hedges, I think. There wasn't anywhere else he could have come from. He was just there, suddenly, and I hit the brakes but I was already right on top of him. It didn't make a bit of difference. I must have been going over fifty when I hit him, and he just . . . he bounced off the car like a ball.

"I stopped, a long way up the road. A hundred yards or so. I got out, and came running back. I was hoping, obviously . . . but he was dead, no question. A boy. About eight or nine years old, maybe. I'd killed a child. Broken him in pieces, inside his skin, so his arms and legs didn't even bend the right way.

"I think I stayed there a long time. I was shaking, and crying, and I couldn't . . . I couldn't get up. It felt like a long time. I wanted to run away, and I couldn't even move."

She looks at the sergeant, now, but the darkness hides her expression almost completely. Only the twisted line of her mouth shows. It reminds him, right then, of the line of his scar.

"But then I did," she says. "I did move. I got up, and I drove away. Locked my car in the garage and went to bed. I even slept, Parks. Can you believe that?

"I never did make up my mind what to do about it. If I confessed, I'd most likely go to jail, and my career would be over. And it wouldn't bring him back, so what would be the point? Of course, I knew damn well what the point was, and I picked up that phone about six or seven times in the next couple of days, but I never dialled. And then the world ended, so I didn't have to. I got away with it. Got away clean."

Parks waits a long while, until he's absolutely certain that Justineau's monologue is finished. The truth is, for most of the time he's been trying to figure out what it is exactly that she's trying to tell him. Maybe he was right the first time about where they were heading, and Justineau airing her ancient laundry is just a sort of palate-cleanser before they have sex. Probably not, but you never know. In any case, the countermove to a confession is an absolution, unless you

221

think the sin is unforgivable. Parks doesn't.

"It was an accident," he tells her, pointing out the obvious. "And probably you would have ended up doing the right thing. You don't strike me as the sort of person who just lets shit slide." He means that, as far as it goes. One of the things he likes about Justineau is her seriousness. He frigging flat-out hates frivolous, thoughtless people who dance across the surface of the world without looking down.

"Yeah, but you don't get it," Justineau says. "Why do you think I'm telling you all this?"

"I don't know," Parks admits. "Why are you telling me?"

Justineau steps away from the parapet wall and squares off against him – range, zero metres. It could be erotic, but somehow it's not.

"I killed that boy, Parks. If you turn my life into an equation, the number that comes out is minus one. That's my lifetime score, you understand me? And you . . . you and Caldwell, and Private Ginger fucking Rogers . . . my God, whether it means anything or not, I will die my own self before I let you take me down to minus two."

She says the last words right into his face. Sprays him with little flecks of spit. This close up, dark as it is, he can see her eyes. There's something mad in them. Something deeply afraid, but it's damn well not afraid of him.

She leaves him with the bottle. It's not what he was hoping for, but it's a pretty good consolation prize.

41

Caroline Caldwell waits until the sergeant and Justineau leave the room. Then she gets up quickly and goes through into the kitchen.

She saw the Tupperware boxes earlier, stacked in the furthest cupboard along – ranged in order of size, so they formed a steep-sided pyramid. Nobody else spared them a second glance, because the boxes were empty. But Caldwell noted them with a small surge of pleasure. Every so often, even now, the universe gives you exactly what you need.

She takes six boxes of the smallest size and six teaspoons, dropping them one by one into the pockets of her lab coat. She brings a torch, too, but doesn't turn it on until she reaches her destination and closes the door.

She breathes in shallow sips. The smell of the human remains, and of years of enclosed decay, freights the air so heavily it's almost a physical presence.

With the spoons, Caldwell takes a range of samples from the hungry that was killed by Sergeant Parks. She's only interested in brain tissue, but multiple samples mean more chance of getting at least one that's not too badly contaminated by

223

flora and fauna from skin, clothes or ambient air.

After sealing each container carefully, she puts them back into her pockets. She discards the soiled spoons, for which she has no further use.

She thinks as she works: I should have done this years ago. Men like the sergeant have their uses, and she knows she could never have collected the test subjects by herself. But if she'd been there with the trappers as part of the team, she wouldn't have had to rely on their inadequate observations and unreliable memories.

So she wouldn't have wasted so much time exploring blind alleys.

She would have known, for example, that although most hungries have only the two states – the rest state and the hunting state – some have a third state that corresponds to a degraded version of normal consciousness. They can interact with the world around them, fitfully and partially, in ways that echo their behaviour before they were infected.

The woman with the baby carriage. The singing man, with his wallet full of photos. These are trivial examples, but they represent something momentous. Caldwell is very close, she knows, to an unprecedented breakthrough. She can't do anything with these samples until she gets back to Beacon and has access to a microscope, but an idea is forming in her mind as to what it is she should be looking for. What shape her research will take, once she's back in a lab and has everything she needs.

Including, of course, test subject number one.

Melanie.

42

Justineau is roused from sleep by a hand shaking her shoulder. She panics momentarily, thinking that she's being attacked, but it's Parks she's struggling against, Parks' grip that she's trying to slap away. And it's not just her. He's waking everyone, telling them to get their arses over to the window. The sun has come up on a pretty ugly and depressing state of affairs, and they need to see it.

The hungries who chased them the day before have not dispersed. They stand two or three deep along the length of the fence around Wainwright House, most of them having stopped dead when they hit that barrier.

The downstairs hall is full of those who didn't stop – who chased their human quarry all the way inside. From the stump of the top stair, you can stand and look down on a crowd of gaunt, gaping monsters, standing shoulder to shoulder like the audience for some sell-out event.

Which would be breakfast.

Tense and scared, the four of them canvass possibilities. They can't shoot their way out, obviously. They could waste all their ammunition and not even make a dent in those numbers.

Besides, loud noise was the trigger that got them into this mess in the first place; producing more of it runs the risk of attracting more monsters from even further afield.

Justineau wonders if maybe they can use that.

"If you were to throw some hand grenades," she suggests to Parks, "say, from the top of the roof. The hungries will target on the sound, right? We could draw them off, and then when the fence is clear we just run in the opposite direction."

Parks spreads his empty hands. "No grenades," he says. "I just had the ones on my belt, and I used them all when I pulled up the drawbridge last night."

Gallagher opens his mouth, shuts it, tries again. "Could make some Molotovs?" he suggests. He nods toward the kitchen. "There's bottles of cooking oil in there."

"I don't believe breaking bottles would make a particularly loud noise," Dr Caldwell says acerbically.

"It might be loud enough," Parks muses, but he doesn't sound convinced. "Even if it wasn't, we could set fire to the fuckers and clear a bit of space for ourselves that way."

"Not the ones downstairs in the hallway," Caldwell counters. "I don't relish the prospect of being trapped in a burning building."

"And there'd be smoke," Justineau says. "Probably a lot of it. If the junkers are still looking for us, we'd be putting up a big sign telling them where we are."

"Just empty bottles, then?" Gallagher says. "No oil. We try to draw them away with the sound."

Parks looks out of the window. He doesn't even need to say it. The distance from the roof and windows of the house to the pavement outside the fence is about thirty yards. You could throw a bottle that far, but you'd need to put your shoulder into it, and you'd want luck and the wind to both be with you. If the thrown bottles fall short, they'll just entice the hungries who stopped at the gates to come on inside.

226

Same thing would have gone for grenades too, of course. They probably would have done more harm than good.

They go back and forth, but nobody can suggest an easy or obvious way out. They've let themselves get cornered, by predators who won't lose interest or wander away. Waiting this out isn't an option, and all the other options look bad.

Justineau goes to check on Melanie. The girl is already on her feet, looking out of the window, but she turns at the sound of footsteps. Probably she's heard their conversation in the next room. Justineau tries to reassure her. "We'll think of something," she says. "There's a way out of this."

Melanie nods calmly.

"I know," she says.

Parks doesn't like the idea, which doesn't surprise Justineau at all. And Caldwell likes it even less.

Only Gallagher seems to approve, and he doesn't do more than nod – seeming reluctant to say anything that directly contradicts his sergeant.

They're sitting in the day room, on four chairs that they've pulled up into a small circle. It provides the illusion that they're actually talking to each other, although Caldwell is off in her own world, Gallagher won't speak until he's spoken to, and Parks listens to nobody but himself.

"I don't like the idea of letting her off the leash," he says, for about the third time.

"Why the hell not?" Justineau demands. "You were happy enough to cut her loose two days ago. The leash and the handcuffs were so she could stay with us. Your idea of a compromise. So from your point of view, there's nothing to lose here. Nothing at all. If she does what she says she'll do, we're out of this mess. If she runs away, we're no worse off than we are now."

Caldwell ignores this speech and makes her appeal directly to the sergeant. "Melanie belongs to me," she reminds him.

"To my programme. If we lose her, it will be your responsibility."

It's the wrong thing to say. Parks doesn't seem to like being threatened. "I spent four years servicing your programme, Doc," he reminds her. "Today is my day off."

Caldwell starts to say something else, but Parks talks over her – to Justineau. "If we let her go, why would she come back?"

"I wish I could answer that," Justineau says. "Frankly, it's a complete mystery to me. But she says she will, and I believe her. Maybe because we're all she knows."

Maybe because she's got a crush on me, and all love is as blind as it needs to be.

"I want to talk to her," Parks says. "Bring her in."

On the leash still, with her hands behind her back and the muzzle over her mouth, she faces Parks like the chieftain of a savage tribe, on her dignity, and Justineau is suddenly aware of the changes in her. She's out in the world now, her education accelerating from a standing start to some dangerous, unguessable velocity. She thinks of an old painting. *And When Did You Last See Your Father?* Because Melanie's stance is exactly the same as the way the kid stands in that picture. For Melanie, though, that would be a completely meaningless question.

"You think you can do this?" Parks asks her instead. "What you said to Miss Justineau. You think you're up to it?"

"Yes," Melanie says.

"It means I'd have to trust you. Set you free, right here in the room with us." He's been holding something in his right hand, shaking it as though it's a dice he was going to throw. He shows it to her now: the key to her handcuffs.

"I don't think it means that, Sergeant Parks," Melanie says.

"No?"

"No. You have to set me free, but you don't have to trust me. You should put the chemical stuff all over your skin first, to make really sure I don't smell you. And you should make

228

Kieran unlock the handcuffs while you aim your gun at me. And you don't have to take the cage thing off my mouth. I just need to be able to use my hands."

Parks stares at her for a moment, like she's something written in a language he doesn't speak.

"Got it all figured out," he acknowledges.

"Yes."

He leans forward to look her in the eye. "And you're not scared?"

Melanie hesitates. "Of what?" she asks him. Justineau is amazed at that momentary pause. Yes or no would be equally easy to say, whether they were true or not. The pause means that Melanie is scrupulous, is weighing her words. It means she's trying to be honest with them.

As if they've done a single thing, ever, to deserve that.

"Of the hungries," Parks says, like it's obvious.

Melanie shakes her head.

"How come?"

"They won't hurt me."

"No? Why not?"

"Enough," Justineau snaps, but Melanie answers anyway. Slowly. Ponderously. As though the words are stones she's using to build a wall.

"They don't bite each other."

"And?"

"I'm the same as them. Almost. Close enough so they don't get hungry when they smell me."

Parks nods slowly. This is where the catechism has been leading all this time. He wants to know how much Melanie has already guessed. Where her head is. He's working his way through the logistics.

"The same as them, or almost the same? Which is it?"

Melanie's face is unreadable, but some powerful emotion flits across it, doesn't settle. "I'm different because I don't want to eat anyone."

229

"No? Then what was that red stuff all over you when you jumped on board the Humvee, day before yesterday? Looked like blood to me."

"Sometimes I *need* to eat people. I never *want* to."

"That's all you've got, kid? Shit happens?"

Another pause. Longer, this time. "It hasn't happened to you."

"Very true," Parks admits. "Still feels like we're splitting hairs, though. You're offering to help us against those things down there, when it seems to me that you'd want to be down there with them, looking up at us, waiting for the dinner bell to ring. So I guess that's what I'm asking you. Why would you come back, and why would I believe you'd come back?"

For the first time, Melanie lets her impatience show. "I'd come back because I want to. Because I'm with you, not with them. And there isn't any way to be with them, even if I wanted to. They're . . ." Whatever concept she's reaching for, it eludes her for a moment. "They're *not* with each other. Not ever."

Nobody answers her, but Parks looks happy with this. Like she got the secret password. She's in the club. The hopelessly-outnumbered-and-surrounded-by-monsters club.

"I'm with you," Melanie says again. And then, as if it needed saying, "Not you, really. I'm with Miss Justineau."

Surprisingly, Parks seems satisfied with this too. He stands, with a decisive air. "I get that," he says. "Okay, kid. We're going to trust you to get this job done. Let's go."

Melanie stays where she is.

"What?" Parks demands. "Something else you need?"

"Yes," Melanie tells him. "I want to wear my new clothes, please."

43

They take her to the top of the stairs. To where the top of the stairs was, before Sergeant Parks exploded them. Melanie peers over the edge.

There are lots and lots of hungries down there. Maybe a hundred or more, all standing together in the hallway. They look up as the two men and two women come into view, their heads all moving together like flowers following the sun.

Sergeant Parks doesn't get his gun out, but he makes Melanie turn away as he unlocks the cuffs, and he tells her not to move. She feels them fall away, and she wants to wiggle her fingers to make sure they still work okay, but she doesn't.

Sergeant Parks unties the leash from around her neck, too, and she turns to Miss J, who's ready with the little bundle of clothes.

It's unpleasant to have the sweater – Miss Justineau's sweater, which she's worn all this time – lifted off over her head. To be momentarily naked again. It's not the scrutiny of the adults she dislikes, it's the feel of air directly on her body. The sensation of being so exposed.

But as Miss J dresses her in her new finery, that feeling goes away. She likes the jeans and the T-shirt very much – and the jacket, which is a little like Sergeant Parks' jacket. It's only the trainers that feel strange. She's never worn shoes before, and the loss of the stream of information her feet receive from the ground is disturbing. It's possible that she and the trainers might not be a long-term thing. But they're so beautiful!

"Done?" Parks says.

"You look great, Melanie," Miss Justineau tells her.

She nods thanks, and agreement. She knows she does.

But they're not done. Not yet. Miss Justineau takes something out of her pocket and holds it out for Melanie to take. It's a tiny thing, made out of grey plastic. Rectangular, with a single round button on it. Around the edge of the button, in red letters are the words SAFE and GUARD. And then underneath, DANGER 150 DECIBELS.

"When you get to the part where you have to make a big noise," Miss Justineau tells her, "this might help."

"What is it?" Melanie asks. She's trying to look casual and calm, like getting a present from Miss Justineau is no big deal.

"It's a personal alarm. From a long time ago. People used to carry them in case they got attacked."

"By hungries?"

"No, by other people. It makes a noise like the end-of-the-day klaxon back at the base, but much, much louder – loud enough to make people panic, so they want to run away. But hungries wouldn't run away, they'd run towards the sound. It might not work at all, after all this time, but you never know."

Melanie hesitates. "You should keep it," she says. "In case you get attacked."

Miss Justineau closes Melanie's fingers over the object, which is still warm from being in her pocket. It's like a little piece of Miss Justineau that she can take out into the world with her. The weight of her new knowledge is still pressing her down, but her heart swells with joy as she puts the alarm into the pocket of her brand-new unicorn jeans.

"Done," she confirms to Sergeant Parks. Sergeant's face says *about time*. He ties the leash up again around Melanie's waist with a different knot.

"Once you're down on the ground," he tells her, "you pull on this end here, and the rope will come away."

"Okay," she says.

"I'm not taking your muzzle off," Sergeant says. "But with your hands free, you could easily release the strap yourself and get it off. You're a smart kid, and I bet you thought of that already."

Melanie shrugs. Of course she has, and there doesn't seem to be any point in trying to explain to him all over again why she won't do that.

"Just so you know," Sergeant Parks says, "if you want to stay with us, you're going to need to keep the muzzle on. Or put it back on when you're done. I don't have any more of them, and as far as I'm concerned, your teeth are a loaded gun. So keep that thing safe, because that's what gets you back in the door. Okay?"

"Okay."

"Okay then. Gallagher, give me a hand here."

The two men move into position at the top of the stairs and get ready to pay out the rope, but at the last moment Miss Justineau kneels beside Melanie again and holds out her arms.

Melanie steps into the embrace, shivers deliciously as Miss Justineau's arms close around her.

But she pulls away after no more than a moment. There's just a tiny trace of the human smell, the Miss Justineau smell, underneath the bitterness of the chemicals. Enough to turn the pure pleasure of their proximity into something else entirely; something that threatens to escalate out of her control. "Not safe," she mutters urgently. "Not safe."

"Your e-blockers," Sergeant Parks translates unnecessarily. "You need another layer."

"I'm sorry," Miss Justineau murmurs – not to Sergeant Parks, but to Melanie.

Melanie nods. She was scared for a moment there, but it's okay. It was a very faint scent, and now that it's gone, the hungry feeling is back under her control.

Sergeant Parks tells her to sit down on the top step, and then to push herself away. He and Kieran lower her down into the waiting crowd of hungries.

Who don't react at all. Some of them follow the movement as she comes down, but Sergeant Parks makes sure that her descent is really slow and gradual, so it doesn't get the hungries too excited. Their gaze sweeps over her without lingering. Or else they stare right through her, not registering her presence at all.

As soon as her feet are on the ground, she loosens the rope with a tug. Sergeant Parks draws it up again, just as slowly and gradually as he let it down.

Melanie glances up. Sees Sergeant Parks and Miss Justineau peering down at her. Miss Justineau waves; a slow opening and closing of her hand. Melanie waves back.

She threads her way carefully through the hungries, un-noticed, unmolested.

But she was lying when she said she wasn't afraid. To be right here in the middle of them – to look up at their bowed heads and half-open mouths, their off-white eyes – is very frightening indeed. Yesterday she thought that the hungries were like houses that people used to live in. Now she thinks that every one of those houses is haunted. She's not just surrounded by the hungries. She's surrounded by the ghosts of the men and women they used to be. She has to fight a sudden urge to break into a run, to get out of here into the open air as quickly as she can.

She makes it to the door, pushing between the packed-together bodies. But the doorway itself is completely impassable. Too many hungries have squeezed themselves into the narrow

234

space between the doorposts, and she's not strong enough to break up that logjam. But the floor-to-ceiling windows to either side of the door have been shattered, every last sliver of glass forced out of their frames by the hungries charging through. Some of those closest to Melanie bear the slash marks from that difficult passage on their arms and bodies. From the new wounds a sluggish brown liquid has oozed. It doesn't look much like blood.

Melanie pushes her way out through the left-hand window. More hungries are standing out on the driveway, but they're not so tightly clustered and it's easier for her to make her way through.

To the gates, and then out on to the street.

She walks past more hungries. They don't turn as she goes by or seem to notice her at all. She crosses to the overgrown green and walks in among the trees and tall grass.

Melanie likes it here. If she were free, if she had lots of time and nothing that she needed to do, she'd like to stay here for a long time and pretend that she's in the Amazon rainforest, which she knows about from a lesson with Miss Mailer, a long time ago, and from the picture on the wall of her cell.

But she's not free, and time is pressing. If she takes too long, Miss Justineau might think she's run away and left her, and she'd rather die than let Miss Justineau think that even for a second.

She's hoping for a rat like the one that scared Dr Caldwell, but there are no rats. No birds, even, but in any case a bird probably wouldn't do for what she needs.

So she looks further afield, walking up and down the streets, through the open doors of houses, through the jumbled, desecrated remains of vanished lives, trying not to be distracted by the ornaments, the photos, the hundreds and thousands of inscrutable objects.

In a room silted up a foot deep with old brown leaves, she startles a fox. It leaps for a broken window, but Melanie is on it so quickly that she catches it in mid-air. She's thrilled at her own speed.

And at her strength. Though the fox is as big as she is, when it squirms and thrashes in her arms she just tightens her grip, closing down its range of movement, until it stills, quivering, whining, and lets her take it where she wants.

Back up the street to the green. Across the green to the fence where the hungries are clustered, every face turned away from her, every body still.

Melanie screams. It's the loudest sound she can make. Not as loud as Miss Justineau's personal alarm would be, but both her hands are full of fox and she doesn't want to let it go until all the hungries are looking at her.

When the heads turn, she opens her arms. The fox is away like an arrow flying out of Ulysses' bow.

Primed by the sound, awake and alert for prey, the hungries obey their programming. They start into violent motion, run after the fox as though they're joined to it by taut strings. Melanie backs out of the way quickly, into a doorway, as the first wave goes by her.

There are so many of them, crowded in so tightly together, that some of them get knocked down and trampled on. Melanie sees them trying again and again to get up, only to be trodden underfoot each time. It's almost funny, but the grey-brown froth that's forced out of their mouths, like wine from grapes, makes it sort of sad and horrible too. When the rest of the horde have run on down the road, almost out of sight, some of these fallen struggle to their feet and limp and crawl after them. Others stay where they fell, twitching and scrabbling but too badly broken to get up off the ground.

Melanie skirts around them carefully. She feels bad for them. She wishes that there was something she could do to help them, but there isn't anything. She goes back in through the gates and walks up to the house. She enters the hall, which is completely deserted now, and calls up to Sergeant Parks, who

236

is exactly where he was when she left. "It worked. They've gone now."

"Stay there," Sergeant Parks calls down. "We'll join you."

And then, after looking at her hard for a few moments longer:

"Good job, kid."

44

Getting everyone down to street level is easy enough, with the ropes. Sergeant Parks decides the order: Gallagher first, so there's someone on the ground who knows how to use a gun, then Helen Justineau, then Dr Caldwell, with himself bringing up the rear. Dr Caldwell is the only one who presents any kind of a problem, since her bandaged hands won't allow her to grip the rope. Parks makes a running knot, which he ties around her waist, and lowers her down.

They could retrace their steps, but it's easier to keep going through the town. There are any number of places where they can pick up the A1 again, and they'll actually get out from among the buildings more quickly if they steer east of south, past a region of desolate industrial estates. Not many people ever lived out here, and after the Breakdown the pickings were thin for uninfected survivors, whose needs ran more to food than to heavy plant, so they don't see many hungries at all. Of course, they're also following roughly the same line that the fox took, at least to start with. That irresistible moving target cleared the way for them very effectively.

So that's twice now that the hungry kid has saved their

bacon. If she makes the hat-trick, maybe Parks will even start to relax a little around her. Hasn't happened yet though.

They discuss logistics as they walk, in low, measured voices that won't carry too far. Parks feels they should stick to Plan A, despite the clusterfuck they just experienced.

His reasons are the same as they were. The direct route through London will save them at least two days' travel, and they still need shelter when they stop and sleep.

"Even given that the shelter can turn into a trap?" Dr Caldwell asks tartly.

"Well, that's an issue," Parks allows. "But on the other hand, if we'd been out in the open when those hungries came for us last night, we wouldn't have lasted ten fucking heartbeats. Just a thought."

Caldwell doesn't attempt a comeback, so he doesn't have to remind her that it was her striking up an acquaintance with a female hungry out on the street that got them into trouble in the first place. And nobody else seems inclined to argue. They continue on their way, the conversation dying out into wary silence.

Over the course of the morning, their line stretches out unacceptably. Gallagher takes point, as Parks ordered him to do. Helen Justineau sticks with the kid, who manages a reasonable pace despite her shorter legs, but keeps being distracted and slowed by the things they pass. Dr Caldwell is slowest of all, the gap between her and the others gradually but steadily increasing. She quickens her stride whenever Parks asks her to, but always slows again after a minute or two. That desperate fatigue, so early in the day, worries him.

They're moving now through a burn shadow, another artefact of the Breakdown. Before the government fell apart entirely, it passed a whole series of badly thought-out emergency orders, one of which involved chemical incendiaries sprayed from helicopter gunships to create cauterised zones that were guaranteed free from hungries. Uninfected civilians were warned in advance by sirens and looped messages, but a lot of them died anyway because they weren't free to move when the choppers flew in.

The hungries, though, they ran ahead of the flame-throwers like roaches when the light goes on. All the incendiaries could do was to move them on a few miles in one direction or another, and in some cases to destroy infrastructure that might have saved a lot of lives. Luton Airport, for instance. That got torched with about forty planes still on the ground, so when the next memo came round – about evacuating the uninfected to the Channel Islands using commercial carrier fleets – all the army could do was shrug its collective shoulders and say, "Yeah, we wish."

The buildings on this part of their route are foreshortened stumps, not so much burned down as rendered into tallow. The monstrous heat of the incendiaries melted not just metal but brick and stone. The ground they're walking on carries a thin black crust of grease and charcoal, the residue of organic materials that burned and sublimed, took to the air and settled again wherever the hot winds of combustion took them.

The air has a sour, acid tang to it. After ten minutes or so, your breath is rasping in your throat and there's an itchy feeling in your chest that you can't scratch because it's inside you.

It's more than twenty years on and still nothing grows here, not even the hardiest and most bad-ass of weeds. Nature's way of saying she's not stupid enough to be caught like that twice over.

Parks hears the kid asking Justineau what happened here. Justineau makes heavy weather of the question, even though it's an easy one. *We couldn't kill the hungries, so we killed ourselves. That was always our favourite party trick.*

The burn shadow goes on for mile after mile, oppressing their spirits and draining their stamina. It's past time they stopped, grabbed some rest and rations, but nobody's keen to

240

sit down on this tainted ground. By unspoken consensus, they press on.

It's really sudden, when they reach the edge of it, but the shadow's got one more miracle to show them. Over the space of a hundred steps they go from black to green, from death to hectic life, from dry-baked limbo to a field of massive this-tles and dense hollyhocks.

But there was a house here on the borderland that burned but didn't fall. And against its rear wall there are heat shadows, where something living collapsed against the hot brick and burned with different colours, different breakdown products. Two of them, one large and one small, painted in deep black against the grey-black of their surroundings.

An adult and a child, arms thrown up as though they were caught in the middle of an aerobics workout.

Fascinated, the hungry kid measures herself against the smaller shape. It fits her pretty well.

45

What she thinks is: *this could have been me.* Why not? A real girl, in a real house, with a mother and a father and a brother and a sister and an aunt and an uncle and a nephew and a niece and a cousin and all those other words for the map of people who love each other and stay together. The map called *family*.

Growing up and growing old. Playing. Exploring. Like Pooh and Piglet. And then like the Famous Five. And then like Heidi and Anne of Green Gables. And then like Pandora, opening the great big box of the world and not being afraid, not even caring whether what's inside is good or bad. Because it's both. Everything is always both.

But you have to open it to find that out.

46

They stop and eat, setting their faces against the dead zone they've just crossed.

Sergeant Parks has brought some of the tins from the kitchen in Wainwright House with him in his pack. Miss Justineau and Dr Caldwell and the soldiers eat cold sausage and beans and cold Scotch broth. Melanie eats something called Spam, which is a bit like the meat she had the night before, but not so nice.

They face south, away from the thing that Miss Justineau called a burn shadow — but Melanie keeps turning her head to look back the way they've come. They're on a rise in the ground, so she can see a long way to the north, all the way back to the town where they slept last night and where she loosed the fox. Mile after mile of gentle rise and fall, baked and blackened to charcoal. She catechises Miss Justineau again to make sure she understands, the two of them talking in low voices that don't carry.

"Was it green before?" Melanie asks, pointing.

"Yes. Just like the countryside we passed through right after we left the base."

"Why did they burn it?"

243

"They were trying to keep the hungries contained, in the first few weeks after the infection appeared."

"But it didn't work?"

"No. They were scared, and they panicked. A lot of the people who should have been making the important decisions were infected themselves, or else they ran away and hid. The ones who were left didn't really know what they were doing. But I'm not sure there was anything better they could have done. It was too late, by then. All the evil shit they were afraid of had already happened, pretty much."

"The evil shit?" Melanie queries.

"The hungries."

Melanie contemplates this equation. It may be true, but she doesn't like it. She doesn't like it at all. "I'm not evil, Miss Justineau."

Miss J is penitent. She touches Melanie on the arm, gives her a brief but reassuring squeeze. It's not as nice as a hug, but also not so dangerous. "I know you're not, sweetheart. I wasn't saying that."

"But I *am* a hungry."

A pause. "You're infected," Miss J says. "But you're not a hungry, because you can still think, and they can't."

That distinction hasn't struck Melanie until now, or at least hasn't weighed much against the planetary mass of her realisation. But it *is* a real difference. Does it make other differences possible? Does it make her not be a monster after all?

These ontological questions come first, and loom largest. Another, more practical one peeps out from behind them.

"Is that why I'm a crucially important specimen?"

Miss J makes a hurting face, then an angry one. "That's why you're important to Dr Caldwell's research project. She believes she can find something inside you that will help her to make medicine for everyone else. An antidote. So they can't ever be turned into hungries, or if they're turned, they can be changed back again."

Melanie nods. She knows that's really important. She also knows that not all the evils that struck this land had the same cause and origin. The infection was bad. So were the things that the important-decision people did to control the infection. And so is catching little children and cutting them into pieces, even if you're doing it to try to make medicine that stops people being hungries.

It's not just Pandora who had that inescapable flaw. It seems like everyone has been built in a way that sometimes makes them do wrong and stupid things. Or *almost* everyone. Not Miss Justineau, of course.

Sergeant Parks is signalling to them to stand and start walking again. Melanie walks ahead of Miss Justineau, letting the leash run taut as she revolves all these dizzying things in her mind. For the first time she doesn't wish that she was back in her cell. She's starting to see that the cell was a tiny piece of something much bigger, of which everyone who's with her here used to be a part.

She's starting to make connections that build outwards from her own existence in some surprising and scary directions.

47

London swallows them very slowly, a piece at a time.

It's not like Stevenage, where you basically walk in from open fields and open roads and find yourself suddenly in the heart of the town. For Kieran Gallagher, who found Stevenage pretty big and impressive, this is an experience at once so intense and so drawn out that it's hard to process.

They walk, and they walk, and they walk, and they're still coming into the city – whose heart, Sergeant Parks tells him, is at least another ten miles south of them at this point.

"All the places we've passed through today," Helen Justineau tells Gallagher, taking pity on his awe and unease, "they used to be separate towns. But the developers just kept building outwards from London, as more and more people came to live there, and eventually all those other towns just got absorbed into the mass."

"How many people?" Gallagher knows he sounds like a ten-year-old, but he still has to ask.

"Millions. A lot more people than there are in the whole of England now. Unless . . ."

She doesn't finish the sentence, but Gallagher knows what

she means. *Unless you count the hungries.* But you can't. They're not people any more. Well, except for this weird little kid, who's like . . .

He's not sure what she's like. A live girl, maybe, dressed up as a hungry. But not even that. An adult, dressed as a kid, dressed as a hungry. Weirdly, probing his feelings the way you stick your tongue into the place where a tooth fell out, Gallagher finds himself liking her. And one of the reasons why he likes her is because she's so different from him. She's as big as four-fifths of five-eighths of fuck all, but she takes no bullshit from anyone. She even talks back to the Sarge, which is like watching a mouse bark at a pitbull. Frigging amazing!

But he and the kid have got this much in common: they both walk into London with their mouths hanging open, barely able to process what they're seeing. How could there ever have been enough people to live in all these houses? How could they ever have built their towers so high? And how could anything in the whole world ever have conquered them?

As the fields beside the road give way to streets, and then more streets, and then a hell of a lot more streets on top of that, they sight more and more hungries. The Sarge has already told him about the density law. The more living people there once were in any place, the more hungries will probably be there now, unless it's a place where burn patrols have been through or bombs have been dropped. And that's just what they find.

But the thing about the hungries is that they cluster, just like they did in Stevenage, and with that near-disaster fresh in his memory, the Sarge isn't taking any chances. They go slowly, doing recce along parallel streets and choosing the ones where the hungries aren't. If you're prepared to fake and double a little bit, you can stay clear of the mouldy bastards for long stretches. He and Parks take point on this at first, but increasingly they use the kid because (a) she runs no risk and (b) they know after Stevenage that she'll come back. She's the perfect advance scout.

The first few times, Sergeant Parks undoes the leash each time and then ties her up again when she comes back. Then one time he forgets to tie her up, or decides not to, and after that the leash just stays tucked in his belt. She's still got the muzzle on, and her hands cuffed behind her, but she walks along with the rest of them, free to stride ahead or dawdle along behind.

The density of hungries holds high but steady through most of that afternoon. And then, weirdly, it starts to come down again. It's after they've passed through a place called Barnet, and they're walking down a long straight road strewn with abandoned vehicles. It's the sort of terrain that the Sarge hates, and he's watchful, keeping them in a tight group as they thread their way through the saloon car Sargasso.

But they barely see a single hungry, all the way down the road. Even though this area is all built up and ought to be crawling. And when they do get a sighting, mostly the dead-beats are a long way off, sprinting across the street north of them in pursuit of a stray cat, or just loitering at corners like streetwalkers from some apocalyptic nightmare.

The kid – Melanie – is walking beside Gallagher, for part of the way. She catches his gaze and then points, with her eyes, up and right. When he looks, he sees another marvel. It's like a cross between a car and a house. Bright red, with two rows of windows, and – he can see them very clearly – a flight of stairs inside it. But it's on wheels. The whole thing is on wheels. Insane!

The two of them, Gallagher and the kid, go up and examine it together. This takes the kid further away from Helen Justineau than she's been at any time since they left Stevenage, but Justineau is looking at something else and talking with the Sarge and the doctor. They're free, for a moment, to follow their shared curiosity.

The two-storey car has crashed into the front of a shop. It's canted over on its side, just a little, and all of its windows are shattered. The perished tyres have fallen away in curved strips like the grey-black rinds of some weird fruit. There's no blood, no bodies, nothing to indicate what happened to this awkward, towering chariot. It just reached the end of its journey here, probably a very long time ago, and it's stood here ever since.

"It's called a bus," Melanie tells him.

"Yeah, I knew that," Gallagher lies. He's heard the word, but he's never seen one. "Of course it's a bus."

"Anyone could ride on them, if they had a ticket. Or a card. There was a card that you could put into a machine, and the machine would read it and let you on to the bus. They'd stop and start all the time, to let people get on and off. And there were special parts of the road that only buses could go on. They were a lot better for the environment than everyone driving their own cars."

Gallagher nods slowly, like none of this is news to him. But the truth is, this vanished world is something he's profoundly ignorant of, and barely ever thinks about. A child of the Breakdown, he was a lot less interested in tales of the glorious past than in how he could cadge a bit of someone else's bread ration. He uses the artefacts of the past all the time, obviously. His gun and knife were made back then. So were the base's buildings, and the fence, and most of the furniture. The Humvee. The radio. The fridge in the rec room. Gallagher is a squatter in the ruins of empire, but he doesn't interrogate the ruins any more than you'd interrogate the meat you eat to try to guess what animal it came from. Most of the time it's better not to know.

In fact, the ancient relic that most excited his curiosity was a porno mag that Private Si Brooks had under the mattress of his bunk. Leafing reverently through its pages, for the standard price of one and a half ciggies, Gallagher had wondered at length whether the women of the pre-Breakdown world really had bodies with those colours and those textures. None of the women he's ever seen look like that. He blushes to remember

249

this now, with the little girl beside him, and he glances down to make sure that his thoughts haven't surfaced in some readable way on his face.

Melanie is still looking at the bus, fascinated by its construction.

Gallagher decides enough is enough. They should go back to the others. Almost unconsciously, he reaches out a hand to take hers. He freezes in the middle of the gesture. Melanie hasn't noticed, and she couldn't take his hand in any case because her own are cuffed behind her back, but what a stupid, stupid thing to do. If the Sarge had seen . . .

But the Sarge is still in deep and earnest conversation with Justineau and Dr Caldwell, and hasn't seen a thing. Relieved, shaken, sheepish, Gallagher joins them.

Then he sees what it is that the other three are looking at, and these thoughts slip from his mind. It's a hungry, lying full length on the ground, in an alcove formed by the entrance of a shop.

Sometimes they fall down and can't get up, when the rot inside them fucks up their nervous system to the point where it doesn't really work any more. He's seen them sprawled on their sides, random shudders passing through them like jolts of electricity, their grey-on-grey eyes staring at the sun. Maybe that's what happened to this one.

But something else has happened to it too. Its chest has broken wide open, forced open from within by . . . Gallagher has no idea what that thing is. A white column, at least six feet high, flaring at the top into a sort of flat round pillow thing with fluted edges – and with bulbous growths on its sides like blisters. The texture of the column is rough and uneven, but the blisters are shiny. If you tilt your head when you look at them, they've got an oil-on-water sheen to them.

"Jesus Christ!" Helen Justineau says, in a kind of a whisper.

"Fascinating," Dr Caldwell murmurs. "Absolutely fascinating."

250

"If you say so, Doc," the Sarge says. "But I'm thinking we should keep the hell away from it, right?"

Fearless or foolhardy, Caldwell reaches out to touch one of the growths. Its surface indents a little under the pressure of her finger, but fills out quickly to its original shape once she draws her hand back.

"I don't think it's dangerous," she says. "Not yet. When these fruits ripen, that may be a very different matter."

"Fruits?" Justineau echoes. She says it in exactly the same tone that Gallagher would have used. Fruits out of a dead man's rotten, broken-open body? Where would you have to go to get sicker than that?

Melanie squeezes in beside Gallagher, peers around his leg at the fallen hungry. He feels bad for her, that she has to see this. It's not right for a little kid to be made to think about death.

Even if she's, you know, dead. Kind of.

"Fruits," Caldwell repeats, firmly and with satisfaction. "This, Sergeant, is the fruiting body of the hungry pathogen. And these pods are its sporangia. Each one is a spore factory, full of seeds."

"They're its ball-sacks," the Sarge translates.

Dr Caldwell laughs delightedly. She was looking really beaten up and exhausted the last time Gallagher glanced at her, but this has brought her to life. "Yes. Exactly. They're its ball-sacks. Break open one of these pods, and you'll be having an intimate encounter with *Ophiocordyceps*."

"Then let's not," Parks suggests, pulling her back as she goes to touch the thing again. She looks up at him, surprised and seeming ready to argue the point, but the Sarge has already turned his attention to Justineau and Gallagher. "You heard the Doc," he says, like it was her idea. "This thing, and any more of them we see, they're off-limits. You don't touch them, and you don't go near them. No exceptions."

"I'd like to take some samples—" Caldwell starts to say.

251

"No exceptions," Parks repeats. "Come on, people, we're wasting daylight. Let's move out."

Which they do. But the interlude has left them all in a weird mood. Melanie goes back to Justineau and walks right at her side, as though she was back on the leash again. Dr Caldwell blathers on about life cycles and sexual reproduction until it almost sounds like she's coming on to the Sarge, who lengthens his stride to get away from her. And Gallagher can't keep from looking back, every now and again, at the ruined thing that's become so weirdly pregnant.

They see a dozen more of these fallen, fruiting hungries in the next couple of hours, some of them a lot further gone than the first one. The tallest of the white columns tower way over their heads, anchored at the base by a froth of grey threads that spills over the hungries' bodies and almost hides them from sight. The central stems get thicker as they get taller, widening the gap in the hungry's ribs or throat or abdomen or wherever they first broke through. There's something kind of obscene about it, and Gallagher wishes to Christ they'd gone some other way so they didn't have to know about this.

He's a little freaked out too, by what seems to be happening to the round growths on the fungal stems. They start out as just bumps or protuberances on the main vertical shaft. Then they get bigger, and fill out into shiny pearly-white spheroids that hang like Christmas tree ornaments. Then they fall off. Beside the tallest and thickest stems, there are thin scatterings of them around which they step over with gingerly care.

Gallagher is happy when the sun drops below the horizon and he doesn't have to look at the bastard things any more.

48

The third night, for Helen Justineau, is the strangest of all.

They spend it in the cells of a police station on the Whetstone High Road, after Sergeant Parks has ordered a short detour to explore it. He's hoping that the station will have an intact weapons locker. Their ammunition has been depleted by the skirmish in Stevenage, and every little helps.

There's no weapons locker, intact or otherwise. But there's a board with keys hanging on it, and some of the keys turn out to be for the remand cells in the basement. Four cells, strung out in a row along a short corridor with a guardroom at the further end of it. The door that opens on to the stairwell is a two-inch thickness of wood, with a steel panel riveted on to the inside.

"Room at the inn," Parks says.

Justineau thinks he's joking, but then she sees that he's not and she's appalled. "Why would we lock ourselves in here?" she demands. "It's a trap. There's only one exit, and once we lock this door we're blind. We wouldn't have any way of keeping track of what's going on above us."

"All true," Parks admits. "But we know those junkers followed us from the base. And now we're getting into an area that had the densest population out of anywhere in the country. Wherever we stop, we're going to want to maintain some kind of a perimeter. Locked steel door is the most discreet perimeter I can think of. Our lights won't show, and any sound we make probably won't reach the surface. We stay safe, but we don't draw any attention to ourselves. Hard to imagine anything better, on that score."

There's no vote, but people start putting their packs down. Caldwell slumps against the wall, then slides down it into a squatting position. It might not even be that she agrees with Parks' argument. She's just too tired to walk any further. Private Gallagher is unpacking the last few cans of food from Wainwright House, and then he's opening them.

It's carried on the nod, and there's no point in arguing.

They close the door so they can put their torches on, but they don't lock it at first; claustrophobia is already setting in, for most of them, and turning the key seems like too irrevocable a step. As they eat, the desultory conversation winds down into silence. Parks is probably right about their voices not carrying, but they still sound way too loud in this echoing vault.

When they're done, they slip away one by one into the guardroom to do whatever they need to do. No torches in there, so they've got something like privacy. Justineau realises that Melanie never needs to take a bathroom break. She vaguely remembers, somewhere in the briefing pack she was given when she arrived at the base, some notes by Caldwell on the digestive systems of the hungries. The fungus absorbs and uses everything they swallow. There's no need for excretion, because there's nothing to excrete.

Parks locks the door at last. The key sticks in the lock, and he has to apply a lot of force to turn it. Justineau imagines – probably they all do – what would happen to them if the shank broke off in the lock. That's a bloody solid door.

They split up to sleep. Caldwell and Gallagher take a cell each, Melanie goes with Justineau and Parks sleeps at the foot of the stairs with his rifle ready to hand.

When the last torch clicks off, the darkness settles on them like a weight. Justineau lies awake, staring at it.

It's like God never bothered.

49

Melanie thinks: *when your dreams come true, your true has moved.* You've already stopped being the person who had the dreams, so it feels more like a weird echo of something that already happened to you a long time ago.

She's lying in a cell that's a bit like her cell back at the base. But she's sharing it with Miss Justineau. Miss Justineau's shoulder is touching her back, and she can feel it moving rhythmically with Miss Justineau's breath. On one level, that fills her with a happiness so complete that it's stupefying.

But this isn't anywhere they can stay, and live. It's just a stop on the journey, which is full of uncertainties. And some of the uncertainties are inside her, not out in the world. She's a hungry, with a driving need that will always come back no matter what she does. She has to be kept in chains, with a muzzle over her face, so she won't eat anybody.

And they lived together, for ever after, in great peace and prosperity.

That was how the story she wrote ended, but it's not how this real-life story will end. Beacon won't take her. Or else it will take her and break her down in pieces. Miss Justineau's happy ending isn't hers.

She'll have to leave Miss J soon, and go off into the world to seek her fortune. She'll be like Aeneas, running away from Troy after it fell and sailing the seas until he comes to Latium and founds the new Troy, which ends up being called Rome.

But she seriously doubts now that the princes she once imagined fighting for her exist anywhere in this world, which is so beautiful but so full of old and broken things. And she already misses Miss J, even though they're still together.

She doesn't think she'll ever love anyone else quite this much.

50

The fourth day is the day of the miracle, which falls on Caroline Caldwell out of a clear sky.

Except that it's not clear, really. Not any more. The weather has turned. A thin rain is soaking through their clothes, there's no food left, and everyone is in a dismal, surly mood. Parks is worried about the e-blocker, and taking it out on everybody. They're running low on the stuff, and had to go sparingly when they anointed themselves before unlocking the door. And they've still got at least three days' journey ahead of them. If they don't manage to restock at some point, they'll be in dead trouble.

They're still walking south, with the whole of north London and central London and south London to get through. Even for the young private, Caldwell sees, some of the shock and awe has drained away. The only one who's still looking at every new thing they pass with indefatigable wonder is test subject number one.

As for Caldwell, she's thinking about lots of things. Fungal mycelia growing in a substrate of mammalian body cells. The GABA-A receptor in the human brain, whose widespread and vital operation concerns the selective conduction of chloride ions across the plasma membranes of specific neurons. And the more immediate issue of why they're seeing so few hungries now, when yesterday morning they were seeing clusters of several hundred at a time.

Caldwell hypothesises a number of possible answers to this question: deliberate clearance by uninfected humans, competition from an animal species, the spread of a disease through the hungry population, an unknown side effect of *Ophiocordyceps* itself, and so on. Obviously the existence of the fallen, fruiting hungries is a factor – they've seen a lot more since they set out that morning, so many that new sightings arouse no comment – but it's unlikely that this is the sole explanation. For that, there would have to be hundreds of thousands of the things, not just dozens. To Caldwell's intense annoyance, she comes across no observational evidence that would help her to choose between the various scenarios she's theorised.

Moreover – and this distresses her even more – she's finding it hard to concentrate. The pain from her damaged hands is now a persistent and agonising throbbing, as though she had an extra heart beating in each of her palms in very imperfect synchrony. The ache in her head tries to keep pace with both at once. Her legs feel so weak, so insubstantial, she can hardly believe that they're carrying her weight. It's more like her body is a helium balloon, bobbing along above them.

Helen Justineau says something to her, the rising inflection suggesting a question. Caldwell doesn't hear, but nods her head in order to prevent any further repetition.

Perhaps *Ophiocordyceps* induces different behaviours in the mature stage than in its neotenous, asexual form. Migratory behaviours or sessile ones. Morbid photosensitivity or some parallel to the height-seeking reflex of infected ants. If she knew where the hungries had gone, she could begin to construct a model of the mechanism, and that might lead her

259

to an understanding of how the fungus–neuron interface ultimately functions.

The day has a drifting, dreamlike feel. It seems to come to Caldwell from a great distance, only reporting in occasionally. They find a cluster of fallen hungries, who have fruited in the same way as the others – but in this case, they've lain down so close together that the trunks or stems that grow out of their chests are now joined together by rafts of mycelial threads.

While the others stare at the fungal glade in sick fascination, Caldwell kneels and picks up one of the fallen sporangia. It looks and feels solid enough, but weighs very little. There's a pleasing smoothness to its integument. Nobody sees as she slips it, very carefully, into the pocket of her lab coat. The next time Sergeant Parks glances around at her, she's fidgeting with her bandages again and looks as though she's been doing it the whole time.

They walk on endlessly. Time elongates, fractures, rewinds and replays in stuttering moments that – while they have no coherent internal logic – all seem drearily familiar and inevitable.

The GABA-A receptor. The hyperpolarisation of the nerve cell, occurring after the peak of its firing and determining the lag time before it's ready to reach action potential again. So precariously balanced a mechanism, and yet so much depends on it!

"Approach with caution," Sergeant Parks is saying now. "Don't assume it's empty."

In her lab at the base, Caldwell has a voltage clamp of the SEVC-d variety, which can be used to measure very small changes in ion currents across the surface membranes of living nerve cells. She never trained herself to use it properly, but she knows that the *Cordyceps*-infected display both different levels of excitation from healthy subjects and different rates of change in electrical activity. Variation within the infected community is large, though, and unpredictable. Now she's wondering

260

whether it correlates with another variable that she's failed to detect.

A hand touches her shoulder. "Not yet, Caroline," Helen Justineau says. "They're still checking it out."

Caldwell looks on down the road. Sees what's standing there, a hundred yards ahead of them.

She's afraid at first that she might be hallucinating. She knows she's suffering from extreme fatigue and mild disorientation, arising either from the infection contracted when she injured her hands at the base or (less likely) from the untreated water they've been drinking.

Ignoring Justineau, she walks forward. In any case, the sergeant rounds the side of the thing now, and gives the all-clear. There's no reason to hang back.

She raises her hand and touches the cool metal. In curlicues of raised chrome, from under its mantle of dust and filth, it speaks to her. Speaks its name.

Which is Rosalind. Rosalind Franklin.

51

Caroline Caldwell was brought up to believe in the second law of thermodynamics. In a closed system, entropy must increase. No ifs or ands or buts. No time off for good behaviour, since time's arrow always points in the same direction. Through the gift shop to the exit, with no stamp on your hand, nothing that would let you come round and have another ride.

It's twenty years now since Charlie and Rosie went off the grid. Twenty years since they launched – without her – and lost their way in a disintegrating world. And now here's Rosie staring Caroline Caldwell in the eye, as demure as you please.

Rosie is a refutation of entropy just by being here. So long as she's still *virgo intacta*, not looted or torched.

"Door's locked," Sergeant Parks says. "And nobody's answering."

"Look at the dust," Justineau offers. "This thing hasn't moved in a long, long time."

"Okay, I think we should take a look inside."

"No!" Caldwell yelps. "Don't! Don't force the door!"

They all turn to look at her, surprised by her vehemence. Even test subject number one stares, her blue-grey eyes solemn and unblinking. "It's a laboratory!" Caldwell says. "A mobile research facility. If we break the seals, we could compromise whatever's inside. Samples. Experiments in progress. Anything."

Sergeant Parks doesn't look impressed. "You really think that's an issue right now, Doctor?"

"I don't know!" Caldwell says, anguished. "But I don't want to take the chance. Sergeant, this vehicle was sent here to research the pathogen, and it was crewed by some of the finest scientific minds in the world. There's no telling what they found or what they learned. If you smash your way in, you could do untold damage!"

She physically interposes herself between Parks and the vehicle. But she doesn't need to. He's not making any move towards the door.

"Yeah," he says dourly. "Well, I don't think it's going to be an issue. That's some serious plate on that thing. We're not getting in there any time soon. Maybe if we found a crowbar, but even then . . ."

Caldwell thinks hard for a moment, sieving her memory. "You don't need a crowbar," she says.

She shows him where the emergency external access crank is hidden, cradled in two brackets underneath Rosie's left flank, right beside the midsection door. Then, with the crank held awkwardly in her bandaged left hand, she goes down on her knees and gropes under the body of the vehicle, close to the forward wheel arch. She remembers – she thinks she remembers – the position of the socket into which the crank will fit, but it's not where she expects it to be. After a few minutes of blind rummaging, watched in bemused silence by the others, she finally locates the slot and is able to insert the end of the crank into it. There's an override control, but it was only meant to be engaged in conditions of actual siege. The vehicle's designers anticipated a range of situations in which it would be necessary to enter Rosie from the outside without compromising her interior spaces by blasting or forcing a way in.

"How do you know about all this?" Justineau asks her.

"I was attached to the project," Caldwell reminds her tersely. She's lying by omission, but she doesn't blush. The pain of these memories runs much deeper than the embarrassment, and nothing would induce her to explain further.

To reveal that she came out twenty-seventh on the list of possible crew members for Charlie and Rosie. Trained for five months in the operation of the on-board systems, only to be told that she wouldn't, after all, be required. Twenty-six other biologists and epidemiologists had placed higher up the list – had seemed, to the mission's managers and overseers, to possess more desirable skills and experience than those Caldwell had to offer. Since the full complement of scientists for both labs was twelve, that didn't even put her on the list of first alternatives. Charlie and Rosie sailed without her.

Until now, she'd assumed that they'd gone down with all hands – lost in some inner-city fastness, unable to advance or retreat, overwhelmed by hungries or ambushed by junker scavengers. That thought had consoled her a little – not to think that those who'd beaten her had then died for their *lèse majesté*, but because her placing so low on the list had kept her alive.

Of course, that's only a conceptual stone's throw from the thought that her survival is a side effect of mediocrity.

Which is nonsense, and will be seen to be nonsense, when she finds the cure. The story of her failing to gain a berth on Charlie or Rosie will be an ironic footnote to history, like Einstein's alleged bad grades in high-school maths exams.

Only now, the footnote gains an added piquancy. They made this lab for her all along, and they didn't know it. They sent it here to intercept her journey.

Parks and Gallagher are working the crank, which was too stiff and unyielding to move when Caldwell tried it. The door is sliding back, a half-inch at a time. Stale air leaks out, making Caldwell's heart beat fast in her chest. The seal is good. Whatever happened here, whatever may have become of Rosie's crew, her interior environment appears to be sound.

As soon as the gap is wide enough for her to get through, Caldwell steps forward.

Right into Sergeant Parks, who refuses to stand out of her way. "I'm going in first," he tells her. "Sorry, Doc. I know you're keen to take a look at this thing, and you will. Just as soon as I check if anyone's home."

Caldwell starts to state her reasons for believing that Rosie will be empty, but the sergeant isn't listening. He's already gone inside. Private Gallagher stands by the door and watches her warily, clearly afraid that she'll try to barge past him.

But she doesn't. If she's right, there's no risk, but for the same reason no real need for hurry. And if she's wrong, if the vehicle has been breached somehow, then the sergeant will certainly deal more effectively with anything that's inside than she could hope to do. Common sense dictates that she wait for him to complete his search.

But she almost convulses with impatience. This gift is intended for her, and for no one else. There's nobody else who can use what's in there. What *might* be in there, she corrects herself. After so many years, there's no telling what could have happened to the precious equipment in Rosie's labs. After all, what conceivable disaster would have taken out the crew without harming anything around them? The most likely explanation for the sealed door and undamaged exterior is that one or more of the crew became infected while on board. She imagines them running amok through the lab, in a feeding frenzy, toppling delicate imaging frames and centrifuges, trampling on Petri dishes full of carefully incubated samples.

Sergeant Parks emerges, shaking his head. Caldwell is so wrapped up in these disaster scenarios that she takes that for a verdict. She cries out and runs for the door, where Parks steadies her with a hand on her shoulder. "It's fine, Doc. All clear. Only body is in the driving seat, and he seems to have

265

shot himself. But before we go in there, tell me something – because this thing is way outside of my experience. Is there anything in there I should know about? Anything that could be dangerous?"

"Nothing," Caldwell says, but then – the punctilious scientist – she amends that. "Nothing I'm aware of. Let me look around, and I'll give you a definitive answer."

Parks steps aside and she goes in, feeling herself trembling, trying to hide it.

The lab has everything. Everything.

At the far end, facing her, is something she's only ever seen in photographs, but she knows what it is, and what it does, and how it does it.

It's an ATLUM. An automated lathe ultramicrotome.

It's the holy grail.

52

Rosalind Franklin seems to thrill Dr Caldwell and Sergeant Parks, no doubt for different reasons, but Helen Justineau's first impressions are negative. It's cold as hell, it echoes like a tomb, and it smells like embalming fluid. And she can see from Melanie's face that Melanie is even less enthusiastic.

Of course, they've both got recent and unhappy memories of laboratories, especially laboratories with Caroline Caldwell in them. And that's what Rosie, as Caldwell calls this thing, really is – a lab on wheels. Only it's got sleeping berths and a kitchen, so it's also a gigantic motor home. And it's got flame-throwers and turret guns, so it's also a tank. There's something for everyone.

In fact, it's almost big enough to cross time zones. The lab is amidships and takes up nearly half the available space. In front of it and behind it there are weapons stations where two gunners can stand back to back and look out to either side of the vehicle through slit windows like the embrasures in a medieval castle. Each of these stations can be sealed off from the lab by a bulkhead door. Further aft, there's something like an engine room. Forward, there are crew quarters, with a dozen wall-mounted cot beds and two chemical toilets, the kitchen space, and then the cockpit, which has a pedestal gun of the same calibre as the Humvee's and about as many controls as a passenger jet.

Justineau and Melanie stand in the forward weapons station and watch the activity around them, momentarily disconnected from it.

Caldwell is checking equipment in the lab space. She's got a manifest in her hand – it was on the wall of the lab, closest to the door – and she's using it to find specific pieces of equipment, which she then checks for damage. Her expression is rapt, furiously intense. She seems completely oblivious of everyone else's presence.

Parks and Gallagher have gone forward, past the crew quarters, into the cockpit. They're wrestling with something there – presumably the body Parks mentioned. After a while, they carry it through, wrapped in a blanket. It trails a complex raft of unpleasant smells, but they're mercifully old and faint.

"Forward doors are locked," Parks grunts. "Can't open them without power, it looks like. And power's what we haven't got."

They take it out through the midsection door, which is the one they came in through. Justineau notes that there's a complicated arrangement of steel armatures and plastic sheets on the inside of the door. She suspects that what she's looking at is a foldaway airlock. In a cupboard right next to it she finds six sealed environment suits, the helmets huge and cylindrical with a narrow visor, like the heads of robots in a 1950s movie. The people who designed this thing really did think of everything.

But apparently that didn't help the people who rode in it.

Justineau puts a hand on Melanie's arm, and Melanie jumps almost a foot into the air. The extreme reaction makes Justineau start back in her turn.

"Sorry," she says.

"It's all right," Melanie mutters, looking up at her. The girl's blue eyes are wide and fathomless. Normally her emotions are all on the surface, but now, underneath the nerves and the general unhappiness, there are depths that Justineau doesn't know how to interpret.

"We probably won't stay here long," she reassures the girl.

But she hears the hollowness in the words. She doesn't know.

When Parks and Gallagher come back, they talk with Dr Caldwell in hushed, quick tones. Then Gallagher goes into the crew quarters, while Parks walks all the way through to the back of the vehicle.

Curious, Justineau follows him to the engine room.

Where Parks is taking the inspection plate off what looks like a sizeable electrical generator. He prods around inside it for a while, looking thoughtful. Then he starts opening the lockers on the walls, one at a time, and inspecting their contents. The first one has got about a thousand tools in it, neatly mounted in racks. The next contains spools of wire, metal components wrapped in greased muslin, boxes of various sizes bearing long index numbers. The third has manuals, which Parks flicks through with frowning concentration.

"You thinking you can get this working again?" Justineau asks him.

"Maybe," Parks says. "It's not like I'm an expert, but I can probably make shift. They've written these fix-it books for idiots. I can read idiot well enough."

"Might take a while."

"Probably. But Christ, this thing's got more firepower than most armies. Hundred-and-fifty-five-millimetre field guns. Flame-throwers. It's got to be worth trying, right?"

Justineau turns, intending to tell Melanie that they might be staying here longer than expected – but Melanie is already there, standing right behind her.

"I need to talk to Sergeant Parks," she says.

Parks looks up from the manuals, his face impassive. "We got something to talk about?" he demands.

"Yes," Melanie says. She turns to Justineau again. "In private."

269

It takes a moment for Justineau to realise that she's been dismissed. "Okay," she says, trying to sound indifferent. "I'll go help Gallagher do whatever he's doing."

She leaves them to it. She can't imagine what Melanie might have to say to Parks that she doesn't want an audience for, and that uncertainty translates very readily into unease. Parks may have become relaxed about the leash, but Justineau knows he still sees Melanie essentially as a smart but dangerous animal – all the more dangerous for being smart. She needs to watch what she says around him, as much as what she does. She needs Justineau watching her back, constantly.

Gallagher is doing more or less the same thing that Dr Caldwell is doing, which is inventorying supplies – but he's doing it in the crew quarters, and he's already finishing up when Justineau gets there. He shows her the last cupboard he opened. It contains a CD player and two racks of music CDs. Justineau feels memories prickle into stereophonic life as she scans the titles, which are – to say the least – an eclectic mix. Simon and Garfunkel. The Beatles. Pink Floyd. Frank Zappa. Fairport Convention. The Spinners. Fleetwood Mac. 10CC. Eurythmics. Madness. Queen. The Strokes. Snoop Dogg. The Spice Girls.

"You ever hear any of this stuff?" Justineau asks Gallagher.

"A little bit here and there," he tells her, wistfulness in his voice. The only sound system on the base was the one hooked up to the cell block, that played wall-to-wall classical. One or two of the base personnel had digital music players and hand-operated chargers that worked by turning a wheel, but these priceless heirlooms were obsessively guarded by their owners.

"You think there's any way we can play them?" Gallagher asks now.

Justineau has no idea. "If Parks gets the generator going, this thing will probably go live at the same time everything else does. It's been shielded from the weather in here – apart from temperature changes. There certainly isn't any damp, which

270

would have been the worst thing. If the fuse didn't blow and the circuit boards are sound, there's no reason why it wouldn't play. Don't get your hopes up too high, Private, but you might get dinner and a show tonight."

Gallagher looks suddenly cast down. "I don't think so," he says glumly.

"How come?"

He opens his empty hands in a wide shrug, indicating all the cupboards he's already opened and searched.

"No dinner."

53

Parks calls a meeting in the crew quarters, but it only has four attendees.

"Where's Melanie?" Justineau demands, instantly alarmed, instantly suspicious.

"She left," Parks says. And then, in the face of Justineau's ferocious scepticism, "She's coming back. She just had to go outside for a while."

"She 'had to go outside'?" Justineau repeats. "She doesn't get calls of nature, Parks, so if you're saying—"

"She did not," Sergeant Parks says, "go out for a bathroom break. I'll explain later if you insist, but she was actually pretty keen that I didn't tell you about it, so it's your call. In the meantime, we've got some other stuff that we need to discuss, and we need to discuss it now."

They're sitting on the edges of the ground-floor bunks, precariously balanced. The sleeping berths are in vertical stacks of three, so the four of them have to lean forward to avoid bumping their heads on the middle cots, whose steel frames are at exactly the height best calculated to smack someone's brains out. There would have been more room in the lab, but apart from Caldwell, they all seem to prefer not to spend too much time in a space where the potpourri is formaldehyde.

Parks indicates Caldwell with a nod. "From what the Doc says, this thing we're sitting in was some kind of research station, designed to move around freely in inner-city areas and to be secure against attack from hungries or anything else it came up against.

"Which was a great idea, and I'm not knocking it. Only at some point, a couple of things happened – can't be sure in what order. The generator blew. Or something in the power feed blew, maybe, since the generator mostly looks okay to my admittedly shit-ignorant eye."

"Maybe they ran out of fuel," Gallagher hazards.

"Nope. They didn't. The fuel is a high-octane naphtha–kerosene mix, like jet fuel, and they've got about seven hundred gallons of it. And the tanks for the flame-throwers are full too – at a pinch, they would have been able to jury-rig something out of that. So most likely it was a mechanical failure of some kind. They should have been able to fix it, because they've got multiple spares for every damn part, but . . . well, for some reason they didn't. Maybe they'd already taken some casualties, and the people they lost were the ones who were the best mechanics. Anyway, when we get that generator stripped down, we'll see what's what."

"And we are definitely going to do that?" Justineau demands.

"Unless you can think of a good reason not to. This thing is built like a tank. It's everything the Humvee was, and a whole lot more. If we can ride it all the way to Beacon, it could save us a world of heartache."

Justineau can't help noticing that Dr Caldwell's face is wearing a sly, smug little smirk. That makes her push against the idea, even though it's obvious good sense. "We won't exactly be inconspicuous."

"No," Parks agrees. "We won't. People will hear us coming a mile off. And it'll be up to them to get the fuck out of our

273

way, because once we start, we won't be stopping. Hungries, junkers, roadblocks: we just put our foot down and keep rolling. We won't even need to stick to the streets. We could drive right through a house and come out the other side. Only thing that will stop big fat Rosie is rivers, and they've got maps in the equipment locker that show which bridges can take her weight. I think we'd be remiss if we didn't at least try. Worst that can happen is one of those bridges will be down, and we have to drive a bit out of our way. Or she slips a tread or blows a gasket or something, and then we're no worse off than when we started. In the meantime, we get a respite from forced marching, which was taking its toll on all of us and the Doc most of all."

"Thank you for your solicitude," Caldwell says.

"I don't know what that is, but you're very welcome."

"Two things," Justineau says.

"Sorry?"

"You said two things went wrong. The generator was one. What was the other?"

"Yeah," Parks says. "I was coming to that. They ran out of food. The cupboards are completely bare. As in, not one damn crumb. So my disaster scenario goes like this. They lose the generator, and they can't fix it. They sit here for a few days or weeks, waiting to be rescued. But the Breakdown's still raging, and nobody comes. Finally one of them says, 'Screw this,' and they pack their bags and hit the road. One of them stays back, presumably on guard duty. The rest walk off into the sunset. Maybe they make it somewhere, maybe they don't. Most likely they don't, because the stay-behind kills himself and nobody comes back for the salvage. Which is our good fortune."

He looks from face to face. "Except that we run the risk of going the same way," he concludes. "I don't know how long it will take to fix that generator, if we can fix it at all. But until we can do it, or until we give up, we're staying right here. So we need food, just like the original crew did. We used up the last of the tins we took from that house in Stevenage, and we didn't pass any place coming down here that hadn't been looted, torched or flattened. Still got a fair amount of water, but we have to drink it sparingly because there's no place to stock up between here and the Thames. So we need to forage, and we need a quick score. Ideally, a supermarket that no grab-bagger teams or junkers ever found, or a house where the homeowners stocked up big-time for the apocalypse and then got taken out early."

Justineau winces at that cold-hearted calculation. "We'd be looking in the same places the original crew looked," she points out. Parks turns to stare at her, and she shrugs. "I mean, it's safe to assume they took a good look around before they abandoned this super-fortress and went out on the open road. If there was food that was lying there waiting to be found, they would have found it."

"Can't argue with that," Parks says. "So the supply problem might be a serious one. Serious whether we move on or not, of course, but certainly more of a problem if we stay put here, for a day or two days or whatever, while I mess with that generator. So it's a big decision, maybe life-or-death, and it affects all of us equally. I'd be happy to make the call, but as you were keen to remind me a couple of days back, Miss Justineau, you're not under my command. No more is the Doc. So I'm happy, just this once, to put it to a vote.

"Should we stay or should we go? Show of hands for trying to fix the generator and ride home in style?"

Caldwell's hand is up in a moment, Gallagher's slightly slower. Justineau is in a minority of one.

"Okay with that?" Parks asks her.

"I don't have much choice, do I?" Justineau says. But the truth is she was already on the fence. Her wariness about Rosie has a lot more to do with Melanie's visible tension and the events of the last day at the base than with any rational objection. She can certainly see the attraction of making the rest of the journey in the safety and comfort of a humongous tank. No more ambushes. No more exposure. No more starting at every sound or movement, and looking over your shoulder every couple of seconds to see what's coming up behind you.

On the other hand, Caldwell is still wearing her cat-that's-anticipating-the-cream expression. Justineau's mind and stomach rebel against the thought of being stuck in an enclosed space with the doctor for any longer than she has to. "I'd like to be on scavenger duty," she tells Parks. "I mean, assuming you don't need me to help with the generator. I'll go with Gallagher and look for food."

"I had you both down for that," Parks agrees. "Can't start on the generator until I know what I'm doing, so right now I'm mainly reading through the manuals so I can identify all the bits and pieces I need. Still got three hours of daylight left, so if you're up for it, I think the two of you should go ahead and use it. Keep in touch via the walkie-talkies. If you run into any trouble, I'll get to you as quick as I can. Dr Caldwell, I'm letting you off that duty because your hands are still in a bad way and you probably won't be able to carry very much. Plus, we've only got the two packs."

Justineau is surprised that the sergeant bothered to justify himself. He's looking at Caldwell thoughtfully, like maybe there's something else on his mind.

"Well, there are plenty of things I can do here," Caldwell says. "I'll start with the water filtration system. In theory, Rosie was able to condense water from ambient air. Once the generator's working, we might be able to get that up and running again."

"Good enough," Parks says, and turns back to Justineau. "You better hit the road if you want to be back before dark."

But she's not ready to head out just yet. She's worried about Melanie, and she wants the truth. "Can I speak to you," she asks Parks, conscious of the echo, "in private?"

Parks shrugs. "Okay. If it's quick."

276

They go back into the engine room. She starts to speak, but Parks forestalls her by handing her his own walkie-talkie. "In case you and Gallagher get split up," he explains. "Rosie's cockpit has a full comms rig, and it's a lot more powerful than these portables, so you can take one each."

Justineau pockets the unit without even looking at it. She doesn't want to be derailed by a discussion of logistics. "I'd like to know what Melanie said to you," she tells Park. "And where she's gone."

Parks scratches his neck. "Really? Even when she told me not to say?"

She holds his gaze. "You let her go out there on her own. I already know damn well that you don't see a risk to Melanie as worth taking into account. But I do. And I want to know why you thought it was okay to send her out there."

"You're wrong," Parks says.

"Am I? About what?"

"About me." He plants his butt against the opened cowling of the generator, folds his arms. "Okay, not that wrong. A couple of days ago, I said we should cut the kid loose. She pulled our irons out of the fire twice since then, and on top of that she's turned into a really good scout. I'd be sorry to lose her."

Justineau opens her mouth to speak, but Parks isn't finished. "Also, since she can lead people back to us, letting her wander around on her own out there is not a decision that comes without consequences. But after what she told me, it seemed like the least worst option."

Justineau's mouth has gone a little drier than it already was. "What did she tell you?" she demands.

"She said our e-blocker isn't worth fuck any more, Helen. We put it on way too thin this morning, because we've only got half a tube left between the four of us. I thought this rig would have some, but it doesn't. It's got the blue goop that Dr Caldwell uses in the lab, but that's just a disinfectant. It's not going to kill scent in the same way.

277

"So the kid's been smelling us all day, and she's been going half crazy with the hunger all that time. She was scared shitless she was going to get loose and bite one of us. You particularly. And that was why she didn't want me to tell you any of this. She doesn't want you to think of her like that, as a dangerous animal. She wants you to think of her as a kid in your class."

Justineau feels dizzy all of a sudden. She leans back against the cold metal of the wall, waits for her head to stop spinning.

"That . . ." she says. "That *is* how I think of her."

"Which is what I told her. But it didn't make her any less hungry. So I cut her loose."

"You . . .?"

"Took her outside. Took off the cuffs, and off she went. Got them right here, ready for when she comes back." He opens one of the lockers and there they are, laid down all neat and tidy next to the coiled leash. "I showed her how to take the muzzle off for herself, like she didn't figure that out already. It's just a couple of leather straps. She's going to stay out until she finds something to eat. Something big. The plan is for her to gorge herself to bursting. Not come back until her belly's full. Maybe that will keep the feeding reflex at bay for a while."

Justineau thinks back to the way Melanie was behaving before she left – the violent starts and the general unease. She gets it now. Understands what she must have been suffering. What she doesn't get is Parks changing his mind about the muzzle and the cuffs. She's both bewildered and a little resentful. It seems, in some way, to threaten the bond she's developed with Melanie to have the other members of the party – especially Parks! – extending the same trust to her.

"You weren't worried she'd bite you?" she asks him. She hears the snide insinuation in her own voice and it suddenly sickens her. "I mean . . . you think we can keep her with us, even if she's hungry?"

"Well, no," Parks says, deadpan. "That's why I let her leave. Or do you mean was I afraid when I took the cuffs off? No, because I kept my gun on her. The kid's unusual – unique's maybe a better word – but she is what she is. What makes her unique is that she knows it. She doesn't cut herself any slack. Lot of people could take an example from that."

He hands her his pack, which he's emptied.

"You mean me?" Justineau demands. "You think I'm not pulling my weight?"

It would feel good to have a stand-up argument with Parks right then, but he doesn't seem keen to play. "No, I didn't mean you. I meant in general."

"People in general? You were being philosophical?"

"I was being a grumpy bastard. It's what I wear to the office most days. I guess you probably noticed that."

She hesitates, wrong-footed. She didn't think Parks was capable of self-deprecation. But then she didn't think he was capable of changing his mind.

"Any more rules of engagement?" she asks him, still hurting in some obscure way, still not mollified. "How to survive when shopping? Top tips for modern urban living?"

Parks gives the question more consideration than she was expecting.

"Use up the last of that e-blocker," he suggests. "And don't die."

54

Gallagher wishes he was on his own.

It's not that he doesn't like Helen Justineau. If anything, it's the opposite. He likes her a lot. He thinks she's really beautiful. She's had star or co-star billing in a number of his sexual fantasies, mostly playing the role of the highly experienced and wildly perverted older woman picking up a boy young enough to be her son and showing him the ropes. A lot of times, the ropes weren't even metaphorical.

But that makes it all the more awkward to be out on a patrol with her. He's scared of saying or doing something really stupid in front of her. He's scared of being in a position where he has to make a quick decision and not being able to think of one because he's thinking too much about her. He's scared of not being able to hide how scared he is.

It doesn't help that they can't even talk to each other. Okay, they exchange a terse murmur every now and then, when they've come to the end of a street and they have to decide where to go next. But the rest of the time they walk along in complete silence, in the slo-mo shuffle that Sergeant Parks has taught them.

It sort of feels like overkill right then. In the first hour after they leave the armoured truck with the stupid name, they only see four live hungries, and none of them close up.

Then they find the first dead one. It's fruited like all of those others, except that it's fallen down on its stomach and the big white stem has punched its way out of the poor bastard's back. Helen Justineau stares down at it, all sick and sombre. Gallagher guesses she's thinking about the little hungry kid. Like a mother before the Breakdown, thinking the world's a big place and there's lots of sick people in it and where's my baby girl?

Yeah. Full of sick people, the world. He's related to a whole lot of them. And he met a whole lot more when the base fell. A part of his unease right now – maybe the biggest part – comes from the feeling that he's not moving in a direction that makes any sense. Sure, he's going home. But that's like putting your foot back in a trap after you've somehow got free of it. They can't go back to the base, obviously. There isn't any base, not any more, and the bastards who tore it down might still be chasing them. But Gallagher can't see Beacon as a refuge. He can only see it as a mouth opening in front of him to swallow him down.

He tries to shake off the mood of despair. He tries to look and feel like a soldier. He wants Helen Justineau to be re-assured by his presence.

They've been working their way down a long road with shops on both sides, but the shops have all been ransacked long ago. They're way too obvious – easy targets for anyone who came this way. Probably most of them got looted during the early days of the Breakdown.

So now they turn their attention to the houses in the side streets, which are harder to get into and harder to search. You have to do a recce for hungries first of all. And you have to make as little noise as you can breaking in, because obviously noise is going to bring them if there are any of them around. Then once you're inside, you have to do another recce. Could

281

be a whole nest of hungries in any of these houses – former residents or uninvited guests.

It's slow going, and it preys on your nerves.

And it's depressing because the rain has set in solidly now. They're getting pissed on out of a grim, grey sky.

And last of all, it's boring, if something can be both really scary and boring at the same time. The houses all seem the same to Gallagher. Dark. Musty-smelling with squishy carpets underfoot, mouldering curtains and sprays of black mildew up interior walls. Cluttered up with millions of things that don't do anything except get in your way and almost trip you over. It's like before the Breakdown people used to spend their whole lives making cocoons for themselves out of furniture and ornaments and books and toys and pictures and any kind of shit they could find. As though they hoped they'd be born out of the cocoon as something else. Which some of them were, of course, but not in the way they hoped.

In most of the houses, Justineau and Gallagher stay just long enough to check the kitchen. In some, there's a utility room or a garage that they check too. They stay resolutely away from the fridges and freezers, which they know will be filled with a riot of stinking, festering shit. It's canned goods and packet goods that are the jackpot here.

But they don't find any. The kitchens are bare.

They move on to the next street, with similar results. At the very end of it, there's a lock-up garage with a bright green door, which they almost walk past. But it's right next to a looted corner shop, and Justineau slows to a halt.

"You thinking what I'm thinking?" she asks Gallagher.

He wasn't thinking anything until she said it, but he thinks fast now, so he has something to say besides *huh?*

"The lock-up might belong to the shop," he guesses.

"Damn straight. And it doesn't look like anyone's been in there. Let's take a look, Private."

They try the garage door, which is locked. It's made of some light, thin metal, which is good in one way (it's not going to be hard to break it down) and bad in another (anything they do to it is going to make a hell of a lot of noise).

Gallagher gets his bayonet wedged in under one corner of the door and pulls back on it. With a loud, shrill squeal, the metal folds. When it's far enough away from the frame, they get their fingers around the edge of it and pull, slowly and steadily. It's still making that same grinding noise, but there's nothing they can do about that.

They bend back a triangular flap about three feet on its longest side. Then they look in all directions and listen, tense as hell. No sign or sound of anything coming, from either end of the street.

They go down on hands and knees and crawl inside. Gallagher clicks his torch on and plays it around.

The garage is full of boxes.

Most of them are empty. Out of the ones that have stuff in them, most turn out to be not food but papers and magazines, kids' toys, stationery. The rest . . . well, there is food, but it's snack food mostly. Packets of crisps, peanuts, pork scratchings. Chocolate bars and biscuits. Boiled sweets in tubes about the length of a rifle bullet. Individually wrapped Swiss rolls.

And bottles. All kinds of bottles. Lemonade and orangeade and limeade, cola and blackcurrant juice and ginger beer. Not water, but pretty much everything else you could imagine, as long as your imagination restricts itself to saccharine and carbon dioxide.

"You think any of this is still good?" Gallagher whispers.

"Only one way to find out," Justineau whispers back.

They carry out a blind-taste challenge, ripping open plastic packets and nibbling cautiously on what's inside. The crisps are foul, soft and crumbly, with a sour, sweaty tang to them. They spit them out hastily. The biscuits are okay, though. "Hydrogenated oils," Justineau says, spraying crumbs. "Probably last until the heat death of the fucking universe." The peanuts are best of

283

all. Gallagher can't believe their taste, as salty and intense as meat. He eats three packets before he can stop himself.

When he looks up, Justineau is grinning at him – but it's a friendly grin, not a mean one. He laughs out loud, pleased that the two of them have shared this ridiculous feast – and that in the twilight of the garage she can't see him blushing.

He shouts out to the Sarge on the walkie-talkie and tells him they're bringing home the bacon. Or at least some stuff that's got bacon flavouring in it. Parks says to load up and come back in, with his heartiest congratulations.

They fill up the backpacks and their pockets, and each of them takes a couple of boxes besides. When they emerge cautiously into the street again, ten minutes later, they've still got it to themselves.

They head for home in a mood of euphoria. They've done the hunter-gatherer thing, and they've done it well. Now they're bringing the mammoth back to the cave. A campfire will be lit against the dark, and there'll be carousing and stories.

Well, maybe not that. But a locked door, a decent meal and Fleetwood Mac if their luck is in.

55

Dr Caldwell unpacks the six Tupperware containers containing brain tissue from the male hungry at Wainwright House and lays them side by side on the newly disinfected surface in front of her. The lab worktops are made of a synthetic marble substitute which mixes marble dust with bauxite and polyester. It's not as cold as real stone. When she momentarily lays her hot, throbbing hands on it, it offers her little relief.

She prepares slides from each of the samples. She doesn't call the ATLUM into play for this, because Rosie still has no functional power source – and also because the material has been scooped out of the hungry's skull with a spoon. It doesn't lie in its natural layers, and little would be gained by slicing it so very finely.

She'll need the ATLUM later, but not for these samples.

For now, she spreads tiny amounts of the brain tissue across the slides as thinly as she can, adds a single drop of staining agent to each, and drops the covers on with gingerly care. The bandages impede her movements, so this takes longer than it should.

Six tissue samples. Five available staining agents, which are cerium sulphate, ninhydrin, D282, bromocresol and *p*-anisaldehyde. Caldwell has the highest hopes of the D282, a fluorescent lipophilic carbocyanine with proven efficacy in throwing fine neuron structures into high relief. But she's not going to ignore the other stains, since she has them to hand. Any of them has the potential to yield valuable data.

The natural thing to do now would be to power up the transmission electron microscope, which sits in the corner of the lab like the bastard offspring of a road drill and an Imperial Stormtrooper from the *Star Wars* trilogy – all white ceramic and smooth, sculpted curves.

But there's that whole absence-of-power thing again. The microscope is not going to wake up and serve her until Sergeant Parks feeds it.

In the meantime, she turns her attention to the sporangium. The lab boasts a number of manipulator tanks, with two circular holes along one side. The holes are sphinctered. Elbow-length rubber gloves can be inserted through them and rendered airtight by a mixture of sealant gel and mechanical adjustments.

Once the sporangium is safely sequestered from the rest of the lab inside one of these tanks, Caldwell begins to examine it. She tries to open it with her gloved fingers and fails. Its outer shell is tough and elastic and very thick. Even with a scalpel it's not easy going.

Inside, endlessly infolded, is a fine, fractal froth of spores like grey soap bubbles that spills out through the opening she's made. Curious, she dips her finger in. There's no resistance. Even as densely packed together as this, the spores seem to have no mass at all.

She becomes aware, while she's doing this, that she's no longer alone in the lab. Sergeant Parks has entered and is watching her in silence. He has his gun – not the rifle, but the sidearm – in his hand, as casually as such a thing can be carried in a civilised space such as a lab, where it has no conceivable place.

286

Caldwell ignores him for a while as she continues to cut carefully into the grey gourd to examine its interior structure.

"The good news," she observes, her eyes and her attention staying on the contents of the tank, "is that the sporangium's integument appears to be extremely resilient. None of the ones we saw on the ground had broken open, and it's impossible to tear them open with your bare hands. They appear to require an external environmental trigger in order to germinate, and so far that trigger hasn't materialised."

Parks doesn't answer. He still hasn't moved.

"Did you ever consider a scientific career, Sergeant?" Caldwell asks him, still with her back to him.

"Not really," Parks says.

"Good. You're really far too stupid."

The sergeant looms at her side. "You think I'm missing something?" he demands. Caldwell is very conscious of the gun. When she glances down, it's there, directly in her line of sight. The sergeant is holding it in both hands, ready to fire.

"Yes."

"What am I missing?"

She puts down the scalpel and withdraws her hands, very slowly, from the gloves and from the tank. Then she turns to look him in the eyes. "You see that I'm pale and sweating. You see that my eyes are red. You see that I'm slowing down, as I walk."

"Yeah, I see that."

"And you're ready with your diagnosis."

"Doc, I know what I know."

"Ah, but you don't, Sergeant. Not really." She's begun to undo the bandages on her left hand. She holds it up for him to see. As the white linen falls away, her flesh is laid bare. The hand itself is fish-belly white and a little puckered. Red lines begin at the wrist and climb her arm – climb downwards, since her hand is raised, but gravity's no guide here. The poison is finding its way to her heart, and it pays no mind to the vagaries of local topography.

"Blood poisoning," Caldwell says. "Severe inflammatory sepsis. The first thing I did when we arrived here was to give myself a massive dose of amoxicillin, but it's almost certainly far too late. I'm not turning into a hungry, Sergeant. I'm only dying. So please leave me alone to get on with my work."

But Parks stays where he is for a few moments longer. Caldwell understands. He's a man with a strong preference for the sorts of problem that have a simple, unitary solution. He thought Caldwell was such a problem, but now he realises she isn't. It's hard for him to cope with the shift in perspective.

She understands, but she can't really help. And she doesn't really care. What matters now is her research, which – after so long a period of stagnation – is finally starting to look promising.

"You're saying these fruit things aren't dangerous?" he asks her.

Caldwell laughs. She can't help herself. "Not at all, Sergeant," she assures him. "Unless the prospect of a planet-wide extinction event troubles you."

His face, as open as a book, announces relief, then confusion, finally suspicion. "What?"

Caldwell is almost sorry to have to burst the precious bubble of his ignorance. "I already told you that the sporangia contained the spores of the hungry pathogen. But you don't seem to have taken in what that means. In its immature, asexual form, *Ophiocordyceps* toppled our global civilisation in the space of three years. The only reason it didn't achieve global pandemic status at once, the only reason any pockets of uninfected humans were able to survive, was because the immature organism can only propagate – neotenously – in biofluid."

"Doc," the sergeant says, looking pained, "if you're gonna talk like a fucking encyclopaedia . . ."

"Blood and spit, Sergeant. It lives in blood and spit. It doesn't

288

like to venture out into the open air, and it doesn't thrive there. But the adult form . . ." She waves a hand over the innocuous white globe nestling at the bottom of the tank. "Well, the adult form will take no prisoners. Each sporangium contains, at a rough estimate, from one to ten million spores. They will be airborne and light enough to travel tens or hundreds of miles from their place of origin. If they float into the upper atmosphere, as some of them will, they could easily cross continents. They will be robust enough to survive for weeks, months, perhaps years. And if you breathe them in, you'll be infected. You can see a hungry coming, but you'll have a harder time with an organism less than a millimetre across. A harder time seeing it, and a harder time keeping it out. I estimate that what's left of Humanity 1.0 will close up shop within a month of one of these pods opening."

"But . . . you said they won't open," Parks says, stricken.

"I said they won't open by themselves. This species is a sport, a mutant form, and its development is haphazard. But sooner or later, the trigger event — whatever it is — will happen. It's only a matter of time, with the probability rising gradually towards a hundred per cent."

Parks doesn't seem to have anything to say to that. He withdraws at last, and leaves her to it. And although she didn't let his presence slow her down too much, she's a lot happier to be alone.

56

Helen Justineau enjoyed the foraging expedition more than she thought she was going to. Found that time spent in the company of Kieran Gallagher was surprisingly bearable.

But when they get back to Rosie, with only ten minutes of daylight to spare, and they find Melanie hasn't returned yet, the worry drops on her like a ten-ton weight in an old Monty Python sketch. Where the hell could she be all this time? How hard would it have been for her to rustle up something to eat?

Justineau remembers the fox, back in Stevenage. She hadn't seen Melanie catch it, but she'd seen her walking along with the animal squirming in her arms, shifting its weight as it struggled so that she wouldn't lose her balance. If you can catch a fox, then a rat or a stray dog or a cat or a bird ought to be no trouble at all.

There's no telling what Melanie might have run into out there. Justineau should have tried to find her, instead of staying with Private Function and looking for food.

She's instantly contrite about that instinctive surge of contempt for Gallagher. His only faults, really, are that he's young, green as grass, and flat-out idolatrous when it comes to Sergeant Parks.

Who is somewhat taciturn and withdrawn, Justineau realises now. He took the barest glance at what they'd found, commended them with a nod and a grunt, and then went back into the engine room.

She follows him there. "What do we do if she doesn't come back?" she demands.

The sergeant has his head down in the guts of the generator, which he's started to dismantle. His voice comes back muffled. "What do you think?"

"I'm going to go and look for her," Justineau says.

That gets Parks right way up again pretty quick, which is why she said it. She's not seriously contemplating going out into the dark. There'd be no point. She wouldn't be able to use the torch without announcing her presence and location to anyone and everything else on the streets. Without the torch she'd be blind – and with it only marginally less so. The hungries would home in on the moving light, or on her scent, or on her body heat, and it would all be over in a minute.

So when Parks tells her these things, in slightly cruder and more emphatic terms, she doesn't even bother to listen. She waits him out and then says again, "Then what do we do?"

"There isn't anything we can do," Parks says. "She's a lot safer out there than you or I would be, and she's a smart kid. With the night coming on, she knows enough to go to ground and wait for daylight."

"What if she can't find her way back? What if she gets turned around in the dark, or just forgets the way? We have no idea how far she went, and these streets probably all look alike to her. Even in daylight, she might not be able to locate us again."

Parks is looking at her hard. "I'm not sending up a flare," he says. "If that's what you're thinking about, forget it."

291

"What do we lose?" Justineau demands. "We're in a frigging *tank*, Parks. Nothing can touch us."

He throws down the manual he's been clutching all this time and picks up a wrench. For a moment she thinks he's going to hit her with it. She realises, with sharp surprise, that he's as tense as she is. "They wouldn't have to touch us," he points out grimly. "They'd just have to camp out on the doorstep for a day or so. We're not well placed to stand up to a siege, Helen. Not with salted peanuts and Jaffa Cakes."

She knows he's right, as far as that goes. It doesn't matter, since she's already swiped the flare pistol from the mess of stuff Parks dumped on the floor when he gave her the pack. She's tucked it into the back of her jeans, where it barely makes a bulge. So long as she stays out of the light, she's fine.

But whatever is eating Parks, it's different from what's eating her. Not knowing makes her uneasy. "What's the matter?" she demands. "Did something happen while we were out?"

"Nothing happened," Parks says too quickly. "But we've got no e-blockers left, and nothing here we can use instead. From now on, any time we step outside, we're leaving a scent trail that leads right back to our front door. And if the kid does come back, we'll need a lot more than a muzzle and a leash to keep her under control. She's going to be smelling us all the time. What do you think that's going to do to her?"

That question winds its way viciously and insinuatingly through Justineau's mind. For a moment she can't speak. She remembers what the feeding frenzy did to Melanie back at the base. She imagines Melanie losing control like that again, inside Rosie.

How will they even let her in to put the muzzle and handcuffs back on her?

Knowing Parks the way she does – as a man who sees the angles and dots the i's, she wonders how much of this he thought through beforehand. "Is that why you let her go so easily?" she demands. "Did you think you were releasing her into the wild?"

"I told you what I was thinking," Parks says. "I'm not in the habit of lying to you."

"Because this is *not* her natural fucking habitat," Justineau goes on. It feels like there's something bitter that she swallowed, that she has to talk around. "She has no clue about this place. Less than we do, and God knows we don't have much. She might be able to find food for herself, but that's not the same as surviving, Parks. She'd be living with animals. Living like an animal. So an animal is what she'd be. The little girl would die. What would be left would be something a lot more like all the other hungries out there."

"I let her loose so she could eat," Parks says. "I didn't think past that."

"Yeah, but you're not an idiot." She's come right up close to him, and he's actually backed away a little, as far as he can in that narrow space. All she can see of his face in the torch's angled beam is the tight set of his mouth. "Caroline can indulge the luxury of not thinking. You can't."

"Thought the Doc was meant to be a genius," Parks mutters, with unconvincing nonchalance.

"Same thing. She only sees what's at the bottom of her test tubes. When she calls Melanie test subject number one, she means it. But you know better. If you took a kitten away from its mother, then dumped it back again and the mother bit its throat out because it didn't smell right, you'd know that was your fault. If you caught a bird and taught it to talk, and then it escaped and it starved to death because it didn't know how to feed itself, you'd be absolutely clear that was on you.

"Well, Melanie's not a cat, is she? Or a bird. She might have grown up into something like that, if you'd left her where you found her. Something wild that didn't know itself and just did whatever it needed to do. But you dropped a net over her and brought her home. And now she's yours. You interfered. You took on a debt."

Parks says nothing. Slowly Justineau reaches behind her and draws the flare gun from where she hid it. She brings it out and lets him see it, in her hand.

She walks to the door of the engine room.

"Helen," Parks says.

She goes through the aft weapons stations to the door. It's locked but unguarded. Caldwell is in the lab, and Gallagher is in the crew quarters flicking through the old CDs like they were porn.

"Helen."

She disengages the lock. It's the first time she's done it, but it's not hard to figure out how the mechanism works. She glances back at Parks, who's got his handgun out and pointed right at her. But only for a second. The hand falls to his side again, and he puffs out his cheeks in a sigh, like he's put down a heavy weight.

Justineau opens the door and steps out. She puts her arm up over her head and pulls the trigger.

The sound is like a firework going off, but more drawn out. The flare whistles and sighs to itself as it ascends into the utter blackness above her.

There's no light, nothing to see. The pistol was a good few years old, after all. Pre-Breakdown, like most of Parks' kit. It must be a dud.

Then it's like God turned on a light in the sky. A red light. From what she knows about God, that's the colour he'd favour.

Everything is as clearly visible as in daylight, but this is nothing like daylight. It's the light of an abattoir, or a horror movie. And it must have reached the interior spaces of Rosie, even though someone has pulled the light-proof baffles down over the tiny reinforced windows, because now Gallagher is looking out through the door right next to Parks, and Caroline Caldwell has deigned to step out of the lab too and is standing

294

behind them, staring out in bewilderment at the crimson midnight.

"You'd better get back inside," Parks tells Justineau in a voice of flat resignation. "She won't be the only one that sees that."

57

Melanie isn't lost, but the sight of the flare cheers her.

She's sitting on the roof of a house half a mile away from Rosie. She's been sitting there for some hours now, in a steady downpour that's already soaked her to the skin. She's trying to make sense of something she saw late in the afternoon, just after she'd finally filled her belly. She's been running it through in her mind ever since in endless, silent replay.

What she ate, after searching rain-slicked alleyways and sodden gardens for an hour and a half, was a feral cat. And she hated it. Not the cat itself, but the process of chasing and catching and eating it. The hunger was driving her, and driving her hard, telling her exactly what to do. As she ripped the cat's belly open with her teeth and gorged herself on what came tumbling out, a part of her was entirely satisfied, entirely at peace. But there was another part that kept itself at a distance from the horrible cruelty and the horrible messiness. That part saw the cat still alive, still twitching as she crunched its fragile ribs to get at its heart. Heard its piteous miawling as it clawed at her uselessly, opening shallow cuts in her arms that didn't even bleed. Smelled the bitter stench of excrement as she accidentally tore open its entrails, and saw her strew the guts in the air like streamers to get at the soft flesh underneath.

She ate it hollow.

And as she did, she dodged through all kinds of irrelevant thoughts. The cat in the picture on the wall of her cell, peacefully and intently lapping up its milk. The proverb about all cats being black at night, which she didn't understand and Mr Whitaker couldn't explain. A poem in a book.

I love little kitty, her coat is so warm.
And if I don't hurt her, she'll do me no harm.

She didn't love little kitty all that much. Little kitty didn't taste half as nice as the two men she ate back at the base. But she knew that little kitty would keep her alive, and she hoped that the hunger would quiet down a little now and not try to order her around so much.

Afterwards, she wandered the streets, feeling both miserable and agitated, unable to keep still. She kept coming back within sight of Rosalind Franklin to make sure it was still there, then veering off again into this or that side street and getting herself lost for an hour or so. She didn't want to go back yet. She was starting to feel as though she'd need to eat again before she did that.

With each loop she walked a little further, and dragged her feet a little more. She was probing the edges of her hunger, exploring the feel and the urgency of it in the way Sergeant Parks explored the rooms at Wainwright House with his rifle in his hands and his eyes going backwards and forwards. It was enemy territory and she had to get to know it.

On one of her outward swings, she found herself in front of a big white building with lots of windows. The windows on the ground floor were enormous, and all broken. There were more windows higher up that were still in their frames. The sign in front of the building said ARTS DEPOT – a little ARTS and then a much bigger DEPOT, sitting right above the door. And the door used to be made of glass, so now it wasn't

297

really there at all. It was just an empty frame, gripping a few fragments of broken glass at its very edges.

There were noises coming from inside – shrill, short bursts of sound, like the yelps of a hurt animal.

A hurt animal would go down very nicely right around then, Melanie thought.

She went inside, into a room with a very high ceiling and two staircases at the end of it. The staircases were metal, with rubbery bits for you to put your hands on. There was another sign at the bottom of them. The light was starting to fade now, and Melanie could only just read it. It said: CHILDREN MUST BE CARRIED ON THE ESCALATOR.

She walked up the stairs. They gave a metallic groan when she first put her weight on them, and shifted slightly with each step she took as though they were about to fall down. She almost turned back, but those shrieks and squeals from inside the building were louder now and she was curious as to what sort of creature was making them.

At the top of the stairs there was a big room with pictures on the walls and lots of chairs and tables. The pictures were impossible to understand, containing words and pictures that seemed to bear no relationship to each other. One said *Twisted Folk Autumn Tour*, and showed a man playing a guitar. But then it showed the same man in the same position playing lots of other things – a dog, a chair, a tree, another man and so on. Some of the tables had plates and cups and glasses on them, but the cups and glasses were all empty and there was nothing on the plates except for indeterminate smears from food that had rotted away a long, long time ago so that now even the rot was gone.

Nothing seemed out of place up here, or alive for that matter. Melanie could hear sounds of rapid movement now as well as the squealing, but the room was so big and so full of echoes that she couldn't tell which direction the sounds were coming from.

She looked around. There were staircases and doors every-where. She took another staircase at random, then a door, then she walked along a corridor and through two other doors that swung open at her touch.

And stopped at once, the way you might stop when you suddenly saw that you'd got too close to the edge of a cliff.

The space she was in now was much, much bigger than the room downstairs, big as that had seemed. It was completely dark, but she guessed its size from the change in the echoes, and from the movement of the air in front of her face. She didn't even have to think about these things. She just knew this place was vast.

And the sounds were coming from below her, so that vast-ness extended in three dimensions, not two.

Melanie held her hands out in front of her at chest height and stepped forward – little baby steps that brought her very quickly to the edge of a platform. Under her fingers was the cold metal of a rail or balustrade.

She stood silently, listening to the squeals, the pounding of feet, and other rhythmical slaps and booms that came and went.

Then someone laughed. A high, delighted trill.

She stood rooted to the spot, amazed. She could feel that she was trembling. That laugh could have been made by Anne or Zoe or any of her friends in the class. It was a little girl's laugh – or just possibly a little boy's.

She almost shouted out, but she didn't. It was a nice laugh, and she thought that perhaps the person who made it must be nice too. But it couldn't just be one person making all that noise. It sounded like lots and lots of people running around. Playing a game, perhaps, in the dark.

She waited for so long that something strange happened. She started to be able to see.

There wasn't any more light to see by. It was just that her eyes decided to give her more information. She'd been told in a lesson once about something called accommodation. The rods and cones of the eye, especially the rods, change their zone of sensitivity so that they can see details and distinctions in what previously looked like total darkness. But there are functional limits to that process, and the resulting picture is mostly black and white because rods aren't good at gradations of colour.

This was different. It was like an invisible sun came up in the room, and Melanie could see by its light as well as she could see by day. Or like the space below her went from black ocean to dry land over the space of a few minutes. She wondered if this was something only hungries could do.

She was in a theatre. She'd never seen one before, but she knew that was what it had to be. There were rows and rows of seats all facing the same way – and where they were facing there was a wide flat place with a wooden floor. A stage. There were more seats on a balcony on top of the first lot of seats, and that was where Melanie was – at one end of the balcony, standing at the edge where it looked down into the main auditorium below.

And she was right about there being more than one person down there. There were at least a dozen.

They weren't playing a game, though. What they were doing was quite different.

Melanie watched them in silence for a long time – perhaps as long as she'd listened to them, or a little more. Her eyes were wide, and her hands gripped very tight on to the balcony rail as though she were afraid of falling down.

She watched until the noises and the movement died away. Then she slipped out, as quietly as she could, through the swing doors and down the stairs.

Out on the street, where it was raining harder than ever, she walked a few faltering steps and came to a halt in the shadow of a wall whose ancient graffiti had faded to ghost patterns of black and grey.

Something was happening to her face. Her eyes were burning,

her throat convulsing. It was almost like the first breath you take in the shower room after the showers have been turned on and the air fills with bitter spray.

But there was no spray here. She was just crying.

The part of her mind that had stayed detached and watched her eat the cat watched this performance too, and mourned a little that – because of the rain – it was impossible to determine whether her weeping involved actual tears.

58

The night crawls past arthritically and aimlessly after a supper that – despite its perilously high salt and sugar content – nobody seems able to taste.

Justineau sits in the crew quarters, twisted round in the seat so she can look through one of the slit windows at the street outside. Behind her she can hear Gallagher's fitful snoring from the sleeping recess. He chose one of the top bunks, and stole blankets from most of the others to make himself a nest. He's completely invisible up there, barricaded away from the world behind ramparts of dreams and polycotton.

He's the only one who sleeps at all. Parks is still stripping the generator, and he doesn't seem inclined to stop. Intermittent clattering from back there tells Justineau that he's making progress. Intermittent swearing announces his temporary setbacks.

In between them is the lab, where Caldwell works in silence, putting slide after slide under a Zeiss LSM 510 confocal microscope with its own built-in battery (the scanning electron microscope still awaits the quickening touch of electric current from Rosie's generator), writing annotations for each in a leather-backed notebook, then racking it in a plastic box whose compartments she carefully numbers.

When the sun comes up, Justineau is silently amazed. It seemed entirely plausible that this ontological impasse would go on for ever.

Through the red dawn a tiny figure walks out of a side street and crosses to Rosie's door.

Justineau gives an involuntary cry and runs to open it. Parks is there ahead of her, and he doesn't move out of her way. There's a thin, muffled sound: bare knuckles, knocking politely on the armour plating.

"You're going to have to let me handle this," Parks tells her. He's got shadows under his eyes and oil smudges on his forehead and cheeks. He looks like he just murdered someone who bled India ink. There's a weary, defeated set to his shoulders.

"What does 'handle it' mean?" Justineau demands.

"It just means I talk to her first."

"With a gun in your hand?"

"No," he grunts irritably. "With these."

He shows her his left hand, in which he holds the leash and the handcuffs.

Justineau hesitates for a second. "I know how handcuffs work," she says. "Why can't I be the one to go out to her?"

Parks wipes his dirty brow on his dirty sleeve. "Jesus wept," he mutters under his breath. "Because that's what she asked for before she left, Helen. You're the one she's concerned about hurting, not me. I'm nearly certain she's okay, because she just knocked on the door instead of clawing at it and bashing her head against it. But whatever kind of mood she's in, the one thing she won't want to see when it opens is you standing there. Especially if she's got blood on her mouth or her clothes from feeding. You understand that, right? After she's cleaned herself up, and after she's got the cuffs back on, then you can talk to her. Okay?"

Justineau swallows. Her throat is dry. The truth is that she's afraid. Mostly she's afraid of what the last twelve hours might have done to Melanie. Afraid that when she looks into the girl's eyes, she might see something new and alien there. For that very reason, she doesn't want to put the moment off. And she doesn't want Parks to look first.

But she does understand, whether she wants to or not, and she can't go against what Melanie specifically asked for. She has to step back, and around the bulkhead wall, while he opens the door.

She hears the bolt slide back, the smooth sigh of hydraulically assisted hinges.

And then she flees, through the aft weapons stations to the lab space. Dr Caldwell looks up at her, indifferent at first. Until she realises what Justineau's agitation must mean.

"Melanie is back," the doctor says, coming to her feet. "Good. I was concerned she might have—"

"Shut your mouth, Caroline," Justineau interrupts savagely. "Seriously. Shut it now, and don't open it again."

Caldwell continues to stare at her. She makes to walk aft, but Justineau is in her way and she stays there. All that aggression that's building up in her, it's got to come out.

"Sit down," Justineau says. "You don't get to see her. You don't get to talk to her."

"Yeah, she does," says Parks, from behind her. She turns, and he's standing in the doorway. Melanie is behind him. He hasn't even put her cuffs on yet, but she's already replaced her muzzle. She's sodden, her hair plastered to the side of her head, her T-shirt clinging to her bony body. The rain has petered out now, so this is from last night.

"She wants to talk to all of us," Parks goes on. "And I think we want to listen. Tell them what you just told me, kid."

Melanie stares hard at Justineau, then even harder at Dr Caldwell. "We're not alone out here," she says. "There's somebody else."

59

In the crew quarters, they choose places to sit. Even though
Rosie's full complement was meant to be a dozen, it feels way
too small. They're aware of each other's proximity, and none
of them looks any more comfortable with that than Justineau
feels.

She's sitting on the edge of a lower bunk. Caldwell sits on
its counterpart, directly opposite. Gallagher is cross-legged on
the floor, and Parks leans in the doorway.

Standing at the forward end of the narrow space, Melanie
addresses them. Justineau has dried her hair with a towel, hung
out her jacket, jeans and T-shirt to dry and put another towel
around her as a temporary bathrobe. Her arms are inside the
towel – behind her back, because Parks has cuffed her hands
again. It was her idea. She turned her back to him, arms held
together, and waited patiently while he did it.

There's massive tension in her face, in the way she stands.
She's struggling to keep herself under control – not in the
feeding frenzy way, but in the way someone might be if they'd
just been mugged on the street or witnessed a murder.
Justineau has seen Melanie scared before, but this is something

new, and for a little while Justineau struggles to identify it. Then she realises what it is. It's uncertainty.

She speculates for the first time on what Melanie could have been, could have become, if she'd lived before the Breakdown. If she'd never been bitten and infected. Because this is a child here, whatever else she is, and she's never lost that sense of her own centre before except when she smelled blood and turned, briefly into an animal. And look at how pragmatically, how ruthlessly, she's coped with that.

But Justineau only pursues this train of thought for a moment. When Melanie starts to speak, she commands their full attention.

"I should have come back sooner," she says, to everyone in the room. "But I was scared, so I ran away and hid at first."

"They don't need a dramatic build-up, kid," Parks drops into the ensuing silence. "Just go ahead and tell them."

But Melanie starts at the beginning and rolls right on, as though that's the only way she knows how to tell it. She recounts her visit to the theatre the night before in spare and functional sentences. The only sign of her agitation is in the way she shifts from foot to foot as she speaks.

Finally she reaches the point where she looked down from the balcony with her dark-adapted eyes and saw what was below her.

"They were men like the ones I saw at the base," she says. "With shiny black stuff all over them and their hair all spiked up. In fact, I think they were exactly the same ones from the base." Justineau feels her stomach lurch. Junkers are maybe the worst news they could get right now. "There were lots and lots of them. They were fighting each other with sticks and knives, except that they weren't. Not really. They were only pretending to fight. And they had guns too – like yours, in big racks on the walls. But they weren't using them. They were just using the sticks and the knives. First knives, then sticks,

306

then knives again. The man who was in charge of the fighting told them when to use sticks and when to change over. And someone asked when they could stop and he said not until I say so."

Melanie shoots a glance at Caroline Caldwell. Her expression is unreadable.

"Did you get an idea how many there were?" Parks asks.

"I tried to count, Sergeant Parks, and I got to fifty-five. But there could have been more, underneath where I was standing. There was a part of the room that I couldn't see, and I didn't want to move in case they heard me. I think there were probably more."

"Jesus!" Gallagher says. His voice is hollow with despair. "I knew it. I knew they wouldn't stop!"

"What made you think," Caldwell asks, "that this was the same group who attacked the base?"

"I recognised some of them," Melanie says promptly. "Not their faces really, but the clothes they wore. Some of them had patches and bits of metal on them, and they made patterns. I remembered the patterns. And one of them had a word on his arm. *Relentless.*"

"A tattoo," Parks translates.

"I think so," Melanie says, her eyes on Dr Caldwell again. "And then, while I was watching, three more men came in. They talked about a trail that they were following, and they said they'd lost it. The leader got really angry with them and sent them straight back out again. He said if they didn't bring back prisoners, he was going to let the other men use them to practise on with their knives and sticks."

That seems to be the end of the story, but Melanie waits, tense and expectant, in case there are questions.

"Christ almighty!" Gallagher moans. He buries his head in his folded arms, and keeps it there.

Justineau turns to Parks. "What do we do?" she asks him.

Because like it or not, he's the one who's going to

307

formulate their strategy. He's the only one who really has a chance of bringing them out of here, now that they've run out of e-blocker and there's an army of murderous lunatics camped on their doorstep. She's heard stories about what the junkers do to people they take alive. Probably bullshit, but enough that you'd want to make sure they took you dead.

"What do we do?" Gallagher echoes, unfolding from his crouch. He stares at her like she's crazy. "We get out of here. We run. Now."

"Not yet we don't," Parks says deliberately. And then when they turn to him, "Better to roll than to run. I'm maybe an hour away from getting the generator working – and from where I stand, this bucket still gives us our best chance. So we don't make a break for it. We lock down until we're good and ready."

"It's anomalous behaviour," Caldwell muses.

Parks gives her a shrewd glance. "From the junkers? Yeah, it is."

"They were in convoy when we saw them. Using the base's vehicles to cover the ground fast. Switching to a fixed base – a command post of some kind – makes no sense. A group that size is going to find it hard to live off the land. Scavenging has proved difficult enough even for the four of us."

Justineau can just about find room to be surprised. "Wow," she says, shaking her head. "Why don't you go and tell them that, Caroline? They nearly made a really stupid mistake there. They need someone with your wisdom and foresight to smack their heads together and get them thinking straight."

Caldwell ignores this sally. "I think we may be missing something that would make sense of this," she says, forensically precise. "It doesn't make sense as it stands."

Parks comes away from the door-frame, rubbing his shoulder. "We lock down," he says again. "Nobody goes out there until further notice. Private, did you find any duct tape in those lockers?"

Gallagher nods. "Yes, sir. Three full rolls, one started."

"Tape up the windows. No telling how good those flare-baffles are."

When he mentions flares, Justineau feels a rush of shame and retrospective dread. When she fired that flare last night, she could have brought the junkers right down on their heads. Parks should have shot her when he had the chance.

"And check how we're doing for water," he's saying now. "Doc, you were going to see if there was any in the filtration tank."

"The tank is full," Caldwell says. "But I wouldn't advise drinking from it until the generator is running. There's algae in there, and probably a lot more contaminants besides. We can rely on the filters to do their job, but only once they get some power."

"Then I guess I'd better get back to work," Parks says. But he doesn't leave. He's looking at Melanie. "What about you?" he demands. "Are you holding up? Been most of a day now since any of us put any blocker on."

"I'm fine now," Melanie tells him in the same pragmatic tone – as though they were discussing some problem external to both of them. "But I can smell all four of you. Miss Justineau and Kieran a little, you and Dr Caldwell a lot. If I can't go out to hunt again, you'd better find some way to lock me up."

Gallagher looks up quickly when Melanie says she can smell him, but he doesn't say anything. He's looking a little pale around the gills.

"Handcuffs and a muzzle aren't enough?" Parks asks.

"I think I could pull my hands out of the handcuffs, if I had to," Melanie tells him. "It would hurt, because I'd have to scrape the skin all off, but I could do it. And then it would be very easy to get the muzzle off."

"There's a specimen cage in the lab," Dr Caldwell says. "I believe it's big enough, and strong enough."

"No." Justineau spits out the word. The anger that went to

sleep while Melanie was talking yawns and stretches, awake again in an instant.

"It sounds like a good idea," Parks says. "Get it ready, Doc. Kid, stay close to it. Like a hop and a jump away. And if you feel anything . . ."

"That's absurd," says Caldwell. "You can't expect her to self-monitor."

"Any more than we can expect you to," Justineau says. "You've been itching to get your hands on her ever since we left the base."

"Since before that," Caldwell says. "But I've resigned myself to waiting until we reach Beacon. Once we're there, the Survivors' Council can hear us both out and make a determination."

Justineau is two syllables into an obscene rejoinder when Parks claps his hand down on her shoulder and turns her round to face him. The brusqueness of it takes her by surprise. He's almost never touched her, and never since his abortive pass on the roof of Wainwright House.

"Enough," he says. "I need you in the engine room, Helen. The rest of you, you know what you're doing. Or you should do. The kid goes in the cage. But you don't touch her, Doc. For now, she's off-limits. You cut her, you'll answer to me. Trust me, all those slides you spent last night making up will not survive the encounter. Understood?"

"I've said I'll wait."

"And I believe you. I'm just saying. Helen?"

Justineau lingers for a moment longer. "If she comes near you," she says to Melanie, "just scream and I'll be right there."

She follows Parks all the way aft to the engine room, where he closes the door and leans his weight against it.

"I know things are bad," Justineau says. "I'm not trying to make them worse. I just . . . I don't trust her. I can't."

"No," Parks agrees. "I don't blame you. But nothing's going to happen to the kid. You've got my word."

It's a relief to hear him say that. To know that he recognises Melanie as an ally, at least for now, and won't let her be hurt.

"But I'd like you to do me a favour in return," Parks goes on.

Justineau shrugs. "Okay. If I can. What?"

"Find out what she really saw."

"What?" Justineau is mystified for a moment. Not angry or exasperated, just at a loss to understand what Parks is saying. "Why would she lie? Why would you even think that she . . .? Shit! Because of what Caroline said? Because she fancies herself as an anthropologist? She doesn't know shit. You can't expect psychopaths like the junkers to make rational decisions."

"Probably not," Parks agrees.

"Then what are you talking about?"

"Helen, the kid's talking hairy-arsed nonsense. I'm pretty sure she saw something last night. And it was probably something that scared her, because she's really sincere about wanting us to leave. But it wasn't junkers."

Justineau is getting angry again. "Why?" she demands. "How do you know? And how many times does she have to prove herself to you?"

"None. No times. I think I've got a pretty good handle on her now. But her story doesn't hold together at all."

He picks up one of the manuals he's been working from, which he's left lying on the cowling of the generator, and sets it aside so he can sit there. He doesn't look happy.

"I can see why you wouldn't want to face up to this," Justineau says. "If they followed us from the base, it means we screwed up. We left a trail."

Parks gives a sound that could be a laugh or just a snort. "We left a trail you could follow facing backwards with your head in a bucket," he says. "It's not that. It's just . . ."

He raises a hand and starts counting off on his fingers.

"She says she saw all men, no women, which means this is a temporary camp. So why don't they put up a perimeter?

311

How come she can walk right in there and walk right out again without being seen?"

"Maybe they have lousy security, Parks. Not everyone has your skill set."

"Maybe. And then we have those guys conveniently coming in just at the right moment and saying they're following someone. And the tattoo. Private Barlow, back at the base, he had that same word on his arm. Some coincidence."

"Coincidences happen, Parks."

"Sometimes they do," Parks agrees. "But then there's Rosie."

"Rosie? What's Rosie got to do with this?"

"She hasn't been touched. We found her standing right here in the street, and there isn't a mark on her. Nobody tried to jack the door open, or to lever out one of the windows. There was all that dirt and grime on her, and not so much as a handprint or a smudge. I'm having a hard time believing that fifty junkers could walk through here and not see her. Or that they could see her and not want to take a look inside. Come to think of it, I'm having a hard time believing that you and Gallagher managed to do your foraging yesterday without bumping into them. Or that they didn't see your flare. If they really are following our trail, they're missing a hell of a lot of tricks."

Justineau is looking for counterarguments, and finding some, when she runs right into the one piece of evidence that Parks didn't see. Those sidelong looks at Caldwell . . . it was as though Melanie was really aiming her story at an audience of one all along. Talking to the doctor over the heads of everyone else in the room.

So she doesn't argue. There's no point when she's more than half sold. But she doesn't let it rest there either. She's not going to go off and interrogate Melanie without knowing what Parks' play is.

"Why did you do that then?" she demands. "Back in there?"

"Why did I do what?"

312

"Order a lockdown. If Melanie is lying, there's no danger."

"I didn't say that."

"But you didn't try to get to the truth. You acted like you believed every word. Why?"

Parks takes a moment to think about that. "I'm not going to bet our lives on a hunch," he says. "I think she's lying, but I could be wrong. It wouldn't be the first time."

"Bullshit, Parks. You don't second-guess yourself like that. Not from what I've seen. Why didn't you at least call her on it?"

Parks rubs his eyes with the heel of his hand. He looks really tired all of a sudden. Tired, and maybe a little older. "It meant something to her," he says. "I don't know what, but unless I'm dead wrong, it's something she's way too scared to talk about. I didn't push her, because I don't have a bastard clue what kind of something that might be. So I'm asking you to find out, because I think you can get her to tell you what scared her without making it any worse for her than it is already. And I don't think I can. We don't have that kind of relationship."

It's the first time since Justineau met Parks that he's actually surprised her.

Without thinking about it, she leans forward and kisses him on the cheek. He freezes just a little, maybe because where she kissed is mostly scar tissue, or maybe just because he didn't see the move coming.

"Sorry," Justineau says.

"Don't be," Parks replies quickly. "But . . . if you don't mind me asking . . ."

"It's just that you talked about her like a human being. With feelings that might sometimes have to be respected. It felt like that was an occasion that ought to be marked somehow."

"Okay," Parks says, trying that on for size. "You want to sit around and talk about her feelings some more? We could—"

"Later maybe." Justineau heads for the door. "I wouldn't want to distract you from your work."

Or get your hopes up, she adds to herself. Because Parks is still someone she mostly associates with blood and death and cruelty. Almost as strongly as she associates herself with those things. It really wouldn't be a good idea for the two of them to get together.

They might breed, or something.

She goes through into the lab where she sees that Caldwell has already set up the specimen cage. It's a fold-out structure, like the airlock, but sturdy. A cube of thick wire mesh about four feet on each side, supported by solid steel uprights that lock into place in brackets set into the walls of the lab. It stands in the forward corner, where it doesn't impede access to work surfaces or equipment.

Melanie is sitting in the cage, knees hugged to her chest. Caldwell is doing very much what Parks is doing with the generator – overhauling a complicated piece of equipment, one of the largest in the lab, so deeply and completely absorbed that she doesn't hear Justineau come in.

"Good morning, Miss Justineau," Melanie says.

"Good morning, Melanie," Justineau echoes. But she's looking at Caldwell. "Whatever you're doing," she says to the doctor, "it's going to have to wait. Go take a cigarette break or something."

Caldwell turns. Almost for the first time, she lets her dislike of Justineau show on her face. Justineau greets it like a friend; it's really something to have got through that emotional barricade.

"What I'm doing is important," Caldwell says.

"Is it? Too bad. Get out, Caroline. I'll tell you when you can come back."

For a long moment they're face to face, almost squaring off against each other. It looks like Caldwell might go for it, damaged hands or not, but she doesn't. It's probably just as well. She looks bad enough right now that a stiff wind would knock her down, never mind a stiff punch in the head.

314

"You should examine the pleasure you take in intimidating me," Caldwell says.

"No, that might spoil it."

"You should ask yourself," Caldwell persists, "why you're so keen on thinking of me as the enemy. If I make a vaccine, it might cure people like Melanie, who already have a partial immunity to *Ophiocordyceps*. It would certainly prevent thousands upon thousands of other children from ending up the way she has. Which weighs the most, Helen? Which will do the most good in the end? Your compassion, or my commitment to my work? Or could it be that you shout at me and disrespect me to stop yourself from having to ask questions like that?"

"It could be," Justineau admits. "Now do as you're told and get out."

She doesn't wait for an answer. She just bundles Caldwell to the forward end of the room, pushes her through into the crew quarters and closes the door on her. The doctor is so weak that it isn't even hard. The door doesn't lock, though. Justineau waits there for a moment or two in case Caldwell tries to come back in, but the door stays closed.

Finally, satisfied that they've got as much privacy as they're going to get, she goes back to the cage and kneels beside it. She stares through the bars at the small, pale face inside.

"Hi," she says.

"Hi, Miss Justineau."

"Is it okay if we . . ." she starts to say. But then she thinks better of it. "I'm coming in," she says.

"No!" Melanie yelps. "Don't. Stay there!" As Justineau puts her hand on the door and slides back the bolt, the girl scrambles to the other end of the cage. She presses herself hard into the corner.

Justineau stops, with the door half open. "You said you could only smell me a little bit," she says. "Is it enough to be uncomfortable for you?"

"Not yet." Melanie's voice is tight.

"Then we're okay. If that changes, you tell me and I'll get out. But I don't like you being in a cage like an animal with me out there looking in. This would feel better for me. If it's okay with you."

But it's clear from Melanie's face that it's not okay. Justineau gives up. She closes the door and locks it again. Then she sits down and leans her shoulder against the mesh, legs crossed.

"Okay," she says. "You win. But come on over here and sit with me at least. If you're inside and I'm outside, that should be fine, right?"

Melanie advances cautiously, but she stops halfway, evidently fearful of a situation that could spiral quickly out of her control. "If I tell you to get further back, you have to do it right away, Miss Justineau."

"Melanie, there's a wire-mesh screen in between us and you've got your muzzle on. You can't hurt me."

"I don't mean that," Melanie says quietly.

Obviously. She's talking about changing, in front of her teacher and her friend. Ceasing to be herself. That prospect scares her a lot.

Justineau feels ashamed, not just about the thoughtless comment but about what she's come here to do. Melanie must have lied for a reason. Breaking down the lie feels wrong. But so does the thought of some new random factor out there that Melanie wants them all to run away from. Parks is right. They have to know.

"When you went into the theatre last night . . ." she begins tentatively.

"Yes?"

"And saw the junkers . . ."

"There weren't any junkers, Miss Justineau."

Just like that. Justineau's got her next few lines already prepared. She stares stupidly, mouth open. "No?" she says.

316

"No."

And Melanie tells her what she really saw.

Running between the mildewed seats and across the booming stage. Naked as the day they were born. And filthy, although their skin underneath the dirt was the same bone white as her own. Their hair hanging lank and heavy, or in a few cases standing up in spikes. Some of them had sticks in their hands, and some of them had bags – old plastic bags, with words on them like *Foodfresh* and *Grocer's Market*.

"But I wasn't lying about the knives. They had those too. Not stabbing knives like Sergeant Parks' and Kieran's. Knives like you might cut bread or meat with in a kitchen."

Fifteen of them. She counted. And when she made up the story of the junkers, she just added forty more.

But they weren't junkers. They were children of every age from maybe four or five to about fifteen. And what they were doing was chasing rats. Some of them beating the floor and the seats with their sticks to get the rats running. Others catching them when they ran, biting off their heads and drop-ping the limp bodies into the bags. They were much faster than the rats, so it wasn't hard for them. They made it into a game, laughing and taunting each other with shrieks and funny faces as they ran.

Children like her. Children who were hungries too, and alive, and animated, and enjoying the thrill of the hunt. Until they sat down, at last, and feasted on the small, blood-drenched corpses, the big ones choosing first, the little ones pushing in between them to snatch and steal. Even that was a game, and they were still laughing. There was no threat in it.

"There was a boy who seemed to be the leader. He had a big stick like a king's sceptre, all shiny, and his face was painted in lots of different colours. It made him look sort of scary, but he wasn't scary to the little ones: he was protecting them. When one of the other big kids showed her teeth to one of the little

317

ones and looked like she was going to bite him, the painted-face boy put his stick on the big kid's shoulder and she stopped. But mostly they didn't try to hurt each other. It seemed like they were a family almost. They all knew each other, and they liked being together."

It was a midnight picnic. Watching it, Melanie felt like she was looking at her own life through the wrong end of a telescope. This was what she would have been if she hadn't been taken away to the base. This was what she was supposed to be. And the way she felt about that kept changing as she thought about it. She was sad that she couldn't join the picnic. But if she hadn't gone to the base, she would never have learned so many things and she would never have met Miss Justineau.

"I started to cry," Melanie says. "Not because I was sad, but because I didn't know if I was sad or not. It was like I was missing all those kids down there, even though I'd never even met them. Even though I didn't know their names. They probably didn't *have* names. It didn't seem like they could talk, because they just made these squeaking and growling sounds at each other."

The emotions that cross the little girl's face are painfully intense. Justineau puts her hand up against the side of the cage, slides her fingers through the mesh.

Melanie leans forward, letting her forehead touch the tips of Justineau's fingers.

"So . . . why didn't you tell us all this?" It's the first thing Justineau can think of to ask. She skirts around Melanie's existential crisis with instinctive caution, afraid to confront it head on. She knows Melanie won't let her go into the cage and hug her, not with that fear of losing herself, so all she has is words, and words feel inadequate for the job.

"I don't mind telling you," Melanie says simply. "But it has to be our secret. I don't want Dr Caldwell to know. Or Sergeant Parks. Or even Kieran."

318

"Why not, Melanie?" Justineau coaxes. And gets it as soon as she's asked. She holds up her hand to stop Melanie from saying it. But Melanie says it anyway.

"They'd catch them and put them in cells under the ground," she says. "And Dr Caldwell would cut them up. So I made up something that I thought would make Sergeant Parks want to go away really fast, before anyone finds out they're here. Please say you won't tell, Miss Justineau. Please promise me."

"I promise," Justineau whispers. And she means it. Whatever comes of it, she won't let Caroline Caldwell know that she's sitting right next door to a new batch of test subjects. There'll be no culling of these feral children.

Which means she'll have to go back to Parks and maintain the lie. Or bring him in on it. Or come up with a better one.

The two of them are silent for a moment, both presumably thinking about how this changes things between them. Back when they first left the base, she'd offered Melanie the choice between staying with them and going into one of the nearby towns. "To be with your own kind," she'd almost said, and stopped herself because she realised even as she was saying it that Melanie didn't *have* a kind.

But now she does.

While she's still thinking through the implications of what Melanie has just told her, Justineau starts to shake. For a surreal and terrifying moment she thinks it's just her – that it's some sort of seizure. But the vibration settles into a throbbing rhythm that she recognises, and there's a low rumble in her ears that crests and then dies. The throbbing dies with it as quickly as it came.

"My God!" Justineau gasps.

She scrambles up off the floor and runs, heading aft.

Parks stands over the generator, his oily hands hovering as though he's just performed a blessing. Or an exorcism. "Got it," he says, giving Justineau a fierce grin as she comes into the room.

319

"But it died again," she says.

Caldwell follows her into the room. The generator's magical resurrection has brought her running too.

"No, it didn't. I cut it off. Don't want the noise to carry until we're ready to drive out. You never know who's listening, after all."

"So we can leave!" Justineau says. "Keep going south. Let's roll, Parks. To hell with anything else."

He gives her a wry look. "Yeah," he says. "Don't want to have to tangle with those junkers. We might have to . . ." He stops and looks past the two women, his face serious all of a sudden.

"Where's Gallagher?" he demands.

60

Gallagher is in the wind. He's bolted. The pressure that had been building in him exploded outwards, all at once, and carried him out of there before he even registered what he was doing.

It's not that he's a coward. It's more like a law of motion. Because the pressure, for him, was coming from in front as well as from behind – from the thought of what he was going back to. He just got squeezed sideways.

Yeah, but it's also the thought of locking the door, turning out the lights and waiting for the junkers to find them. Like anyone could possibly miss them, just standing out there in the street.

When the base fell, Gallagher saw Si Brooks – the man who rented out his precious vintage porno mag to the whole barracks, and was privately in love with the girl on page twenty-three – get his face split open with the butt of a rifle. And Lauren Green, one of the few female privates he could talk to without getting tongue-tied, was stabbed in the stomach with a bayonet. And he would have got a helping of that too, if Sergeant Parks hadn't grabbed him by the shoulder and hauled him away from the corner of the mess hall, where he was hiding, with a terse "I need a gunner."

Gallagher has no illusions about how long he would have lasted otherwise. He was nailed to the spot with pure terror. But nailed was the wrong word, because what he was actually feeling right then was more like vertigo – as though if he moved, he was going to fall in some random direction, slant-wise across the tilting world.

So he's ashamed, now, to be running out on the Sarge, his saviour. But this is how you square the circle. Can't go back. Can't go forward. Can't stay put. So you pick another direction and you get out from under.

The river is going to save him. There'll be boats there, left over from the old days before the Breakdown. He can row or sail away and find an island somewhere, with a house on it but no hungries, and live on what he can grow or hunt or trap. He knows that Britain is an island, and that there are others close to it. He's seen maps, although he doesn't remember the fine detail. How hard can it be? Explorers and pirates used to do it all the time.

He's heading south, with the aid of the compass from his belt. Or rather he's trying to, but the streets don't always help. He's left the main drag, where he felt way too exposed, and is zigzagging his way through back streets. The compass tells him which way to go, and he follows its advice whenever the maze of avenues, crescents and cul-de-sacs allows him to. They're mercifully empty. He hasn't seen a live hungry since he flung open Rosie's door and fled. Just a couple more of the dead ones with the trees growing out of them.

He'll get to the river, which can only be another five miles or so, and then he'll take stock. As he walks, the rain clouds roll on past and the sun comes out again. Gallagher is surprised, in a dislocated kind of way, to see it again. The warmth and the light seem to have nothing in common with the world he's journeying through. It even makes him a little uneasy

322

– dangerously exposed, as though the sun is a spotlight focused on him, keeping pace with him as he walks.

Something else too. He sees movement in the street ahead of him that makes him jump like a hare and all but piss himself. But then he realises it's not in the street at all. There's nothing there. It was the shadow of something moving behind and above him, up on one of the rooftops. A junker? Didn't look big enough for that, and he's pretty sure he would have been shot in the back already if they were on him. More likely a cat or something, but shit, that was a bad moment.

He's still shaking, and his stomach feels like it's going to do something that might be slightly projectile. Gallagher finds a place where the rusting remains of a car screen him from the street, and sits down for a moment. He takes a drink from his canteen.

Which is almost empty.

He's aware suddenly that there are a whole lot of things he could really do with right now, and flat-out doesn't have.

Like food. He didn't feel like he could steal one of the backpacks when he left, so he's got nothing. Not even the packet of peanuts he'd slipped under the pillow of his bunk for later.

Or his rifle.

Or the empty tube of e-blocker he was going to peel open so he could rub the last nubs of gel over his underarms and crotch.

He's got his sidearm and six clips of ammunition. He's got a little water left. He's got the compass. And he's got the grenade, which is still in the pocket of his fatigues where it's sat ever since they abandoned the Humvee. That's it. That's the whole inventory.

What kind of idiot goes for a hike through enemy territory with just the clothes he's standing up in? He's got to resupply, and he's got to do it fast.

The lock-up garage where he and Justineau found the snack

323

foods is a couple of miles behind him now. He hates to double back and lose time. But he'd hate starving to death a whole lot more, and there's no guarantee that he'll find another mother lode like that between here and the Thames.

Gallagher stands up and gets himself moving again. It's not easy, but he immediately feels better, just to be doing something. He's got a defined goal, and he's got a plan. He's going backwards, but only so he can go forwards again and get further this time.

After five or six turns, compass or not, he's totally lost.

And he's pretty much certain now that he's not alone. He doesn't see any more moving shadows, but he can hear shuffling and skittering sounds coming from somewhere really close by. Whenever he pauses to listen, there's nothing, but it's right there behind the sound of his own footsteps when he starts walking again. Someone is moving when he moves, stopping when he stops.

It sounds like they're almost on top of him. He ought to be able to see them, but he can't. He can't even be sure what direction they're coming from. But the shadow he saw . . . that was definitely cast by something up on the roof. If he's being stalked, Gallagher thinks, that would be a great way for the stalker to stay close to him without being seen.

Okay. So let's see them jump clear across the street.

He breaks into a run, without warning. Sprints across the street and then sidelong into an alley.

Across a sort of parking area behind some burnt-out shops. Through one of the gaping back doors, into a narrow hallway. A vulcanised rubber swing door, rotten and sticky to the touch, takes him on to the sales floor, which Gallagher crosses quickly and . . .

Slows. Then stops.

Because this is some sort of mini-market, with about six cramped aisles and shelves from floor to ceiling.

On the shelves: toilet brushes, eggcups in the shape of smiling chicks, tin bread bins decorated with Union Jacks, wooden mousetraps with their name ("The Little Nipper") stamped on their sides, cheese graters with easy-grip handles, chopping boards, tea towels, novelty condiment sets, bin liners, car seat protectors, magnetic screwdrivers.

And food.

Not much of it – just one section of shelving at the end of an aisle – but the tins and packets don't seem to have been touched. They're still neatly arrayed by type, all the soups on one shelf, foreign cuisine on another, rice and pasta on a third. Just as some anonymous and probably long-dead retail grunt set them out on what must have seemed like an ordinary morning, in a world that nobody thought could end.

The tins are blown, every one of them. They're full in the sun right now, as they must have been on every sunny day going back to before Gallagher was even born.

But there are packets too. He examines them first with hope, and then with excitement.

Gourmet's Feast Chicken Curry with Rice – just add water!
Gourmet's Feast Beef Stroganoff – just add water!
Gourmet's Feast Mixed Meat Paella – just add water!

In other words, desiccated foods in airtight sachets.

Gallagher tears one open and takes a tentative sniff. It smells pretty bloody good, all things considered. And he really doesn't care whether or not this stuff ever met a chicken or a cow, as long as he can keep it down.

He pours in about a third of his remaining water, grips the neck of the sachet tight and shakes it for half a minute or so. Then he opens it and squeezes a dollop of the resulting paste straight into his mouth.

It's delicious. A gourmet's feast, just like it says on the label. And he doesn't even need to chew. It slides down as easy as soup. The slight grittiness doesn't bother him either, until some of the unmixed powder accidentally goes down his throat and he breaks into a fit of explosive coughing, anointing all the packets left on the shelf with brown flecks of curried spit.

He finishes off the packet, with a bit more caution. Then he rips open a few more of them, discarding the cardboard sleeves and stuffing his many pockets with the food sachets. When he reaches the river, he'll celebrate with two or three of them chosen at random. A mix-and-match supper.

Speaking of which, he should really get going. But he can't resist casting a quick eye over the rest of the store, wondering what other marvels it might contain.

When he finds the magazine rack, Gallagher's heart leaps. The entire top shelf – ten feet or more of display space – is full of porno mags. He takes them down, one after another, and turns the pages as reverently as if they contained holy writ. Women of inconceivable beauty smile back at him with love, understanding and welcome. Their legs and hearts are wide open.

If he were still at the base, this treasure trove would make him rich beyond measure. Pilgrims would come from every barracks to pay him in tobacco and alcohol for a half-hour in the company of these ladies. The fact that he doesn't smoke and fears alcohol almost as badly as he fears hungries and junkers does nothing to tarnish this dazzling vision. He'd be the man, nonetheless. One of those guys who gets a nod or a word from everybody when he walks into the mess hall, and takes it as his due. A man whose acknowledgement, when granted, confers status on those who get a nod or a word in return.

The creak of a floorboard startles Gallagher back from eternal glory into the here and now. He lowers the magazine that's in his hands. Ten feet away, hidden until that moment by the magazine although she's not making any effort to conceal herself, is a girl. She's tiny, naked, skinny as a bag of sticks. For a startling moment, she looks like a black and white photograph, because her hair is jet and her skin is pure, unmitigated white. Her eyes are as black and bottomless as holes drilled through a board. Her mouth is a straight, bloodless line.

She could be five or six years old, or an emaciated seven.

She just stands there, staring at Gallagher. Then, when she's sure she's got his attention, she holds out her hand and shows him what she's holding. It's a dead rat without a head.

Gallagher looks from the rat to the girl's face. Then back to the rat. They stand like that for what feels like a long time. Gallagher sucks in a long, tremulous breath.

"Hey," he says at last. "How are you doing?"

It's about the stupidest line you could come up with, but he's having a really hard time believing this is happening. This little girl is a hungry, that's obvious. But she's one of the Melanie kind of hungries, that can think and doesn't have to eat people if it doesn't want to.

And she's giving him a peace offering. A pretty major one, given how agonisingly thin she is.

But she doesn't make a move towards him, and she doesn't say anything. Can she even speak? The kids at the base were more like animals when they were first brought in. They learned to talk pretty quickly once they heard other people talking, but he remembers them squealing like little piglets or chittering like chimps to start with.

Doesn't matter. There's other stuff. Body language.

Gallagher gives the girl a big wide smile and a friendly wave. She's still not moving, and her face is as rigid as a mask. She just jiggles the rat at him, the way you'd do for a dog.

"You're a very pretty little girl," Gallagher tells her inanely. "What's your name? My name's Kieran. Kieran Gallagher."

The rat jiggles again. The girl's mouth opens and closes as though she's miming eating.

This is ridiculous. He's going to have to take the rat, or the impasse will go on for ever.

Gallagher puts down the porno mag very slowly – face down, as if this living dead kid was capable of being embarrassed or corrupted by the bare breasts on the cover. He shows her his empty hands. Moving in the gradual, strolling gait Sergeant Parks taught him, he advances on her, one step at a time. He's careful to keep his hands in full view and the smile on his face the whole time.

He reaches out one hand, very slowly, for the rat.

The little brat hauls it back, out of his reach. Gallagher stops dead, wondering if maybe he's misunderstood.

Pain explodes in his left leg, then his right, sudden and astonishing. He screams and falls, both legs buckling under him so that he hits the floor as heavy and ungainly as a toppled wardrobe. Diminutive figures flee away on both sides of him from the intersecting aisle where they'd been crouching hidden. He doesn't get a good look at them because he's in pain and he's angry and he's too thoroughly confused even to realise at first what it is that's just happened.

He levers himself up on one elbow and looks down at his feet, but he can't process what he's seeing. There's red everywhere. Blood. It's blood. And it's his. He knows that because he can feel it now as well as see it. The backs of his calves pulse and throb agonisingly. From the knees down, his trousers are already saturated.

What did they do? he wonders dazedly. *What did they just do to me?*

He catches a blur of movement in his peripheral vision, and he turns. Another little kid is rushing on him. His face is a bright splash of random colour, in which his eyes show out as two black pinpricks. His arm is raised high, and he's holding a shining metal something over his head that glints blindingly in the slanting afternoon light.

Gallagher flinches away with a shriek of terror as the boy swings. For a crazy moment he thinks the weapon is a sword, but as it flashes past him he sees that it's too fat, too solid. The metal shelf unit takes most of the force of the blow. Gallagher brings his arm up to smack the kid in the chest backhanded,

328

and the kid weighs nothing so the blow sends him spinning head over heels. The weapon — it's an aluminium baseball bat — flies out of his hand and clatters at Gallagher's feet.

Which are now in an actual puddle. A puddle of his own blood.

The painted-face kid scrambles away, but there's two more of them running in now from either side, one with a knife and the other swinging what looks like a butcher's cleaver. Gallagher screams again at the top of his voice, and snatches up the baseball bat.

The hungry kids abort their attack runs, back-pedal right out of his reach.

But they're everywhere now. Gallagher can't see how many but it seems like dozens. Hundreds, maybe. Little pale faces peer at him through the gaps in the shelves, duck in and out of view. Bolder ones crowd the ends of the aisle, staring at him openly. They're armed with everything under the sun, from knives and forks to broken branches. They're mostly stark naked like the girl, but some are wearing weirdly assorted clothes that must have been looted from shop displays. One boy has a leopard-print bra fastened diagonally across his upper body, tied at the bottom end to a webbing belt from which a whole bunch of ornamental key rings are hanging.

The little girl he saw first is still standing there, Gallagher sees now. She's just stepped back a little to give the ones with the weapons a bit more room. She's chewing on the dead rat, calm and patient.

Gallagher tries to get up, but his legs won't bear his weight. He can't take his eyes off the kids in case they attack again, so he reaches down with his free hand to try and figure out by feel what it is that's happened to him. There's a broad rent in the right leg of his trousers, halfway between knee and ankle. Gingerly he reaches through it to touch the edges of the wound. It's not wide, but it's long and it's straight and you have to figure it's deep.

Same with the left leg.

The rat wasn't a peace offering. It was bait. And it shouldn't have worked because he doesn't eat rat, but hey, what do you know? He's a sucker for a pretty face. The little moppet manoeuvred him into position, and then two of her friends sliced him up from behind.

He's been hamstrung.

He's not walking out of here.

He may never walk again.

"Fuck!" Gallagher is surprised when the word comes out of him as a whisper. In his mind it was a shout.

"Listen," he says, aloud. "Listen to me. This is not . . . you're not going to do this to me. You understand? You can't . . ."

The faces he's seeing don't change. The same expression on all of them. Wild, aching need, somehow reined in, somehow not acted on.

They're waiting for him to die, so they can eat him.

He takes out his sidearm and points it. At the girl. Then at the kid who dropped the baseball bat. He looks to be one of the oldest. He's got incongruously red, full lips, where most of them barely have lips at all. You don't notice that at first because of the paint all over his face, which Gallagher realises is not abstract. It's another face, kind of a monster's face painted over his own, the open mouth encompassing everything from his nose to his chin. The work is smudgy enough and wobbly enough to suggest that he did it himself, probably in marker pen. His lank, black hair hangs straight down over his eyes, giving him a louche, rock-star look. He's so skinny, Gallagher can count every rib.

And the gun doesn't bother him at all. He stares right past it, unblinking, into Gallagher's eyes.

Gallagher waves the gun at the other kids, one by one. They don't even seem to see it. They don't know what a gun is or why they should be afraid of one. He's going to have to shoot at least one of them to make them get it.

Better do it quick too. His hand is trembling and there's a

sort of fuzzy static behind his eyes. The world's starting to jump a little, like a car on a bumpy road. He tries to focus through the shakes.

Painted-face boy. The one who dropped the baseball bat. He's right at the front of the crowd, and he's probably the one in charge of Operation Eat-Kieran-Gallagher, so fuck him, he's duly nominated.

But he keeps moving. They all keep moving. Might hit the little girl if he's not careful. For some reason, Gallagher doesn't want to do that, even though she set him up. She's too small. It would feel too much like murder.

There he is, the little bastard. Target acquired. The gun feels like it weighs a couple of hundredweight but Gallagher only needs to hold it on the right line for a couple of seconds. Just time enough to squeeze, squeeze, and . . .

The trigger doesn't move.

The clip's empty.

Gallagher used it up on the second day when they were running through the crowd of hungries to get into that hospital place. Wainwright House. Then he switched to the rifle, and it's the rifle he's had in his hands ever since whenever it seemed like they might have to fight. He's never reloaded.

He almost laughs. The kids haven't even reacted because the gun doesn't mean a damn thing to them. It's the baseball bat that's keeping them at bay.

Except it's not. Not any more. They're advancing slowly from both ends of the aisle, creeping in closer to him a step or two at a time, like they're on a dare. Painted-face boy is leading the pack, even though he doesn't have a weapon any more. His bony fingers flex and contract.

Numbness is creeping over Gallagher now, seeping up through his body from his wounded legs. But the terror effervescing in his mind keeps it back, and brings a sudden inspiration. Quickly he shifts on to his left side, so he can feel in the pockets of his fatigues for . . .

331

Yes! There it is. His hand closes on the cold metal. *Hail Mary*, he thinks incredulously, *full of grace.*

The kids are really close. Gallagher pulls the grenade from his pocket and holds it out for them to see.

"Look!" he yells. "Look at this!" The inexorable advance slows and stops, but he knows it's the shout and not the danger that has made the kids hesitate. They're gauging how much fight he has left in him.

"Boooooom!" Gallagher mimes an explosion, throwing his arms out wildly. Silence for a moment. Then painted-face boy barks back at him. He thinks it's just a threat display. A pissing contest.

And the kids are moving again. Closing in for the kill.

"It's a bomb!" Gallagher shouts desperately. "It's a fucking grenade. It will rip you apart. Go and eat a stray dog or something. I'll do it. I mean it. I'll really do it."

No reaction. He takes the pin between thumb and forefinger.

He doesn't want to kill them. Just to make sure his own exit is a white light and a sudden shock, rather than something drawn out and horrible, beyond his capacity to endure. It's not like they've left him a choice. He doesn't have any choice at all.

"Please," he says.

Nothing.

And when it comes to it, he can't do it. If he could make them understand what it was he was threatening them with, maybe it would be different.

He drops the baseball bat, and the feral children take him like a wave. The grenade is knocked out of his hand and rolls away.

"I don't want to hurt you!" Gallagher shrieks. And it's the truth, so he tries not to fight back as they clutch and bite and tear at him. They're just kids, and their childhood has probably been as big a load of shit as his was.

In a perfect world, he would have been one of them.

61

Parks is determined to search even though he knows the chance of finding Gallagher is close to zero. They can't shout and they can't throw up any kind of a grid, because it's just the three of them – himself, Helen Justineau and the kid. Dr Caldwell claimed she was too weak to walk very far, and since she looks as though a harsh word would break her in two, he didn't argue the point.

But they don't need a grid. Melanie turns herself around like a weathercock, sniffs the wind a couple of times. She ends up facing a little bit west of south.

"That way."

"You're sure?" Parks asks her.

A nod. No wasted words. She leads the way.

But the trail goes all over the place, up one road and down another, mostly keeping southerly at first, but then not even that. Gallagher seems to have doubled back on himself, when he was only a mile or so out from Rosie. Parks wonders if the kid might be stringing them along for some reason – to look important, maybe, and to have the grown-ups' attention. But that's bullshit. Maybe a ten-year-old with a pulse would

333

pull a trick like that, but Melanie's more grounded. If she didn't know where Gallagher went, she'd just say so.

There's something else going on though, and it's between Melanie and Justineau – a dialogue of scared glances that reaches a crescendo at the point where the trail crosses a street into a back alley.

The kid stops and looks at him. "Get out your gun, Sergeant," she says quietly. She's gone way solemn.

"Hungries?" He doesn't care how she knows. He just wants to be clear about what he's walking into.

"Yes."

"Where?"

The kid hesitates. They're in a sort of parking apron behind some shops. Lots of doorways on three sides of them, mostly broken open or broken down. A rusting car off on one side that's up on bricks, probably already immobile long before the Breakdown silenced the roads. Wheelie bins laid out in a long line for a collection that never came.

"There," Melanie says at last. The doorway she nods towards is at first glance no different from any of the others. Second glance takes in the trodden-down weeds right in front of it, one of them a monster thistle that's still wet with sap where it was broken.

Parks goes to silent running. Better late than never, he figures. He taps Justineau's hand, indicates that she should take out her handgun. The two of them approach the door like cops in a pre-Breakdown TV drama, exaggeratedly furtive despite the crunch and grind of their footsteps on the broken ground.

Melanie steps in between and turns to face them.

"Cut me loose," she says to Parks.

He looks her in the eye. "Hands?"

"Hands and mouth."

"Not that long ago, you asked me to tie you up," he reminds her.

"I know. I'll be careful."

She doesn't need to say the rest out loud. If they're walking into an enclosed space full of hungries, they'll probably need her. Can't argue with that. Parks unlocks the cuffs, slides them into his belt. Melanie undoes the muzzle for herself and hands it to him.

"Will you look after this for me, please?" she asks.

He pockets it, and Melanie walks before them into the darkness.

But they're coming late to the party. Whatever happened here, it's already over. A broad smeared trail of blood leads from the centre of an aisle into a corner out of the sun, which is where the hungries took Gallagher so they could eat him. He stares straight at the ceiling with a look of patient suffering on his face, like the more mannerly depictions of Christ on the cross. Unlike Christ, he's been chewed down to the bone in most places. His jacket is gone. No sign of it anywhere. His shirt, ripped wide open, frames the hollow chasm of his torso. His dog tags have fallen among exposed vertebrae. The hungries appear somehow to have eaten his throat without breaking the steel chain – like that party trick where you whip out the tablecloth without disturbing the crockery.

Justineau turns away, tears squeezed out from her closed eyes, but she makes no sound. Neither does Parks, for a moment or two. All he can think of is that he had a command of one and he let the boy die alone. That's the sort of sin you go to hell for.

"We should bury him," Melanie says.

For a moment his anger turns on her. "Fuck's the point?" he growls, glaring at her. "They didn't leave enough to bury. You could scoop him up and drop him in a frigging litter bin."

Melanie meets him more than halfway. Teeth bared, she snarls right back at him. "We have to bury him. Or dogs and other hungries will get him and eat even more of him. And there

335

won't be anywhere to show where he died. You should honour a fallen soldier, Sergeant!"

"Honour a . . . Where the fuck did that come from?"

"The Trojan War, most likely," Justineau mutters. She wipes her eyes with the heel of her hand. "Melanie, we can't . . . there isn't anywhere. And we don't have the time. We'd just be making ourselves into targets. We're going to have to leave him."

"If we can't bury him," Melanie says, "then we have to burn him."

"With what?" Justineau demands.

"With the stuff in the big barrels," Melanie says impatiently. "From the room with the generator in it. It says *Inflammable* on it, and that means it burns."

Justineau says something else. Trying to explain, maybe, why dragging twenty-gallon drums of aviation fuel through the streets is another activity that they won't be engaging in.

But Parks is thinking, with a sort of dull wonder: as far as the kid is concerned, the world never ended. They taught her all these old, old things, filled her head with all this unservice-able shit, and they thought it didn't matter because she was never going to leave her cell except to be dismantled and smeared on microscope slides.

His stomach lurches. He has a sense, for the first time in his soldiering career, of what a war crime might look like from the inside. And it's not him who's the criminal, or even Caldwell. It's Justineau. And Mailer. And that drunken bastard Whitaker, and all the rest of them. Caldwell, she's just a butcher. She's Sweeney Todd, with a barber's chair and a straight razor. She didn't spend years twisting kids' brains into pretzels.

"We can say a prayer for him," Justineau is saying now. "But we can't drag one of those fuel drums all the way here, Melanie. And even if we could—"

"Okay," Parks says. "Let's do it."

336

Justineau looks at him like he's gone mad. "This isn't a joke," she tells him grimly.

"Do I look like I'm joking? Hey, she's right. She's making more sense than either of us."

"We can't—" Justineau says again.

Parks loses it.

"Why the hell not?" he roars. "If she wants to honour the fucking dead, let her do it! School's out, teacher. School's been out for days now. Maybe you missed that."

Justineau stares at him in bewilderment. Her face is a little pale. "You shouldn't shout," she mutters, making shushing motions with her hands.

"Did I get moved to your class?" Parks asks her. "Are you my teacher now?"

"The hungries that did this are probably still close enough to hear you. You're giving away our position."

Parks raises his rifle and squeezes off a round, making Justineau flinch and yelp. The shot punches a hole in the ceiling. Clods of damp plaster thud down, one of them bouncing off Parks' shoulder and leaving a white streak where it hit. "I would welcome a word or two with them," he says.

He turns to Melanie, who's watching all this with wide eyes. It must be like seeing Mummy and Daddy quarrel. "What do you say, kid? Shall we give Kieran a Viking funeral?"

She doesn't answer. She's caught between a rock and a hard place, because if she says yes, then she's siding with him against Justineau – and there's no way that crush is subsiding any time soon.

Parks takes silence for consent. He goes around behind the counter, where he's already seen a box of disposable lighters. They're still full of fluid – only a few ccs in each one, but there are about a hundred of them. He brings them back to the pathetic remains.

Being a man of a practical turn of mind, he takes the walkie-talkie from Gallagher's belt and transfers it to his own before breaking open the little plastic tubes one at a time and emptying the lighter fluid out on to Gallagher's corpse. Justineau watches, shaking her head. "What about the smoke?" she asks him.

"What about it?" Parks grunts.

Melanie turns her back on the two of them and walks down the aisle, all the way to the front of the shop. She comes back a moment later carrying a bright yellow cagoule in a plastic wrapper.

She kneels and puts it under Gallagher's head. She's kneeling in his blood, which isn't even dry yet. When she stands again, red-black streaks adorn her knees and calves.

Parks gets to the last lighter. He could use it to light the pyre, but he doesn't. He pours it on, like the rest, then strikes a spark with his tinderbox to start the blaze.

"God bless, Private," he mutters, as the flames consume what little is left of Kieran Gallagher.

Melanie is saying something too, but it's under her breath – to the dead body, not to the rest of them – and Parks can't hear. Justineau, to do her justice, waits in silence until they're done, which is basically when the greasy, stinking flames force them back.

They make the return trip to Rosie a lot more widely spaced than on the outward journey, and with a lot less to say to each other. The shop blazes behind them, sending up a thick pillar of smoke that spreads, far over their heads, into a black umbrella.

Justineau is treating Parks like a dog that's showing a little foam around the gums, which he feels is probably more than fair right then. Melanie walks ahead of them both, shoulders hunched and head lowered. She hasn't asked for her cuffs and muzzle to be replaced, and Parks hasn't offered.

When they're most of the way back, the kid stops. Her head snaps up, suddenly alert.

"What's that?" she whispers.

Parks is about to say he can't hear anything, but there is a vibration in the air and now it assembles itself into a sound. Something stirring into wakefulness, sullen and dangerous, asserting its readiness to pick a fight and win it.

Rosie's engines.

Parks breaks into a run, turning the corner of the Finchley High Road in time to see the distant speck grow in seconds into a behemoth.

Rosie weaves a little, both because there's debris in the road and because Dr Caldwell is driving with her thumbs hooked into the bottom of the steering wheel. Every twitch of her arm translates into a yawing roll of the long vehicle.

Without even thinking about it, Parks steps into the road. He has no idea what Caldwell is doing, what she might be fleeing from, but he knows he has to stop her. Rosie lurches like a drunk to miss him, smashing into a parked car, which is dragged along with it for a few yards before breaking apart in a shower of rust and glass.

Then it's gone by. They're staring at the mobile lab's tail lights as it accelerates away from them.

"What the fuck?" Justineau exclaims in a bewildered tone.

Parks seconds that emotion.

62

As soon as Parks and Justineau go off in search of Private
Gallagher, taking test subject number one with them, Caroline
Caldwell crosses to Rosie's midsection door, opens up a
compartment beside it at about head-height and pulls a lever
from the vertical position to the horizontal. This is the override control for the external emergency access. Nobody can
now enter the vehicle unless Caldwell lets them in herself.

That done, she goes to the cockpit and powers up one of
three panels. The generator, twenty yards behind her in the
rear of the vehicle, starts to hum – but not to roar, because
Caldwell isn't sending the power to the engine. She needs it
in the lab, which is where she goes next. Since she'll be working
directly with infected tissue, she puts on gloves, goggles and
face mask.

She boots up the scanning electron microscope, works her
way patiently and punctiliously through the setting and display
option screens, and mounts the first of her prepared slides.

With a pleasant tingle of anticipation, she puts her eyes to
the output rig. The central nervous system of the Wainwright
House hungry is instantly there, laid out before her avid gaze.

Having chosen green as the key colour, she finds herself strolling under a canopy of neuronal dendrites, a tropical brainforest.

The resolution is so perfect, it takes Dr Caldwell's breath away. Gross and fine structures are rendered in pin-sharp detail, like an illustration in a textbook. The fact that the brain tissue was so badly damaged before she was able to take her sample mainly shows itself by the presence, as she shifts the slide minutely under the turret, of foreign matter – dust motes, human hair and bacterial cells as well as the expected fungal mycelia – among the neurons. The nerve cells themselves are completely and thrillingly laid out to her gaze.

She sees what other commentators have seen, but what she has never been able to verify with the inadequate and jury-rigged equipment available to her at the base. She sees exactly how the cuckoo *Ophiocordyceps* builds its nests in the thickets of the brain – how its mycelia wrap themselves, thread-thin, around neuronal dendrites, like ivy around an oak. Except that ivy doesn't whisper siren songs to the oak and steal it from itself.

Cuckoos? Ivy? Sirens? *Focus, Caroline*, she tells herself fiercely. *Look at what's in front of you, and draw appropriate inferences where the evidence exists to support them.*

The evidence exists. Now she sees what other eyes have missed – the cracks in the fortress (*focus!*), the places where the massively parallel structures of the human brain have regrouped, forlorn and outnumbered, around and between the fungus-choked nerve cells. Some uninfected clusters of neurons have actually grown denser, although the newer cells are bloated and threadbare, ruptured from within by jagged sheets of amyloid plaque.

Caldwell's scalp prickles as she realises the significance of what she's seeing.

It would have happened quite slowly, she reminds herself. The earlier researchers didn't chart this progression because, immediately post-Breakdown, it hadn't yet reached a point where it could be visually verified. The only way anyone could have found it would have been by guessing it might be there and testing for it.

Caldwell lifts her head and steps back from the imaging rig. It's hard, but necessary. She could stare into that green world for hours, for whole days, and keep on finding new wonders there.

Later, perhaps. But later is starting to be a word that has no referent for her. Later is another day or two of rising fever and loss of function, followed by a painful, undignified death. She has the first half of a working hypothesis. Now she has to finish this project, while she still can.

In Caldwell's lab back at the base there are – or were – dozens of slides taken from the brain tissue of test subject sixteen (Marcia) and test subject twenty-two (Liam). If these were still available to her now, she'd use them. She's not profligate with resources, despite the comment she once made in desperation to Justineau about amassing as many observations as she could in the hope that some pattern might finally emerge. Now she has her pattern – has, at least, a hypothesis that can be tested – but all her existing samples from the test subjects at the base, the children who seem to have a partial immunity to the effects of *Ophiocordyceps*, have been taken from her.

She needs new samples. From test subject number one.

But she knows that Helen Justineau will resist any attempt she makes to dissect Melanie, or even to take a biopsy from her brain. And both Sergeant Parks and Private Gallagher have, as Caldwell feared from the start, developed unacceptably close relationships with the test subject through repeated interaction in a partially normalised social context. There's no guarantee, now, that if she announced an intention to obtain brain tissue samples from Melanie, she would be supported by anyone in the group.

So she makes her plans on the assumption that she has already issued that announcement and been refused.

She unfolds and assembles the collapsible airlock around the midsection door. Its ingenious multi-hinged construction makes this relatively straightforward, despite the clumsiness of her hands. It's not just the bandages now; the earlier tenderness of the inflamed tissue has given way to a general loss of sensation and response. She tells her fingers to do something, and they react late, move fitfully, like a car starting in winter.

But she perseveres. Fully extended, the airlock bolts into eight grooved channels, four in the ceiling of the vehicle and four in its floor. Each bolt needs to be shot home and then anchored with a sleeve bracket that tightens by the turning of a wheel. Caldwell has to use both hands and a wrench. Eight times. Long before she's finished, feeling has returned to her hands in the form of intense and unremitting pain. The agony makes her whimper aloud in spite of herself.

The sides and front of the airlock are made of an ultra-flexible but extremely strong plastic. Its top and bottom now need to be sealed with a quick-hardening solution shot from a hand-held applicator. Caldwell has to hold it in the crook of her left elbow, using the thumb of her right hand to depress the trigger.

The result is a mess, but she verifies that the seal is perfect by pumping the air out of the airlock and watching the pressure gauge drop smoothly to zero.

Very good.

She pumps fresh air in, bringing the airlock to normal pressure. She takes manual control of the doors and routes it to her own computer in the lab. She leaves both doors closed, but only the inner door locked. Then she manhandles a cylinder of compressed phosgene gas into the airlock's reserve chamber. She had already noted the cylinder's presence during her initial search of the lab's contents, and assumed that it was there to assist in the synthesis of organic polymers. But it has other uses, of course, including the rapid and effective suffocation of large lab animals without widespread tissue damage.

343

Now she waits. And while she waits, she examines her own feelings about what she's about to do. She's reluctant to dwell on the effects of the gas on her human companions. Phosgene is more humane than its close relative, chlorine, but that's not saying very much. Caldwell is hoping that Melanie will enter the airlock first, and that it will be possible to lock the outer door before anyone else follows her in.

She's aware, though, that this is unlikely. It's far more probable that Helen Justineau will either enter alongside Melanie or else precede her into the vehicle. This prospect doesn't trouble Caldwell too much. There's even a certain rightness to it. Justineau's many interventions have contributed very substantially to the present absurd situation – in which Caldwell has to plot to recover control of her own specimen.

But she hopes, at least, that it won't be necessary to kill Parks or Gallagher. The two soldiers will probably bring up the rear, covering Justineau and Melanie until they're inside Rosie. By which time, the door can be locked against them.

None of this is perfect. It's not as though she wants to commit what more or less amounts to murder. But her hypothesis is so huge in its implications that to shrink from murder would be a crime against humanity. She has a duty, and she has an interval of time in which she can still work. That interval is most likely measurable not in days, but in hours.

Caldwell has pulled back the baffles from the window in the lab so that she can peer out into the street and see the rescue party when it returns. But the pain in her hands and arms has exhausted her. Despite her best efforts, she dozes. She drifts in and out of consciousness. Every time she forces her eyelids open, they lower themselves again by subliminal increments.

After one of these times, Caldwell finds herself meeting – at a distance, through the window – the gaze of a small child, who is standing in a doorway almost directly opposite her.

A hungry, obviously. Age at time of primary infection, no more than five. Naked, scrawny and indescribably filthy, like a

344

disaster victim in a charity appeal broadcast before the Breakdown, in those innocent days when a few thousand dead felt like a disaster.

The little boy is watching Caldwell avidly and unblinkingly. And he's not alone. It's late afternoon now, and the long shadows provide a lot of natural cover. But like the details in a puzzle picture, the other hungries emerge from the background one by one. An older, red-haired girl behind the rusting hulk of a parked car. A black-haired boy, older still, crouched in the remains of a shop window display with an aluminium baseball bat clutched in his hands. Two more behind him, in the shop itself, on hands and knees underneath a rack of sun-bleached and mouldering dresses.

A whole pack of them! Caldwell is enthralled. She'd always known, when Parks and his people said the supply of test subjects in the wild had dried up, that it could mean many things. One possibility – at the time she thought it implausible, but she's not so certain now – was that the feral infected children had been intelligent enough to perceive the sergeant and his trappers as a threat and to move on to new hunting grounds.

Now Caldwell watches as the black-haired boy signals to the two behind him with a toss of the head, and they come up level with him to see what he's seeing. He's the leader, obviously. He's also one of the very few who are not completely naked. He wears a camouflage jacket on his narrow, bony shoulders. At some point, he's brought down a soldier and taken a fancy to his hide as well as his flesh. His face is a riot of smudged colour – a tribal display of status and potency.

Caldwell sees how the hungry children operate as a pack. How they signal using silent gestures and facial expressions. How they coordinate their efforts against this unfamiliar thing in their midst.

Perhaps it's the sound that has brought them, the steady hum of the generator. Or perhaps they've been watching Rosie for a while now, having followed Justineau or Gallagher back here after one of their excursions. But whatever it was that attracted their attention, now they've seen her.

And having seen her, they're stalking her.

Even though she's immured behind unbreakable glass in an oversized battle tank whose armaments could blast the buildings all around into rubble and powder. Even though there's no obvious way to reach her, and no way of quantifying the risk she poses. Even though, crucially, they can't *smell* her through steel and glass and polymer and airtight seals.

They recognise her as prey, and they're responding accordingly.

Caldwell is not immediately conscious of having made the decision as she rises to her feet and walks softly out of the lab towards the midsection door. But it's a good decision. She can justify it on any number of grounds.

She returns the door-control functions to the panel beside the airlock itself. Then she slides the outer door open and closed again, several times over, testing its operation at various speed settings. She watches the hydraulic valves, as thick as her forearms, sliding smoothly backwards and forwards at the top and bottom of the door. Even at the third speed setting – there are seven that are faster – she estimates that the valves are exerting in excess of five hundred foot-pounds of pressure. The inner door, by contrast, is operated by simpler mechanical servos. It was never anticipated that the airlock would have to function as a second restraint cage.

Caldwell takes into account a number of highly pertinent factors. There's no telling whether test subject one will even return from the expedition. If she does, it's far from certain that the ambush Caldwell has already mounted will work. Or if it works, how any survivors would respond to the deaths of those caught in the airlock.

But the truth – or at least part of it – is that she can't resist. These monsters are hunting her. She wants to hunt them in return and to enfold their efforts effortlessly in her wider stratagem.

With the outer door opened fully, she slides the inner airlock door open halfway. She stands up against the opening and waits.

Her body is still sticky with sweat from her earlier exertions. Her pheromones, she knows, are now spreading outward from her body on the turbulent gradients of the cooling afternoon air. With every breath, the hungry children are inhaling her. Sentient they may be, and cooperative, and sly. But their nature being what it is, it's only a matter of time before they respond.

It's the red-haired girl who moves first. She comes out from behind the car, walks straight into the open and advances towards Rosie's inviting doorway.

The boy in the camouflage jacket makes a sound like a bark. The red-haired girl slows, reluctantly, and turns to face him.

The younger boy from the shop doorway shoots past her at a dead run and flings himself directly at the door. It's so sudden and so fast that Caldwell – even though this is exactly what she's been waiting for – barely has time to react.

Her thumb closes on a switch.

The hungry boy leaps the sill of the outer door and throws himself at Caldwell like a missile, arms outstretched to catch and clutch.

Before he can reach her, the inner door slams shut.

Caldwell has underestimated the power of the servos. The door closes on the hungry's upper body like a nutcracker, crushing its ribs. The hungry opens its mouth to scream, but its lungs are terminally and irreversibly deflated. Screaming is no longer an option. It's been trapped with one arm behind its torso, inside the airlock, the other thrust forward. It's still straining futilely to reach Caldwell, its slender fingers stretched out. One of them actually flicks the sleeve of her lab coat, but the infection can't be contracted from a scratch, only from

347

blood or saliva. With her goggles and face mask in place, she's not at risk.

The creature's head, Caldwell notes, is completely undamaged. She feels a dizzying surge of elation, and she laughs aloud.

She *half* laughs. The rest of the sound is choked off as something streaks in from the street and smacks into her jaw, ripping right through the wire and paper of the face mask. The agony is astonishing. Caldwell's mouth fills up with blood in which broken-off pieces of tooth grate against each other with a dull, shipwrecked sound.

The stone clatters along the floor, dark red with her spilled blood. The red-haired girl is already loading another into the strip of faded cloth or leather she's using as a sling.

The boy's crushed body is wedging the door open about three inches, the outer door is still gaping wide, and the hungries outside, its cohort, its friends, are racing into the breach with their makeshift weapons raised.

Caldwell's hand lashes out by pure reflex, hitting the controls for the outer door. It starts to close, but she's forgotten to raise the speed from level three to level ten. At the last moment, the tip of the baseball bat is thrust into the narrowing gap, where it wedges tight. The hydraulics whine, and the edge of the door bites deep into the metal of the bat, starts to slice it in two. But now, little hands come groping around the edges of the door, some of them reaching for Caldwell, most of them wrestling with the door to keep it from closing.

They can't get to her. But they're pulling at the door determinedly, shifting their position to allow more hands to get a grip, to add their efforts. Caldwell knows how strong that door is, so when she sees it start to open again, the sudden shock makes her body rebel against her will. She staggers back, fists coming up to her mouth as though she could hide behind them.

The painted face of the black-haired boy appears in the gap of the outer door. He fixes her with baleful, bloodshot eyes, telling her in wordless grimaces that this is personal now.

Which means he thinks of himself as a person. Amazing.

Caldwell sprints for the cockpit, where she slams down two more levers, engaging wheels and weapons. She can't operate both at once, of course. She'll be lucky if she can remember how to drive this thing, on a few days' training received two decades ago. For a terrifying moment, the entire console seems suddenly alien and meaningless. She has to drag her brain out of the adrenalin flood and back under her conscious control.

The button marked E. That comes first, and it's right there, in the centre of the steering column. It stands for ELEVATE. Rosie's chassis lifts itself eight inches higher off the road, hissing like a snake as the hydraulics kick in. Caldwell sees some of the hungries scatter, but the booming and banging from the midsection tells her that some of them are still at work there.

Panic twists her innards. She has to get out of here. She knows she might be bringing the enemy with her, but if she stays, she's dog meat. They'll get the outer door open eventually, and then the inner door will hold them for a few seconds at most.

Caldwell takes the steering column in her unresponsive hands, pushes hard forward and prays. The brakes disengage without being asked to. Rosie shakes herself like a dog and lurches into motion, so fast and so sudden that Caldwell is thrown backwards into the driving seat. Her hands slip partway off the grips and the behemoth slews across the road, punching into a lamp post and ripping it right out of the ground with a clang like the bell that signals the start of a boxing match.

Caldwell has to grip more tightly and pull hard to bring Rosie straight again. The pain makes her scream aloud, but she can barely hear the sound over the full-throated roar of the engines. She has no idea what's happening at the midsection door, because the engine noise hides those sounds too. So she pushes harder, takes the column all the way to the top of its grooved channel. The street becomes a grey blur.

There's another impact, then a third, but Caldwell is aware

349

of them only as vibrations. Rosie has so much momentum now that she parts the world like water.

Figures in the street, briefly in front of her, then beside her, then gone. More hungries? One of them looked like Parks, but there's no way of finding out without stopping, and she doesn't want to do that. In fact, for the moment she doesn't even remember how.

Some parts of the console, though, are starting to look a lot more familiar now. Caldwell realises that she doesn't have to be blind. Rosie has cameras mounted along her entire length, most of which can be swivelled to look in any direction. She flicks them all on, and scans the left-hand feeds. One of them is dead-centred on the midsection door, where two hungries have managed to keep their grip on the moving juggernaut. One is the leader, his jacket whipping in Rosie's slipstream like a flag. The other is the red-haired girl.

Caldwell swerves right, up a steep incline where a road sign points towards Highgate and Kentish Town. She leaves the turn to the last moment, then yanks the steering column as hard as she can so that Rosie lists sharply, but the incline slows her and the effect isn't as spectacular as she was hoping. The hungries are still hanging on, still wrestling with the partly opened door.

Caldwell has been here before, a long time ago. Pre-Breakdown. Memories stir, filling her mind with surreal juxtapositions. Houses she once aspired to live in flick past her, squat and dark like widows in a Spanish cemetery waiting patiently for the resurrection.

At the top of the hill, she turns again. She misjudges the angle, punches out part of the wall of a pub that stands on the corner. Rosie isn't perturbed, though the rear-view cameras show the building slumping into ruin behind her.

There's a narrow elbow of road, then a long, wide sweep down towards central London. Caldwell piles on the acceleration again, and leans hard over, deliberately scraping Rosie's left flank against the long exterior wall of what looks like a school building. The sign above the gate reads *La Sainte Union*. Pulverised brick powders the windscreen, and there's a shriek of tortured metal even louder than the engine roar. Rosie endures and Caldwell is rewarded by the sight of at least one of the hungries flung loose in the hard rain.

She yells at the top of her voice – a banshee shriek of triumph and defiance. Blood from her wounded mouth flecks the windscreen in front of her.

She veers back out into the centre of the road, glancing at the cameras again. No sign of the hungries now. She has to stop so that she can examine her prize and make sure it's still intact. But the hungries she's just shaken off might still be alive. She remembers the look on the painted face of the black-haired boy. He'll follow her for as long as his legs still work.

So she drives on, more or less due south, through Camden Town. Euston lies beyond, and after that she'll be approaching the river. The streets remain empty, but Caldwell is wary. Eleven million people used to live in this city. Behind these blind windows and closed doors some of them must still be waiting, stuck halfway between life and death.

She's figured out the brakes by this time, and she slows, intimidated by the echoing bellow of Rosie's engines in these desolate landscapes. She feels for a sickening moment that she might be the last human being left alive on the face of a necrotic planet. And that it might not matter after all. To have the race that built these mausoleums lie in them finally, quiet and resigned, and crumble into dust.

Who'd miss us?

It's the comedown after the adrenalin high of taking her specimen and shaking off her enemies. That and the fever. Caldwell shudders, and her vision swims. The road ahead of her seems to dissolve all at once into a grey smear. The dysfunction is sudden and spectacular. Is she going blind? That can't happen. Not yet. She needs another day. A few hours, at least.

She brings Rosie to a jerking, screaming stop.

Locks the column.

And runs a hand over her face, massaging her eyes with thumb and forefinger to clear them. They feel like hot marbles nestling in her skull. But when she ventures to open them and look out through the cockpit's windshield, there's nothing wrong with how they work.

There really is a grey wall, forty feet high, that's been thrown across the road ahead of her. And finally, after a minute or more of baffled awe, she knows it for what it is.

It's her nemesis, her mighty opposite.

It's *Ophiocordyceps*.

63

Miss Justineau is furious, so Melanie does her best to be furious too. But it's hard, for lots of reasons.

She's still sad about Kieran being killed, and the being sad seems to stop the being angry from getting started. And Dr Caldwell driving away in the big truck means that Melanie won't have to see either one of them again, which makes her want to jump up and down and punch the air with her hands.

So while Sergeant Parks is using all the bad words he knows, it seems like, and Miss Justineau is sitting by the side of the road with a sad, dazed face, Melanie is thinking *Goodbye, Dr Caldwell. Drive far, far away, and don't come back.*

But then Miss Justineau says, "That's it. We're dead."

And that changes everything. Melanie thinks about what's going to happen now, instead of just about how she feels, and her stomach goes all cold suddenly.

Because Miss Justineau is right.

They've used up the last of the e-blocker. The food smell is really strong on them, and Melanie is amazed that she's able to be this close without wanting to bite them. She's become used to it somehow. It's like the part of her that just wants to

353

eat and eat and eat is locked up in a little box, and she doesn't have to open the box if she doesn't want to.

But that's not going to help Miss Justineau and Sergeant Parks very much. They've got to keep walking through this city, smelling like food, and they won't walk far before they meet something that wants to eat them.

"We have to follow her," Melanie says, full of urgency now that she sees what's at stake. "We have to get back inside."

Sergeant Parks gives her a searching look. "Can you do it?" he asks her. "The way you did with Gallagher? Is there a trail?"

Melanie hasn't even thought of it until then, but now she breathes in deep – and finds it at once. There's a trail so strong it's like a river running through the air. It's got a bit of Dr Caldwell in it, and a bit of something else that might be a hungry or more than one hungry. But mostly it's the stinky chemical smell of Rosie's engine. She could follow it blind-folded. She could follow it in her sleep.

Parks sees it in her face. "Okay," he says. "Let's get going."

Justineau stares at him, wild-eyed. "She was pushing sixty miles an hour!" she says, her mouth twisted in a snarl. "She's gone. There's no way in God's green earth we're going to catch up with her."

"Won't know unless we try," Parks counters. "Want to lie down and die, Helen, or give it a shot?"

"It's going to come to the same thing either way."

"Then die on your feet."

"Please, Miss Justineau!" Melanie begs. "Let's go a little way, at least. We can stop when it gets dark, and find somewhere to hide." What she's thinking is: they have to get out of these streets, where the hungry children who are just like her live and hunt. She thinks she might be able to protect Miss J against ordinary hungries, but not against the painted-face boy and his fierce tribe.

Sergeant Parks holds out a hand. Miss Justineau just stares

354

at it, but he keeps it there in front of her, and in the end she takes it. She lets him haul her to her feet.

"How many hours of daylight have we got left?" she asks.

"Maybe two."

"We can't move in the dark, Parks. And Caroline can. She's got headlights."

Parks concedes the point with a curt nod. "We follow until it's too dark to see. Then we hole up. In the morning, if there's still a strong trail, we carry on. If not, we look for some tar or creosote or some other shit like that to mask our scent, the way the junkers do, and we keep on heading south."

He turns to Melanie. "Go ahead, Lassie," he says. "Do your stuff."

Melanie hesitates. "I think . . ." she says.

"Yeah? What is it?"

"I think maybe I'll be able to run a lot faster than the two of you, Sergeant Parks."

Parks laughs – a short, harsh sound. "Yeah, I think so too," he says. "We'll do the best we can. Keep us in sight, that's all." Then he has a better idea, and turns to Justineau. "Let her have the walkie-talkie," he tells her. "If we lose her, she can call us and talk us in."

Justineau hands the rig to Melanie, and Sergeant Parks shows her how to send and receive with it. It's simple enough, but designed for much bigger fingers than hers. She practises until she gets it right. Then Parks shows her how to hook it on to the waistband of her pink unicorn jeans, where it looks ridic-ulously large and cumbersome.

Miss Justineau gives her a smile of encouragement. Underneath it Melanie can see all her fears, her grief and exhaustion. How close she is to empty.

She goes up to Miss J and gives her a short, intense hug. "It'll be all right," she says. "I won't let anything hurt you."

It's the first time they've hugged like this – with Melanie giving comfort rather than receiving it. And she remembers

355

Miss Justineau making the same promise to her, although she couldn't say exactly when. She feels a pang of nostalgia for that time, whenever it was. But she knows that you can't be a child for ever, even if you want to be.

She sets off at a run, and slowly accelerates. But she holds herself to a speed that the two grown-ups can just about keep up with. At each junction she waits until they jog into sight before setting off again. Walkie-talkie or not, she's not going to leave them to their own devices with the night coming on – a night that she knows contains so many terrible things.

64

Caroline Caldwell gets out of Rosie using the cockpit door rather than the midsection door. The midsection door still has the airlock attached and her hungry specimen jammed into it.

She walks twenty paces forward. That's as far as she can go, more or less.

She stares at the grey wall for a long time. For whole minutes, probably, although she doesn't really trust her time sense any more. Her wounded mouth throbs in time with her heartbeat, but her nervous system is like a flooded carburettor; the engine doesn't catch, the confused signals don't coalesce into pain.

Caldwell registers the wall's construction, its height and width and depth – the depth is just an estimate – and the time it must have taken to form. She knows exactly what she's looking at. But knowing doesn't help. She's going to die soon, and she'll die with this . . . *thing* in front of her. This gauntlet, flung down by a bullying, contemptuous universe that allowed human beings to grope their way to sentience just so it could put them in their place that bit more painfully.

Caldwell makes herself move, eventually. She does the only thing she can think of to do. She picks up the gauntlet.

Returning to Rosie, she lets herself back in through the cockpit door, which she closes and locks. She goes through the crew quarters and the lab to the midsection. She stops briefly in the lab to replace her face mask, which was ripped when the slingshot stone smacked into it. She scrubs up and dons surgical gloves, takes a bone-saw from a rack and a plastic tray from a shelf. A bucket would be better, but she has no bucket.

The hungry she caught is still moving sluggishly, despite the horrific damage the door mechanism has done to the muscles and tendons of its upper body. Seen from this close, the size of the head in relation to the body suggests that it may have been even younger at the time of initial infection than Caldwell had previously estimated.

But then she's about to test that hypothesis, isn't she?

The hungry's right arm is jammed behind it, inside the airlock space. Caldwell secures the left arm by catching it in a noose of plasticated twine and tying the free end of the twine to a bracket on the wall. She wraps the twine around her own forearm three or four times and uses her body weight to pull it tight against the hungry's struggles. The loops of twine bite deep into her arm, where the flesh has gone from angry red to sullen purple. She feels very little pain, which is a bad sign in itself. Nerve damage in necrotised flesh is irreversible and progressive.

As quickly as she can, but carefully, she saws off the hungry's head. It grunts and snaps its jaws at her throughout the whole of this process. Both of its arms flail violently, the left one within a tight circular arc defined by the free play of the twine. Neither arm can reach her.

The fragile upper vertebrae yield to the saw almost instantly. It's the muscle, on which the blade alternately sticks and slides, that's hardest. When Caldwell is through the vertebrae, the hungry's head sags suddenly, opening the incision wide to show the severed nubs of bone, shockingly white. By contrast, the liquor that drips down from the wound on to the tray and the floor all around is mostly grey, shot with rivulets of red.

The last thin ribbon of flesh tears under the head's own weight, and the head abruptly falls. It hits the edge of the tray, flipping it over, and rolls away across the floor.

The hungry's body is still moving very much as it did when the head was still attached. Its arms windmill uselessly, its legs step-slide on the airlock's grooved metal floor. Colonies of *Cordyceps* anchored to the spine are still trying to commandeer the dead child and make it work for the greater good of its fungal passenger. The movements slow while Caldwell bends to retrieve the head, but they haven't entirely stopped when she straightens again and takes the head through into the lab.

Safety first. She leaves the head on the work surface for a moment or two while she returns to clear the airlock, flinging the still-twitching headless corpse out on to the road. It lies there like a reproach not just to Caldwell but to scientific endeavour in general.

Caldwell turns her back on it and slams the door. If the road to knowledge was paved with dead children – which at some times and in some places it has been – she'd still walk it and absolve herself afterwards. What other choice would she have? Everything she values is at the end of that road.

She closes the doors, returns to the lab and sets to work.

65

Melanie is waiting when Justineau and Parks finally turn into the long road that has Euston station at the other end of it. Wordlessly she points, and Justineau looks. Breathless, lathered in sweat, her legs and chest knotting in agony, it's all she can do.

Halfway along the broad avenue, Rosie has slewed to a halt on a steep diagonal, practically touching the kerb on both sides. Directly in front of the vehicle a huge barricade blocks the street. It rises to a height of forty feet or so, which puts it higher than the houses on either side. In the low, slanting sunlight, Justineau can see that it continues over the houses, into them and beyond them. It looks like a sheer vertical, at first, but then its subtle tones resolve themselves and she can see that it's a slope like the side of a mountain. It's as though a million tons of dirty snow has fallen in this one spot.

Parks joins her and they continue to boggle in unison.

"Any idea?" the sergeant asks at last.

Justineau shakes her head. "You?"

"I prefer to look at all the evidence first. Then I get someone smarter than I am to explain it to me."

They go forward slowly, alert for any hostile movement. Rosie has been in the wars, and they can see the aftermath. The dents and scrapes on the armour plating. The blood and tissue plastered around the midsection door. The small, crumpled body lying in the street, right beside the vehicle.

The body is a hungry. A child. Male, no older than four or five. His head is gone – no sign of it anywhere nearby – and his upper body is crushed almost flat, as though someone put his narrow chest in a vice and tightened it. Melanie kneels to examine him more closely, her expression solemn and thoughtful. Justineau stands over her, searching for words and not finding any. She can see that the boy wears a bracelet of hair, perhaps his own, on his right wrist. As a badge of identity, it couldn't be clearer. He was like Melanie, not like the regular hungries.

"I'm sorry," Justineau says.

Melanie says nothing.

A movement in Justineau's peripheral vision makes her turn her head. Sergeant Parks is looking the same way, towards Rosie's central section. Caroline Caldwell has stripped the duct tape away from the lab window and slid back the light baffles. She's staring out at them, her expression hard and impassive.

Justineau goes over to the window and mouths: *What are you doing?*

Caldwell shrugs. She makes no move to let them in.

Justineau hammers on the window, gestures to the midsection door. Caldwell goes away for a few moments, then comes back with an A5 notepad. She holds it up to show Justineau what she's written on the top sheet. *I have to work. Very close to a breakthrough. I think you might try to stop me. Sorry.*

Justineau throws out her arms, indicating the empty street, the long shadows of late afternoon. She doesn't have to say or mime anything. The message is clear. *We're going to die.*

Caldwell watches her for a moment longer, then once again closes the baffles right across the window.

Parks is on his knees now, a few feet to Justineau's left. He's working the crank to open the door. But it's not opening, even though he's encouraging it with a continuous stream of bad language. Caldwell must have disabled the emergency access.

Melanie is still kneeling beside the beheaded body, either grieving or else so lost in thought that she's not aware right now of what's going on around her. Justineau's stomach is churning and she feels sick. From the hard running, and now from this lethal smack in the face. She walks on a little, trying to outdistance the nausea, until she comes to the outermost reaches of the wall.

It's not a wall at all but an avalanche, a formless sprawl of matter in slow-motion advance. It's made from the tendrils of *Ophiocordyceps*, from billions of fungal mycelia interwoven more finely than any tapestry. The threads are so delicate that they're translucent, allowing Justineau to peer into the mass to a depth of ten feet or so. Everything within is cocooned, colonised, wrapped in hundreds of thicknesses of the stuff. Outlines are softened, colours muted to a thousand shades of grey.

Justineau's dizziness and nausea return. She sits, slowly, rests her head in her hands until the feelings stop. She's aware of Melanie walking past her, skirting the edge of the thing and then seemingly about to walk into it.

"Don't!" Justineau yells.

Melanie looks at her in surprise. "But it's only like cotton, Miss Justineau. Or like a cloud that's come down to the ground. It can't hurt us." She demonstrates, bending to run a hand lightly through the fluffy mass. It parts cleanly, retains a perfect image of the hand's passage. The threads she's touched cling to her skin like spiderwebs.

Justineau scrambles up to pull her away, gently but firmly. "I don't know," she says. "Maybe it can, maybe it can't. I don't want to find out." She asks Melanie to brush the stuff off her hands, very carefully, on to a tuft of grass that's sprouting up

362

from the ruined pavement nearby. The fungal threads are wrapped around the grass stalks too, and most of it appears to be dead – much more grey than green showing.

They go back to Parks, who's given up on trying to open the midsection door and is now sitting with his back to Rosie, leaning against one of her rear treads. He's holding his canteen, weighing it carefully in his hands. He takes a swig as they approach, then hands it to Justineau to do likewise.

When she takes it, she realises from its weight that it must be almost empty. She gives it back. "I'm good," she lies.

"Bullshit," Parks says. "Drink and be merry, Helen. I'm gonna go look around these houses shortly. See if there's anything left standing in rain buckets or gutters. God will provide."

"You think?"

"He's known for it."

She drains the canteen and slumps down beside him, dropping it into his lap. She looks up at the sky, which is darkening. Sunset's maybe half an hour away, so Parks is probably bluffing about looking for standing water – which anyway would likely be full of all kinds of bad shit.

Melanie sits cross-legged between them and facing them.

"What now?" Justineau asks.

Parks makes a non-committal gesture. "I guess we wait a while longer, and then we pick one of these houses. Secure it as far as we can before it gets dark. Try and fix up some kind of a barricade, because we've got to be leaving a scent trail now as well as a heat trail. Hungries will find us long before morning."

Justineau is torn between despair and choking rage. She goes with the rage because she's afraid the despair will paralyse her. "If I get my hands on that bitch," she mutters, "I'll beat her brains out, and then mount the best parts on microscope slides." Moved by some atavistic reflex, she adds, "Sorry, Melanie."

"It's all right," Melanie says. "I don't like Dr Caldwell either."

When the sun touches the horizon, they finally force

363

themselves to move. The lights are on in the lab by this time, a little of their glow spilling around the edges of the baffles so that the windows look as though they've been drawn on Rosie's side in luminous paint.

The rest of the world is dark, and getting darker.

Parks turns to Melanie, very abruptly, as though he's been nerving himself up to something. "You sleepy, kid?" he asks her.

Melanie shakes her head for no.

"You scared?"

She has to think about this one, but it's no again. "Not for me," she qualifies. "The hungries won't hurt me. I'm scared for Miss Justineau."

"Then maybe you could run an errand for me." Parks points at the lowering grey mass. "I don't fancy our chances going through that stuff. I don't know whether it could infect us or not, but I'm pretty sure it could choke us to death if we breathed enough of it in."

"So?" Melanie demands.

"So I'd like to know if there's a way around it. Maybe you could go check it out, once we've found a bolt-hole for ourselves. Might make a difference tomorrow if we know where we're going."

"I can do that," Melanie says.

Justineau is unhappy at the thought, but she knows it makes sense. Melanie can survive out here in the dark. She and Parks definitely can't.

"Are you sure?" she asks.

Melanie is very sure.

66

She's even keen to do it, because she's restless and unhappy about everything that's happened today. Kieran dying – dying because her story, her lie, frightened him away. And then Dr Caldwell driving off and leaving Miss Justineau with nowhere safe to sleep. And then the finding of the little corpse, the body of a child much younger than her, with his head cut off.

She thinks maybe Dr Caldwell cut his head off, because that's the sort of thing that Dr Caldwell does. Underneath the unhappiness, she finds a pure, white anger. Dr Caldwell has to be made to *stop* doing these things. Someone has to teach her a lesson.

The wild children are just the same as she is, except that they never got to have lessons with Miss Justineau. Nobody ever taught them how to think for themselves, or even how to be people, but they're learning without that help. They've already learned how to be a family. And then Dr Caldwell comes and kills them as though they're just animals. Maybe they tried to kill her first, but they don't know any better and Dr Caldwell does.

It fills Melanie with a rage so strong it's almost like the

hungry feeling. And discovering that she can feel like that makes her afraid.

So she doesn't mind at all going out to explore the grey stuff. She thinks moving will be a lot better for her than staying still.

Sergeant Parks and Miss Justineau find a loft in one of the houses of a three-storey Victorian terrace a few streets away from where Rosie stopped. There's a ladder that leads up there, but once Sergeant Parks and Miss Justineau have climbed up, Melanie takes the bottom of it while the two grown-ups take the top and they manage between the three of them to rip it out of the metal brackets that hold it in place. Melanie catches it as it falls and lowers it carefully to the floor so that it doesn't make too much noise.

"I'll see you later," she calls up to them softly. She takes the walkie-talkie from her belt and waves it to show that she hasn't forgotten about it. She'll be able to talk to them, even if she goes far away.

Miss Justineau whispers a reply. Goodbye, or good luck, or something like that. Melanie is already running lightly back down the stairs, her bare feet silent on the rotten, moss-covered carpet.

She picks a starting point at random and follows the edge of the grey mass. She starts off at a walk, but she's still filled with a sense of restlessness and urgency, so after a while she breaks into a trot and then into a run. She goes a long way, detouring wherever she has to and then finding the wall again as soon as she can.

It seems to go on for ever. Its outer surface isn't totally straight; it goes in and out a lot, throwing out salients along the narrower streets, falling back a little where there are open spaces that offer less to cling to. But there's no sign of a break and nowhere where Melanie can glimpse anything on the further side of the barrier.

After she's been running for more than an hour, she stops.

366

Not to rest – she could go on for a while yet without discomfort – but to check in with Miss Justineau and Sergeant Parks.

She presses the stud on the walkie-talkie and says hello into it. For a long time it just crackles, but then Sergeant Parks' voice answers. "How are you doing?"

"I went east," Melanie tells him. "Quite a long way. The wall just goes on and on."

"You've been walking all this time?"

"Running."

"Where are you now? Can you see any street signs?"

Melanie can't, but she walks on until she reaches another crossroads. "Northchurch Road," she says. "London Borough of Hackney."

She hears Parks breathing hard. "And it goes on further than that?"

"A lot further. As far as I can see. And I can see a long way, even in the dark." Melanie isn't boasting; it's just something Sergeant Parks needs to know.

"Okay. Thanks, kid. Come on back. If you feel like taking a look to the west, too, I'd be grateful. But don't wear yourself out. Come on back here if you're feeling tired."

"I'm fine," Melanie says. "Over and out."

She retraces her steps and goes the other way, but it's exactly the same. If they go around the wall, they'll have to go a very long way either to the east or to the west, and it's not clear where they'll be able to start going south again.

Finally Melanie finds herself standing directly in front of the wall, a few miles away from where they first met it. It's as thick here as it is anywhere, but the angle of its fall is different. An outcrop of grey froth leans forward a long way, right over her, and she can see the moon shining down through it. The stark white glow is like a promise, an encouragement. If she pushes forward through the wall, she might be able to find the further side before she loses the light.

Miss Justineau said it was dangerous, but Melanie doesn't

367

see how, and she's not afraid of it. She takes a step forward, and then another. The grey threads are up to her ankles, then up to her knees, but they offer no resistance at all. They just tickle a little as she pushes through them, parting with the smallest sigh of not-quite-sound.

The moon follows her, a moving spotlight in which everything opens itself up to her gaze. The grey threads quickly get thicker and thicker. Objects that she passes – rubbish bins, parked cars, post boxes, garden hedges and gates – are swathed in endless layers, turned into granite statues of themselves.

Twenty feet in, Melanie finds the first fallen bodies. She slows to a halt, amazed at what she's seeing. The hungries have fallen down in the middle of the street, or slumped at the bases of walls – just like the bodies they saw when they were walking into London. But there are so many more of them here! From their split skulls and exploded heads, grey stems about six inches in diameter have sprouted like the trunks of trees. The stems grow straight upwards to incredible heights, and the threads pour out from them at all angles in endless proliferation. Some of them connect to whatever other stems are nearest, making a dense net like a million spiderwebs all woven together. Others wrap around whatever is in their path, or if there's nothing, they shelve gently down to the ground. Wherever the threads touch the ground, another trunk appears, but these trunks are a lot thinner and shorter than the trunks that grow straight out of the bodies of the hungries.

Melanie goes closer. She can't help herself. The sad husks at the bottom of each fungus tree don't scare her. There's nothing of humanity left in them, nothing to remind anyone that they were once alive. They're more like clothes that someone has taken off and left lying on the ground.

Close up, she can see the grey fruit that hangs on these ghost trees. She reaches up to touch one of the spherical growths, which is just a little higher up on the trunk than the top of her head. Its surface is cool and leathery, and gives very slightly under the touch of her fingers. She presses hard, and makes an indentation. When she takes her hand away, the mark slowly disappears. The surface of the ball is elastic enough to spring back into shape. After a slow count of ten, it looks exactly the same as it did before she touched it.

Melanie wanders on through the grey wilderness. It doesn't seem to have a further side; it just keeps going. And it keeps getting thicker. After a while, there's only just enough space between the trunks for her to slide her skinny body through, and the moonlight is dripping down like dirty water through a raft of threads so tightly intertwined they're almost like a solid mass.

Melanie's shoulder bumps into one of the grey balls and it falls to the ground with a muffled plop. She stoops to pick it up. There's a puckered ring where it was attached to the trunk, but the rest of the surface is smooth and unbroken. She squeezes it in her hand, and once again it returns quickly to the shape it had before she touched it.

If she goes any further, she'll be bumping into the trunks. She touches one and finds that it feels unpleasantly clammy. She recoils a little. She was expecting the trunks to be smooth and dry like the fruit they bear, which in Melanie's opinion would have been a lot less disgusting.

Something moves off to her left and she starts violently. She thought she had this twilit world to herself. A strange figure stumbles towards her, silhouetted in the dull moonlight. From the neck downwards it looks like a man – but it has no shoulders or neck or head. Its upper body is just an undifferentiated lump.

She backs away from the thing, scared more than anything by its utter strangeness. But it's not attacking her. It doesn't even seem to know she's there.

As it passes her, she recognises it for what it is. It's a hungry whose torso has started to split open. The first foot or so of one of the upright trunks is thrusting upwards from its chest, splintered spars of rib protruding outwards from its point of origin. Threads have blossomed profusely from the trunk, disguising what's left of the hungry's head, which has been forced sideways at a steep angle by the relentless upward growth.

Melanie stares at the apparition, both relieved – because the horror of the unknown is more frightening than any horror you can understand – and revolted at this strange violation of human flesh.

The hungry shambles on past her, its zigzag course dictated by the trunks it bumps into and bounces off. It's almost more ridiculous than it is horrible. It will fall down soon, Melanie imagines – and then the trunk will be pointing sideways. It will have to find some way to right itself.

This whole forest grew from the ruined dead. This is where the hungries end up after all their faithful service to the infection that made them what they are.

Melanie sees her future, and accepts it. But she's not ready to die with so many important things still to be done.

She turns and walks back the way she came, following the tunnel of her own cleared path through the crowding grey filaments.

67

Dr Caldwell works on through the night, feverishly busy. The fever is literal, and it's currently running at 103 degrees.

Extracting the hungry boy's brain takes a lot longer without Dr Selkirk to help – and Dr Caldwell's hands are so clumsy that it's virtually impossible to take it out without damaging it. She does the best she can, removing most of the skull in inch-wide jigsaw pieces before she finally screws up her courage and severs the brain stem.

When she lifts it out, although her hands tremble violently, it comes clean.

She powers up the microtome and takes slices from the brain, choosing cross-sections that will allow her to examine most major structures. She mounts her slides, awed at how perfectly the microtome has done its job. The slices are exquisite, with no crush damage or smearing despite their ethereal thinness.

Caldwell labels each slide, and then examines them in sequence – a virtual tour of the hungry boy's brain beginning at its base and proceeding upwards and forwards.

She finds what she expected to find. The null hypothesis is

shot to pieces. She knows what the children are, and where they came from, their past and their future, the nature of their partial immunity, and the extent (close to a hundred per cent) to which her own labours over these past seven years have been a waste of time.

She feels a moment of pure happiness. If she'd died yesterday, she would have died blind. This discovery redeems everything, even if what she's found is so bleak and absolute.

A sound from close by dynamites her train of thought and brings her instantly to her feet. It's an innocuous enough sound – just a few clicks and whispers – but it's coming from inside Rosie!

Dr Caldwell is not given to excessive flights of imagination. She knows that Rosie's doors are sealed, and that anything powerful enough to open them would have been loud and protracted, alerting her long before this. But she's still trembling a little as she follows the sound forwards, through the crew quarters to the cockpit.

There's a lit-up section of the console, off to the right-hand side, and that's where the sound is coming from. From the radio. She slips into the seat and leans her head forward to listen.

There's not much to hear. Mostly static, pops and hisses and whoops of sound, like the chaos between stations on an ancient analogue wireless set. But a few words stand clear of the aural swamp. ". . . days out from Beacon . . . saw your . . . identify . . ." The voice is hollow, inhuman, warped by echo and distortion.

The beam of an electric torch moves quickly across the cockpit's forward shield, and then it's gone again. No sounds penetrate from outside, but she sees movement. Just a shadow, thrown down momentarily by the torch's moving beam. A figure moving briskly down Rosie's left flank.

". . . just a wreck . . . think there's any . . ."

Caldwell heads quickly for the midsection door. Halfway

there, she realises she could have gone out through the cockpit. She stops, turns around. But she knows the midsection door's mechanism better. The sounds from the cockpit radio fizzle and die. With a yelp of alarm, Caldwell runs back to the console and replies on the same channel on which the voice came through.

"Hello?" she cries. "Who's there? This is Caroline Caldwell of base Hotel Echo, in region 6. Who's there?"

Just static.

She tries the other channels in turn, and gets the same response.

She runs through to the midsection again. But when she gets there, she's irresolute. She hasn't applied any e-blocker since the day before, and she can smell her own sweat. If she opens that door, she might bring the hungries down on herself and her would-be rescuers.

The cupboard next to the airlock contains six biohazard suits. Caldwell was trained in their use back when she was still on the expedition list, and although it takes her ten minutes to put one on, she's confident that she's done it correctly. Her scent is completely masked, and her body heat at least temporarily contained.

When she pushes the door open, she sees nothing moving outside. "Hello?" she calls. She steps out into the street. Nobody. But the light is at Rosie's aft end now, and it's still moving, flicking to left and right.

"Hello?" Caldwell says again. Perhaps the suit's helmet is muffling her voice. She walks on shaky legs down the flank of the vehicle, the skin of her neck prickling. She rounds the aft end. The light is in her eyes for a moment. She speaks to whoever is behind it. "My name is Caroline Caldwell. I'm a scientist attached to base Hotel Echo in region 6. I'm here with . . ."

The light turns away from her, and Caldwell runs out of words. Nobody is carrying the torch. It's just been attached by

373

its strap to a metal rail on Rosie's rear. It's moving in the wind, not in someone's hands.

Fury at the childish trick gives way to the pure terror of realisation. This is an ambush. And since nobody is attacking her, the target must be Rosie. The doctor takes to her heels and runs back the way she came, sprinting for the midsection door, expecting a cadre of junkers, or perhaps Sergeant Parks, to burst out from hiding (except where would they hide?) and race her for the prize.

Nothing moves. She gets inside and slams the door, engages the lock and the failsafes. Then the airlock, for good measure. And then the bulkhead door that seals off the weapons station.

Finally she stops shaking. There's no sound, no sign of anyone. She's safe. Whoever was outside went away and just left the torch. Perhaps it really was a search-and-rescue team from Beacon. Perhaps they got eaten. Caldwell has no idea, but whatever happens, she's not leaving Rosie again. Not for the siren song of a voice on the radio, not for actual humans showing their actual faces, not for marching bands and ticker-tape parades. She walks through into the lab, loosening the seals on the environment suit's helmet as she goes.

Melanie is sitting in her chair, in front of the microscope, reading her notes. She looks up. "Hello, Dr Caldwell," she says politely.

Caldwell has stopped dead in the doorway. Her first thought is: *Is she alone, or did the others arrive with her?* Her second: *What can I use as a weapon?* The cylinder of phosgene gas is still screwed into place in the airlock's feed chamber. Since she's still wearing the environment suit, she'd be immune to its effects. If she could get to that . . .

"I'll stop you," Melanie says, in the same courteous and level tone, "if you move. I'll stop you if you pick up a gun or anything that's sharp, or if you try to run away, or if you try to shut me in the cage again. Or if you do anything else that I think might be meant to hurt me."

374

"That . . . that was you?" Caldwell asks her. "On the radio?"

Melanie indicates with a nod the walkie-talkie sitting beside her on the work surface. "I kept trying all the different channels. It took a long time before you answered."

"And then . . . then you . . .?"

"I lay down underneath the door. You stepped out over me. As soon as you went past me, I came inside."

Caldwell takes off the helmet and sets it down, very gently, on a work surface. A few feet away is the squat bulk of the microtome lathe, an exquisitely engineered guillotine. If she could trick Melanie into walking close to it, and topple her on to its cutting bed, this could be over in an instant.

Melanie frowns and shakes her head, seeming to guess her intentions. "I don't want to bite you, Dr Caldwell, but I've got this." She holds up a scalpel, one of the ones that Caldwell used in the dissection of the hungry specimen and hasn't yet found time to disinfect. "And you know how fast I can move."

Caldwell considers. "You're a good girl, Melanie," she essays. "I don't think you'd really hurt me."

"You tied me to a table so you could cut me up," Melanie reminds her. "And you cut up Marcia and Liam. You probably cut up lots of children. The only reason I ever had for not hurting you was that Miss Justineau and Sergeant Parks probably wouldn't have liked it. But they're not here. And I don't think they'd mind so much now, even if they were."

Caldwell is inclined to believe this. "What do you want from me?" she asks. It's clear from Melanie's agitated manner that she wants *something*, has something on her mind.

"The truth," Melanie says.

"About what?"

"About everything. About me, and the other children. And why we're different."

"Can I take off this suit?" Caldwell temporises.

Melanie gestures for her to go ahead.

"I have to do it in the airlock," Caldwell says.

375

"Then keep it on," Melanie says.

Caldwell gives up on the idea of retrieving the phosgene. She sits down on one of the lab chairs. As soon as she does so, she realises how exhausted she is. Only willpower and bloody-mindedness have kept her going this long. She's close to crashing now – too weak to resist this hectoring monster child. She has to gather her strength and choose her time.

She's expecting Melanie to interrogate her, but Melanie continues to read the notes: the observations Caldwell has jotted down about her two sets of brain tissue samples, and about the sporangium. She seems particularly fascinated by the sporangium notes, lingering over Caldwell's labelled diagrams.

"What's an environmental trigger?" she demands.

"It defines any factor external to the sporing body that causes or predisposes towards the onset of sporing," Caldwell says coldly. It's the tone she uses to put Sergeant Parks in his place, but Melanie takes it very much in her stride.

"Anything outside?" she paraphrases. "Anything outside the pod that makes the seeds come out of the pod?"

"That's right," Caldwell says grudgingly.

"Like the Amazon rainforest."

"I'm sorry?"

"There are trees in the Amazon rainforest that only shed their seeds after a bushfire. The redwood and the jack pine do that too."

"Do they?" Caldwell's tone is brittle. It's actually a perfectly good example.

"Yes." Melanie sets the notes down. She's looked at each page exactly once, stopped when she got to the front of the stack again. "Miss Mailer told me, back at the base."

She holds Caldwell's gaze with her unblinking, bright blue eyes.

"Why am I different?" she asks.

"Narrow down the question," Caldwell mutters.

"Most of the hungries are more like animals than people.

376

They can't think or talk. I can. Why are there two kinds of hungries?"

"Brain structures," Caldwell says.

But she's at war with herself. Part of her wants to guard the secret, to give away no more than she's asked, to force Melanie to dive deep for every pearl. The other part is desperate to share. Caldwell longs for an auditorium of geniuses, sages both living and dead. She gets a child who's neither, or both. But the world is winding down, and you take what you're given.

"The hungries," she says, "including you, are infected with a fungus named *Ophiocordyceps*." She assumes no prior knowledge, because there's no telling what Melanie has understood, or failed to understand, from those notes. So she begins by describing the family of hot-wiring parasites – organisms that fool the host's nervous system with forged neurotransmitters, hijacking the host's living brain and making it do what the parasite needs it to do.

Melanie's questions are infrequent, but right on topic. She's a smart kid. Of course she is.

"But why am I different?" she presses again. "What was special about the children you brought to the base?"

"I'm coming to that," Caldwell says testily. "You've never studied biology or organic chemistry. It's hard to put this stuff in words you can understand."

"Put it in words *you* understand," Melanie suggests, in much the same tone. "If it's too hard for me, I'll ask you to explain it again."

So Caldwell delivers her lecture. Not to Elizabeth Blackburn, Günter Blobel or Carol Greider, but to a ten-year-old girl. That's humbling, in a way. But only in a way. Caldwell is still the one who made all the connections and found what was there to be found. Who entered the jungle and brought the hungry pathogen back alive. *Ophiocordyceps caldwellia.* That's what they'll call it, now and for ever.

As the sky pales outside, she talks on and on. Melanie stops her every so often with pertinent and focused questions. She's a receptive audience, despite her lack of a Nobel prize.

To the newly infected, Caldwell says, *Ophiocordyceps* is utterly without mercy. It batters down the door, breaks and enters, devours and controls. Then finally it turns what's left of the host into a bag of fertiliser from which the fruiting body grows.

"But we were wrong about how quickly the human substrate is destroyed. The fungus targets different brain areas with differing speed and severity. It shuts down higher-order thought. It enhances hunger and the triggers for hunger. But we'd assumed that all drives outside of that – all behaviours that didn't serve the parasite's agenda – were embargoed at the same time.

"When I saw that woman in the street in Stevenage, and the man in the care home, I could see that wasn't the case. Both of them were still making connections, haphazardly, to their former lives. They were engaging in behaviours – pushing a pram, singing, looking at old photographs – that were completely without function as far as the parasite was concerned."

Caldwell looks up at Melanie. Her mouth is unpleasantly dry, despite the sweat that's running freely down her face. "Can I have a glass of water?" she asks.

"When you've finished," Melanie promises. "Not yet."

Caldwell accepts the verdict. She reads nothing in Melanie's face that would give her room for negotiation. "Well," she says, her voice faltering a little, "that made me think. About you, and the other children. Perhaps we'd missed the obvious explanation for why you're so different."

"Go on," Melanie says. Her voice is level, but her eyes betray her fear and excitement. It comforts Caldwell a little – in the absence of the physical control she used to enjoy – to have at least this degree of power over her.

"I realised that you might have been *born* with the infection. That your parents might already have been infected when you were conceived. We thought that was impossible – that hungries couldn't have a sex drive. But once I'd seen the survival of other human drives and emotions – mother love, and loneliness – it didn't seem impossible at all.

"With that in mind, I went back to the cytological evidence. I was fortunate enough to be able to obtain a fresh sample of brain tissue—"

"From a boy," Melanie says. "You killed him and cut off his head."

"Yes, I did. And his brain was very different from a normal hungry brain. With the equipment I had back at the base, it was pretty much all I could do to verify and map the presence of the fungus. With this . . ." – she indicates with a nod of the head the microtome, the centrifuge, the scanning electron microscope – "I could look at individual neurons and how the fungal cells interacted with them. The boy here, and the man from the care home, they were so different there was almost no way to compare them. The fungus utterly wrecks the brain of a first-generation hungry. Goes through it like a train. The chemicals it secretes – the brute-force triggers that turn specific behaviours on and off – they cause terrible damage as they accumulate. And the fungus is drawing nutrients from the brain tissue too. The brain is progressively hollowed out, sucked dry.

"In the second generation – that's you – the fungus is spread evenly throughout the brain. It's thoroughly interwoven with the dendrites of the host's neurons. In some places it actually replaces them. But it doesn't *feed* on the brain. It gets its nourishment only when the host eats. It's become a true symbiote rather than a parasite."

"Miss Justineau said my mother was dead," Melanie objects. It's almost a protest – as though a lie from Helen Justineau is a thing that can have no place in the world.

"That was our best guess," Caldwell says. "That your parents were junkers or other survivors who'd never made it to Beacon, and that you and they had all been fed on and infected at the same time. We had no model for hungries copulating. Still less for them giving birth in the wild, and the babies somehow surviving. You must be much hardier and more self-sufficient than normal human infants. Perhaps you were able to feed on the flesh of your mother until you were strong enough to—"

"Don't," Melanie says sharply. "Don't talk about things like that."

But talking is all that Caldwell has left now, and she can't stop herself. She talks about her observations, her theory, her success (in working out the pathogen's life cycle) and her failure (there's no immunity, no vaccine, no conceivable cure). She tells Melanie where to find her slides and the rest of her notes, and who to give them to when they get to Beacon.

When it becomes harder for Caldwell to talk, Melanie comes closer and sits at her feet. The scalpel is still clutched in her hand, but she doesn't bully or threaten now. She just listens. And Caldwell is full of gratitude, because she knows what this lethargy that's flooding through her means.

The septicaemia is entering its final phase. She won't live to write her findings down, to astonish the remaining scientific minds of humanity's doomed rearguard with the spectacle of her clear-sightedness and their idiocy. It's just Melanie. Melanie is the messenger sent by providence in her last hour to carry her trophies home.

68

It's a bad night.

The room contains nothing except a table and a metal cistern that was once part of the house's central heating system. Every movement makes the bare boards creak loudly, so for the most part Justineau and Sergeant Parks sit still.

Their first visitors arrive about an hour after Melanie pulled the ladder away. A few minutes after she calls them on the walkie-talkie from the wilds of Hackney. Justineau can hear the hungries stumbling and scrabbling about in the room below, moving restlessly back and forth. The source of the smell, the chemical gradient they're following, is above them, but they can't get up there. All they can do is charge around, driven by eddies of air, random shifts in the intensity of the chemical trigger.

Justineau keeps hoping they'll leave, or at least stop moving around, but this isn't like Stevenage. At Wainwright House, the hungries were drawn by sound and movement. When the signals stopped, they stopped too, waiting for the fungus in their brains to give them further orders. Here, the orders are coming through continually, keeping them in constant, restless motion.

At first Parks opens the trap to peer down at them every so often, shining the light of the torch down into the dark to illuminate slack, grey faces, upturned, their milky eyes wide and their nostrils flared like the mouths of tunnels. But the view never changes, and after a while he gives up.

An hour or so after that, they hear thuds through the walls from whatever rooms are alongside of them. More hungries, following the scent or the heat trail as assiduously as the first bunch, but betrayed by local geography into going up the wrong stairwell, taking the wrong turn.

They're at the centre of a great volume of space, filled with things that want to eat them.

No, Justineau corrects herself. *Not the centre. There's nothing up on the roof. Not yet, anyway.*

She finds a skylight and climbs up on a table to look out of it. A hunter's moon illuminates the wide sweep of streets southward towards the river. Fungal froth fills them to the brim, and it goes on as far as she can see. London is a no-go area, an exclusion zone for the living. Only hungries can thrive here. God alone knows how far east or west they'll have to trek to get around it.

Well, God and maybe Melanie. They try to contact her on the walkie-talkie, but there's no reply and no trace of her signal. Parks thinks it's possible that she's switched to another frequency, although he can't think of any good reason why she'd do that.

"You should try to sleep," he tells Justineau. He's sitting in a corner of the room now, cleaning his gun by the light of the electric torch. It shines on the underside of his chin and eye sockets, and most unsettlingly of all on the diagonal furrow of his scar.

"Like you?" Justineau asks laconically. But she climbs down. She's sick of looking at the endless grey escarpments.

She sits beside him. After a moment, she touches his arm, low down near the wrist. Then, with a slight feeling of unreality, she slips her hand into his.

382

"I haven't been fair to you," she says.

Parks laughs out loud. "I don't think fairness was what I was looking for exactly."

"Still. You got us this far, against all the odds, and for most of the way I've treated you like the enemy. I'm sorry about that."

He takes her hand and raises it to head height. She thinks he's going to kiss it, but he just turns it this way and that to let the torchlight shine on it. "It doesn't matter," he says. "Actually, it's probably better this way. I could never respect any woman who had low enough standards to sleep with me."

"That's not funny, Parks."

"No. I guess it isn't. It is okay to call me Eddie, by the way."

"Are you sure about that? It feels like fraternising."

She's actually angling for the laugh this time, and she's pleased when it comes.

Does she want this? She doesn't even know. She wants something, clearly. She didn't hold Parks' hand out of some abstract need for human contact. She held it to see what, if anything, his touch would do to her. But what it does is equivocal.

The scar doesn't bother her. If anything, it takes his face out of the category of symmetrical and ordered things to which everybody else's face belongs. It's a face like the throw of a dice. She likes that arbitrariness, instinctively. It's something she's drawn to.

What she doesn't like is the cruelties in his past, and in hers, over which she'll have to crawl to get to him. She wishes she'd never told him that she was a murderer. She wishes that she was pristine, in his mind, so that touching him might feel like booting up a different version of herself.

But that's not how you get reborn, if you ever can.

She pulls out of Parks' grip. Then, holding his head between her hands, she kisses him on the lips.

After a moment, he turns off the torch. She knows why, and makes no comment.

383

69

Sometime in the middle of the night, the quality of the sounds from beneath them changes.

Up to then, it's been random – the thuds and judders of stampeding hungries bouncing off each other again and again in a Brownian cascade. What they're hearing now has a definite rhythm to it, a persistence. And there are grunts and clicks and whistles, mixed in with the sounds of effort and impact. Hungries don't vocalise.

Parks disentangles himself from Justineau's heavy, sleepy embrace and crawls to the trap. He lifts it up and flicks the torch on, already pointed straight down.

Framed in its beam is a face out of nightmare. It seems to leap up at Parks out of the blackness. Dark-eyed, pale-skinned, piebald with dots and slashes of colour. Its wide mouth hangs open to display slender pointed teeth like the teeth of a piranha.

Then it really does leap up, reacting to the light with instant, murderous rage. Something parts the air in a whickering blur right in front of Parks' face – something that shines in the torchlight, and hits the mouth of the trapdoor with a resonant clang.

384

Parks leans back, but he doesn't flinch away from the misjudged blow, so he sees what's happening behind his attacker. Children, boys and girls both, are swarming over the lurching hungries, pulling them down and quickly dispatching them with a range of weapons that's both wide and eclectic.

But this isn't what they came for. This is just clearing the ground. They didn't find this place by accident. It's the loft room, and what's in it, that brought them here. The dark eyes flick upwards again and again, locking stares with Parks.

He flings the trap shut again. Justineau is already stirring, but he pulls her quickly to her feet.

"We've got to go," he says. "Now. Get dressed."

"Why?" Justineau demands. "What's . . .?" She doesn't finish the sentence, because she's heard the sounds from below. Maybe she guesses instantly what they mean. She knows they mean trouble, anyway, and she's not so stupid that she'll ask for an explanation that could take up the time they need for an escape.

The trapdoor doesn't have a lock, but Parks manages to topple the metal cistern on top of it. He's barely in time – the trap was already being pushed open when the tank crashed down across it. A shriek from below tells him that whoever was climbing up didn't enjoy being swatted back down.

In seconds, the trap is thumping and juddering as the hungry children bring their strength to bear on it. Parks has no idea how they're managing to reach it. Climbing on each other's shoulders, or on the piled bodies of the other hungries they've just harvested? It doesn't matter. They're too strong and too determined for the cistern to hold them back for long.

He jumps up on to the table and thrusts his head out of the window, which Justineau has left open. There's nobody up on the roof. He gets his shoulders through and levers himself up on to the slates. Justineau is already following, and although he offers his hand, she doesn't need it.

The sloping slates aren't wet, but they're still as slippery as hell. The two of them climb up to the roof ridge with their limbs splayed like frogs, pressing their bodies hard against the treacherous surface.

Once they reach the ridge, it's easier. There's a single skin of brickwork making a narrow walkway, so they can stand upright and stumble along like drunken trapeze artists, using the breastwork of chimneys and the pipes of heating vents to steady themselves.

Parks is aiming to get to the end of the terrace and find another window to climb in through. Before they're halfway there, loud scuffling and shrill shrieks from behind them warn him that they're no longer alone. He turns to look. Small, limber shapes, clearly defined in the moonlight, are swarming up on to the roof from the room the two of them just left. They're not making for the ridge; they're crab-shuffling diagonally towards Parks and Justineau, taking the shortest route to their prey.

Parks waits until he reaches the next chimney before he takes out his gun. He fires twice, at the closest of the children. The first shot is a direct hit. The kid is slammed backwards, goes tumbling down the slope and over the edge before he can stop himself. The other shot goes wide, but the children scatter, panicked, and another one falls.

The rest retreat quickly. Not quickly enough, though. Parks has plenty of time to pick off a few more.

"Don't kill them!" Justineau shouts. "Don't, Parks! They're running away!"

They're changing tactics is what they're doing. But Parks doesn't bother to argue. Better to save the bullets, because they're going to need them when they get to the ground.

If they get to the ground.

Something hits the brickwork of the chimney right next to Parks' head, and splinters fleck his cheek. From behind chimneys and gables, the hungry kids let loose with what must be

386

slingshots – but with the whiplash speed of a hungry arm behind them, the stones hit like bullets. One of them cleaves the air so close that he can feel it, and hear its mosquito whine as it goes by his ear.

Enough.

He unships his rifle and fires two wide bursts. The first sprays the chimney stacks, forcing the kids back into hiding. The second shatters the slates between him and them on a sweeping, ruinous arc. They'll have a hard time coming across that stretch of roof, if they decide to risk it.

"Keep moving," he yells to Justineau. He points. "Down! Down that way. Find a window!"

Justineau is already sliding back down the tiles towards the rain gutter, arms spread to slow herself, feet scrabbling. Parks follows her on hands and knees, facing backwards up the ridge, ready to shoot at anything that moves. But nothing moves.

"Parks," Justineau says below him. "Here."

She's found a window that's not just open but gone, frame and all. All they have to do is let themselves down from the roof, taking their weight on their elbows, and step off on to the sill. Then it's the work of a second to duck and snake inside.

Seconds count now. They've got to make it to the ground before the kids do. Get as good a head start as they can manage. They stumble through the dark, looking for a staircase.

That's when the walkie-talkie goes off. Parks doesn't stop – doesn't dare to – but he snatches it up from its holster on his belt and answers.

"Parks. Go."

"I heard shots," Melanie says. "Are you okay?"

"Not so much."

Justineau grabs his shoulder, drags him sideways. She's found some stairs. They launch themselves into the lightless well, stumbling and almost falling. He should stop and get the torch from his backpack, but using it would probably just bring the kids down on them more quickly.

"Some hungry kids found us," he says, through panting breaths. "Armed to the teeth. Kind of like you, only harder to get along with. They're still on us."

"Where are you?" Melanie asks. "Where I left you?"

"Further. End of the street."

"I'm coming to find you."

Good news. "Come fast," he suggests.

They can tell when they're on the ground floor, because the house's street door is gaping open. They're heading right for it, but the moonlight frames a silhouette as it pops up right in front of them. Four feet tall, a knife in each hand, ready to carve.

Parks fires, and the slight shape ducks away. Last bullet in the mag, or maybe second to last. He slides to a ragged, flailing halt. Justineau slams into his back. In full reverse, they head for the rear of the house.

Through one mouldering cave after another. The functions of the rooms are impossible to guess and of no damn interest to Parks at all. He's just looking for a back door. When he finds it, he kicks it open and they burst out into – what he was praying for – the walled-in wilderness of an urban garden twenty years gone to seed.

They dive into head-high brambles, leaving flesh and cloth as tribute. An ululation from behind tells them that the kids are close at hand and still coming. Parks wishes them joy of it. Most of them are bollock naked, so they're more exposed to the inch-long thorns, which are thickest close to the ground.

He looks behind. The doorway they just ran through is already lost in the inky dark, but he can see some vague movement back there. He fires into it and something shrieks. Fires again and the slide springs back with a barren click. Does he have another mag in his belt? Is he going to stop and reload, in the dark, with those cute little moppets climbing right up his arse?

A garden wall. "Go! Go!" he shouts. He boosts Justineau over it, then jumps, misses, jumps again. He finds the top on his third try and she's hauling him up by the neck of his shirt.

Something punches him in the shoulder. Another something explodes against the brickwork next to his hand. Justineau grunts in pain and she's gone from the top of the wall, toppled as clean as a target on a gunnery range.

Parks slides over the top and jumps down after her, on to the cracked, weed-choked asphalt of a car park. The remains of a four-by-four lies beside them, its front wheels gone, looking like a steer down on its knees and waiting for the bolt gun to be pressed to its head. The coup de grâce.

Justineau is down, and not moving. He feels her forehead gingerly, and his fingers come away wet.

She's no lightweight, but Parks manages to get her up on to his shoulder. He can't keep her there one-handed, though, so it's either run or fight.

He runs. Then figures out immediately that it was the wrong thing to do. Half a dozen low, lithe forms come sprinting around the side of the house into view, and they don't even slow as they head for him. More are squirming up on to the garden wall and dropping down on to the asphalt behind him.

He runs in the only direction he can see that's clear, out into the open, where he's a sitting duck for the slingshots. Right on cue, they start up again. He takes another hit, low down on his back, and it feels like someone punched him in the kidney. He staggers, just about stays upright.

And he's tackled, run right off his feet, by the fastest of the kids. It launches itself at him in a flying dive, lands on the small of his back and clings there, letting its momentum topple him. Parks goes sprawling, trying to twist his body around

389

under Justineau's to cushion the landing, but they part company somewhere along the way.

As Parks goes down, the hungry is already clawing for his throat. He punches it in the face, as hard as he can, and it falls away, giving him space to get his foot up and kick it away into midfield. He's doing fine now. Got space enough to grab his rifle and bring it round.

Something smashes down on to his shoulder – the same shoulder that took the slingshot stone – with shocking force. The rifle falls from his fingers, but he only knows that because he hears it hit the ground. For a second or two he doesn't feel anything, not even pain. Then the pain rushes in and fills him to the brim.

He's sprawled on the ground, the rifle next to his head, and though he's trying to move, nothing very much is happening. His right arm is useless, his right side a barbed-wire tangle of complex agonies. The painted kid in the flak jacket kneels at his side. The others are massed behind him, waiting, as he leans in with his mouth gaping wide. From this close up, there's no doubt about it: those teeth have been filed.

They meet in Parks' forearm. It's the right arm, so it doesn't hurt; there's no free space on that side of his body for new pains to be inserted. But he screams, all the same, as the boy's head bobs back up again, a lump of Parks' flesh gripped raw and bloody in his jaw.

This is the signal for the feast to commence. The other kids come skipping in, as though they've been called to a picnic. One of them, a tiny blonde girl, scrambles on to Helen Justineau's chest, grips her hair to tilt her head right back.

Parks' left hand finds the handgun tucked into Justineau's belt. He pulls it out and fires. Blind. The kid goes spinning away into the dark, the hollow-point shell whipping her like a top.

The hungry kids freeze for a moment, startled by the booming report at such close quarters.

390

Into that moment, something new inserts itself.
Deafeningly.
Terrifyingly.
Spitting fire and screaming like all the demons of hell.

70

Melanie did her best with the limited materials that were available to her.

She advances on the feral children on tiptoe, straining for height, making herself look as little like a girl and as much like a god or a Titan as she can. She's naked from the neck down – *sky-clad* – but she wears on her head the oversized helmet from the environment suit, whose polarised view-plate completely hides her face.

Her body is bright blue and glistening, anointed from head to foot with the disinfectant gel that Dr Caldwell employs – used to employ – in her dissections.

In her left hand, she carries Miss Justineau's personal alarm, which is doing exactly what Miss Justineau said it would do. A hundred and fifty decibels of sound hammer the ears and hector the brains of everyone in the vicinity, making clear thought impossible. It's doing this to Melanie too, of course, but at least she knew it was coming.

In her right hand she carries the flare pistol, and she fires it now directly at the painted-face boy who stole Kieran Gallagher's jacket. The flare shoots right past his head and the smoke from its passage falls over him, over all of them, like a shawl dropping out of the sky.

Melanie flings the personal alarm at the boy's feet, and he takes a step back, flailing at the air as though he's being attacked.

She throws herself at him. She doesn't really want to. She wants him to run away from her, because then all the other kids will run too, but he's not doing it and she's reached him and she's all out of ideas now.

She catches him under the chin with the butt of the flare pistol, a solid blow that snaps his head back and makes him stagger. But he doesn't fall. Shifting his stance, he swings the baseball bat with all his strength.

And connects. But he's been fooled by the helmet, which is way too big for Melanie and sitting very loosely on her slender shoulders. He thinks she's six inches taller than she is. His devastating blow, which would have staved in the side of her skull if it had connected, ploughs into the top of the helmet instead and whips it right off her head.

The boy seems surprised to find that she's got another head underneath, and he hesitates, the baseball bat poised for a backhand slash. The sound of the personal alarm is still shrilling in their ears. It's as though the whole world is screaming.

Melanie clicks the flare gun a quarter-turn, loading another pellet. She shoots the boy in the face with it.

To the other kids, watching, it must look as though his face has caught fire. The flare pellet is lodged in his eye socket, shining like a piece of the sun that's fallen to the ground. Smoke pours out of it, straight upwards at first, then breaking into a tight spiral as the boy bends backward from the knees. He drops the baseball bat to clutch at his face.

Melanie uses the baseball bat to finish him.

By the time she's done, the other kids have finally run away.

71

Melanie leads the way and Sergeant Parks comes after, carrying Miss Justineau on his left shoulder. His right arm hangs straight down at his side, swinging very slightly with the rhythm of his walking. He doesn't seem to be able to move it.

Miss Justineau is unconscious, but she's definitely still breathing. And there's no sign that she's been bitten.

The kids are getting their courage back, a little at a time. They don't dare to press an attack just yet, but stones whistle out of the dark to clatter at Melanie's feet. She keeps to the same level pace, and Sergeant Parks does too. If they run, Melanie thinks, the children will chase them. And then they'll have to fight again.

They turn a corner at last, and Rosie is before them. Melanie walks just a little faster so she can get there first and open the door. Sergeant Parks staggers over the threshold and sinks to his knees. With Melanie's help, he puts Miss Justineau down. He's exhausted, but she can't let him rest yet.

"I'm sorry, Sergeant," she tells him, kicking the door closed. "There's something we still need to do."

Sergeant Parks gestures, left-handed, at the ragged rent in

his shoulder. His face is pale, and his eyes are already a little red at the corners.

"I . . . have to get out of here," he pants. "I'm—"

"The flame-throwers, Sergeant," Melanie interrupts urgently. "You told Miss Justineau there were flame-throwers. Where are they?"

He doesn't seem to understand what she wants at first. He meets her gaze, breathing hard. "The wall?" he hazards. "The . . . the fungus stuff?"

"Yes."

Sergeant gets to his feet and stumbles through to the aft weapons station. "You need to power up," he tells her.

"I did that before I came to get you."

Sergeant wipes his face with the heel of his hand. His voice is a whisper. "Okay. Okay." He points to two toggles. "Primer. Feed. You light the primer, then you uncap the feed, then you fire. Jet stays alight until you let go of the throttle here."

Melanie stands on the firing platform. She can reach the controls, but she's not tall enough to put her eye to the sights or even to peep over the lower edge of the viewing port. Sergeant can see that she's not going to be able to do this by herself.

"Okay," he says again, hollow with pain and exhaustion.

She stands down, and he climbs up in her place, stumbling and almost falling off the platform. With one hand useless, firing the flame-thrower seems to be a lot harder to do than it was to explain. Melanie helps him, working the toggles while he manhandles the gun itself.

The turret turns with servos, following the movement of the gun barrel, so at least that part is easy. Sergeant targets on the dull grey mass of the fungus forest, which is impossible to miss because it fills half of the horizon.

"Anywhere?" he asks her. His voice is slow and slippery, the way Mr Whitaker's voice sometimes used to be.

"Anywhere," Melanie confirms.

"Kid, there's miles and miles of that stuff. It won't . . . it won't penetrate. Not all the way. It's not going to punch a way through."

"It doesn't have to," Melanie says. "The fire will spread."

"I fucking hope so." Parks leans on the barrel to aim, and depresses the trigger. Fire streaks through the sky, horizontally at first, dipping at the end of its arc to slice through the grey mass like a sword twenty metres long.

Filaments that stand directly in the path of the flame just disappear. It's only to the sides that the fire catches and spreads. And it spreads faster than they can turn their heads to see. The fungal mat is as dry as tinder. It seems to *want* to burn. In the light of the fierce flames, some of the nearer trunks can now be seen even from this far off, straight-edge shadows that shift wildly as the heart of the fire roams like a wild animal through the fungus forest. With more moisture inside them than the filaments, they smoulder and spit sparks for a long time before they catch too and pass from shadow into eye-hurting light.

After a full minute, Melanie touches Sergeant's arm. "That should be enough," she says.

Gratefully he releases the trigger. The fiery sword retracts itself in the space of a second back into the flame-thrower's barrel.

Sergeant steps down off the platform, his knees buckling a little under him.

"You've got to let me out," he mumbles. "I'm not safe any more. I . . . It feels like my fucking head is splitting apart. For the love of God, kid, open the door."

He doesn't seem to be able to find it by himself. He turns one way, then another, blinking his bloodshot eyes and grimacing against the light. Melanie takes his good left hand and leads him to the door.

Miss Justineau is sitting up now, but she doesn't seem to notice them as they walk by. There's a puddle of vomit at her feet, and her head is hanging down between her knees.

396

Melanie stops to kiss her, very softly, on the top of her head. "I'm coming back," she says. "I'll take care of you."

Miss Justineau doesn't answer.

Sergeant's hand is on the handle of the outer door, but Melanie's hand closes over his, gently, trying not to hurt him, but stopping him from pulling back on the handle and opening the door. "We have to wait," she explains.

She cycles the airlock, following the instructions written on the wall right next to the controls. Sergeant Parks watches, mystified. The light goes from red to green and she opens the outer door.

They walk out into a mist so fine it's like someone laid a lace curtain across the world. The air tastes the same as it ever did, but it feels a little gritty on the tongue. Melanie keeps licking her lips to clear the rime from them, and she sees Sergeant Parks do it too.

"Is there somewhere I can sit?" he asks her. He's blinking a lot, and a red tear has leaked down out of one of his eyes.

Melanie finds a black plastic wheelie bin and tips it over. She sits Sergeant down on it. She sits herself down beside him.

"What did we do?" Sergeant's voice is hoarse, and he looks around urgently, as though he's lost something but he can't remember what it is. "What did we do, kid?"

"We burned the grey stuff. We burned it all up."

"Right," Parks says. "Is . . . is Helen . . .?"

"You saved her," Melanie assures him. "You brought her back inside, and she's safe now. She didn't get bitten or anything. You saved her, Sergeant."

"Good," Sergeant says. And then he's quiet for a long time. "Listen," he says at last. "Could you . . . Kid, listen. Could you do me a favour?"

"What is it?" Melanie asks.

Sergeant takes his sidearm out of its holster. He has to reach across his body to do this with his left hand. He ejects the empty magazine, and gropes around in his belt until he finds a fresh one, which he snaps home. He shows Melanie where to put her fingers, and he shows her how to take off the safety. He chambers a round.

"I'd like . . ." he says. And then he goes quiet again.

"What would you like?" Melanie asks him. She's holding the big gun in her tiny hands and she knows, really, what the answer is. But he has to say it so she's sure she's right.

"I've seen enough of them to know . . . I don't want that," Sergeant says. "I mean . . ." He swallows noisily. "Don't want to go out like that. No offence."

"I'm not offended, Sergeant."

"I can't shoot left-handed. Sorry. It's a lot to ask."

"It's all right."

"If I could shoot left-handed . . ."

"Don't worry, Sergeant. I'll do it. I won't leave you until it's done."

They sit side by side while the dawn comes up, the sky lightening by such tiny increments that you can't tell when the night stops and the day begins.

"We burned it?" Sergeant asks.

"Yes."

He sighs. The sound has a liquid undertow.

"Bullshit," he groans. "This stuff in the air . . . it's the fungus, right? What did we do, kid? Tell me. Or I'll take that gun away from you and send you to bed early."

Melanie resigns herself. She didn't want to trouble him with this stuff when he's dying, but she won't lie to him after he's asked her for the truth. "There are pods," she says, pointing towards where the fungus wall is still burning. "In there. Pods full of seeds. Dr Caldwell said this was the fungus's mature form, and the pods were meant to break open and spread the seeds on the wind. But the pods are very tough, and they can't open by themselves. Dr Caldwell said they needed something to give them a push and make them open. She called it an environmental trigger. And I remembered the trees in the

398

rainforest that need a big fire to make their seeds grow. I used to have a picture of them, on the wall of my cell back at the base."

Parks is struck dumb with the horror of what he's just done. Melanie strokes his hand, contrite. "That's why I didn't want to tell you," she says. "I knew it would make you sad."

"But . . ." Parks shakes his head. As hard as it is for her to explain, it's a lot harder for him to understand. She can see that it's hard for him even to frame the words. *Ophiocordyceps* is demolishing the parts of his mind it doesn't need, leaving him less and less to think with. In the end he settles for, "Why?"

Because of the war, Melanie tells him. And because of the children. The children like her – the second generation. There's no cure for the hungry plague, but in the end the plague becomes its own cure. It's terribly, terribly sad for the people who get it first, but their children will be okay and they'll be the ones who live and grow up and have children of their own and make a new world.

"But only if you *let* them grow up," she finishes. "If you keep shooting them and cutting them into pieces and throwing them into pits, nobody will be left to make a new world. Your people and the junker people will keep killing each other, and you'll both kill the hungries wherever you find them, and in the end the world will be empty. This way is better. Everybody turns into a hungry all at once, and that means they'll all die, which is really sad. But then the children will grow up, and they won't be the old kind of people but they won't be hungries either. They'll be different. Like me, and the rest of the kids in the class.

"They'll be the *next* people. The ones who make everything okay again."

She doesn't know how much of this Sergeant has even heard. His movements are changing. His face slackens and then twists by turns, his hands jerking suddenly like the hands of badly animated puppets. He mutters "Okay" a few times, and Melanie

399

thinks that might mean he gets what she said. That he accepts it. Or it might just mean that he's remembered she was talking to him and wants to reassure her that he's still listening.

"She was blonde," he says suddenly.

"What?"

"Marie. She was . . . blonde. Like you. So if we'd had a kid . . ."

His hands circle each other, searching for a meaning that evades them. After a while he goes very still, until the sound of a bird singing on a wire between the houses makes him sit bolt upright and swivel his head, left and then right, to locate the source of the sound. His jaw starts to open and close, the hunger reflex kicking in sudden and strong.

Melanie pulls the trigger. The soft bullet goes into Sergeant's head and doesn't come out again.

72

Helen Justineau comes back to consciousness like someone trudging home after a twenty-mile hike. It's exhausting, and it's slow. She keeps seeing familiar landmarks, and thinking that she must be almost there, but then she'll get lost again and have to keep slogging on through her own shattered thoughts – reliving the events of the night in a hundred random re-sequencings.

Finally she realises where she is. Back inside Rosie, sitting on a steel grating by the midsection door, in a puddle of her own sick.

She struggles to her feet, throwing up a little more in the process. She goes through Rosie's various spaces, looking for Parks and Caldwell and Melanie. She scores one out of three. The doctor's body, stiff and cold, lies on the floor of the lab, curled up into a post-mortem question mark. There's a little dried blood on her face, from a recent injury, but it doesn't seem likely that that could have killed her. Then again, from what Parks said, she was already dying of blood poisoning from the infected wounds on her hands.

On one of the lab's work surfaces sits a child's head from

which the top of the skull has been removed. There are chunks of bone and bloody tissue in a bowl beside the head, along with a discarded pair of surgical gloves crusted with dried blood.

No sign of Melanie, or of Parks.

Looking out of the window, Justineau can see that it's snowing. *Grey* snow. Tiny flakes of it, more like a sifting of dust really, but coming down endlessly out of the sky.

When she realises what it is she's seeing, she starts to cry.

Hours pass. The sun climbs in the sky. Justineau imagines that its light is dimmed a little, as though the grey seeds are making a curtain in the upper air.

Melanie comes walking back to Rosie, through the tidal flurries of the end of the world. She waves to Justineau through the window, then points to the door. She's going to come inside.

The airlock cycles very slowly, while Melanie carefully sprays her already disinfectant-covered body with a layer of liquid fungicide.

I'm coming back. I'll take care of you.

Justineau understands what that means now. How she'll live, and what she'll be. And she laughs through choking tears at the rightness of it. Nothing is forgotten and everything is paid.

Even if she could, she wouldn't haggle about the price.

The airlock's inner door opens. Melanie runs to her and embraces her. Gives her love without hesitation or limit, whether it's earned or not – and at the same time pronounces sentence on her.

"Get dressed," she says happily. "Come and meet them."

The children. Sullen and awkward, sitting cross-legged on the ground, cowed into silence by Melanie's fierce warning glares. Justineau has only the haziest memories of the night before, but she can see the awe in their eyes as Melanie walks among them, shushing sternly.

Justineau fights a queasy wave of claustrophobia. It's quite

402

hot inside the sealed-environment suit, and she's already thirsty, even though she just drank about half her own weight in water from Rosie's filtration tank.

She sits down on the sill of the midsection door. She has a marker pen in her hand. Rosie herself will be her whiteboard.

"Good morning, Miss Justineau," Melanie says.

A murmur rises and falls as some of the other children – more than half – try to imitate her.

"Good morning, Melanie," Justineau replies. And then, "Good morning, class."

She draws on the side of the tank a capital *A* and a lower-case *a*. Greek myths and quadratic equations will come later.

Acknowledgements

This novel grew out of a short story, "Iphigenia in Aulis", which I wrote for a US anthology edited by Charlaine Harris and Toni Kelner. So I have them to thank for its existence, and for the encouragement and feedback they gave me when I was writing it. I'd also like to give huge thanks to Colm McCarthy, Camille Gatin and Dan McCulloch for some wonderful brainstorming sessions when we were turning the short story into a movie pitch. We found different approaches and solutions for the movie, but some of the clarity of their vision and the vigour of their imaginations rubbed off on me and – I'm sure – transferred themselves to the novel. And thanks, finally, to my family – Lin, Lou, Davey and Ben, Barbara and Eric – who were my test bed and wind tunnel for most of the story's key moments and who never complained once. Not even if they happened to be recovering from major surgery at the time.

About the author

M. R. Carey is a pen name for an established British writer of prose fiction and comic books. He has written for both DC and Marvel, including critically acclaimed runs on *X-Men* and *Fantastic Four*, Marvel's flagship superhero titles. His creator-owned books regularly appear in the *New York Times* graphic fiction bestseller list. He also has several previous novels and one Hollywood movie screenplay to his credit.

Find out more about M. R. Carey and other Orbit authors by registering online for the free monthly newsletter at www.orbitbooks.net.